From *The History and A̶̶̶̶̶̶̶̶̶̶̶̶̶̶̶̶̶̶ ̶̶̶̶̶̶̶̶̶bire*
by Lady Melicent Beaumont

Fortune's Folly, population 856, is a large village in north Yorkshire some twelve miles from the market town of Skipton. The village was originally called Fort-tun from the Old English, meaning a fort built on the site of an earlier farm. It is referred to as Fortune in a document from 1232 and has been known by that name ever since. The word *Folly,* from the Old French *fol,* meaning a fool, was added in 1455 when George Fortune, the lord of the manor, tried to repel a Lancastrian attack during the Wars of the Roses and accidentally blew up his own garrison instead.

The current lord of the manor is Sir Montague Fortune, baronet, who resides at Fortune Hall with his brother Thomas and half sister Lady Elizabeth Scarlet. Sir Montague is considered by all the populace to be very much in the mould of his ancestor George Fortune.

Other major houses in the village are The Old Palace, once the property of the prior of Fortune and currently the residence of Laura, Dowager Duchess of Cole, and the attractive modern villa Spring House, which was recently purchased by the heiress Miss Alice Lister of Harrogate.

There is a lively social season in Fortune's Folly that centres on the spa baths, the assembly rooms and the circulating library. There are two inns—The Granby Hotel, which is for the discerning visitor, and The Morris Clown for those slightly less plump of pocket and not too discriminating about the quality of their fellow guests. Whichever category you fall into, we hope you enjoy your visit!

NICOLA CORNICK

is an international bestselling author and a
RITA® Award finalist. Her sensational and sexy novels
have received acclaim the world over

"A rising star of the Regency arena."
—*Publishers Weekly*

"Nicola Cornick creates a glittering, sensual world of
historical romance that I never want to leave."
—Anna Campbell, author of *Untouched*

"Ms. Cornick has a brilliant talent for bringing her
characters to life, and embracing the reader into her
stories."
—*RomanceJunkies*

Praise for Nicola's previous HQN titles

"A powerful story, rich, witty and sensual—
a divinely delicious treat."
—Marilyn Rondeau, Reviewers International
Organization, on *Deceived*

"If you've liked Nicola Cornick's other books, you are
sure to like this one as well. If you've never read one—
what are you waiting for?"
—*Rakehell* on *Lord of Scandal*

"RITA® Award-nominated Cornick deftly steeps her
latest intriguingly complex Regency historical in a
beguiling blend of danger and desire."
—*Booklist* on *Unmasked*

NICOLA CORNICK

❧ THE BRIDES OF FORTUNE ❧

THE CONFESSIONS *of a* DUCHESS

HQN™

If you purchased this book without a cover you should be aware that this book is stolen property. It was reported as "unsold and destroyed" to the publisher, and neither the author nor the publisher has received any payment for this "stripped book."

Recycling programs
for this product may
not exist in your area.

ISBN-13: 978-0-373-77377-0

THE CONFESSIONS OF A DUCHESS

Copyright © 2009 by Nicola Cornick

All rights reserved. Except for use in any review, the reproduction or utilization of this work in whole or in part in any form by any electronic, mechanical or other means, now known or hereafter invented, including xerography, photocopying and recording, or in any information storage or retrieval system, is forbidden without the written permission of the publisher, Harlequin Enterprises Limited, 225 Duncan Mill Road, Don Mills, Ontario M3B 3K9, Canada.

This is a work of fiction. Names, characters, places and incidents are either the product of the author's imagination or are used fictitiously, and any resemblance to actual persons, living or dead, business establishments, events or locales is entirely coincidental.

This edition published by arrangement with Harlequin Books S.A.

® and TM are trademarks of the publisher. Trademarks indicated with ® are registered in the United States Patent and Trademark Office, the Canadian Trade Marks Office and in other countries.

www.HQNBooks.com

Printed in U.S.A.

**For an exclusive prequel to
The Brides of Fortune series visit
www.eHarlequin.com**

**Upcoming titles in
The Brides of Fortune series**

The Scandals of an Innocent (July 2009)
The Undoing of a Lady (August 2009)

Also available from

NICOLA CORNICK

and HQN Books

Deceived
Christmas Keepsakes
"A Season for Suitors"
Lord of Scandal
Unmasked

Other titles from Harlequin Historical

The Last Rake in London
Lord Greville's Captive
The Rake's Mistress
One Night of Scandal
The Notorious Lord

**Browse www.eHarlequin.com for
Nicola's full backlist**

To all the wonderful writers I have met through the U.K. Romantic Novelists Association and the Romance Writers of America.

THE CONFESSIONS of a DUCHESS

PROLOGUE

Go, take thine angle, and with practiced line
Light as the gossamer, the current sweep;
And if thou failest in the calm, still deep,
In the rough eddy may a prize be thine.
— Thomas Doubleday

Brooks's Club, London, July 1809

"SHE REFUSED ME!"

Sir Montague Fortune swept through the library of
Brooks's Club, scattered the gambling counters on the
faro table with the edge of his sleeve and gave no apology,
and deposited himself in an indignant flurry in a chair
beside the Earl of Waterhouse. He smoothed one shaking
hand over his hair and beckoned impatiently to a club
servant to fetch him brandy.

"Ungrateful minx," he muttered. "That I, one of the
Fortunes of Fortune's Folly should seek to ally myself
with the servant classes and be rejected!" He swallowed
half the glass of brandy in one gulp and gave the assembled group a furious glare. "Do you know what she called
me? A bibulous country squire with watery eyes!" He
reached for the brandy bottle that the servant had thought-

fully left on a low table beside him, refilled his glass and frowned slightly. "What does bibulous mean?"

"Damned if I know," Nathaniel Waterhouse said comfortably. "Dex was the one who shone at Oxford whilst the rest of us were running wild. Dex?"

Dexter Anstruther, thus applied to, raised his shrewd blue gaze from *The Times* and looked from the squire of Fortune's Folly to the brandy bottle and back again.

"It means that you drink too much, Monty," he drawled. He looked across at Miles, Lord Vickery, the fourth member of the group, who was smiling quizzically at Montague Fortune's indignation.

"Am I missing something here?" Miles inquired. "Who is the discerning lady who has rejected Monty's suit?"

"You've been in the Peninsular so long you've missed the *on dit,* old fellow," Waterhouse said. "Monty here has been paying ardent court to Miss Alice Lister, a former housemaid, if gossip is to be believed, who is now the richest heiress in Fortune's Folly. He offered her his hand and his heart in return for her money but the sensible female has evidently rejected him." He turned to Monty Fortune. "Surely you have not traveled all the way up to London just to bring us the bad news, Monty?"

"No," Montague Fortune huffed. "I have come up to consult my lawyer and study the Fortune's Folly estate papers."

"Very laudable," Dexter murmured. "Exactly what one would hope for in a responsible landowner."

Monty Fortune glared at him. "It is not for the benefit of my tenants," he protested. "It is so that I can get my hands on the money!"

"Whose money?" Dexter asked.

"Everyone's money!" Sir Montague barked. "It is not appropriate that half the population of Fortune's Folly should be richer than the squire!"

The others exchanged looks of covert amusement. The Fortunes were an old gentry family, perfectly respectable but with an inflated view of their own importance, and Sir Montague's single-minded pursuit of money was considered by some to be very bad *Ton*.

"What does Tom think of your plans, Monty?" Dexter asked, referring to Sir Montague's younger brother.

Sir Montague looked annoyed. "Said I was a grasping leech on other people's lives and went off to spend my substance at the gambling tables," he said.

The others laughed.

"And Lady Elizabeth?" Nat asked lazily. Lady Elizabeth Scarlet was Sir Montague's debutante half sister and a veritable thorn in his side.

"I cannot repeat Lizzie's language to you," Sir Montague said primly. "It is far too shocking!"

The laughter of the others increased.

Miles leaned forward. "So what are you planning, Monty?"

"I intend to assert my rights as lord of the manor," Sir Montague said, self-importantly. "There is a medieval law called the Dames' Tax that has never been repealed. It permits the lord of the manor to levy a tithe on every unmarried woman in the village."

Miles's lips formed a soundless whistle. "How much is the tithe?"

"I can take half their fortune!" Sir Montague announced triumphantly.

There was a shocked silence around the group.

"Monty," Dexter said slowly, "did I understand you correctly? It is in your power to levy a tax of half their wealth on all unmarried women in Fortune's Folly?"

Sir Montague nodded, eyes bright.

"How?" Dexter demanded. "Why?"

"I told you." Sir Montague's greedy gaze swept the group. "Medieval laws. Because Fortune's Folly belonged to the church it was exempt when the secular laws were repealed in the seventeenth century. I discovered quite by accident that all the tithes and taxes are still applicable. In recent centuries they have not been collected only through the goodwill of the squire."

"And you do not have any goodwill," Nat said dryly.

"Not now that Miss Lister has refused me," Sir Montague said, the virtuous expression on his face sitting oddly with the avarice in his eyes. "Had she accepted me I am sure that I would have been the most generous of village squires."

"And one of the richest," Dexter murmured.

"Every single woman… Half their fortunes…" Nat Waterhouse was spluttering into his brandy. "That's…" His mathematical ability, never strong, failed him. "That's potentially a huge amount of money, Monty!" he protested.

"I know." With a self-satisfied smile, Sir Montague settled back in his chair. "I have not quite worked it out yet but Miss Lister's fortune is rumored to be in the region of eighty thousand pounds and Mrs. Everton pocketed a cool fifty thousand under the terms of her husband's will—"

Miles shot him a sharp glance. "It applies to widows as well as spinsters?"

"All unmarried women," Sir Montague confirmed.

"But I have a cousin living in Fortune's Folly," Miles protested. "You can't fleece her, Monty! It's not socially acceptable, old fellow—not acceptable at all!"

Dexter raked a hand through his disordered tawny hair in a characteristic gesture. "Presumably if the ladies of Fortune's Folly choose to marry they are exempt from the tax?"

Sir Montague nodded. "That's it, Dexter. Got it in one. I can see why the government employs you."

Dexter's lips twitched. "Thank you, Monty. I am glad that my powers of deduction are still as acute as I thought. So." He paused. "You announce the introduction of the Dames' Tax and the ladies of Fortune's Folly have to decide whether they wish to give away half of their money to you in tax or all of it to their husbands in marriage."

Nat winced. "They will be as mad as wet hens to be forced into this situation, Monty. I hope you are prepared."

Sir Montague shrugged expansively. "They can't do anything about it. The law is on my side. I tell you, the plan is perfect."

The others exchanged looks. "Monty, old chap," Miles said softly, "much as I disapprove of your avarice, I do believe that you have just made Fortune's Folly a veritable marriage mart, a positive haven for those of us who are—"

"Impecunious," Dexter said. "Improvident, penurious—"

"Flat broke," Nat said, "and looking for a rich wife."

"You're right," Sir Montague said, beaming. "I have made Fortune's Folly the marriage mart of England!"

CHAPTER ONE

Fortune's Folly, Yorkshire, September 1809

DOWAGER. It was such a lonely word.

Most people thought of dowagers as faintly comic figures, diamonds displayed on their shelflike bosom, possessing a long, patrician nose to look down.

Laura Cole thought of dowagers as the loneliest people in the world.

It was Laura's loneliness that had prompted her to go down to the river that day, dressed in a pale blue muslin gown with a warm navy-blue spencer over the top, a wide-brimmed straw bonnet on her head and a novel in her hand. She had read somewhere that the beauties of nature were supposed to soothe a troubled spirit and so she had decided to take the rowing boat out and float in bucolic peace under the willow branches that fringed the water's edge.

However, the nature cure was proving to be a disappointing failure. For a start the boat was full of fallen yellow leaves, and once Laura had brushed them off the seat her gloves were already dirty. She sat down and opened her book, but found herself unable to concentrate on the trials and tribulations of her heroine because her mind was full of her own difficulties instead. Every so often, golden-brown leaves would float down and adorn the page. The wind was surprisingly chilly. Laura frowned at her lack of attentiveness and tried all the harder to enjoy herself.

Laura loved the countryside. She had grown up in this wild Yorkshire landscape and had lived in the county for much of her life, though she had spent the previous two years in London. She had hoped that returning to her childhood home would lessen the feeling of emptiness that dogged her steps these days, but it had not, and she could not understand it. It was not as though she was alone in the world. She adored her three-year-old daughter, Harriet, and spent an unfashionable amount of time with her. Fortune's Folly was a busy little village and she had made many new friends there. And she also had a huge extended family with a tribe of cousins in every rank of the *Ton*. It was not even the case that she missed her late husband, Charles, for they had lived apart for the majority of their marriage. She had been shocked when Charles had died, of course. All of Society had been shocked that a man could be so profligate that he over-turned his curricle and killed three of his mistresses as well as himself. But Laura had not missed the errant duke. She had felt enormous relief when she had heard that he had died.

Relief.

Guilt.

Excitement.

She had felt a thrill of anticipation that she and Hattie were free and then she had felt guilty again and lonelier than she had ever done in her life.

It was to forge a future for herself and Hattie that Laura had come to Fortune's Folly. She wanted her daughter to grow up in the country, so after a year of formal mourning she had left London, where people insisted on trying to commiserate with her about Charles's death, and had come to this Yorkshire village near to Skipton, where her grandmother had left her a modest house, The Old Palace. It sounded grand but Laura privately thought that it should have been renamed Old Place rather than Palace because it was an ancient and inconvenient medieval building no doubt suited to a not-so-ancient but impoverished dowager duchess who was trying to make a new start in life. Her brother and sister-in-law had pressed her to live with them but Laura had a vision of what that would be like—the dowager aunt taken in through charity, deferring to her brother's will at every turn—and she knew that even solitary poverty had to be better than genteel dependence. Hattie's situation would be even more intolerable than her own as she grew up as a poor relation. It was not to be borne. Skimping and scraping, growing her own fruit and vegetables, keeping bees, making and mending, just herself and Hattie and a few servants had to be preferable to being her brother's pensioner.

Her daughter was a constant joy and revelation to her. And though she sometimes wished that Hattie had brothers or sisters with whom to share her childhood, Laura thought this wildly unlikely now. In order to have more children she would need to take a new husband and it would take an exceptional man to persuade her into marriage again after her experience with Charles. She and ould fend quite well for themselves and soon, she was sure, her feelings of isolation would start to fade. She did not want her melancholy to affect Hattie. Hattie was such a happy child.

She cast the book aside and untied the mooring rope. Since she could not seem to concentrate on reading, she would take the boat for a short row on the river. Physical activity would help to occupy her and she could admire the autumnal countryside at the same time. She pushed the boat off from the bank and sat back to enjoy the gentle flow of the river.

As soon as the boat left the shelter of the bank the current caught it with quite unexpected strength. The water flowed deep and fast here. Nervous now, Laura gritted her teeth and tried to use the oars to steer back to the side, but she was clumsy and the river was too powerful. One of the oars slid from the rowlock and floated away. The boat began to make its rather erratic way down the river quite of its own accord.

Life, Laura thought helplessly, as she watched the oar bob away from her, so seldom turned out as planned. Here she was, a widow of four and thirty with a small daughter, virtually penniless and with an uncertain future. And now her immediate prospects scarcely looked better than her long-term ones. In fact they looked very wet and unpleasant indeed. She needed to start thinking about how she was going to get out of this situation without compromising her life, if not her dignity.

The boat scraped against the stony bed of the river and Laura made a grab for an overhanging branch, missed it and felt the sleeve of her spencer rip. Damnation. She could not afford to buy any new clothes. She would be the only duchess in the country who would be wearing darned clothing. People would commend her for her frugality to her face and talk about her poverty behind her back. Even in the small society of Fortune's Folly there was a great deal of gossip, and not much of it was kind.

Laura plied her one remaining oar with energy but little direction and felt the boat start to turn in a slow circle in the water, which was not what she had intended at all. She rowed a little harder and the boat turned more quickly, picking up momentum, swinging around in a way that made her feel slightly sick. She grabbed for another branch in a last attempt to save herself. The sunlight was in her eyes and the shadows danced against her lids, blinding her, and the bark of the tree scored her fingers. She had just managed to gain a faint purchase when she felt the boat lurch as though someone had pushed it hard. The branch snapped, hitting her on the back of the head as it fell into the water. She heard the snap of breaking twigs and a scuffle as though someone were running away.

The boat rocked and Laura's head spun with nausea. She let go of the second oar and clutched the sides. She could only hope that the boat would steady and the current would take her back in to the bank for she was momentarily too disoriented, and felt too sick, to do anything else.

But the boat did not steady. Instead it lurched out into the center of the river and headed toward the fish weir. The current was flowing faster and faster now. Laura knew she should jump but she had left it too late. The river was too strong for her here. She thought that she heard someone shouting but the sound was lost in the roar of the water and the grating of the stones of the weir beneath the hull of the boat. It rolled violently and then Laura was pitched over the side and the river closed over her head. The noise was in her ears and the water filled her lungs so she could not breathe. She had a last, vivid picture in her mind of her daughter's smiling face and then everything went dark.

CHAPTER TWO

DEXTER ANSTRUTHER was fishing.

Such a mild autumn day in the rocky reaches of the River Tune was perfect for grayling. Dexter liked fishing because it was a peaceful, soothing and solitary occupation, in contrast to the frequently disturbing, violent and unpleasant matters that he had to deal with in his work for the Home Secretary. Only the previous week Dexter had masterminded the capture of a brutal criminal who specialized in theft and extortion. He had hoped that after that success Lord Liverpool, the Home Secretary, would finally be persuaded to allow him some much-needed leave. But Liverpool had another plan.

"Need you to go to Yorkshire and deal with some damned murdering criminal," Lord Liverpool had said, snapping a quill pen irritably between his fingers and casting the parts aside with a muttered curse. "You remember the death of Sir William Crosby, Anstruther?"

"Yes, my lord," Dexter said. Sir William Crosby, a Yorkshire magistrate, had shot himself whilst out hunting a month before. "I thought," he added, "that that had been an accident?"

Lord Liverpool shook his head. "Murder," he said, with gloomy relish. "It was dressed up to look like an accident but Crosby was left-handed and the angle of the bullet made it impossible for him to have tripped and fallen. Blasted nuisance, but the fact is that these blackguards can't be allowed to get away with it."

"Quite, my lord," Dexter said. "But if it is a straightforward case of murder, surely this is a matter for the local constable rather than the Guardians—" He stopped as Liverpool shook his head crossly and reached for another quill to decimate.

"Can't allow some bungling local official to deal with this, Anstruther," he had barked. "It's complicated. Warren Sampson may be involved. Crosby was investigating some business that implicated Sampson when he died. Convenient, eh?"

Dexter pursed his lips on a soundless whistle. That did put a different complexion on matters. For several years there had been rumors that Warren Sampson, a disgustingly rich Yorkshire mill owner and businessman, was involved in stirring up civil unrest and sedition in the North of England. Sampson was clever about it and there was nothing that could be pinned on him; he worked through intermediaries and it was thought that he encouraged mill riots so that he could steal business from his rivals and that he had perpetrated various insurance frauds and other swindles. Lord Liverpool was near apoplectic because the authorities had been unable to trap Sampson.

"There is a rumor that one of Sampson's henchmen is a member of the local gentry," Liverpool said disgustedly. "The bored son of some rustic squire looking for excitement and extra cash, perhaps. He may well be the murderer, Anstruther. The whole thing is a damned nuisance, but the case needs careful handling."

Dexter had sighed. "Do we have any idea of the location of this aristocratic delinquent, my lord?"

"Sampson owns land around Peacock Oak and Fortune's Folly," Lord Liverpool said, "and Crosby lived close by. The trouble is that every petty criminal in the country is hanging out there at the moment. Natural enough when that dashed fool Monty Fortune has put about town the fact that he has made the place the marriage mart of England. The town is crowded with visitors and every villain for miles around wants to get their share of the spoils."

Dexter saw the problem. Even the impecunious fortune hunters who flocked to the village might have a watch or a snuffbox worth stealing and the homes of the rich heiresses would yield fine pickings. It was a temptation many criminals would not wish to resist and in amongst the petty thieves might lurk a more dangerous malefactor with Warren Sampson pulling his strings.

"Whilst you are there you could also turn your attention to finding yourself a rich wife, Anstruther," Lord Liverpool had added. "Don't think that I don't know your family finances are in a parlous state. Your mama can no more retrench than she could swim the Thames, your sisters need to be launched into society and your brothers are damned expensive to educate. You need to wed an heiress. Penniless men are vulnerable to blackmail and I cannot have that in a man working so closely with me."

"I would not dream of succumbing to blackmail, no matter how desperate my situation, my lord," Dexter said coldly. He clenched his hands into fists to prevent himself from telling his employer how offended he was at the suggestion.

"No need to get touchy with me, lad," Liverpool grunted, noticing the gesture. "I know you're sound as a bell but others in your family may not be and where there is a weakness…" He shook his head. "Get you to Fortune's Folly. If you cannot catch yourself a rich wife there, then I wash my hands of you. But make sure that you find our miscreant before you succumb to the lures of some young lady. I don't want you distracted, Anstruther. This Fortune's Folly marriage mart business is the perfect cover for your presence in Yorkshire but make sure you keep your mind on your work first and your fortune hunting second."

"Yes, my lord," Dexter said.

"I'll give you two months," Lord Liverpool said. "Want the matter tied up by Christmas, Anstruther. That should give you plenty of time. If you're lucky you might even fit in some fishing, as well. Catch the murdering miscreant fair and square, see that he implicates Sampson, as well, and if you also come back with a wealthy wife you will have done a good job."

"Yes, my lord," Dexter said, heart sinking. There was no reasoning with Lord Liverpool when he was in this sort of mood. And truth to tell, Dexter knew that he should not be arguing the case anyway. Lord Liverpool was right—he desperately needed a rich wife and ever since Monty Fortune had made his announcement in Brooks's Club that night he had been thinking of going to Yorkshire to find one.

The problem, Dexter reflected, as he cast his line again, was that he was a reluctant suitor. Hence the fact that he was fishing today rather than paying court to any of the ladies gathered in the winter gardens and the pump rooms. Blatant fortune hunting offended his sense of honor. But, as Miles Vickery had helpfully pointed out to him, honor could be an expensive commodity and one that, in this context, Dexter really could not afford.

Dexter's father had died five years before, having gambled away a fortune that he did not have. The Honorable James Anstruther had staggered out of his club on his way to a low tavern to drown his sorrows, and had finished the whole sorry business of his life by stumbling, blind drunk, in front of a carriage and leaving his eldest son with a pile of debts and six siblings to take care of. By great good fortune he had staved off his ruin until Dexter had completed his studies at Oxford, which at least ensured he could get a job in the government, but it was not well paid and the widowed Mrs. Anstruther and his younger brothers and sisters were ruinously extravagant and expensive.

Some people are blessed with one irresponsible parent; Dexter had two. In that respect The Honorable Mr. Anstruther and his wife were extremely well suited, with their gambling, their affairs and their general decadence. Dexter, the eldest child and the only one of the seven members of the "Anstruther Collection" who could definitely be assumed to be his father's son, had watched his parents lurch from financial crisis to emotional disaster for as long as he could remember. From the age of twelve he had determined that his life was going to be the opposite of his father's: rational, controlled and with no dangerous emotions to cloud his judgment. He would marry responsibly to a woman who would be faithful to him and his children would know exactly who their parents were. He would never tolerate for his offspring the kind of stigma and ignominy that had attached to him and his siblings: the covert smiles, the knowing looks, the veiled references to his parents' disastrous affairs and their own illegitimacy.

Such a rational approach to life had stood him in good stead until the age of twenty-two, when he had succumbed to one spectacular, exhilarating episode of sexual abandon, during which he had lost his heart as well as his virginity and fallen hopelessly in love. The incident had been a disaster, reinforcing in the end all his beliefs about the need for a calm and controlled life. In his youth and inexperience he had miscalculated badly and thought his feelings were returned. Disillusioned and angry when he had discovered they were not, he had sought solace in liaisons with courtesans that he could ill afford until Lord Liverpool had called him gruffly to account.

There was no sound but for the call of a moorhen by the riverbank and the splash of a fish farther upstream. The day was extremely peaceful. Dexter cast his line again, thinking of the calm and rational future marriage he had planned.

"Try not to make as big a hash of this case as you did that Glory business, Anstruther," Liverpool had said caustically as he bade Dexter farewell. "That whole affair was an utter disaster."

Dexter shifted slightly now as he reflected on the conversation. The "Glory business" Lord Liverpool had referred to had indeed been an unfortunate case. Four years previously, Dexter and his colleague Nick Falconer had failed to capture the highwaywoman Glory, a popular heroine who was the darling of the Yorkshire Dales. Glory had fought for justice in her own inimitable style, righting wrongs, settling scores, taking from the rich to give to the poor in true Robin Hood style. Even now, Dexter could not quite think of Glory as anything other than a heroine, a piece of sentimentality that irritated him profoundly when he should not have been thinking about her at all.

The bobbin on the end of his fishing line dipped, indicating that a fish had taken the bait. Dexter started to reel it in.

He heard a splash followed by an expletive and then an oar drifted lazily past him, tangling briefly with the fishing line and dislodging his catch. Dexter swore, too, and again as a second oar came sailing past, knocking his fishing rod off the bank. He made a grab for it and reeled it in just as Laura, Dowager Duchess of Cole, floated past in a rowing boat.

Dexter straightened up and watched curiously.

The rowing boat was spinning slowly in the current, heading toward the fish weir. He could see Laura sitting bolt upright, clutching the sides of the boat. She seemed stunned. Dexter doubted that she could swim. Most women could not, for it was not something that they were taught. And she was perfectly right to be worried, of course. He calculated quite coolly that in a minute, two at the most, the boat would tumble over the weir and Laura would fall into the water and might well drown. She might hit her head as she fell, or her long skirts might become entangled and pull her underwater, or any number of fatal things might happen to her.

Which, arguably, was what Laura Cole deserved for giving him such a perfect night of love four years before and then shattering his heart immediately afterward, showing herself to be no more than a cold, calculating, selfish and hypocritical creature into the bargain.

Not that he was bitter.

He did not care. Laura Cole could drown, for all he cared.

Hell and the devil.

Laura Cole would drown in approximately one minute and he was standing here watching it happen.

Dexter threw down the fishing rod and wrenched off his jacket. There was no time to stop to remove his boots. He strode into the river—it was shallow at the edge but deep in the middle—just as the boat reached the top of the weir and stopped with a rather sickening crunch as the wooden frame caught on the stones at the top.

"Jump!" he shouted.

Laura turned toward him. Her face was a pale blur. She was gripping the edge of the boat so tightly that Dexter could see her knuckles white against the dark wood. She did not move.

The water was up to his chest now and the current was frighteningly strong, threatening to pull him over the top of the weir. The mossy stone of the riverbed slid beneath his feet, treacherously uneven, as he struggled to stay upright.

Dexter made a grab for the boat but in that second the keel slid with a grating roar across the stones at the top of the weir, tipped up at a steep angle and decanted Laura into the river. She disappeared over the top of the weir in a cacophony of water, her bonnet tumbling off and one of her shoes flying through the air in a perfect arc before landing with a plop in the water beside Dexter's head. Muttering a curse, Dexter gave in and allowed the current to take him over the weir and into the deep green pool at the bottom. Even as he did it he wondered what on earth possessed him to take such a dangerous risk. He felt as though all the air had been pummeled from his body in the fall. There was the sound of rushing water in his ears, cold water that chilled him bone-deep. It filled his lungs, smothering him. He stumbled upright, shaking the water from his eyes, searching desperately for Laura.

Then he saw her.

She was struggling like a madwoman against the heavy, dragging weight of her skirts, which threatened to pull her under. He grabbed hold of her and held her hard against him, protecting her from the tow of the current. His hand was firm in the hollow of her back, their lower bodies pressed intimately together. The water splashed cold around them, but where their bodies touched and clung together he could, suddenly and surprisingly, feel the heat in her. Her breasts were resting against his chest and through his soaking shirt and her drenched clothes he could feel her nipples tight and hard, pressing against him. Despite the cold water and the extreme discomfort of their situation, he felt his body start to stir as he remembered that other occasion on which she had been clasped close in his arms, naked, warm and enticing.

Dexter had not anticipated this happening to him when—if—he ever met Laura Cole again. Certainly it was not his usual response to a soaking-wet female. But now the memories of his night with Laura swelled like a dam that was about to burst and in combination with her wet and seminaked state made his erection swell in proportion. He felt simultaneously hugely aroused and furiously angry with himself for that instant and very inappropriate arousal. He tried to think of icy winds and how chilly the water was, but his body felt like a furnace. He could not control it. And the more he tried to exert self-control the more excited his errant body seemed to become, as though it were asserting its independence and its right to find Laura attractive if it chose. Dex was enraged.

Laura could evidently feel his response, as well. She raised a hand and dashed the wet strands of honey-brown hair back from her face. Her hazel eyes snapped with anger and discomposure. A hint of color touched her cheekbones. She looked as though she was as uncomfortable with his proximity as he was with hers. It was the reaction of the perfect, respectable duchess that he had always imagined her to be. And indeed she had been utterly perfect in his bed and nowhere near as virtuous as she pretended to be out of it…

"Mr. Anstruther! What are you *doing?*" Laura hit exactly the right note for an outraged dowager duchess and Dexter admired the apparent ease with which she could assume the role. No one hearing her now would ever guess that she had taken him into her bed and made mad, ecstatic, explosive love to him for an entire afternoon, evening and night. It might be something that, with hindsight, he deplored ever happening, but it seemed he could not forget it.

"I am saving you from drowning, your grace," Dexter said politely. "However, if you object I can let you go." He suited actions to words by loosening his grip on her.

Laura gave a muffled squeak and clung to him all the more tightly, her fingers digging into the muscles of his upper arms. Dexter was immediately reminded of the sensation of her fingernails scoring his back as she had moved in sensual abandonment beneath him. He tried to ignore the thought and erase the memory—and failed dismally. His body hardened still further until he felt as though he might burst—or throw her down on the river-bank and make love to her. He struggled for some ration-ality but his body still felt as though it was under independent ownership, hot, tight and desperate for sat-isfaction. He almost groaned aloud. It was a long time since he had had a woman—since his fall from grace and subsequent recovery he had avoided casual *affaires*—and none of the women he had known had ever affected him in the stunningly physical way that Laura did. That had been part of the problem. The awareness between them was unwanted, it was infuriating, but it was undeniable.

"Mr. Anstruther, do you always find situations such as this so arousing?" Laura's tone was frigid enough to turn the most ardent man limp.

"Always," Dexter said grimly. He bent, slid an arm beneath her knees and swept her off her feet and up into his arms. Judging by the startled look on Laura's face, he guessed that no one had ever done that to her before. Perhaps it was not surprising for she was a tall woman. He stood at over six feet and she was a bare few inches shorter than him. Many men, he was aware, would find that intimidating.

Buffeted by the current, he strode toward the bank and deposited her gently on the ground. She was still wearing one shoe, the match for the one that had floated off down the river. He noticed that her other foot, in its soaked silk stocking, was large for a woman, but nevertheless deli-cately shaped with an elegantly high instep. For some reason Dexter found the fact that Laura had big feet to be rather endearing. He wished now that the contrast between her size and her apparent fragility did not appeal to him so much. He did not like her and he did not want to be attracted to her any more but reason, the main-spring of his life, seemed to desert him when Laura was around. It was most inconvenient and quite inexplicable.

"Thank you for your assistance." Laura's tone was still arctic. "You may leave me now."

Dexter had had every intention of doing precisely that, but her dismissal grated on him. He stood watching as she wrung the water from her skirts. It was a fairly point-less exercise. Her entire gown was soaking, damp, he was quick to appreciate, in ways that went far beyond the practice followed by fashionable whores. The drenched muslin clung to every one of her curves—and those who declared Laura Cole to have no figure were clearly mistaken for she had the most entrancingly small, rounded, tip-tilted breasts and a deliciously arched line to her hips.

But Dexter knew that already.

He had seen those curves.

He had traced every last one of them with his hands and his lips and his tongue. He had worshipped her with his body....

Suddenly the mild autumn day seemed sweltering. Dexter's brain ceased to function at any coherent level as his mind finally gave up the resistance and was swamped with erotic images of Laura lying naked on her tumbled bed at Cole Court whilst he followed every lush, tempting line of her body with his lips. The memories seemed indelibly imprinted on his mind. No attempt at erasure ever seemed to work, no matter how he had tried, or how he had pretended to forget her.

He had wondered what would happen if and when he met Laura Cole again. It was a natural enough matter to speculate about. In the encounters he had envisaged, he had variously been civil, cold, contemptuous and indifferent. In none of them had his throat dried with lust and his eyes been riveted to her slender figure as she stood dripping wet and unbearably seductive before him. Another hot wave of desire surged through him even as he shivered as the breeze flattened his wet trousers against his thighs. There was no concealing his enormous erection now.

And Laura had stopped wringing out her skirts, the material falling from her hands as she straightened up, and was looking at him with a mixture of shock and outrage.

"Mr. Anstruther, a gentleman does not *stare* at a lady in that frank and boorish manner. Nor does he demonstrate such a strong reaction…" She stopped, making a vague flapping gesture with her hands toward his groin.

Dexter could have put her right on that. No matter how much he fought it, no matter how much he wished to suppress his desires, he was obliged to admit that any man with a pulse would be staring when a figure straight from his most heated fantasies was standing before him. That same man would, as Laura herself had put it, develop a strong and well-nigh irresistible reaction to what he saw. From the confrontational tilt of her chin, however, he suspected that Laura would not take kindly to being corrected. She had started to shiver and looked both upset and defiant. Whilst he had no time for her false protestations of respectability—not with the things that he knew about her—he could see that this might not be the moment to discuss the matter.

With one stride Dexter had reached her side and swung her up in his arms again. She went absolutely rigid as soon as he touched her.

"Where are you staying?" he inquired.

"I live at The Old Palace," Laura said, "but there is absolutely no need for you to carry me home in this fashion. Unhand me at once, Mr. Anstruther. I insist!" She was at her most peremptory. Most people, Dexter was aware, would obey such a command from a dowager duchess. He ignored it and did not even break his stride as he marched purposefully across the water meadow toward the gate that led to The Old Palace.

Laura's hair was starting to dry now in honey-brown wisps about her face. She had had it cut since Dexter had first known her and the cluster of curls in the nape of her neck was extremely becoming. One of them brushed his cheek like a feather across his bare skin. Dexter felt the shiver down to his toes. It was so light a touch to have so profound an effect on him. But it seemed impossible not to be aware of every last inch of her. She smelled of fresh air and roses; the scent was in her hair and on her skin and it made him want to bury his face in the curve of her neck and to taste her. He wondered if she would taste the same as he remembered. He wondered if she would kiss the way he remembered. He imagined not. These days he was inclined to believe—or to hope for the sake of his peace of mind—that in his youthful infatuation he had imagined her to be so much more perfect than she really was. The dazzling, physical compatibility that he had thought existed between them would prove to be a product of his inexperience. A kiss was just a kiss. She would not be special and he would not lose his head over her again.

But he would give a lot to know...

As though sensing his feelings, Laura tried to hold herself away from him and put some distance between their bodies.

"Do not be alarmed," Dexter said. "You are perfectly safe. All I mean to do is convey you home. I have no intention of ravishing you. I do not even like you."

Laura arched her brows. "Indeed? Parts of you seem to like me well enough, Mr. Anstruther."

"True," Dexter said. "They always did. But then not all of me is as discerning as my mind."

Laura gave a snort of disgust. "Then spare yourself further bodily inconvenience and permit me to walk home unaided. I do not need your help. Indeed, I had no notion that you were even visiting Fortune's Folly."

"Nor I you."

"A pity," Laura said acidly. "If only we had known we could each have chosen a different destination and spared ourselves the unpleasantness of having to meet."

Dexter ignored her comments again, kicking open the paddock gate with one booted foot and striding across the field toward the house. A little social discomfort was the least she owed him. Anger and contempt licked through his blood again. Laura had thrown him out of the house the very morning after their passionate night together. He had begged her to run away with him and she had told him he was no more than a stupid youth. She had laughed at his suggestion, taking all that new and untried love for her that he had only just discovered and making it seem tawdry. Her words were etched in his memory:

"Did you imagine that this meant more to me than a brief and pleasant interlude? What a great deal you have to learn, Mr. Anstruther. It was but sport...."

He had been ridiculously naive, and she an experienced woman to whom he was, no doubt, just one in a long line of liaisons and infidelities. He knew that was how many of the bored wives of the *Ton* passed their time, going from husband to lover as the fancy took them. But at the time he had thought Laura different and the whole business had left him feeling stupid and betrayed, and vowing never again to allow his physical passions to cloud his emotions and swamp his good judgment. He had thought himself a man of firm principles until he had met Laura Cole but now he thought bitterly that in her company his strength of character lasted just as long as it took him to take his clothes off.

Cynically, he supposed that he should actually be grateful to her. If she had not shown her true colors, if she had not discarded him with careless disdain but had taken him at his word and run away with him, he would have made an almighty mess of his life and one from which he might never have recovered his rational, calm and logical course. No indeed, he should thank Laura for turning him down so brutally and making him see that passion had no place in his life.

Laura shifted in his arms and sighed again. Dexter almost sighed himself. His body was still clamoring for satisfaction even as his mind despised her. It was a small revenge to make her so uncomfortable through his proximity and not a particularly sensible idea, but he felt she deserved it.

"You know, you really should not go out alone in a boat if you cannot swim," he observed softly into the tumble of curls that tickled his chin.

"I *can* swim." Laura wriggled crossly, which did nothing for Dexter's concentration and a great deal for his bodily torment.

"I was brought up around here and swam in the river from the age of three," she said. "Unfortunately I do not have an extensive wardrobe and prefer not to swim in a muslin gown."

"How like a woman," Dexter said. "Given a choice between jumping in the water and ruining her gown or escaping drowning, she prefers not to jump."

Laura clenched her lower lip between her teeth. Dexter felt his body jolt. He had fantasized often enough about feeling that mouth against his own again.

"I had forgotten that you are an expert on women these days, Mr. Anstruther," Laura said. "How fortuitous that your experience gained in bawdy houses and brothels across London has given you such an insight into the female mind. You *have* changed."

"I have." Anger flickered within Dexter again. He tried to quench it. Anger was not a proper response to this situation. It was dangerous and threatened his control in much the same way that his lust did. Laura could try to goad him as much as she wished but he would not rise to her provocation.

"I am not the same man you knew before," he said.

"Evidently," Laura said. "Four years can change a man."

"Is it four years?" Dexter was not going to admit that he could tell her the precise length of their time apart in days and months, and possibly hours if he was honest. "I had forgotten."

"Of course you had," Laura said. He saw a faint bitter smile touch her lips. "Men always do."

Well, no doubt she knew the truth of that with her experience. Dexter tried not to care. He wrenched open the garden gate and marched up the path.

The grounds at The Old Palace were empty and overgrown. The house seemed shuttered and still. Dexter looked around. "Where are your servants?"

Laura seemed discomfited. "I do not have a large staff. They are probably busy about the house somewhere and my daughter is out in the village with her nursery maid, so no one will be about."

Dexter had yet to meet a duchess who had less than a regiment of servants. They seemed to think that being waited upon hand and foot was their inalienable right. But perhaps Charles Cole had left Laura without a feather to fly and no means to support her young daughter. The new duke held the title now and there was apparently no love lost between Henry Cole and his cousin's widow, so he would not be financing her, either. At any rate, no one answered the door to Dexter's increasingly forthright knocking.

"Oh, put me down!" Laura said, clearly losing patience and slipping from his arms before Dexter could stop her. "I can open a door for myself and I am chilled to the bone, dripping here." She looked at him. "You are very damp, as well, Mr. Anstruther. Do you require a change of clothing? I do believe there are some old clothes of my grandfather's somewhere about the place should you need them."

"Thank you, your grace," Dexter said, with a slight bow, "but I shall collect my fishing gear and walk back to the inn as I am."

Laura looked at the pool of water that was dripping steadily from his shirt onto the slate of the path. "Surely that will cause conjecture if anyone sees you?"

"Not as much as the sight of me walking back to the Morris Clown Inn dressed in your grandfather's Georgian fashions, I imagine," Dexter said.

"My grandfather was quite the beau," Laura said. "You might find that you start a new style. Not that that is likely to appeal to you, I suppose, Mr. Anstruther. Fashion is far too shallow an interest for one of your serious nature, is it not? Or have you changed in that respect, as well?"

Dexter was almost drawn into replying to that. He admitted ruefully to himself that he was finding it hard to resist Laura's provocation. She had a way of getting under his skin unmatched by anyone else he had ever met.

She looked exquisite, he thought, standing there in damp disarray. Others overlooked Laura because her beauty was not of the obvious variety that society admired. Her appeal for him lay in the fine, direct gaze of those hazel eyes and the rich creaminess of a skin that was sprinkled with endearing freckles. It was in the soft curl of that honey-chestnut-colored hair and the upward turn of her lips, as though she was always on the edge of a smile. The fact that she was not in the first flush of youth and had a tracery of fine lines about her eyes only enhanced her beauty for him because it added character.... Dexter caught himself up before he got too carried away. There was no point in standing here catching a chill whilst he rhapsodized about Laura's outward beauty. It was not a fair guide to the woman beneath, whom he had discovered was actually a calculating and manipulative whore.

"On second thoughts, I will accept your offer of a change of clothing, thank you," he said, following her into the stone flagged hallway of The Old Palace. "The breeze is chilly today and there is no sense in taking cold. One must be practical."

"Of course," Laura said. "I know that you pride yourself on your practicality, Mr. Anstruther."

The house was silent, the floors muffled in ancient rugs, the walls smothered in equally dark and old tapestries on which were depicted a variety of bloodthirsty war and hunting scenes. A huge suit of medieval armor dominated one corner. From the wall above the fireplace glared a bad-tempered stag's head whilst a moth-eaten stuffed fox prowled the stone windowsill. There was a child's rocking horse in one corner and a rather beautiful porcelain-faced doll sitting in a small chair.

"I see that your grandfather had martial tastes as well as sartorial ones," Dexter said, looking at the shields hanging rather precariously from the walls.

Laura shook her head. "No, that was my grandmother. She rode to hounds every day and could shoot a longbow. She said that one of them had to think about more than the cut of their clothes." She pointed to two portraits hanging on the far wall. "There they are."

The late Lord Asthall looked every inch the eighteenth-century dandy, Dexter thought. He had hazel eyes and black hair, a pronounced nose and strong chin, and his expression was arrogant and amoral. His features were also vaguely familiar. Dexter's paternal family had come from Yorkshire several generations back and there had been a rumor in the family that there was bastard Asthall blood in the line somewhere. Certainly Dexter's brother Roly and his father's so-called "ward" Caro had the same coloring. Dexter reflected ruefully that that was probably where his father had got his libertine tendencies from, as well. Lord Asthall looked a complete cad. Still, Lady Asthall was, quite frankly, a fearsome Amazon of a woman in her archery dress, so perhaps they had been well matched.

"Were they happy together?" he asked.

"I do not believe so. My grandfather was a terrible rake," Laura said, confirming Dexter's suspicions. "I am surprised that Grandmama did not shoot him with her bow and arrow."

"And does your daughter inherit the same sporting prowess as her great-grandmother?" Dexter asked.

Laura paused. There was a rather odd silence. Looking at her, Dexter thought she looked pinched and cold, as though he were trespassing on a subject she did not want to discuss.

"Hattie is still very young." Laura spoke stiffly. "She can sit a small pony if I walk beside her and she loves her rocking horse, so perhaps one day she will be a rider."

There was another silence. Dexter could hear the loud hum of a bumblebee trapped against the windowpane and the rush of the river over the weir. He felt a little disquieted to think of Laura rattling around in this ancient place all on her own with her small daughter, but then there did not seem much of value to steal here. It seemed that his speculation about Charles Cole leaving Laura with no money had been close to the mark. She was penniless, alone and unprotected. He was disturbed at how uneasy the thought made him.

The door at the end of the dark corridor opened and a butler shuffled forward into the patch of sunlight that was making patterns through the diamond windowpanes.

"Your grace! I did not hear the bell."

Dexter was shocked to recognize Carrington, the butler from Cole Court. Four years ago the man had been vigorous and healthy. Now he looked old and broken. He stooped. His hands shook and his voice was a whisper. Dexter doubted that he could hold a tray, let alone announce visitors.

"It does not matter, Carrington," Laura spoke softly. "Please could you show Mr. Anstruther down to the warming room whilst I find some dry clothing for him? We have had a small mishap."

The butler's gaze darted from one to the other like a furtive rabbit. "An accident? Oh, madam—"

"There is nothing to cause distress," Laura interrupted firmly. "It was no more than a fall in the river. If you would be so good…"

The butler nodded and drew himself up with a sad echo of his former authority. "This way, sir, if you please."

CHAPTER THREE

DEXTER FOLLOWED the tottering butler down the old stone stair. On more than one occasion he put out a hand to steady the man when it appeared he was about to tumble down the steps to the bottom. He could not believe the change in Carrington and was tempted to ask him what had happened except that the butler seemed confused and did not appear to recognize him at all. He showed Dexter into the little warming room, where a fire burned hot in the grate and the air was scented with lavender from the drying sheets, and promptly disappeared.

Dexter stripped off his sodden shirt with some relief, for little trickles of water were still running down his chest and they felt icy cold. His boots were also full of water and it was one of the most unpleasant things he had ever experienced. He hoped that they were not ruined. They were almost new and he could not afford to buy another pair. He had invested in several new items of clothing to add credence to his role as a fortune hunter since he did not think he could turn up to pay court to an heiress looking like the beggar he was. Lord Liverpool gave such expenses short shrift, so now his wallet was empty.

He heard a knock and a step in the doorway and turned

to find Laura there, her arms full of clothes. She was staring at his naked torso and a deep pink color stained her cheeks. There was shock in her eyes. The clothes slipped from her hands and she made a grab for them even whilst her gaze was still riveted on him.

"I've brought… Um… Did you…"

Dexter was surprised that she was acting like a startled virgin when she was an experienced woman, a widow with a child. Surely there was no need for any pretense between them after all that had happened? And surely she did not possess an ounce of modesty? In bed with him four years previously she had been open and generous, warm and wanton. Her sweet, seductive shamelessness had been one of the reasons that he had fallen so disastrously in love with her. It had seemed so honest and unguarded at the time.

But she had put him right quickly enough on that score. She had no use for him and his devotion, so she had said. And when she had had him in her bed once it seemed that she had no further use for him in that respect, either.

"It would be best for you to leave now," she had said in the morning, with a cool, aristocratic disdain that had made him feel utterly insignificant. *"I would not wish the servants to find you here.…"*

Yet now it seemed that she had forgotten her indifference to him, since she was staring like a woman who had never seen a half-naked man before and looking flustered and more than a little intrigued. Her glance stirred something sensual in Dexter, reviving the fire he had only just managed to damp down.

Somewhere at the back of his mind a voice was cautioning him that to take this any further would be dangerous and irresponsible. He ignored it. He wanted to know if what he had experienced before with Laura had been no more than vivid imagining. He *needed* to know. Once he had exorcised the power she had over him, once he had proved that there was nothing special about Laura at all, he would be free of the past. He was no longer an inexperienced youth. He was at no risk of falling in love with Laura Cole all over again.

Very deliberately he bent down and eased off his boots. When he straightened up Laura was still staring. With calculated intent, he started to unfasten his trousers.

"Did you want me to take these off, as well?" His voice had a rough edge to it now.

Laura's eyes met his and there was a confused and heated expression in them that made the lust slam through him, tightening its grip on him even as he cautioned himself against it.

"Stop! No!" Laura seemed to wake from a trance. She thrust the pile of clothes down on the table and glared at him. "What are you *doing?*"

"I am removing my wet clothes," Dexter said. He allowed his gaze to drift over her appraisingly. "You should do the same, your grace. You look—" his voice dropped "—most disheveled."

He saw Laura swallow hard. Her hazel eyes darkened further and the unconscious desire in them sent another jolt of lust through him. The warmth of the room, the intimacy of the small space, the heady scent of lavender and his seminakedness were a powerful blend. Dexter took a step toward her.

He had not intended this when first they had met.

He had certainly not meant to provoke Laura or tease her or make love to her. Such a course of action was completely irrational. But she was standing there with her hair tumbled about her shoulders and the damned gown still clinging to every curve and he wanted her with all the raw longing he had known four years before. And he wanted to prove that he could master that longing and take one kiss and that it would mean absolutely nothing.

He took another step toward Laura. She took a step back so that she was trapped between his body and the warming room door. She was clutching one of the shirts to her breast now like armor.

"Mr. Anstruther," Laura said, her voice a thread of sound, "this is most improper."

"You were swift enough to help me out of my clothes the last time we met," Dexter said, "and we both know that your concessions to propriety are only for outward show."

He took the shirt from her hands and tossed it carelessly aside, closing the space between them.

He saw the expression flare in Laura's eyes, pain as well as heat. "I did not invite you here to—"

"To take up where we left off?"

Dexter was so close to her now that he could see the rapid rise and fall of her breasts beneath the damp muslin of her gown and the pulse that beat in the hollow of her throat. He wanted to rip the dress from neck to hem and expose her pale body to his sight and touch. The violence of his reaction shocked him, a man who prided himself on his self-control, even as the shock was swept away by the desire that ran through his blood in a ravening tide.

"Perhaps you did not intend this." His words were a

breath against her lips. "But now that I understand what it is that you want…"

Confusion flickered in the hazel eyes so close to his. "What *I* want?"

"Yes. An affair. No complications, no involvement. Four years ago you told me that sex was nothing more than sport to you. So that is what I am offering now—a love affair, nothing but pleasure."

She put a hand against his chest and pushed him away from her. "I never said an affair was what I wanted!"

Anger and lust warred in Dexter. The feeling was utterly alien to him. He did not want to talk. His need for her had pushed him beyond that but still the bitterness in him could not be denied. His voice was harsh. "Four years ago I asked you to elope with me and instead you laughed at me and threw me from the house. It was clear that you did not wish for any emotional entanglement."

"No, I did not…." Her voice caught. "But I did not intend you to interpret that as a desire for an affair."

"No?" His anger increased by several notches. It seemed as uncontrollable as his need for her and his lack of restraint only served to inflame him further.

"So all you sought was one night of passion," he said bitterly. "I realize that when your appetite was slaked you wanted nothing other than for me to leave."

He did not give her the opportunity to reply. His delusion of self-restraint vanished and he bent his head and kissed her, determined now to prove that there was nothing unique or exceptional in his response to her and there never had been.

As soon as they touched he knew he had lost.

His mouth slanted over hers with the same precise perfection that he remembered. They matched as though they were made for one another. Their bodies came together gently, flawlessly, with the same exquisite sense of rightness as before.

The thought knocked the breath from Dexter's body as powerfully as any physical reaction. There was no uncertainty between them. Their bodies recognized each other with an instinct older than time. The sense of belonging together was strong and dangerously seductive. Old feelings and emotions started to awaken.

"This is how it was always meant to be..."

Dexter knew that such thoughts and emotions were an illusion. They *had* to be. He might achieve physical bliss with Laura Cole but there was no more to it than that. There was no real sense of rightness, no belonging, no *love*. Love was a misnomer for infatuation anyway, and he was too old and experienced to feel that now. But in trying to banish the need he felt for her all he had managed to achieve was to awaken every last yearning, every last desire. He ached with the need for satisfaction. He wanted Laura so much it actually hurt. He closed his mind to complicated emotion and allowed himself simply to feel.

He deepened the kiss, coaxing her lips apart, his tongue sliding inside to search and caress and seduce. She tasted sweet as honey. He sensed a hesitation in her beneath the hot, helpless response that she could not deny, and he almost drew back, but a moment later her uncertainty had gone and she pressed closer against him, meeting his demands with a heated need of her own. Her hands slid across his bare chest, raising sensations in him that roused a firestorm of physical desire. This was the secret duchess that he remembered, the woman who responded to him without fear or modesty, who gave all of herself, in contradiction of her cool public persona, and aroused an answering ache of need in him. He had wondered if he had imagined their response to one another or if, in his innocence, he had made it more powerful and extraordinary than it really was. Yet now there was the same cascade of sensation and emotion, an explosion of feeling, sparks of fire in his blood. He was not a fanciful man but the force of it almost swept him away.

But as he reached for her to draw her closer still, she drew back with a gasp.

"No! I cannot do this." She took a step back and raised one hand to her forehead. A frown dented the smooth skin between her brows as though she had a sudden headache. "I do not want this."

Some of the white-hot fever eased within him and this time when Dexter made a determined effort to regain rational control, he succeeded. He too took a step back, his hands falling to his sides. So it seemed that what had felt so real, so *right* to him had been no more than an illusion. Once again it had meant nothing to her.

"Forgive me," he said with biting sarcasm, "but I was under the impression that you kissed me back, *your grace*. Were you merely curious to see if all that whorehouse experience had changed me?"

She flinched. The color flooded her cheeks. Her lips were deep pink and slightly swollen from his kisses and she pressed a hand to them. "I have my reputation to consider," she said steadily. "Fortune's Folly is a small place and I cannot afford to lose my good name—"

Dexter laughed. "You were not so careful of it last time and I would swear you still want me."

She bit her lip hard. "That is beside the point. There is more at stake now."

"You are no more than a hypocrite," Dexter said brutally. "You always were concerned for nothing but outward show." The anger licked through his blood. He was in danger of making the same mistakes all over again and being carried away by his lust. His self-restraint where Laura Cole was concerned seemed as wafer-thin as before. He wondered bitterly why it took him so long to learn. Sanity was clearing his mind now and with it came a mixture of fury and perplexity that he had even thought of pursuing her again. He was in Fortune's Folly for work and also to swallow his pride and find a rich, conformable wife who would fit into his life without causing any trouble. He did *not* want to behave in a way that reminded him of his parents' disastrous indiscretions. The thought of such emotional incontinence made him feel cold to the bones. He had put all that behind him.

He grabbed his wet shirt and forced his feet into his soaking boots, wincing as the leather creaked in protest. "I won't trouble you for those spare clothes," he said. "I'll walk back as I am."

"Like that? From my house?" Laura was clearly taken aback.

It gave him the greatest pleasure to provoke her. "Indeed. If anyone gossips you may tell them that I have been fixing your medieval plumbing."

"You are absurd."

"And as I have said, you were always concerned with preserving public propriety when beneath the surface you broke every rule." He gave her a brusque nod. "Good day, your grace."

"Mr. Anstruther." Her voice halted him before he reached the door and he stopped, deploring the fact that even now a part of him wanted her to call him back, back into her arms, back into her bed.

"I think it would be better," she said, "if we avoided each other in future."

That was going to be the devil of a problem in a small village like Fortune's Folly but Dexter was not going to argue. In fact he would do his utmost to oblige her. He wanted to keep out of her way and forget that anything had ever occurred between them though he knew it would be the devil's own job to do so.

"Of course," he said. "It will be my pleasure."

This time he walked out on her without being invited to leave.

CHAPTER FOUR

HE HAD CHANGED. The Dexter Anstruther she had known before would never have spoken, acted or behaved like that. He had become a man who was hard, experienced and cynical. And she had taken her part in making him so.

Laura, her soaking gown and underclothes changed for a clean, dry set, sat before her mirror combing the tangles out of her hair. Her body still hummed gently, frustratingly, with a pulse of thwarted desire. Her breasts felt heavy and full and her whole body was flushed with arousal. Woken from four years of celibacy, it was demanding satisfaction.

With an uncharacteristic impatience, she slammed the comb down on the dressing table. Damn Dexter Anstruther! It would have been better if she had never met him.

When first she had known him, Dexter had been sent to catch the notorious highwaywoman Glory and bring her to justice. For that reason alone Laura, who had ridden out on more than one occasion with the Glory Girls, had kept out of his way. Rumor whispered that Dexter was one of the shadowy Guardians, the men who worked for the Home Secretary to keep the country safe against threats to law and peace within its own borders. The war against Napoleon had made everyone acutely aware of the danger from abroad but equally important and equally secret was the threat of civil unrest.

It seemed strange now to recall that when Dexter had first joined their house party at Cole Court she had barely noticed him as a man, except to register the fact that he was very handsome. That had been a fact that was difficult to miss, for he had dark, tawny, golden hair, sapphire-blue eyes and an impressive physique. All the housemaids had been in love with him and probably some of the footmen, too. His good looks had in fact initially made Laura wary, for she was familiar with being the plain one at the ball, the girl whom everyone overlooked. She would never in her wildest dreams have expected to draw the attention of a man who was as sinfully attractive, as utterly gorgeous, as Dexter Anstruther.

But slowly and so subtly she was still not sure how it had happened, Laura had started to become aware of Dexter in a different way. He was thoughtful, kind and he *listened*. Laura, accustomed to being ignored by her husband, found that being the sole focus of Dexter's attention was extremely seductive. She had allowed herself to spend time with him; she had fallen in love with him without even really noticing and once it had happened it was far too late to save her heart.

She had struggled hard against her feelings. Her involvement with the Glory Girls was one secret she absolutely had to keep. And not only was she eight years Dexter's senior, she was also a married woman, a duchess, and as far as everyone knew, a pillar of the community. There were endless reasons why her foolish passion for Dexter was doomed and so she had tried to ignore it, and him, as best she could.

Then, one afternoon, Dexter had found her alone and distraught after Charles had betrayed and deserted her and she had lost one of her closest friends. Dexter had comforted her and she had turned to him absolutely. She did not know when comfort had turned to desire and desire to passion. It had ambushed her utterly, taking her into uncharted waters.

But in the morning the fever had gone from her and she had seen her actions for what they really were. She had hidden her guilt and criminality from Dexter. Worse than that, she had been unfaithful to her husband, she had taken the virginity of a man eight years her junior; she had used him to ease her pain.

For Laura, unfamiliar with sensual pleasure, the night had been unimaginably blissful. But it was still dreadfully *wrong.* And when Dexter had begged her to elope with him, to run away from Charles and leave all her unhappiness behind, she had known that although she found the idea dangerously appealing, it would be the worst thing that she could do.

She could still see the expression on Dexter's face when he had pleaded with her to go with him. He had looked eager and hopeful, with the kind of shining, new happiness about him that she remembered from when she, too, had been young. When she saw it, it made her feel every one of those eight years' difference in their ages. She knew that if she took what he was offering she would ruin him forever. For a man of his age at the start of his career, with no money or connections, with nothing but a good name and integrity of spirit, to run away with a married duchess considerably older than he was himself, would be absolute disaster. The scandal would ruin him and he would never recover.

She had sent him away.

She had not done it gently. She had been deliberately cruel, for she judged that if she had explained her reasons he would have tried to override them and she would have been all too easily persuaded. She had hurt him and in the process she had broken her own heart as well as his. She had made him think her a faithless wanton. And now, four years later, she had had to send him away again still thinking she was a hypocrite and a whore.

Laura got to her feet and took an anxious turn across the room. When she had sent Dexter away before she had thought that would be the end of the matter. She had never imagined that the outcome of that passionate encounter would be her beautiful, precious daughter, Harriet.

It had taken her a long time to realize that she was pregnant. At first when she had missed her courses she had assumed that the misery and loss she had suffered had affected her cycle. She had been married to Charles for over ten barren years and during that time had gradually come to assume that there would be no children. Her childlessness had been a terrible grief to her, made all the more painful because she knew there was probably no cause for it other than the fact that her husband never came to her bed. When she had fallen pregnant with Hattie she had suffered no sickness in the mornings and had been out riding until her sixth month. Thinking back over that time, she wondered whether she had simply been denying her situation or had been so transfixed to find herself *enceinte* after all those years that she was afraid even to think about it in case it was all an illusion. Whatever the case, she said nothing until her friend Mari Falconer had challenged her gently about the pregnancy and then she had finally admitted to her oldest friend that the baby was not Charles's child.

Laura put her hands to her head for a brief moment and then allowed them to fall. Her pregnancy had been a thing so precious and so closely guarded that she was afraid that if anyone or anything should threaten her baby or her future happiness she would surely run quite mad. And then Charles had arrived and had done precisely that. He had sworn to take the child away from her as soon as it was born. He had shouted at her and hit her, pushing her down the stairs…

Laura closed her eyes for a second to blot out the memory of that appalling scene. She told herself fiercely that she did not need to think about it now, or ever again. Charles was dead and his hatred could no longer touch either herself or Hattie. But she still felt unsettled and disturbed and she knew that the reason was Dexter. She had never imagined that he would come to Fortune's Folly. She had never thought to see him again.

Dexter could never be allowed to know about Hattie for if the truth ever came out her daughter would be branded a bastard and her life ruined forever.

Laura felt cold even to think of it. She shuddered, feeling the goose bumps breaking out on her skin. She did not have any fears for herself or her own reputation if the truth were known; that mattered nothing compared to Hattie's future. Nor did she believe that Dexter would ever deliberately hurt an innocent child, as Charles had threatened to do. But if Dexter knew Hattie was his daughter he might want some say in her upbringing. He might wish to acknowledge her openly. Infidelity and illegitimacy had made his family a laughingstock throughout his life. His parents' offspring had borne the stigma of not knowing the truth of their lineage and she could not imagine Dexter would wish the same fate on his own children. He might suggest that Hattie be brought up with his own family.

He might try to take Hattie away from her.

A powerful wave of protectiveness swamped Laura. She would die before she relinquished her child. And she would do everything in her power to make sure that no rumor or whisper of scandal would ever taint Hattie's future with her mother's disgrace.

So she could never tell Dexter about his daughter. Hattie had to be protected at all costs. She had to remain forever unquestionably and officially the offspring of the late Duke of Cole. For the past three years Laura's sole purpose had been to shield and safeguard her child and that would not change now.

Laura walked slowly through the connecting door that linked her bedchamber with her daughter's room. Her sister-in-law, who had made sure that her children's nursery was not only on a different floor but in a different wing of the house, had told her quite plainly that she was mad to spend so much time with Hattie.

"You are storing up trouble for yourself in future," she prophesied gloomily. "The child will grow up thinking it natural to spend time with you and will be forever hanging on your skirts. Best to get her a good nurse and then leave her upbringing to the servants."

Which, Laura thought, probably accounted for the

dislike in which her niece and nephew seemed to hold their parents.

She picked up the framed charcoal drawing of Hattie that stood on the chest of drawers and studied it for a moment. Hattie was smiling, all round pink cheeks, tiny rosebud mouth and tumbled black curls. She did not look like Dexter. She had Laura's hazel eyes and Laura's grandfather's coloring, but apart from that Laura thought she resembled no one in particular. She was her own person.

Laura's heart eased slightly. Perhaps Dexter would not even recognize Hattie were he to see her in the village. Why should he, when she did not resemble him? Perhaps, Laura thought with a flash of bitterness, he would not believe Hattie to be his even if she *did* tell him. Since he thought Laura herself to be a faithless wanton he would think Hattie's father could be one of any number of men.

But even so, she could not risk it. She would not hide Hattie away, of course, for people would notice that and talk, but she would have to be very careful.

She was so deep in her thoughts that she missed the sound of the front door opening and footsteps on the stair. A moment later the door of the room burst open and Hattie flung herself on Laura, a sticky, stripy piece of candy clutched in her hand. Judging by the way her cheeks were bulging, Laura suspected that the rest of the sweet—a rather large piece by the looks of it—was already in her mouth. She bent and scooped Hattie up in her arms.

"Mama, Mama! Candy!"

"So I see," Laura said, smiling over her daughter's

curls at the nursemaid, who had followed Hattie up the stairs and was standing in the doorway. "Have you had fun, darling? I hope you were good for Rachel."

"Mr. Blount gave Lady Harriet some sweets, ma'am," Rachel said. "I hope you do not mind. And Mrs. Morton gave her some lilac ribbons for her hair and a little scrap of lace to make a doll's dress. Very generous, people are."

"Yes, they are." Laura kissed Hattie's bulging cheek and smoothed a hand over her soft curls. She knew most of the shopkeepers in Fortune's Folly pitied her the lack of a husband and her straitened circumstances, but because they felt uncomfortable giving a duchess charity they would always slip Hattie presents instead. Almost all of Hattie's clothes were made from off cuts from Mrs. Morton's gown shop and Hattie was likely to develop a very sweet tooth as a result of the grocer's generosity, for scarcely a day went past without him leaving a small bag of sweets for her, or a packet of biscuits or a new cake recipe he was apparently trying out. Mrs. Carrington, who acted as cook housekeeper for Laura these days, grumbled that she was quite capable of making her own cakes, thank you, but she said it quietly because she knew as well as everyone else that without the generosity of their neighbors the household would in all probability starve.

"Mr. Wilson gave me two turnips," Rachel said with a giggle. "He said Lady Harriet would enjoy making a lantern from one for Halloween and Mrs. Carrington can turn the other into soup."

"That sounds delicious," Laura said, "though I do not know how you managed to carry everything home."

She smiled at Hattie. "Will you enjoy making a lantern, darling?"

"Yes," Hattie said, wriggling to be freed. Laura put her down and she turned her face hopefully toward Rachel. " Can we make it now?"

"Not now, milady," Rachel said firmly. "It's time for nuncheon."

"Don't tell me," Laura said resignedly. "Mr. Blount also gave you some hot-cross buns."

"And some oaten biscuits and strawberry jam," Rachel said. "He said it would only go to waste if I did not take it." She held out her hand to Hattie. "Come along, madam. Time to wash all that candy from your fingers."

"I can do it myself," Hattie said with dignity, spurning her helping hand, and Laura smothered a smile.

"Proper independent, she is," Rachel said. "You mind, madam. She'll be walking into the village all on her own one of these days if we give her half a chance. Strong-minded, she is, the poppet."

Laura listened as Rachel took Hattie off to the closet to wash, her daughter chattering all the while about making the turnip lantern and wheedling a promise from Rachel that if she was a good girl they would go down to the water meadows to play. Laura listened with half an ear, tidying and folding Hattie's clothes as she did and feeling a mixture of contentment and a strange poignancy that she could not quite place. Strong-minded, Rachel had said. Little Hattie, independent and bold and happy, with her ebony curls and her fearless nature… Pride and a kind of astonishment rose in Laura that she had produced such a miracle as her daughter, that she and Dexter together had created something so exquisite and extraordinary. She doubted she would ever stop feeling that sense of awe.

Guilt stirred in her. Dexter was denied the pleasure of knowing his daughter and of seeing her growing up. She was denying him that right and she wished she did not have to do so, but she had no choice. Never for a single moment could she risk Hattie's future, her happiness and her security.

The echoing jangle of the doorbell broke her thoughts.

"Hello?" A feminine voice wafted up the stairs to her. "Laura? Are you at home?"

Glad of the distraction, Laura hurried down the stone stair and out into the hall. Carrington was nowhere to be seen. Yet again he had not heard the bell. Laura sighed. There was no point in bemoaning the shortcomings of either her butler or her housekeeper since she had deliberately kept them on to save them from an uncertain future. The health of both Mr. and Mrs. Carrington had been ruined in the last few years by the constant and excessive demands of the new Duchess of Cole and Laura, guilty that she had left her servants to Faye Cole's mercy, had subsequently offered the Carringtons a new home. After a year, however, she was reflecting that it would have been better to employ servants to wait on *them*. Both Mr. and Mrs. Carrington were broken, shadows of their former selves.

Miss Alice Lister, Laura's neighbor from Spring House, a neat villa whose garden bordered Laura's own, was standing in the hall and peering through the door of the drawing room. She had a straw bonnet on her corn-colored hair and was clad in an extremely pretty cream-and-yellow-striped muslin gown with matching pelisse.

Laura liked Alice very much. Miss Lister had been ostracized by most of village society, especially those who were keenly aware of rank and status and were appalled that a woman reputed to be a former maidservant had come into money, bought herself a fine house and come to live amongst them. Such events went much against the natural order and the good ladies of Fortune's Folly were not prepared to give Alice countenance. Then Laura had arrived, the biggest fish in the small pool of Fortune's Folly, and she and Alice had become friends immediately. Laura liked Alice because she was neither servile nor ingratiating and she told things exactly as she saw them whether speaking to a duchess or a stable hand alike. Laura, surrounded by toadies for much of her life, found it refreshing.

"I did knock," Alice said. "I thought perhaps you might be down by the river this afternoon—" She stopped. "Oh! You have been *in* the river."

"How did you know?" Laura inquired.

"You have a strand of pond weed in your hair. What happened?"

Laura sighed. "I am not quite sure. I was in the rowing boat and I lost an oar, so I tried to paddle back with the remaining one but ended going in circles instead."

"Never try to paddle with only one oar," Alice said. "It does not work."

"As I realize now. I grabbed at a branch and would have been able to steady myself, except that it broke and I drifted into the middle of the river and went over the weir." Laura paused. Had she imagined that someone had given the boat a hefty push? She had seen nothing, for the sun had been in her eyes, but she had thought she had heard footsteps…

No. That had to be pure imagination. She pulled herself together as Alice gave a gasp and clapped her hand to her mouth. "Laura, no! You were not injured?"

"Fortunately not," Laura said. "I should have jumped in and swum ashore but after I bumped my head I felt too sick." She took a deep breath. "It was lucky that Mr. Anstruther was on hand to pull me out."

There—she had mentioned Dexter's name with barely a pang of emotion and felt proud of herself. In a little while, possibly months but hopefully only days, she might even be able to think of him without that complicated mixture of guilt and longing.

"Mr. Dexter Anstruther?" Alice said, eyes wide. "The mysterious gentleman who is staying at the Morris Clown Inn?"

"Yes. He was fishing nearby."

"I thought so," Alice said. "I passed him just as I arrived. He was wet and carrying several fish. That explains a great many questions I was asking myself."

"Such as?"

"Why there was a pool of water on your front step and damp footprints in the hall for a start."

"You have a talent for investigation," Laura said. She hoped that Alice's powers of deduction did not extend as far as working out what she had been up to with Dexter Anstruther in the warming room. She hoped none of her feelings showed on her face.

"I do." A frown wrinkled Alice's brow. "Mr. Anstruther is a little odd, do you not think?"

Odd was not a word Laura would have used to describe Dexter. Wickedly handsome, sinfully tempting and very dangerous perhaps, but never odd....

"Laura?" Alice had her head on one side and was looking curious. Laura gave herself a mental shake.

"In what way is he odd?" she asked cautiously.

Alice waved a hand about in a vague way. "Oh, I am not sure. I sometimes think that he behaves like an older man, for all that he can be no more than seven and twenty."

"He is only six and twenty, actually," Laura said, before she could stop herself. "What do you mean, older?"

"He seems very grave," Alice said, "and responsible."

"He may seem that way," Laura said, "but it was only a couple of years ago that he was spoken of as one of the most reckless libertines in London." A fresh wave of guilt assailed her. She had a terrible fear that Dexter's fall from grace had been her fault. "Though he was extremely responsible beforehand."

"Before what?" Alice's bright gaze was penetrating.

Before I took his virginity and ruined his character...

Laura swallowed hard. "Before...um... Before he became a reckless libertine."

"So he was responsible before, and responsible after, and something happened in the middle that made him behave differently," Alice said thoughtfully. "I wonder what that was?"

"Yes, I wonder." Laura moved a few of the ornaments on the dresser at random.

Alice's bright, intelligent gaze was fixed on her face. "Anyway, how do you know?"

Laura's confusion grew. "How do I know what?"

"Mr. Anstruther's age. How do you know he is only six and twenty?"

"Because I know his mother," Laura said, seeing that she needed to crush this line of conversation if she did not want to give away her feelings utterly. "We are of the same generation."

Alice was diverted, as Laura had hoped she would be. "Oh come now, Laura, that must be nonsense," she said. "You cannot be much above thirty yourself!"

"I am four and thirty to be precise, my child," Laura said. She felt woefully irresponsible, for all her years. A bare thirty minutes before she had almost made love with Dexter Anstruther in her own drying room. How reckless and foolish—and, if she were honest, how utterly enjoyable—had that been?

But Alice had not finished with the subject yet. She lowered her voice and glanced conspiratorially over her shoulder. "The *on dit* is that Mr. Anstruther works for the government, you know."

"There is no need to whisper," Laura said. "Hattie and Rachel are upstairs and there is no one else about except Carrington and Mrs. Carrington, and they are as deaf as two posts."

"You don't seem very interested," Alice said, crestfallen. "The trouble with you, Laura, is that you are so perfectly reserved and composed. Nothing seems to ruffle your calm. I suppose it is the natural consequence of being a duchess."

"I am good at concealing my feelings," Laura allowed. "*That* is the natural consequence of being a duchess."

She privately reflected that she had not been either reserved or composed in Dexter's arms. *Wanton* and *abandoned* were more accurate words to describe her state. But then Dexter was the only one who had unlocked a wild and passionate sensuality in her that she had never imagined existed. She had known passion in other areas of her life—no one who rode as hard as she did or took up the cause of injustice as fiercely as she had done could consider herself to be truly meek and conventional—but she had never imagined that she could make love with such unrestrained ardor. With Charles the idea had been laughable. With Dexter it was a wild reality.

But now for Hattie's sake as well as her own she knew she must turn her back on Dexter and all that might once have been. She had to be the perfect dowager duchess once more, restrained and cool, gracious, a little distant and reserved. Violent passion was in the past.

Alice had brightened again. "At any rate, that was not what I came to talk about. Are you going to offer me a cup of tea?"

"I shall go and make it myself," Laura said, moving toward the servants' stair.

"Is Mrs. Carrington having another of her bad days?" Alice asked sympathetically, trotting along beside her as they went down the stair and into the kitchen.

"I fear so," Laura said. "She was in so much pain that she could not lift the pans at breakfast, so I sent her back to bed with a hot brick."

"You should get some more servants," Alice said, "competent ones. You cannot be forever making the tea yourself."

"I have Molly and Rachel, and they are perfect," Laura pointed out. Molly was Rachel's sister and acted as both maid of all work and Laura's personal maid on the rare occasions she required it. Both girls were capable, good-humored and an asset to the household. "And then there is Bart to do the garden."

"Bart is so old and lame he can scarcely bend,"

Alice pointed out. "You do the garden yourself, Laura. Don't think I haven't noticed. With the exception of Rachel and Molly you run a home for incapable servants here."

"Well, there is no reason why I shouldn't make the tea myself," Laura pointed out, a little defensively. She lifted the copper kettle and placed it on the hob. "There is no great mystery about making tea—or about cooking or dressing oneself, or growing vegetables, for that matter."

"But you are a *duchess*," Alice said, in horrified tones. "It is not right."

Laura laughed. "I am a penniless dowager. And that is the marvelous thing. As a dowager duchess I can do as I wish. My relatives cannot interfere and tell me what to do—though they try—and I have no social obligations now that Henry and the dreaded Faye are Duke and Duchess of Cole. And after all, Queen Marie Antoinette played at being a milkmaid, did she not?"

"And look what happened to her," Alice said gloomily.

"I have no intention of losing my head," Laura said firmly, "either metaphorically or practically."

"I almost forgot—I have shocking news." Alice leaned her chin on her hand and fixed Laura with her bright brown gaze. "There is uproar in the town. We are in the most tremendous fix and it is entirely my fault. You will remember that I refused Sir Montague Fortune's offer of marriage in July?"

"Of course," Laura said, reaching for the tea caddy.

"Apparently in revenge he has dug up some ancient law that entitles him to take half our fortunes," Alice said. "Oh, Laura, all unmarried women in Fortune's Folly have either to marry or give Sir Montague their money!"

Laura put the caddy down slowly. "Surely you jest? That cannot possibly be legal. It's iniquitous!"

"Apparently it *is* legal." Alice looked tragic. "Even if we all sold our property and left the village we could not escape because it applies to all single women living here *now.* So I am wondering whether I should marry him in order to save all the other ladies of Fortune's Folly."

"I wouldn't advise it," Laura said, stifling a smile as she measured tea into the pot. "You refused Sir Montague for a reason, did you not?"

"Yes. I don't like him."

"Quite so. You would like him even less if you felt blackmailed into marrying him." Laura took the singing kettle from the hob and added the boiling water to the pot. "Besides, I suspect that now Sir Montague has realized he can take half of the fortune of *every* woman in the village without matrimony, he will not settle for just one woman in wedded bliss."

"I suppose not." Alice raised her eyes to Laura's face. "What is to be done?"

Laura reached the biscuit tin down from the shelf and pushed it toward her guest.

"Try these—oaten biscuits from Mr. Blount." She sighed. "Well, for my own part, Sir Monty will make very little money out of me, for I have nothing but this house and a pittance to keep it up. But that does not mean I wish to give any of it away and I can certainly help the rest of you if you would like me to." She smiled reassuringly at Alice. "I will write to my lawyer at once for advice on countermeasures that we may take. Then we will rally the ladies of the village to oppose Sir Montague. There must be plenty of steps we can take to thwart him. A meeting at the circulating library within the next few days, perhaps…" She felt an unexpected rush of excitement. It was a small thing to be organizing a revolt against their grasping lord of the manor but it made her feel as though she was doing something active and worthwhile. For too long she had lacked a cause.

Alice was looking at her with admiration. "How splendid you are, Laura! So practical! We will soon have Sir Montague retreating in disarray."

"That explains Mr. Anstruther's presence in Fortune's Folly," Laura said, struck by a sudden thought. "He must be here to look for a rich wife." She felt her temper bubble up as she thought about it. The nerve of Dexter Anstruther, coming to the village with the intention of finding a bride and propositioning *her* to be his mistress at the same time. And he had once been a man of principle. He had been right. He *had* changed.

"The blackguard!" she said, her indignation growing. "Everyone knows he is as poor as a church mouse. He is no more than a fortune hunter!"

"He is not the only one," Alice said. "I was tripping over gentlemen down from London on my way to visit you. I could scarcely make my way across the market square without being importuned by some adventurer or other."

"Well," Laura said, stirring the teapot so viciously that the liquid inside splashed onto the table. "They will find that the ladies of Fortune's Folly are no easy target. The arrogance! To think that they can come here with their town bronze and sweep some heiress or other to the altar."

She reached for the cups with a violence that put her ancient china at risk. So Dexter Anstruther had come to

Fortune's Folly hunting a rich heiress. Well, she would show him his mistake. He would rue the day he had come seeking a wealthy wife. She would see he did.

CHAPTER FIVE

DEXTER WAS HOLDING in his hand a letter from the Dowager Duchess of Cole. It reminded him of the Laura Cole he had known four years before, who had been the perfect duchess, elegant and gracious.

Dear Mr. Anstruther, it read, *thank you very much for the service rendered to me earlier today when you rescued me from the river...*

Dexter sighed. Laura Cole was, as ever, presenting the perfect facade of propriety. But what had he expected it to say?

Dear Mr. Anstruther, thank you very much for your offer to be my lover on the basis of mutual convenience and pleasure. Having given the matter my consideration, I fear I must decline. Although I took you to my bed in the past, I no longer have any romantic interest in you...

On calm and mature reflection, Dexter felt that trying to seduce Laura had not been the most intelligent thing that he could have done. He needed to remember that he was in Fortune's Folly to work first and foremost, and also to find a rich wife. Laura Cole was a penniless widow and unsuitable to boot. The fact that he wanted her in his bed now as much as ever was distracting and irrational and he needed to ignore it, particularly since she had made her disdain for him so very clear. Even so, the urge to seek her out again, the need to see her, speak to her, simply be near her, plagued him and would not go away. It felt like a burr against his skin. He shrugged irritably.

"Are we to go to the assembly or not?" Miles Vickery drawled, lounging back in the chair. "Or are you to sit here rereading that note all evening?"

Miles had arrived an hour before with fresh instructions from Lord Liverpool and the express intention of finding himself an heiress as swiftly as possible. News of Sir Montague's dastardly plan to reinstate the Dames' Tax had spread like wildfire around the town even as the place filled up with adventurers from London.

With a sigh, Dexter folded Laura's note and placed it in his inside pocket. "I beg your pardon. I had no notion you were in such a hurry."

"Need to find myself a rich wife," Miles pointed out. "Thought you were in the market for a bride, too."

"Since the ladies have just heard that they are to lose half their fortunes if they do not enter wedlock within a year, I doubt we'll get a very warm welcome," Dexter said dryly.

"We'll persuade them," Miles said. "Seduce them to our point of view if we must. Compromising a lady is a very effective way to secure her fortune."

"And a very dishonorable one," Dexter said. Sometimes he thought that where women were concerned, Miles had neither scruples nor principles.

Not that he could afford the scruples and principles that beset him. Miles had also brought with him a letter from Dexter's sister Annabelle. Written in Belle's loopy, extravagant hand, it had reminded Dexter of all the reasons why he needed to marry money—if reminder was needed.

Belle had written,

Mama was in her cups last night, and she let slip to us that you had gone to Yorkshire not only for the fishing, dear Dexter, but also to offer yourself on the Altar of Matrimony for all our sakes! Such Noble Sacrifice! You are indeed the Best of Brothers!

There was much more in the same vein about how much Belle was looking forward to her come-out ball the following year and how Charley and Roland had lost their shirts at the gambling tables the previous night, and how Mama had an utterly beautiful new peacock-blue morning gown. Dexter shuddered to read the list of all their extravagances.

There was also a short note from his father's ward, Caroline Wakefield, whom everyone knew to be another of the Anstruther Collection masquerading under the false respectability of wardship.

Caro had written crossly,

Dear Dexter, pray do not regard Belle's nonsense. The truth is that if we have no money we shall all have to economize and in the last resort find employment. Belle will not expire over the loss of a season, and your mama would have more to spend on gowns if she did not spend so much on gin. If you choose to marry for money for our sakes then you are a fool.

Dexter smiled ruefully and put the letters in his case. Caro had grown up with no illusions about her place in the world and a far more practical approach to financial matters than his other siblings. He tried to imagine blond featherbrained Belle going out to earn a living—and failed miserably.

"I should stay here and work," he said, gesturing to Lord Liverpool's letter, "and so should you. Liverpool mentions that there is someone who may be able to help us in the matter of Warren Sampson and that you will effect an introduction—"

"Later," Miles said, grabbing his arm and hustling him out of the room. "Anyway, this *is* work, Dexter. You need to listen to the gossip and to meet the suspects. What better way than by mingling with all the fortune hunters and heiresses at the assembly?"

They went out into the market square. It was a blustery night with the wind rising and the moon dodging behind ragged clouds. The Morris Clown Inn, a sprawling coaching inn that dated back to medieval times, was on the southern corner of the square, opposite the town's small but nicely appointed assembly rooms. Fortune's Folly had been little more than a hamlet until fifty years before when Sir Monty's grandfather had taken advantage of the fact that the natural springs around the village were thought to be medicinal. He had created a spa, laid out a small park, built an assembly room and a circulating library and had watched Fortune's Folly grow into an exclusive watering place. There were new houses and shops, and in the summer the town attracted visitors from Harrogate and York. Now that it was the marriage mart of England it attracted a fair amount of riffraff, as well.

"Oh dear," Mr. Argyle, the master of ceremonies, said unhappily, on seeing them. "Not two *more* gentlemen. Disastrous!"

He threw open the doors to the assembly rooms and Dexter immediately saw the problem. The place was packed with men in evening dress and there was scarcely a lady to be seen.

"All the respectable visitors have left town," Mr. Argyle said. "They say that Fortune's Folly is full of fortune-hunting rogues who lower the tone of the place."

"They're not mistaken," Miles said. He caught Dexter's arm. "Look, there's that dashed libertine Jasper Deech. He's been hanging out for a rich wife for years."

"So have you," Dexter pointed out. "So have I."

"That's different." Miles looked affronted. "Deech is very unsavory." He paused. "It's not impossible that Deech could be the one engaged in criminal activities. I have often wondered where his money comes from. And that is Warren Sampson over there—" He gestured toward a middle-aged, florid-looking man who was rocking back on his heels as he surveyed the room. "I cannot believe that he seeks a wife here. He is not in need of a fortune."

"Men like that always want to increase their capital," Dexter said dryly. "I thought he was already married?"

"He buried his second wife last year so perhaps he is looking for a replacement," Miles said. "Speaking of disagreeable characters, is that not Stephen Armitage over there, as well, fawning over Laura Cole? It certainly isn't marriage he's after there! He tried to fix his interest with her in London before she was even out of mourning. Frightfully bad form."

Dexter spun around so quickly that he almost dislodged three glasses of lemonade from a tray carried by one of the servants. He apologized and tried to right the drinks before they splashed all over his and Miles's shoes. It had not occurred to him that Laura would be present that evening but now he wondered why he had made that assumption. The main purpose of the assemblies might be for the young ladies of the neighborhood to meet eligible men, but it was also an opportunity for everyone in the community to meet and mingle and talk, and tonight there was much to talk about.

"Laura is in looks tonight," Miles said, still watching the dowager duchess with deep appreciation. "I always thought she was far prettier than anyone gave credit and now that she is rid of that louse of a husband she positively blooms—" He broke off on a splutter as Dexter took him by the neck cloth and pulled tight.

"You are mighty familiar, bandying about her grace's name with such ease," Dexter said through his teeth. The unbearable thought that Miles might be another of Laura's lovers took hold in his mind and could not be dislodged, no matter how he tried. Miles was a rake of the first order and his conquests were legendary. Dexter knew that it should not matter to him if Laura Cole was simply another name on the list but the fury that clouded his mind was as sudden and uncontrollable as it was unexpected and illogical. Miles, Stephen Armitage, and no doubt a dozen or more others…

"Steady, old fellow," Miles protested, flailing his arms about and wheezing for breath, "Laura is my cousin! Known her since we were children. Why shouldn't I use her name?"

Cousin. The word pierced the rage that seemed to envelope Dexter's mind like a blanketing fog. Laura was Miles's cousin, not his mistress. His grip eased slightly.

"Your cousin?"

Miles's eyes bulged. "That's what I said. Remember when we were in London I told you that I had a cousin living here? And what is it to you, anyway, Dexter?"

Dexter released him slowly. "I didn't know," he said. "I thought that the Duchess of Devonshire was your cousin."

"She is." Miles looked affronted. "What the hell's wrong with you, Dexter? No reason why you should know all the ramifications of my family tree, is there? I have cousins all over the *Ton,* not that it's any of your business."

"Good evening, Miles. Mr. Anstruther…"

Dexter and Miles both jumped. Laura was standing before them in a glorious dark blue silk dress embroidered with tiny diamonds. It was cut discreetly low over the swell of her breasts yet it seemed to Dexter that the very modesty of the design and the tight swathing of the material served only to emphasize the sheer sensuousness of Laura's curves. Whenever she moved, whenever she breathed, the gown shimmered with the radiance of a thousand tiny stars. She looked exquisite. He felt hot just looking at her.

Laura's hair was swept up into a matching diamond clip. It shone with rich golden and chestnut lights and it seemed to beg to be unpinned and touched. Dexter felt his breathing constrict as though all the air had been sucked from his lungs. He stood still and looked at her and absorbed what felt like a physical blow. His habitual cool rationality had never seemed so far away. He could not move. He could not speak.

"Is there some kind of problem?" Laura asked, looking pointedly at where Dexter's hands were still resting on Miles's shoulders.

"Not at all," Dexter said, coming to himself and smoothing Miles's jacket down hastily. "Lord Vickery merely had a small malfunction with his wardrobe."

"Next time you can call my tailor rather than attempting to assist yourself," Miles said, glaring at him. He adjusted the set of his jacket and bowed to Laura, taking her hand and pressing a kiss on it.

"How are you, Laura?" he asked, sounding suspiciously to Dexter as though he was putting extra emphasis on his use of her name. "It is good to see you again. You look divine tonight. That must be one of Madame Hortense's creations, I think."

"I thought," Dexter said sharply, unable to help himself, "that her grace was a relative of yours, Miles?"

"Not a close one," Miles said, smiling wolfishly at Laura.

"Thank you for the compliment, Miles." Laura's smile held a sparkle of mischief. "But you need not waste your time on me when there are other richer and more susceptible ladies about." She stood gracefully on tiptoe to kiss his cheek. "Even so, it is a pleasure to see you, too."

"You are as proper as always," Miles said, smiling at her.

"And as impervious to your flattery," Laura responded, her lips tilting into an irresistible answering smile. "Pray remember I am a dowager duchess, Miles, not a green girl to fall for your compliments."

Miles released her hand with every sign of reluctance. Dexter felt his temper bristle. "You are the most seductive dowager I have ever known," Miles said, "and trust me, I have known many and in every way imaginable."

"Enough, Miles," Laura said, her strict tone giving Dexter a most inappropriate frisson of sexual excitement. "I do not wish to know about your conquests, nor do I have any intention of joining their ranks."

"Oh very well…" Miles sighed. "I hope Hattie is doing well," he said, reverting to a more cousinly tone. "I have brought some gifts for her from Mama. If I might call tomorrow…"

Dexter smiled. The image of an utter rake like Miles traveling from London with a child's toys in his luggage was irresistible. Miles shot him a dark look.

"Of course," Laura said. Dexter felt rather than saw her cast a quick look in his direction. Her tone was slightly strained. "Hattie will be delighted to see you."

"Capital," Miles said.

Laura turned to Dexter and her smile was several degrees cooler than the one she had given her cousin. It felt as though she was only addressing him because socially she had to. Dexter felt excluded. He did not like it. The urge to make her take notice of him, to force a response from her, was strong. This ice maiden could not have been more different from the sensuous woman he had held in his arms only a few hours before.

He caught her eye and for a second the awareness shimmered between them again. The noise from the crowd faded and it was just him and Laura looking at one another. He tried to force his gaze away from her and failed signally to do so.

Miles cleared his throat loudly and they both jumped.

"I wondered what had brought you to Fortune's Folly, Mr. Anstruther," Laura said icily, covering her embarrassment with an arctic chill that Dexter thought might freeze him to the marrow. "I assume that both you and Miles are here because of Sir Montague's outrageous edict? It is the only thing that I can think of that would bring two such *in*eligible gentlemen as yourselves to the north."

"A man has to do what he must," Miles said gloomily, "no matter how repugnant it may seem."

"What an admirable approach to marriage, Miles," Laura said. She was laughing. "And you, Mr. Anstruther—" Once again her tone had chilled as she turned to Dexter. "Do you hold the same sentiments? Your mama has made no secret of the fact that she wishes you to seek a rich and conformable wife." She sounded derisive, as though Dexter were tied to his mother's apron strings.

"Dexter needs to try harder to find a girl to suit him," Miles said, grinning maliciously at Dexter. "He's too damned—sorry, dashed—particular."

"Possibly you cannot find a suitable bride because most young ladies have the wit not to be conformable these days," Laura said. She threw Dexter a mocking look. "Is that what you want, Mr. Anstruther? A henwit?"

What Dexter wanted was to respond to Laura Cole's provocation by shaking her—or possibly kissing her senseless. He felt alarmingly heated, as though his clothes were too tight and were smothering him. He wanted to break out of their restrictions with a roar and grab Laura and carry her off. He wanted to forget that his life was governed by sense and order these days and be decidedly disordered and irrational.

"And what of your own matrimonial prospects, your grace?" he inquired smoothly, clamping down on instincts that were becoming more ungovernable by the moment. "You are, after all, a single woman and a resident of Fortune's Folly. As such you fulfill all the criteria for Sir Montague's tax. Are you resigned to handing over half of your fortune to him?"

Laura laughed. "I most certainly am not, Mr. Anstruther! I have no intention of doing so. But with so small a fortune of my own I imagine that I am a negligible part of Sir Montague's plan."

"I doubt," Dexter said, "that Sir Montague sees any sum of money as negligible, your grace."

"Well, he won't get his hands on mine," Laura snapped.

"Then you *will* marry to avoid the tax?" Dexter enjoyed the flash of anger he had provoked in Laura's eyes.

"That is even less likely than that I would willingly hand over my minuscule fortune, Mr. Anstruther," she said. "I have had one husband and have no wish for a second."

Dexter could well believe that having finally got rid of the ghastly Charles, Laura would not wish to compromise her freedom again. And why should she, when widows could manage their lovers as they pleased as long as they showed a little discretion? The thought did nothing to soothe his aggravation.

"I am fascinated to know how you plan to solve this dilemma," he said. "It is marry or pay, is it not?" He raised his brows. "Are you not trapped, your grace? Sir Montague's edict has the weight of the law behind it, distasteful as it may be. Surely you cannot intend to break that law? You, a dowager duchess and pillar of the community?"

For a moment he thought he saw a hint of amusement in Laura's face before she veiled her expression again.

"The law can be opposed in the courts," she said frostily.

"Ah, I see." Dexter's smile broadened. "You intend to spend a fortune you do not possess on lawyers to thwart Sir Montague?"

"It is the principle of the matter that counts," Laura said.

"And you are such a principled person." Dexter felt a stab of anger at her hypocrisy.

"As are you, Mr. Anstruther," Laura said, her contemptuous gaze sweeping the room full of debutantes and making her meaning explicitly clear. "An excellent way to save time—combining your search for a bride and a mistress in one place!"

As the intensity of their exchange had increased so had they drawn closer together and now Dexter realized that they were almost touching. He could see all the little flecks of gold in Laura's hazel eyes and the shadow of each individual eyelash against her skin. The curve of her cheek would fit so neatly into the caress of his palm, just as her lips had fitted his as though they had been made for that very purpose. He wanted to kiss her again with all the abandonment he had felt earlier. As soon as he thought it he ached for it.

Both of them had forgotten Miles, who was watching this interchange with eyebrows raised.

"Excuse me," he murmured, "I can see that you do not need me here. I think I shall seek out the card room."

Dexter saw the shock in Laura's eyes as she realized how far she had let their exchange go. She wrenched her attention from him. One of her gloved hands crept up to her throat. He could see that she was shaking slightly. The diamonds on her bodice shimmered with each unsteady breath she took and he felt the same shocking uncertainty sweep through him. He had lost himself, forgotten everything in the potency of that moment with her.

A crash and the babble of voices cut across the hum of noise in the room and both of them turned with relief to see that Sir Montague Fortune had come into the ballroom with his brother, Tom, and had been the immediate recipient of a glass of lemonade full in the face. The perpetrator of this outrage was an extremely pretty young lady who looked barely out of the schoolroom. Tom Fortune, a wicked-looking young man who possessed all the humor that his brother lacked, was laughing as he shook the stray drops of liquid from his coat.

"Monty!" the debutante shrieked. "How *dare* you plot to steal my money, you great oaf? I'll see you pay for this!"

"Have you met Lady Elizabeth Scarlet, Sir Montague's half sister?" Laura inquired. "Her mother was married first to Sir Montague's father and then after his death to the Earl of Scarlet. Lizzie is Sir Montague's ward now that her parents are both dead. He has, naturally enough, upset her with his money-grabbing plan. They have a somewhat volatile relationship."

"I would never have guessed," Dexter said. He shook his head disapprovingly. "I should think Sir Montague *deserves* half her fortune in return for having to put up with such a hoyden as a sister."

Laura tutted. "What a stuffed shirt you sound, Mr. Anstruther, six and twenty going on six and seventy. Clearly Lady Elizabeth is one you will need to cross off your list of eligible females. I see what Miles means when he claims you are too particular."

Dexter looked at her suspiciously. "What makes you think that I would have a list, your grace?" he asked.

Laura's hazel eyes sparkled with malicious amusement. "It is the sort of thing you would do. Groundwork, preparation, research…" She waved a dismissive hand. "Those are your trademarks, are they not, Mr. Anstruther? Of course you would have a list. You are the sort of man who thinks he has everything organized only to see it spiral spectacularly and inexplicably out of control."

Her appraisal was so uncannily accurate that Dexter was silenced for a moment.

They both watched as a servant rushed out with a cloth for Sir Montague to mop his face and another to clean up the pools of lemonade on the floor.

"Surely you cannot condone Lady Elizabeth's actions?" Dexter said. "They hardly accord with the idea of public propriety that you yourself pretend to embrace so heartily."

Laura gave him an unfriendly look. "You are correct, of course," she said. "I do not condone the throwing of lemonade. It can stain wooden floors very badly." She watched Sir Montague retire from the room, dabbing ineffectually at his face and clothing with the large white napkin, and sighed.

"Retreating in disarray," she remarked. "If only the war could be won as easily as this first battle."

Suddenly she turned fully to face him.

"If you think to find your innocent little bride here in Fortune's Folly, you should think again, Mr. Anstruther," Laura said. She tapped her closed fan in the palm of her gloved hand in a gesture that betrayed her irritation. "It would be a mistake."

Dexter moved closer to her. She seemed uncomfortable with his proximity and tried to move away but the press of the crowd in the assembly rooms was great now, pushing them together. Her body brushed his, the rub of her skirts sensuous against his thigh. Dexter could feel the heat of her through the thin silk and feel also the tiny quiver that racked her as their bodies touched. It incited a jolt of lust straight through him, a molten hunger sufficient to banish all thoughts of logic and sense and conjure visions of tangled drapes and of Laura's pale nakedness in the moonlight.

"I am fascinated to discover that you take such an interest in my wedding plans, your grace," he said softly.

The pink color stained Laura's cheeks with both anger and reluctant arousal.

"I have no interest in either you or your plans," she said sharply, stepping back as the crowd shifted a little. "I speak only to warn you, Mr. Anstruther. We want no fortune hunters here."

"And you are certain," Dexter said, "that you have no personal concern in my case?"

Laura laughed shortly. "You have a remarkably good opinion of yourself, Mr. Anstruther. Why should I care? I did not seek you out this evening. I do not look for the company of a man hypocritical enough to censure *me* for my behavior and then adhere to a double standard himself." She flicked her fan angrily. "You are just like all the rest, are you not, Mr. Anstruther? As I said earlier, you seek a biddable wife and a complaisant mistress simultaneously."

Dexter laughed. "No one," he said politely, "could call you complaisant, your grace."

"No one will call me your mistress, either!" Laura snapped, her hazel eyes narrowing disdainfully. "And as for the biddable wife, I suggest you forget her, too, and leave Yorkshire at once. I am persuaded that you are far better suited to London. Besides—" she gave her fan another angry swish "—you will have a deal of trouble finding a lady willing to entertain your suit if you put fishing before your bride, as you seem inclined to do. Surely you are aware that real men do not fish?"

Dexter gave her a look that brought the hot blood surging back into her face. "I have had no complaints, madam," he said. "You were the one who rejected a real man earlier because you could not deal with him."

He saw her eyes widen with shock at this outrageous and deliberate provocation. "Why, you—"

She raised her hand and his fingers closed tightly about her wrist.

"Surely you would not strike me in public?" His tone was soft and mocking. He drew her resisting body closer to his, feeling the heat in her and the tension and the anger. His own body was taut; the need for her pounding in his veins, destroying all good sense or cool thought.

"What scandalous behavior that would be from the perfect Dowager Duchess of Cole," he said. "Are you willing to smash that public facade, your grace, or shall I do it for you?"

For a moment they stared deep into each other's eyes and he saw the fury in the depths of hers, and also the shadow of fear that he might just do as he threatened and kiss her here, now, in front of the assembled crowds. He imagined what it would be like to bend her back like a bow against his encircling arm, to take that tempting mouth with his, to drink from her until he was finally sated. Not the actions of a man seeking a conformable wife, perhaps, but very definitely those of a man driven mad with lust by a wanton.

Laura wrenched her wrist from his grasp and took a step back. Her face was flushed as pink as a blown rose and her eyes were bright.

"You forget yourself, Mr. Anstruther," she said. "Where is your self-control?" She smoothed her skirts down with a quick, nervous gesture and Dexter felt a savage satisfaction to see her hands shaking slightly.

"I came over in the first place only to see Miles," she said quietly. "Next time I find you standing beside him, I shall move on."

"So you say," Dexter said, "but your cousin is long gone—" he nodded across the room to where Miles could be seen in the doorway to the refreshment room, engaging Alice Lister in conversation "—yet you are still here with me in spite of your suggestion that we avoid one another."

Laura chewed her lush lower lip. "That can be easily remedied. Good evening, Mr. Anstruther. I hope you will return home soon. You belong in London where your feckless, libertine habits will be more appreciated."

She turned sharply on her heel and walked away from him and Dexter took a deep breath and allowed the tension to ease from his body. The blood still drummed through his veins with an insistent lustful beat but he felt chilled, as well.

"Your feckless libertine habits…"

He was more like his father than he had thought, more like him than he wanted to be. He barely recognized himself when he was with Laura. He lost control and his need for her seemed to distort all else.

He watched as Sir Jasper Deech slithered across to ambush Laura on her way to the door. Lord Armitage hovered in the wings, waiting for an opportunity to cut in on the pair of them. Tom Fortune actually blew her a kiss across the ballroom. Dexter's temper tightened to think that all those men probably viewed Laura as a widow who might provide the sort of amatory entertainments that would ease the tedium of courting a virginal heiress. Perhaps they imagined that they might woo a debutante during the day and sport with a widow at night. Perhaps she might welcome their advances. The fact that he knew it should not matter to him just made it matter all the more.

"Feckless libertine…"

Laura's voice was like a mocking whisper in Dexter's mind. He clenched his fists. Hell and the devil. He had come to Fortune's Folly with the simple aim of investigating a case for Lord Liverpool and finding an heiress bride if he could. How had matters become so complicated so quickly? He had no desire for any of the insipid misses who flocked the ballroom and an all-too-strong desire for the Dowager Duchess of Cole. But indulging in a liaison with Laura was impossible. Besides, it was the type of thing that he, Dexter Anstruther, simply did not do these days. Losing his head, kissing Laura, burning to make love to her—these were the actions of a previous life. They were not the behavior of the responsible, principled man who sought nothing more than a well-ordered existence and a biddable bride.

He saw Lord Armitage lean close to leer down Laura's gown under the guise of kissing her hand. He felt a primal and possessive fury almost swallow him whole. Was he to call out every last libertine in Fortune's Folly? Because if they laid a finger on Laura Cole, that was exactly what he was afraid he would do and that would not be the action of a rational man.

He ran a finger around the inside of his collar, trying to loosen it a little. He had no idea what was making him think like this. It was utterly out of character. Hell, he was out of control already. And for a man who prided himself on his sound judgment it was inexplicable. He had no idea where it would end.

LAURA SURREPTITIOUSLY PRESSED her hands together as she walked away across the ballroom. Her palms felt hot within her evening gloves. Her whole body felt strangely sensitive, her skin prickling and a curl of excitement as well as a barb of anger still deep in her stomach. The impulse to turn round and look back at Dexter Anstruther was so strong that she could barely resist it.

What on earth was wrong with her? As Duchess of Cole she had entertained princes and dignitaries. She had not enjoyed it but the point was that she had fulfilled her role with grace and charm. She had never allowed any man to shake her composure.

Dexter could get under her skin with the slightest word, undermine her with the smallest touch. His presence was like a prickle in the blood, aggravating, provocative, impossible to ignore. She could not bear it. It tormented her. She had sworn to keep away from him and yet he had been right—she had sought his company deliberately and there was no point in pretending otherwise. It was foolish, it was dangerous and it felt irresistible.

She rubbed her wrist where he had held her. She could still feel the imprint of his fingers on her skin and felt an echo of that touch in the hot silken coil of desire in her belly. She wanted to turn around and grab Dexter. She wanted to drag him from the ballroom and take him to her bed and make love to him until they were both exhausted and the torment was soothed at last. She had felt like that from the very first moment she had seen him that evening. She had pretended barely to notice him but it had been precisely that—a pretense. He had looked very smooth and elegant in his black evening coat and pristine white linen, his tawny fair hair cut in a Brutus crop—she imagined that a longer style would demonstrate too little order and restraint—and the planes of his face harder and leaner than she remembered. And yet despite the outward control there was something about Dexter that she recognized instinctively because it was in her, too. It was the wildness beneath the surface, the danger and the power that no amount of elegant black superfine could subdue. Dexter might be determined to impose discipline on his life because of the chaos of his family background but there was a passion in him strong enough to shatter any barriers. He was denying his true self.

She understood him, and that made her feel a treacherous affinity with him. But that affinity was illusory. He thought her heartless for the way she had treated him in the past and she would allow him to continue to believe it because it enabled her to keep her secrets safe from him. She needed to remember Hattie and that it was essential to protect her. She could not risk exposure of her daughter's secret. Keeping Dexter out of her life was an absolute necessity. She should be finding eligible females for him and throwing them at his feet so that she would be free of his troubling presence in her life. But the idea of Dexter finding a conformable wife turned a knife in her. She felt damnably bad-tempered to imagine it.

It did nothing to raise her spirits when she saw the new Duke of Cole, her cousin by marriage, and his wife, Faye, shepherding their daughter Lydia through the crowds in the ballroom. Faye Cole had the unfortunate appearance of a farmer presenting a prize heifer at market, encouraging her daughter along with little shooing motions of her hands, smiling flirtatiously at every gentleman in sight and pushing Lydia forward to meet them. Lydia was two and twenty now, and very definitely considered an old maid, and Laura realized that Faye must be taking advantage of the Dames' Tax to find her daughter a husband at last. The new duke and duchess did not live in Fortune's Folly, but Cole Court was certainly close enough to take advantage of all the suitors flocking to the village. And Lydia, tricked out in unbecoming pink satin, looked as miserable as sin at the prospect.

Laura watched as the Coles paused to return the greetings of Warren Sampson, an occurrence that struck her as odd since Faye Cole was the sort of snob who would normally cut a *cit* dead. Sampson was fulsomely flattering to Lydia, which made the poor girl blush even more uncomfortably. Then Henry Cole's eye fell on Laura herself and he hailed her with surprising enthusiasm.

"Cousin Laura!" Henry kissed her hand with heavy gallantry. Faye was a great deal less affectionate and gave her a tight little nod. Her cold gaze itemized Laura's appearance with pursed lips and narrowed gaze, assessing the gown and jewels as though placing a cost on each. Laura suspected that Faye already knew the gems were paste and was merely judging how good a counterfeit they were.

"I trust we shall see plenty of you, cousin, during our stay in Fortune's Folly," Henry said, and Faye's mouth turned down at the corners.

"Thank you, cousin Henry, but I do not go much into society," Laura said.

"Which is quite as it should be," Faye snapped.

"Dowagers should neither be seen nor heard?" Laura inquired sweetly, and saw Miss Lydia Cole stifle a smile. Then Lydia's gaze fell on Dexter Anstruther and her face lit up, making her look pretty and animated. Laura felt a pang of raw jealousy spike her inside. Dexter and Lydia had met four years before at Cole Court and had seemed to enjoy one another's company. Laura knew that if Dexter genuinely wished to find a conformable bride he could do a lot worse than Lydia Cole. And Henry and Faye were so desperate to see her settled now that they would probably accept a man with an old family name but no fortune. Laura knew it would be a good match for both of them. The fact that she felt sick with envy to think of Lydia and Dexter together was something she would have to keep to herself. Her ungovernable feelings were her own problem.

A tide of panic rose within her as she realized that if Dexter and Lydia married it would bring him into the Cole family and therefore closer to his own daughter. Except that she seldom saw Faye and Henry socially, of course, and they had never showed any interest whatsoever in Hattie. That was the way it would have to stay, Laura thought. But it was damnably awkward for in the small world of the *Ton* people were always falling over distant relations and it was most unlikely she could hide Hattie from Charles's family forever. She sighed as she felt the web of deceit weave a little tighter about her. It was starting to be a tangled web indeed and one that taunted her with a lifetime of emptiness.

"I will leave you to renew your acquaintance with Mr. Anstruther," she said wearily. She had seen how Faye's face had sharpened into interest to have an eligible gentleman in her sights. "I am sure that he will be delighted to see you again."

"He is extremely handsome, but he has no money, has he?" Faye said thoughtfully, sizing Dexter up like a horse trader. "Still, that should make him grateful to secure a duke's daughter in marriage."

"Mama!" Lydia gasped, turning bright red at her mother's barefaced gall.

"What?" Faye looked impatient. "There is no need to be missish, Lyddy. We all know why we are here, so you had better give him some encouragement."

Laura shot Lydia a sympathetic glance as the poor girl looked as though she was about to bolt from the ballroom.

"Yes, Mama," Lydia said, in a stifled whisper.

As Laura went out Faye was already dragging Lydia across to accost Dexter whilst Henry watched with the calculating expression of a man working out how much the wedding was going to cost him. Laura saw Dexter take Lydia's hand and bow over it and the same shocking spear of jealousy pierced her to the core like a physical pain.

When she reached the door she could not prevent herself from looking back. Dexter was leading Lydia into the set that was forming for a country-dance. He did not look at Laura. It seemed he had already forgotten her.

LYDIA COLE WAS an observant girl. She had already noticed that Dexter Anstruther, though pretending to be utterly indifferent to Laura, had watched her covertly all the way out of the ballroom. She had felt the tension in his body as he led her into the country-dance. She had even noticed that although Dexter was making perfectly pleasant conversation with her, part of his mind was pre-occupied with something—or someone—completely different. She was not the main focus of his attention. In truth, she barely had his attention at all.

She was hugely relieved. Dexter Anstruther, with his tawny golden hair, his deep blue eyes, his commanding physique and authoritative presence, scared her to death. He was far too handsome, far too clever and generally far too overwhelming for her.

Lydia understood her mother's absolute determination to marry her off. She also knew that Dexter was looking for a rich wife. It should have been the perfect, convenient combination. Except that it was not, for she was sure that Dexter's feelings were already engaged elsewhere and she… Well, she had formed a *tendre* for a totally unsuitable man. She was almost certain that she had fallen in love at first sight.

She glanced over at Faye and sighed. The duchess had the instinct of a major predator where her daughter's marriage prospects were concerned and was watching Lydia with a mixture of smugness and vague threat as though she was about to pounce on Dexter and carry him off to announce the banns immediately. Matters, Lydia thought, might well become complicated. She had to ensure that she did not end up being bullied into marrying Dexter and she had to try to cure herself of her hopeless passion for another gentleman. She hoped she had sufficient will to succeed. She was not sure that she did.

Lydia glanced at Dexter's face as the steps of the dance brought them together. He smiled at her but she knew he was not thinking of her. She knew that all his interest, all his energies were concentrated on thinking about Laura. She shivered and felt a secret rush of relief that all the complex emotion and ruthless, sensual demand that she sensed in Dexter was not for her. Never in a million years could she deal with that. There was a hardness, a cynicism and a level of experience in him, for all his outward conformity, that she could not begin to handle.

But Laura could. She sensed that, too. She knew they were well matched and that they should be together.

Lydia sighed. She had lived long enough and knew well enough that things that were meant to be did not always happen as they should.

After that brief smile, Dexter's attention had wandered from her again. It did not matter in the least to Lydia, for she was no longer thinking of him, either. Across the ballroom her eyes met those of the gentleman who was the object of her affection. He held her gaze and smiled gently but meaningfully at her and she forgot everything else in that instant. It seemed that he was as interested in her as she was in him. The thought made her heart pound. Love at first sight felt wonderful.

CHAPTER SIX

"SO," LAURA SAID TO her cousin, "when are you going to tell me what is wrong, Miles? You have been like a cat on hot bricks all afternoon."

They were standing in the long gallery watching Hattie as she played with the spinning top Miles had brought for her from Hamley's toy shop in London. Rachel was showing her how to use the little stick to get the top to whirl so fast that its bright colors all merged into a spinning rainbow and Hattie was squealing with excitement. The sun, shining through the mullioned windows, illuminated her eager little face and brought out the chestnut tones in her black hair. At one point she looked up at Laura, her head tilted in precisely the same mannerism that Dexter had. Laura's heart missed a beat at the betraying gesture and she glanced quickly at Miles, but he appeared to be studying one of the portraits of some seventeenth-century Asthall ancestor with intense concentration.

On the threadbare carpet lay Miles's other gifts—a book of nursery rhymes, a set of tiny carved wooden animals and a doll dressed in pink with a matching bonnet. There was also a new dress for Hattie in crimson brocade, but Laura had insisted on putting that aside for

Christmas so that Hattie did not become too ridiculously spoiled. He had also brought some presents for Laura herself—sugared almonds from Gunters and a book she had particularly wanted—and Laura was touched because she knew Miles's financial state was almost as hopeless as her own but he had insisted that she should not reimburse him.

Hattie had monopolized Miles for the first hour of his visit and Laura thought that he had coped admirably well. It was clear that a part of his mind was elsewhere, though, so whilst Hattie played with the top, Laura drew her cousin to one side.

"Miles?" she prompted, and her cousin straightened up and sighed.

"There is something that I need to talk to you about, Lal," he said. His gaze was fixed on Hattie and he spoke softly. "We need your help."

Laura looked at him sharply. She knew that tone, half firm, half apologetic. It meant that she was not going to like what she heard but she was going to have to do it anyway. She walked over to the carved balustrade that overlooked the great hall below and rested her hands on its smooth wood.

"Lord Liverpool?" she asked quietly. "I always knew that though he said it was ended, that would not be the last of the matter."

Two years previously she had helped the Home Secretary in return for a free pardon for her role in the Glory Girls. The matter had been hushed up to avoid scandal and Liverpool had assured her that it would never be mentioned again, but Laura had not been naive enough to believe him. And now here was Miles two years later, asking for her help again, and she knew she could not refuse because Liverpool would always have the whip hand with what he knew about her.

"It is only information," Miles said soothingly. "We need to know anything you can tell us about Warren Sampson. Or rather, Dexter needs to know because this is his case—"

"I have to speak to *Dexter?*" The words were out before Laura could help herself. Both Rachel and Hattie looked up, startled by Laura's horrified gasp, and Miles stopped, raising his brows. Laura moderated her tone quickly. Her heart was slamming now. "Miles, I have no objection to talking to you about Sampson but why must it be Mr. Anstruther?"

"Why not?" Miles said. "This is Dexter's case, Laura. I am in Fortune's Folly on quite another matter."

"I know," Laura said bitterly. "Fortune hunting! I saw you practicing your charm on Miss Lister last night." She lowered her voice still further. "And I *hear* from servants' talk this morning that you spent the night with one of the barmaids at the Morris Clown Inn. I don't approve of you, Miles, and if everyone hears of your rakish ways you will never catch a wife."

Miles laughed. "We are here to talk about the consequences of your misdemeanors, Lal, not of mine. Now, Dexter is leading this case for Lord Liverpool and I am only here to back him up, so he is the one you must speak to."

"But I can't talk to Mr. Anstruther," Laura protested. She felt panicky and breathless at the thought. "He was the person sent to arrest Glory four years ago," she argued. "He has never known that she was me. I mean

that I was her... Oh, you *know* what I mean! How will
he feel to discover—" She broke off in despair. When
Dexter knew the truth he would see her rejection of him
as an even more calculated and manipulative act. She
could hardly bear the thought. "He does not know
already, does he?" she asked.

"Not as far as I am aware," Miles said cheerfully. "Why
does it matter? You have your pardon now, Lal. All you
are doing is helping us with a bit of information. I am sure
that Dexter will see the benefit of it and not feel too
outraged that you evaded capture four years ago."

"I am sure of nothing of the sort!" Laura snapped. She
was feeling very unsettled now. The prospect of going to
Dexter Anstruther and revealing herself to have been
Glory the highwaywoman was intolerable. She spread
her hands in a gesture of despair. "You know how
odiously stiff-necked and upright Mr. Anstruther can be,
Miles! He is bound to lecture me on the evil of my ways
and come over all virtuous and principled! Oh!" She
threw her hands up. "I could not bear it!"

Miles was laughing. "I'll allow that Dexter can be rather
righteous at times," he said, "but you must remind him that
you took the role of Glory to avenge the poor and the
weak. You are not without principle yourself, Lal."

"I doubt Mr. Anstruther will see it like that," Laura said
bitterly.

"What does it signify?" Miles asked. "Unless..."
He eyed her shrewdly. "Unless his good opinion matters to you."

"Hardly," Laura said untruthfully. "He already holds
me in dislike," she added with a sigh. "This will see him
despise me."

"You could have fooled me," Miles said caustically. "I saw you together at the assembly, Lal. Never have I felt so much *de trop*. Dislike is not what Dexter feels for you."

Laura could feel herself coloring up fierily. "Well, he will do after this," she said.

"But you will do it?" Miles pressed.

"Of course," Laura said tartly. "You have presented it as though I have a choice, Miles, but in fact I have none at all." She sighed again. "Tell Mr. Anstruther that I will meet him tonight at Half Moon Inn. I can scarcely have him calling here. All the village tabbies would notice and I am already quite scandalous enough. And please send to warn Josie to put the private parlor aside for us, as well."

"Do you need me to escort you?" Miles asked.

"Of course I do not!" Laura said crossly. "I was a highwaywoman, Miles. I have a brace of pistols and I can look after myself!" She stopped. "I beg your pardon," she said, seeing his quizzical expression. "I am tired and on edge. Thank you for offering but it is quite unnecessary. And I would ask you not to tell Mr. Anstruther my identity in advance, Miles. If anyone has to explain this to him, it is me."

"As you wish," Miles said. "I will send word to Dexter. Thank you, Lal."

"Don't thank me," Laura said wearily. "I am only doing this because you have twisted my arm, Miles. I will tell Mr. Anstruther whatever I can to help his investigation and then it will be finished."

Finished indeed for Dexter and for her, she thought bitterly. In her heart she had known they had no future but this was a different matter entirely. After he learned the truth tonight he would never wish to see or speak to her again.

FOR A MAN who prided himself on his reputation for rectitude, Dexter Anstruther had seen the interior of more seedy alehouses than he cared to remember. Half Moon Inn, an inn on the Skipton road, was a cut above many of the London drinking dens he had slunk around in as part of his work, but it still had a rough clientele. A few heads turned as he entered the taproom that night before men turned back to stare into their pints of ale with studied lack of interest. A strikingly pretty barmaid with a disreputably low-cut blouse smiled warmly on seeing him but her smile faded when he asked for Josie Simmons, the landlady. A moment later, Josie burst through the door, sending the flagons flying, and stood looking him up and down, her hands on her hips. She was a huge woman, not fat but simply built on epic lines. She was as tall as Dexter but about twice as broad and so solid that he understood why so few of the drunks turned nasty when she asked them to leave.

"Mr. Anstruther," she said. She did not sound welcoming. "I understand that Glory wants to see you."

They still spoke of Glory as a legend in the Yorkshire Dales.

"No," Dexter said. "*I* want to see Glory."

Josie almost smiled. "Got blood rather than water in your veins these days, have you, Mr. Anstruther?" She roared. She grabbed his arm in a wrestling hold. "Well, Glory isn't here yet but come through.…" She practically dragged him into a tiny cupboard of a room with faded chairs set before the fire.

"I'll fetch you a drink," Josie said, depositing him in one of the chairs. "Brandy do for you, Mr. Anstruther?"

"No, thank you," Dexter said, a little stiffly. He did not want a drink.

"You're going to need it," Josie said threateningly, disappearing back through the door.

Left alone, Dexter got up and paced across the tiny parlor, stopping to pull back the faded curtains and stare out into the darkness. Never before had he felt so nervous on an assignment. He could not sit still and he certainly did not want a drink. When Miles had first told him that his informant was Glory and that she was willing to meet with him to throw some light on Warren Sampson and his associates, Dexter's jaw had practically dropped to the floor. Miles had flatly refused to answer any of his questions, however, other than to tell him that Lord Liverpool had granted Glory a free pardon several years before and she was helping them out of goodwill alone. Dexter had then been left to watch the clock and to fret and worry fruitlessly about his assignation with a woman who had been, four years before, both his nemesis and his secret heroine.

The door creaked open and Dexter turned. A woman was standing on the threshold wearing a dark blue cloak and matching blue mask. The hood was drawn close about her face. She was very tall and she held herself very straight. Dexter sensed defiance in her, as though she were daring him to make judgments, and something else, too, that could have been anxiety or fear. He straightened, too, and she came forward into the room, closed the door with precision behind her and raised her gloved hands to untie the mask.

He recognized her a second before she put back her hood.

It was Laura Cole. Understanding broke over him then and his heart turned over. It felt deep down as though he had already known the truth and yet had been too slow or too willfully blind to see.

"I am Glory, Mr. Anstruther," she said. "I understand that you want my help."

Laura Cole was the notorious highwaywoman, Glory.

The Dowager Duchess of Cole was a highwaywoman.

Even though he had already accepted that it must be true, Dexter felt another wave of utter stupefaction wash over him as he looked at Laura standing there before him.

He had always thought that he could not be shocked. He had seen so many terrible, desperate and downright dreadful things in his working life that he was sure he had become inured to the feeling. Now he knew that was not true. He was astonished, angry and appalled. He felt as though he did not know *what* to feel.

Laura was standing very straight and proud before him, her chin raised, a defiant gleam in her hazel eyes, but her hands, twisting together nervously in the folds of her dress, told a different story. She was frightened.

Dex cleared his throat, aware that he was finding it difficult to frame a suitable response. "If you are Glory," he said, "then I did want to see you."

Her gaze flickered to his face and away again. "I have been Glory on some occasions."

"What do you mean?"

"I rode as Glory sometimes and my cousin Hester Berry took the part the rest of the time," Laura said.

"And Miles is evidently aware of it." Dexter felt a twist of bitterness that his friend had known all this time and kept the secret from him.

"Miles only knew because he was the one who arranged a free pardon for me from Lord Liverpool two years ago," Laura said. She came forward slowly into the room. She took some logs from the pile by the hearth and built up the fire again, stirring it into flame. She seemed to need to have something to occupy her and though she appeared composed, Dexter thought she was still apprehensive beneath her outward calm. He watched her every move and thought he saw her hands shake a little.

He walked slowly across the tiny parlor then turned back to see her settle herself in one of the chairs before the fire. All the time he was thinking, and wondering how he could have been so stupid not to see the whole picture from the very first. When he and Nick Falconer had gone to Peacock's Oak four years before with the express intention of hunting Glory down, Lady Hester Berry, Laura's cousin by marriage, had been the obvious candidate for the role. Yet the final time that the Glory Girls had ridden out to free Hester's husband, John Teague, somebody else had taken the role of Glory and that person must have been Laura. It was Laura who had held up the carriage conveying Teague to trial, Laura who had held Dexter himself at gunpoint, Laura who, as Glory, had *kissed* him before seducing him so thoroughly in her own persona later that very same day…

His heart lurched again and a sickness seemed to settle deep within him. At last his passionate night with Laura and her subsequent rejection of him made perfect, if painful, sense. She was not simply a bored aristocrat taking and discarding lovers at whim.

She was worse than that.

She had made love to him for the one simple purpose of distracting him from his duty. She had dazzled him, bewitched him and deliberately diverted him so that he would forget all about hunting Glory and would be so utterly wrapped up in her that he would have no room in his mind for anything else at all.

It had worked.

It had worked so well that he had fallen in love with her.

The anger and pain hit Dexter squarely in the solar plexus. He took a harsh breath, concentrating on mastering his fury. What mattered now was to take from her what information he could that would be useful to his investigation. His personal anger had to be controlled. He remembered the secret admiration he had cherished for the woman he had thought of as a popular heroine and the taste of betrayal was bitter in his mouth.

"To think that I never guessed it," he said. "I already knew you could shoot straight."

"Of course," Laura said. "I am a country girl born and bred."

"You can ride like a Cossack, as well." Dexter remembered her proficiency in the saddle and wondered why on earth it had taken him so long to put two and two together. Probably it was because she had been a duchess and as such, above suspicion. He felt an absolute fool.

"There was a weather vane at Cole Court with a highwayman on it," he said, remembering. "Was that your idea of a joke?"

"My wretched sense of humor." Laura's voice had the tiniest quiver in it. "I am afraid that a lot of people do not understand it."

Dexter ran a hand distractedly through his tawny hair. Suddenly, violently, his anger burst out in a huge, unrestrained blast. "Hell and the devil, Laura," he exploded, "what were you thinking? The Duchess of Cole riding out as a highwaywoman?"

She looked disdainful. "Is that your only objection, Mr. Anstruther? That I was a duchess and it was therefore conduct unbecoming?"

Dexter had plenty of objections. For a moment he did not know where to start. He was so incensed that he had to put some physical distance between them to prevent himself from grabbing her and shaking her. He was not accustomed to feeling so unrestrained.

"You know that if I had caught you I would have had to arrest you and hang you," he bit out.

"Fortunate then that you did not." Her self-possession seemed flawless. "But I am not here to discuss the past, Mr. Anstruther. I am here only to see if I may help you in your current investigation. I gave an undertaking only to help in the matter of Warren Sampson. Nothing else is up for debate."

"Oh, is it not?" Dexter felt so hot he thought he was almost boiling with rage.

The door opened and Josie appeared in the aperture. "Going badly, is it?" she said with gloomy satisfaction, looking from Laura's tight face to Dexter's furious one. "Thought as much."

"Is there any other way for it to go?" Dexter demanded.

"Told you that you'd need that brandy," Josie said. She crashed two glasses and a bottle down on the table. "On the house. Must be a nasty shock for you, Mr. Anstruther."

"You could say so," Dexter said shortly. "I know the

Glory Girls stabled their horses here. No doubt I will discover next that Mrs. Carrington rode out with them, too."

Josie opened her eyes wide at Laura. "Missed a trick there, your grace! Bill Carrington was a fine bareback pony rider when he was a lad! His mam always used to say she feared he would run away to the circus. He could have joined us and kept Lenny company. Ah well…" She sighed. "Too late now. I'll leave you in peace." She thundered out.

"I thought," Dexter said, "that the Glory Girls were female. Or is that too obvious?"

Laura smiled, and for a moment he almost forgot that he disliked her. The firelight burnished her hair with rich copper and gold strands and gave her face a soft glow. Her eyes were full of shadows.

"The membership rules were…flexible," she said.

"Like your standards of morality," Dexter said, and the moment of rapport vanished. Laura's smile faded.

"May we speak of Warren Sampson, Mr. Anstruther?" she said. "I am anxious to be here no longer than I need to be."

Dexter's temper flicked him again at her composure and her determination to dictate the terms of their meeting. "Very well," he said briefly. "Tell me what you know of Warren Sampson."

Laura inclined her head. "He was our neighbor at Peacock Oak for a number of years," she said. "He was— and probably still is—a cruel employer and a greedy landowner. I detested him. I still do."

"You did not mix socially with him."

"No. He was a self-made man and I was a duchess."

Her smile mocked him. "We did not meet except in passing, as we did at the assembly last night. Does that suit your sense of propriety, Mr. Anstruther?"

Dexter ignored that. "But you know his character?"

She thought about it. "I consider him harsh and brutal."

"Weaknesses?"

She smiled. "Vanity. And a love of money."

"He does not seek to try and gain social acceptance from the aristocracy?"

"He never tried to gain it from me." Laura considered the matter, her head on one side. "Actually, I do not think Sampson cares for social standing as such, only for money and what it can buy. He is unusual in that. Many men I have met have wanted to trade on their wealth to gain status, but Sampson never has."

That was interesting, Dexter thought, and might provide a motive for Sampson's behavior. If he cared nothing for acceptance but only for money, and he had various lucrative but illegal businesses operating, the threats of a magistrate like Sir William Crosby to unmask him as a criminal would need to be dealt with mercilessly.

"As Glory you burned his fences down," Dexter said. "Or was that Lady Hester?"

"No, I was Glory on that occasion," Laura said. Dexter remembered the tales of Glory the avenger, riding through the sleeping villages on a white horse, torch in hand. Something close to admiration stirred in him and he dismissed it ruthlessly. He knew that if he started to feel sympathy with criminals he was in danger of compromising his principles and chaos would ensue. His father had been just such a man, adapting his view of morality to suit whatever the situation demanded. It was a weakness, not a strength. Dexter would never allow himself to fail in that way.

"That was criminal damage and arson," he said dispassionately. "Those are capital crimes."

"Just so." Laura's lashes fanned across her cheek, hiding her expression.

"Why did you do it?"

Laura stirred. "Because Sampson had enclosed the common land and refused to let the villagers graze their animals there. He is an odious man. He had forced up rents and driven some families to starvation, Mr. Anstruther, and had laughed in their faces when they begged for aid."

"On another occasion you robbed his banker and redistributed the proceeds amongst his workers. Why?"

"I would have thought that was obvious."

"Humor me."

"Because the money was rightfully theirs. He had promised them their wages and then withheld them. We—the Glory Girls—merely redressed the balance."

Dexter was silent. Laura spoke with a passion and conviction that was difficult to resist, even for someone like him who was always at pains to uphold the letter as well as the spirit of the law. But he could not allow such sentiment to influence his thinking. It was his duty and his responsibility to see justice administered. Compromise led to weakness and frailty. It was the beginning of the downward path.

"You broke the law," he said.

"I did," Laura said. "Many times. For the greater good."

"You are not entitled to make judgments like that." Dexter jumped to his feet. "That is the responsibility of officers of the law."

Laura shrugged. "I understand your disapproval, Mr. Anstruther. How could we ever agree on this when you are sworn to uphold the law and I was obliged to break it, even if I did so for what I thought were the best reasons? Anyway, we are here to talk about Warren Sampson, not my misdemeanors."

Dexter sighed. "Very well. So how do we catch him?"

Laura paused. She rubbed her fingers thoughtfully up and down the side of her brandy glass. "Through his vanity and his weakness for money, I think. Set a trap for him. One that is so temptingly financially baited that he cannot resist. He is too clever to be caught otherwise. He works behind a smokescreen of paid thugs and criminals."

"Yes," Dexter said. "One of his hired men may well have killed Sir William Crosby."

"Miles told me Crosby's death was no accident," Laura said. "If it is true that Crosby was working to bring Sampson down then he might well have paid with his life."

Dexter leaned forward. "If it is also true that Sampson has some of the local gentry in his pocket, who do you think they might be?"

Laura was silent for a moment. "I do not know that. Some bored younger son who has not got enough money to fund his gambling habit, perhaps? There are few such scattered through the Dales."

"Name them."

Laura lifted her hazel gaze to his. Her eyes were very clear and candid. Dexter thought of the way she had used him and marveled she could seem so honest when her heart was corrupt.

"There is Sir James Wheeler's son," she said slowly. "The gossip is that his father keeps him short on his allowance. They are forever at odds. Tom Fortune is a rackety young man but I have never thought there was any harm in him. I could be wrong. And then there is Stephen Beynon. He runs with Tom in a fast set." She shook her head. "I do not know. It is difficult because there may be those Sampson has bought off, or has some information on to persuade them to his point of view. I saw him talking to Henry Cole last night and it struck me as odd because Faye would never give a *cit* the time of day unless she had a particularly good reason. She is far too conscious of her position as Duchess of Cole."

"You think that Sampson might stoop to blackmail?"

"I am sure of it, if it benefited him."

"Do you know where Sampson's henchmen meet?" Dexter asked.

"They favor the Red Lion Inn on Stainmoor," Laura said. She looked up suddenly, her voice changing. "Don't go there, Mr. Anstruther. It is too dangerous. Even I would not have set foot in the Red Lion and the locals *liked* me."

Dexter raised a brow. "So you're concerned for my welfare now?"

Laura looked away. "I would not like to see you hurt."

There was a strained silence. Dexter found that he could not keep still. The frustrated fury burned in him too violently for that. Even though he knew they were there to discuss the present case and not the past, he could not prevent his mind from returning to it. He needed an explanation from Laura. His pride demanded one.

He strode over to the fireplace. "Explain something to me," he said harshly. "Was the work of the Glory Girls all a matter of principle of you?"

"No, it was not," Laura said. "It was in part but not entirely." Once again her expression was shadowed, hidden from him. She shifted a little in her chair. "The truth is that when I first rode with the Glory Girls, I did it because of Charles."

She looked up and met Dexter's eyes and he flinched at the pain and honesty he saw reflected there. It was like stripping her back to her soul. "Charles was so indifferent to me that I wanted to shock him," Laura said softly. "I had loved him desperately for so many years and I was frantic to make him take notice of me."

"You wanted your husband to *know* you were a highwaywoman?" Dexter was appalled. It seemed that Charles Cole's indifference to Laura, the neglect that he himself had observed when he had first met her at Cole Court, had driven her to the edge of sanity. Her appetite for destruction had been terrifying.

"Yes, I wanted Charles to know." Laura's hazel eyes were blank. She looked through him as though she was looking back to a past so painful she could not acknowledge it. "I am being very honest with you, Mr. Anstruther," she said. "I hope you understand that. I loved Charles for so long and so deeply that it became a habit with me. I would have done anything to gain his interest. I wanted him to *see* me, not to look through me. I wanted him to notice me." She took a deep breath. "My love for him drove me close to madness, to the point where I did reckless things to gain his attention."

She looked up and her eyes were no longer blank but vivid with so much pain and misery that Dexter reached out toward her instinctively, before his hand fell back to his side.

"But the irony was that Charles *did* know that I was Glory and still he did not care," Laura said softly. A faint, bitter smile curved her lips. "In the end there was nothing I could do to gain his interest, still less his regard. He saw me as an ornament to his dukedom and wanted nothing from me other than that I be a gracious hostess to his guests, that is all. And in the end my love for him died."

"Charles Cole knew that you were Glory and yet he said nothing, did nothing?" Dexter knew he sounded frankly incredulous now. He was appalled. He was worse than appalled. He was astounded. He could not believe that the late Duke of Cole had known his wife was a highwaywoman and yet it had elicited not the slightest response in him. What had been wrong with the man?

"Yes." Laura smiled mockingly. "Are you thinking that he was a Justice of the Peace, and yet he did nothing to stop me? Not everyone has your moral compass, Mr. Anstruther. He did not care."

"So you were not even acting out of principle," Dexter said. He shook his head, trying to get a grip on the feelings her words aroused in him. "You shock me, your grace," he said slowly.

Laura gave him another faint smile. "Do I really? But you will not accept any justification, will you, Mr. Anstruther? When I claimed to have acted out of principle you still dismissed my actions." She stood up, crossing the room to confront him, stopping only inches away so that he was intensely aware of her physical presence.

"The irony is that you and I are not so different really," she said. "Like you I value integrity and honor and would seek to live my life by those standards." She took a few steps away from him then swung sharply back. "I hold to those principles," she repeated, "but I hold to them with humanity, Mr. Anstruther, because without compassion those qualities are worthless. But you…" She shook her head. "You never compromise, do you? You cannot bend."

"I am sworn to uphold the law," Dexter said. "You—the Glory Girls—broke it. It should be as simple as that."

"It should be," Laura said, "but it isn't." She turned away. "Think of the men, women and children who would have starved if the Glory Girls had not redistributed Sampson's pay where it belonged," she said. "Had the Glory Girls not acted, tens, maybe hundreds of people would have died. Yet Warren Sampson would never have been brought to justice for his greed and cruelty. The law would never have touched him." She took a deep breath. "Think of the people whose livelihood is destroyed every day by greedy landowners enclosing common land. Think of the women forced into marriage against their will and the factory workers slaving for a pittance and any number of people ground down and destroyed through the avarice and brutality of their masters. Those are the sorts of injustices that you cannot address through the exercise of the law, Mr. Anstruther. But the Glory Girls could redress them. Perhaps it is not strictly legal but it has a certain morality and a great deal of humanity."

Dexter felt cold. Her words were a dangerous seduction, tempting him to compromise the principles he had always believed in. She spoke with such conviction and he wanted to believe in her. His desire for her and the secret admiration he had always harbored for Glory was like a weakness in the blood, undermining him. If he once bent then he might break and fail. The fear drove out all else. He grabbed her arm and spun her around to face him.

"Fine words, madam," he said harshly. "But the truth is that you are no more than a criminal. You deceived me through and through. You welcomed me to your bed one night and cast me out the next morning. And at last it makes perfect sense to me."

Laura's chin came up sharply. Her gaze was bright and challenging. The awareness sparked between them like a flame set to dry tinder. It was all he could do not to wrench her into his arms. In that moment he wanted her with an ache so deep he did not know how it could ever be assuaged and he hated her with an equally strong passion.

"What do you mean?" she whispered.

Dexter stared down into her eyes for what felt like an eternity. "It was all a pretense, was it not?" he said violently. "It was all a sham. You made love to me merely to distract me from my duty so that I, poor fool, would be so lost in thoughts of you that I had no space in my mind for anything else." He shook his head with bitter disillusion for his own youthful naiveté. "You must have been aware of what I felt for you. I was young and I do not think I was particularly good at hiding my feelings when I was near you. You saw it as your chance to deflect my attention so that I would never imagine you were Glory, never even *begin* to suspect what you had done. You are no more than a heartless whore."

Laura looked at him and his heart turned over at the expression in her eyes. In that shattering moment of awareness he saw her facade splinter and glimpsed the cracks and the pain beneath. And then the glimpse was gone.

"You may believe that if you wish," Laura said. "I am sure that you will."

Once again their gazes locked. Dexter searched her face. She must be false. She had to be. She had tricked him, deceived him from the very first moment they met. But her eyes were so clear and so honest. He could feel his anger melting and doubt, hope and longing taking its place. His hand slid slowly, caressingly, down her arm from elbow to wrist. She shivered under his touch. Her eyes darkened, her lashes fluttered down and the pink heat of arousal flushed her skin. Her lips parted and Dexter leaned closer.

The door slammed back on its hinges as Josie marched into the room and they fell apart as the fire flickered and hissed in the cold draft. Laura cast him one quick, troubled glance and then reached for her cloak, fumbling to tie the bow.

"Your carriage is ready, madam," Josie said, looking from one to the other with massive disapproval, "and a good thing, too. Seems to me Mr. Anstruther has had as much *help*—" she invested the word with scorn "—as he deserves tonight."

Dexter looked at Laura. Her head was bent. He could not see her face except in pure profile, illuminated in the bronze glow of the fire. When she looked up her expression was empty of emotion and it was as though that flash of intense pain he had seen in her had never been and the blaze of powerful awareness between them had not existed.

"Thank you, Josie," she said. She turned to Dexter. "I wish you luck in your investigation. Good night, Mr. Anstruther."

Josie stood aside for her to walk through the parlor door but when Dexter made to follow she blocked his way, as solid as a brick wall.

"Leave her be," Josie said threateningly.

Dexter looked at her. Her protectiveness toward Laura was striking. He wondered how much she knew. When he had been at Cole Court four years before he had noticed how much loyalty Laura commanded from the inhabitants of Peacock Oak and all the surrounding villages. She had been a good and generous employer and a beloved benefactor. If the villagers knew she was Glory, as well, they probably held her in even higher esteem.

"I appreciate your loyalty to her grace, Mrs. Simmons," he said slowly, "but I am sure she can take care of herself."

Josie snorted. "That's all you know, Mr. Anstruther. Or care, I'll wager. You've done enough harm. Blaming her grace for what she's done when there was no one else to stand up for us! You should take your head out of your... nether parts and think a little. Men!" Upon which she stomped out muttering under her breath.

Dexter's thoughts returned to Laura. In that moment when he had looked into her eyes his belief in her guilt had faltered, but cynicism whispered to him that she would always deny deliberately using him. She had been an older, experienced woman who was probably accustomed to taking lovers to her bed to relieve the tedium of her marriage. He had just been one of many and she had used his infatuation with her to her own ends. What had happened between them had finished four years before. Based on secrets and lies, it had never really started. And now he had an investigation to complete and an heiress to court. His life was as simple as that and it was going to stay that way.

But though he assured himself that the matter was tidy, closed, ended now forever, he had the feeling that Laura Cole would not be so easily dismissed no matter how much he tried, and neither were his feelings for her.

CHAPTER SEVEN

"THANK YOU ALL for joining us, ladies," Laura said. She scanned the crowd assembled in the circulating library. It seemed that every female in Fortune's Folly was present, not simply the single women affected by Sir Montague's Dames' Tax. Absolutely everyone was there, from old Mrs. Broad, who lived in the last cottage on the High Street and whose worldly possessions were no more than two chickens and a sheep, to Sir Montague's heiress half sister, Lady Elizabeth Scarlet. Lady Elizabeth sat next to Lydia Cole, her auburn head bent and her hands demurely in her lap in stark contrast to her behavior the previous night.

Laura thought it was extraordinary. Silk mixed with worsted, trade with old money. They chatted and laughed together, united in a single cause. Laura had never seen such a degree of social acceptance in her life. The only exception was her cousin by marriage, Faye, Duchess of Cole, who was looking down her nose in horror at the need to mingle with the common people. Since Henry and Faye did not even live in Fortune's Folly, Laura was tempted to suggest to Faye that she spared herself the unpleasantness of associating with the masses and simply went back home to Cole Court.

Holding up her hands, she called the meeting to order and the room fell obediently silent.

"I didn't expect," she said slowly, "to see so many of you here."

"We thought we would all come to show support," piped Mrs. Lovell, a pert blonde who had been married to a local solicitor for barely more than a year. "After all, if my dearest Archie were to have an accident and die, I would be in the same situation as the rest of you. What Sir Montague is doing is appalling!"

"Thank you," Laura said. She though it unlikely that Archie Lovell, a timid young man whose idea of a dangerous activity was to walk home rather than take the carriage, would meet with a fatal accident in the near future but she appreciated the vote of support.

"My husband is trying to use the opportunity of the Dames' Tax to get poor Mary off our hands," said Lady Wheeler, the faded wife of a minor baronet, with a fond smile at the plain daughter who was sitting blushing at her side. "He is welcoming all kinds of rogues to the house because he says it is the only way to get her a husband. It's iniquitous!"

A murmur of sympathy arose in the room, though Laura was not sure whether it was for Mary Wheeler's plight in being married off by a hardhearted father or being blessed with so insensitive a mother. Lydia Cole reddened and cast a sideways glance at her own mother and Laura remembered the assembly the previous night and Faye's determined attempts to throw Lydia in the path of any man who looked her way. Poor Mary Wheeler was not the only one.

"I am sorry to hear it, ma'am," she said.

"Sir Montague is a toad," Mrs. Broad opined. "He sent his estate manager around this morning to warn me I'd lose one of my chickens and half of the sheep." She folded her arms belligerently. "I asked him which half he wanted, front or back. I'd rather cut my tongue out than marry again, and so I told him. It took Broad long enough to die and leave me in peace!" She looked around the circle of faces and her gaze softened as it fell on Lady Elizabeth Scarlet. "Bless you, child, I'm sorry to speak ill of your brother, but what he is doing is a scandal!"

"Oh, don't mind me," Lady Elizabeth said cheerfully. There was a spark of humor in her green eyes. "Monty is being an absolute cad but he will be sorry for it when I have finished with him!"

"Quite," Laura said hurriedly, remembering the lemonade incident. "I do think, Lady Elizabeth, that whilst direct action may be all very well in some cases, we do need to be careful how we approach this problem."

"Of course, your grace," Elizabeth said with a demureness that did not fool Laura in the least.

"I have been searching the old books in my grandmother's library," Laura continued, "and I have found some countermeasures that may be useful. When Sir Montague invoked the Dames' Tax, he also revived all the other medieval laws of the village, you see."

The ladies did see. Another flutter of debate and speculation swept the room as they discussed which old village customs might be suitable to revive.

"There's pannage," Mrs. Broad said suddenly. "I remember that from my father's time. He used to let his pigs roam in the lord's woodlands."

"I do not see why it should just be pigs," Elizabeth

said, brightening up. "We have plenty of horses in our stable. They would love to graze Monty's flower beds. His autumn planting is his pride and joy and I am sure the flowers taste as sweet as they smell." She looked around. "Does anyone else have any livestock to graze?"

"You can borrow my sheep with my blessing, Lady Elizabeth," Mrs. Broad said, beaming.

"I believe there is also a custom called foldage, by which the sheep manure the lord's land in return for provision of a sheep fold," Laura said.

"My sheep's good at manuring," Mrs. Broad said proudly. "Reckon she could make quite an impression on Sir Montague's lawn."

Laura laughed. Faye Cole's face contracted in disgust and she moved her skirts aside as though the sheep were already making its presence felt. "This is very childish," she murmured. "Surely one should simply accede to the lord of the manor's authority?" She looked at Lydia. "I came here today to say that this is an excellent opportunity for a matchmaking mama who wants what is best for her daughter. Indeed—" she shot a venomous look at Alice Lister "—certain ladies from humble beginnings should not have been so quick to turn down Sir Montague's generous offer in the first place."

There was an awkward silence. Alice took a deep breath and looked fit to burst but Elizabeth forestalled her with a smile. "For my part," she said, "I have always seen Miss Lister as a sister. She need not sacrifice herself to Monty in wedlock in order to make it a formal arrangement."

There was some laughter at this and Faye subsided, looking huffy. She was not going to be seen to contradict an earl's daughter in public but her boot-faced expression made her opinion clear on outspoken chits who needed a firm hand.

"Thank you," Laura said. "It is always useful to hear opposing views. Now, shall we take a vote? All those in favor of introducing pannage and foldage?"

Every lady in the room raised her hand, with the exception of Lydia and Faye, whose hands remained locked firmly in her lap. After a moment Lydia tentatively put her hand up, as well, only for Faye to grab her arm and wrestle it down again. A small struggle ensued with Lydia's agonized gasp of *"Mama!"* a fair indication of Faye's surprising amount of strength.

"The vote is carried," Laura said briskly, ignoring them. "Lady Elizabeth, may we rely upon you to discuss grazing with all the ladies who possess livestock and arrange for the transfer of animals to Sir Montague's gardens?"

"Certainly," Elizabeth said, her green eyes sparkling. "It will be a pleasure."

"We will call another meeting in a few days' time," Laura said, "when we shall discuss further action. All ideas welcome, ladies. I leave the matter with you."

"It is a disgrace to see you chairing a meeting like this!" Faye hissed in Laura's ear as the ladies of Fortune's Folly filed out of the circulating library into the autumn sunshine of the market square. "Really, Laura, I wonder at you! You are the Dowager Duchess of Cole. A few years ago you were mixing with the hoi polloi at the Harrogate horticultural society. That was bad enough but now this group of miscreants and renegades! I am shocked."

"It is no wonder that you and Sir Montague are in such

agreement, Faye," Laura observed, trying not to feel too irritated. "You are kindred spirits."

She picked up her file of research papers and tucked it under her arm. Faye's snobbery had been a thorn in her side from the very first time Charles had invited his cousin and his wife to visit Cole Court. "Your attitudes are positively antediluvian," she continued. "The *ladies* of Fortune's Folly are not miscreants. It is Sir Montague who deserves the reproof."

"Nonsense!" Faye claimed, puffing across the market square at Laura's side, dragging a reluctant Lydia in her wake. "If Miss Lister had been properly grateful for Sir Montague's condescension in offering marriage, none of this would have happened. I could not believe that she dared show her face at the meeting today."

"Why should she not?" Laura said crossly. She hated Faye's appalling snobbery. "She is as much affected by the Dames' Tax as the rest of us."

"Yes," Faye said, "but she is not a *lady,* is she?"

Laura gritted her teeth to physically keep in her response.

"Anyway," Faye continued, blissfully oblivious to Laura's anger, "I suppose that now this has all happened it is the perfect opportunity for girls such as dear Lydia to find a husband. Mr. Anstruther could barely tear himself from her side at the assembly and he walked with us in the Promenade Gardens yesterday, as well. He was complimenting Lyddy on being in excellent looks. Why, he was quite *épris!*"

"Really?" Laura said. She tried to keep her voice steady even though she had no desire to be treated to every last detail of Dexter's courtship of Lydia and felt decidedly snappy. The autumn day suddenly seemed less sunny and the wind had a biting edge. She told herself that this was no news to her—she had seen Dexter and Lydia together at the assembly, after all—but the sick feeling inside her did not go away.

"He has been paying my Lydia a vast amount of attention from the first," Faye said complacently. "He mentioned how sparkling was her conversation and how pleased he would be to visit Cole again now that you are no longer there, Laura—"

"I don't think he said anything of the sort, Mama," Lydia said. She was still rubbing her arm where Faye had grabbed her earlier and was looking a little defiant. "We had one dance together at the assembly and yesterday he asked after my health very politely, but that was all."

"Well," Faye said, viciously spiking a stray leaf with the tip of her umbrella, "I am sure he *would* have paid you compliments if you had been a little more forthcoming with him, Lyddy. A gentleman likes a little encouragement."

Laura thought of the brazen encouragement that she had given Dexter that day in her warming room and felt rather hot at the memory. It was not the sort of response that a gentleman looked for from his suitable, virgin bride. Could she be any further from Dexter Anstruther's ideal of a wife? She doubted it. But then beneath the surface Dexter was nothing like the austere and rational man he appeared on the outside. It was simply that he denied that part of his character because he was so determined to be the responsible man his father had failed to be. But one thing was for sure—his suitable virgin bride would get the shock of her life if treated to the volcanic passion Laura had unleashed in him.

"Mr. Anstruther should be grateful to have the opportunity to marry into the Coles of Cole Court," Faye continued. "He is a pauper and when all is said and done, has no more than good looks and an old name to his credit and some pointless job as clerk to that old fool Liverpool. His father was a sadly unsteady fellow and Mr. Anstruther himself seemed to be heading the same way a few years ago with his courtesans and his actresses and his liaisons with married women—"

"Mama!" Lydia besought, blushing to the ears. "I cannot believe that you wish me to marry a man you seem to hold in nothing but contempt."

She had a fair point, Laura thought, but Faye, with her elephant hide, saw no contradiction in her attitude.

"Nonsense, Lyddy," she said bracingly. "A female is nothing but a fool if she does not expect a man to have his little fancies and you must remember that he is marrying you for your money and you are marrying him for…" She paused, as though she were trying to come up with a good reason.

"To escape your mother," Laura said under her breath.

"Because he is the only one who will have you!" Faye finished triumphantly. "There he is now!" she trilled, speeding up toward the entrance to the pump rooms. "Cooeee! Mr. Anstruther!"

Laura's heart sank. She had hoped to have a few more days' grace in which to regain her composure before she was obliged to see Dexter again. Her awareness of him had been so intense that night at Half Moon Inn. She had told herself then that she was only meeting with Dexter because Lord Liverpool had the means to twist her arm, but seeing Dexter—talking over times past—had inevitably unleashed memories that were barely buried at all.

"If you will excuse me—" she began, but Faye caught her arm in a clawlike grip and dragged her forward.

"Must you be so selfish?" she hissed. "Show some family feeling and help us to catch Mr. Anstruther for Lyddy!"

Since the only alternative was to indulge in an undignified tussle in the street—a temptation she just managed to resist—Laura gave in with what good grace she could muster and allowed Faye to pull her along to the pump room steps. Dexter and his companion, Nat Waterhouse, paused obligingly as Faye bore down on them like a galleon with the wind in its sails. Both gentlemen were impeccable in morning dress. Laura tried hard not to look at Dexter but it seemed impossible. The more she tried to look away, the more her gaze was drawn to him: to his fair hair, ruffled by the autumn breeze, to his broad shoulders encased in an elegant coat of green this morning and down to the muscular thighs beneath the skintight pantaloons. Suddenly she felt more than a little weak at the knees. She closed her eyes for a second in defense against the awareness he aroused in her.

When she opened her eyes again and raised her gaze, she realized that Dexter had caught her staring and, even worse, read her mind with disturbing accuracy. His brows lifted in a look of quizzical inquiry that was not particularly friendly but was certainly challenging. There was a flame of sensual arousal deep in his eyes that made Laura feel even more flustered. She licked her lips nervously, saw his gaze drop to her mouth and felt her stomach quake.

"Oh, Mr. Anstruther," Laura heard Faye say, "Lydia has been looking forward to seeing you *so* much this morning! Did we not all have a *delightful* time at the park yesterday?"

"Delightful," Dexter said. He wrenched his gaze from Laura at last and sketched a bow. "You have arrived most opportunely, ladies. I had promised to introduce Lord Waterhouse to the pleasures of the sulphur water spa, but he seems strangely reluctant to sample it. Now that you are here, though, he will no doubt yield to a sweeter persuasion than mine."

"You must excuse me from your excursion," Laura said. Dexter's gaze had swept the group and included her briefly and impartially in the invitation and his sudden switch from arousal to apparent indifference made her feel decidedly cross. She had no wish to sit and watch him make eyes at Lydia across a beaker of mineral water.

"I have work to do and no intention of inflicting the spring waters on anyone," she said. She gestured to Faye. "I am sure, however, that her grace and Miss Cole would be delighted to accompany you."

Faye looked torn between disapproval of Laura's cavalier dismissal of the benefits of Fortune's Waters and gratification that she and Lydia would have both gentlemen to themselves. Her smile faded, though, as Nat ushered her up the steps to the pump room but Dexter fell back, catching Laura's arm.

"You returned safely from our meeting at Half Moon Inn the other night, I hope," he murmured. His touch on her arm was firm. Laura felt a shiver of response that was impossible to deny.

"As you see," Laura said coolly. "And you, Mr. Anstruther. Have you had chance yet to call at the Red Lion on Stainmoor?"

"I have," Dexter said. He smiled ruefully. "I thought Half Moon Inn was rough but the Red Lion was another matter again. I was lucky to escape with my life—and that was before they knew why I was there."

Laura looked at him. He did not look to have suffered much by the experience. There was something tough, durable and dangerous about Dexter Anstruther that suggested that he would be a good man in a tight corner, and not at all disadvantaged in a fight with Warren Sampson's thugs.

"I did warn you," she said. "I hope it was worth it."

"You did," Dexter agreed, "and I fear it was not. I gained no useful information." He looked at her. "It reminded me of when I was hunting Glory. No one would talk to me."

"No one spoke of Glory through loyalty," Laura said. "No one speaks of Sampson through fear, Mr. Anstruther. There is a difference." She removed her arm from his grip with deliberation. "Excuse me. I must not keep you from your pursuit of Miss Cole's money—I beg your pardon—from your courtship of Miss Cole."

Dexter smiled. "What can be so pressing that it has you hurrying off with those papers?" he inquired.

"Nothing in particular," Laura said. "You have a suspicious mind, Mr. Anstruther, which I suppose is no surprise in your line of work, but I assure you there is nothing more interesting here than legal business." She gave him a mocking look. "I hope you do not find it too lowering that I infinitely prefer my papers to the company of yourself and Lord Waterhouse."

A stray gust of wind caught the edge of the file and Laura jumped and dropped the papers on the ground. They scattered across the cobbles of the market square, catching the breeze and fluttering in all directions. As she ran about trying to recapture them, Dexter stooped and picked some up, his keen blue gaze scanning the pages.

"Medieval laws and taxes... Foldage... Pannage..."

"Give those back!" Laura said, dignity abandoned, making a grab for the papers in his hand. Infuriatingly Dexter held them out of her reach and smiled patronizingly down at her. It made her want to stamp her foot, preferably on his toes.

"So you are playing Sir Montague at his own game," he said slowly. "Now that is very clever of you."

"I *am* clever," Laura said, flustered. The last thing she wanted was to give away secrets to the enemy. She could imagine Dexter going to Fortune Hall and telling Monty Fortune everything that they planned, ruining their revenge.

"Yes," Dexter said. "You are." He looked at her appraisingly. "It would be a foolish adversary who underestimated you, as I did." He handed the file to her with exemplary courtesy. "You do appreciate, though, that if you declare war on the gentlemen of the town they will respond in full measure?"

"I can hardly wait," Laura said truthfully. "The ladies of Fortune's Folly are ready to do battle."

A smile that was not in the least comfortable curved Dexter's lips. "It will be battle royal," he promised. "You may regret engaging us." His voice fell. "Speaking for myself, I can be very determined when I want something. I do feel the need to even the score with you..."

"Do you indeed," Laura snapped, ignoring the flutter his words sent along her nerves. "Trust a man to be unable to accept when he was bested fair and square." She gestured toward the long picture windows of the pump house, through which Faye Cole could be seen holding court. "May I encourage you to go and be determined with Miss Cole and her mother? I must be getting back."

"To put your plans into action?"

"Precisely."

"But if I tell Sir Montague what you intend that will spike your guns."

It was exactly what Laura had feared. She met his eyes. Beneath the challenge in them she saw the same heat as before. It turned her stomach inside out.

"Tell him and be damned to you," she said.

Dexter laughed. "Sweet of you."

Laura shrugged. "You can deal with it, Mr. Anstruther. I am sure you do not need kind words from me."

"What I need from you…" Dexter mused. The expression in his eyes made explicit just what it was he wanted from her. The flame in them scorched her. "Just now," Dexter said thoughtfully, "what I need is to kiss you to within an inch of your life."

The door of the pump rooms slammed as a couple of ladies came out and glanced at them with curiosity. Laura jumped and turned away from their inquiring glance. Her expression felt too naked.

The interruption had evidently recalled Dexter to his senses, too.

"Are you sure you will not join us for a glass?" he asked, gesturing toward the pump room door. "We could raise a toast to the impending hostilities between the fortune hunters and the ladies of Fortune's Folly."

"No, thank you," Laura said. "The sulphur water is vile stuff and guaranteed to kill off anyone of weakened temperament."

Dexter laughed. "Then I am surprised you do not encourage me to take it by the gallon." He bowed. "Good day then, your grace." He turned away, but paused before he had gone more than a few paces.

"Had you thought of pontage?" he asked. "The right to charge a fee for crossing the bridge over the River Tune? I think that you will find that the bridge belongs to the town rather than the lord of the manor because it was paid for by public subscription. And Monty has to cross the river every time he comes into Fortune's Folly from the Court. You could make a lot of money out of him and annoy him intensely into the bargain…."

Laura narrowed her eyes suspiciously. "And why would you be giving me this advantage, Mr. Anstruther?"

Dexter shrugged easily. "I thought it would make the conflict more even," he said.

Indignation bubbled within Laura. "Because females do not have as much cunning and duplicity as males?" she inquired sweetly.

"Not at all." Dexter thrust his hands into his pockets. "I have observed that the female mind can be unmatched in guile and deceit."

That, Laura thought, was undoubtedly aimed at her. She would do well never to forget that he had an opinion of her that was so low.

"I do believe, however," Dexter continued, "that men are far better at organizing and carrying through a plan.

We have the cool heads, the strength and the determination to succeed."

"And the conceit," Laura snapped, still smarting. "You have just provided the best reason yet to rout the men of Fortune's Folly. We shall puncture that insufferable arrogance of yours. We will see who triumphs, Mr. Anstruther."

DEXTER SAMPLED ANOTHER MOUTHFUL of coffee and reflected that Laura had been right about one thing; it was a great deal more palatable than the spa water on offer at the pump room. He had spent an excruciating hour there earlier in the day paying court to Miss Lydia Cole and almost choking on both the platitudes he was mouthing to her and the sulphur water he was drinking. He was convinced that the famous Fortune Waters were deleterious to the health and probably carried plenty of diseases. If the visitors to the spa started to drop like flies he would know where to begin his investigation.

Meanwhile, it had seemed apparent to Dexter that Lydia had been as unwilling to accept his compliments as he had been to offer them, with the distressing effect that the two of them had struggled to maintain a stilted conversation under Nat's sardonic eye and Faye Cole's indulgent one. Seeing Laura again had undermined him completely and made him see his courtship of Lydia for the hollow sham it was. He hungered for Laura in a way that he did not like, did not understand and could barely restrain. The fact that she had been Glory, the infamous highwaywoman, only seemed to inflame him. It tore his much-vaunted reason and self-control to shreds to be lusting after a woman he did not like and could not have.

But then liking had precious little to do with his desire for Laura. His feelings for her were primitive and intense and angry, far stronger than mere liking or disliking, and far too foreign to him to be at all comfortable. He had sought to master that wild side of his character for so long. He *would not* permit it to dictate to him now.

The others—Sir Montague Fortune and his brother, Tom, Nathaniel Waterhouse and Miles Vickery—were all drinking wine or brandy that afternoon but it was too early for Dexter, who only ever drank in moderation. His father had listed gambling, smoking and drinking amongst his many vices and Dexter had kept away from them as he would the plague. Even in the days of his worst excesses he had not been drawn to the brandy bottle. It seemed that it was only Laura Cole to whom he was attracted with intemperance and excess. Even now he could not keep his mind from her.

"So how goes your plan, Monty?" Miles inquired of their host. "Fleeced any ladies of their fortunes yet? Have there yet been any hastily announced plans to wed?"

"It goes very well indeed," Sir Monty said, rubbing his hands. "My agent is visiting all the properties in the village covered by the Dames' Tax to work out the value of the estate that is due to me.

"The ladies have a year to wed or give me their money, and with the Christmas festivities upon us in a couple months' time there should be ample opportunity for the gentlemen to press their suit—" He stopped, staring out through the library windows. "I say, is that a *sheep* grazing my lawn?"

"There's a whole flock of them," Tom responded helpfully. "Look, they're coming through the paddock gate—

" But Sir Montague had already leaped to his feet and hurried out the door, bellowing for his estate manager as he went.

The others exchanged a look and followed in more leisurely fashion and by the time they had reached the terrace they found Lady Elizabeth Scarlet, Laura Cole and Alice Lister shepherding the last of the flock through the gate and into the gardens.

As soon as he saw Laura, Dexter felt the same slam of awareness that he experienced whenever he was in her presence. She looked every inch his most secret and forbidden temptation. She was dressed very simply in a green gown that brought out the bright hazel of her eyes. Her face was pink from the fresh breeze, her hair escaping its confinement under a bonnet to curl about her face. She was avoiding his gaze and her evasion felt like a challenge. Dexter deliberately kept his eyes on her and saw her glance flicker to him, brief and betraying, before she looked away. The color in her cheeks deepened and he felt a savage surge of satisfaction that she was as aware of him as he was of her, no matter how much she pretended otherwise.

"Have you forgotten that you do not even like me…" Laura's question prickled at his conscience just as her presence chafed at him. His feelings were tangled, lust and caution, sense and desire at war within him. He found it intensely frustrating to be faced with a situation he did not appear to be able to control.

"This is trespass!" Sir Montague shouted, purpling in the face as he ran down the terrace steps. "Stop it at once!"

"Don't be silly, Monty," Lady Elizabeth said. "How can I be trespassing on my own lawn?" She nodded to the others and smiled at Nat Waterhouse. "Good after-

noon, gentlemen. So you are here, as well, Nat! Fortune's Folly is positively stuffed with paupers these days.
Are you looking for a pea-brain to marry, too?"

"Better a pea-brain than a termagant," Nat said. "How
are you, Lizzie?"

"Still too wild for your taste," Lady Elizabeth said.
"But rich, Nat, very rich! Isn't it sickening?"

"It's certainly not remotely tempting," Nat said,
smiling.

"You may not be trespassing, Lizzie, but the sheep
are!" Sir Montague intervened. "Get rid of them!"

"Alas, we cannot, Sir Montague," Laura said, with
every appearance of regret. "Not if we are to conform to
the law. This is foldage, you see. You will find the details
on the same page of the parish history as the Dames' Tax."
Dexter saw her check the sheet of paper in her hand, and
saw the word *strategy* written in large letters at the top.
Laura caught him watching and whisked the paper out of
his line of sight. Dexter grinned at her and she glared
back.

"The sheep are permitted to graze your land in return
for their manure," Laura continued, gesturing to the
nearest sheep, which was neatly illustrating her point on
the lawn.

"But I don't want their ordure!" Sir Montague
lamented. "Stop them!"

"I don't think one can stop a sheep doing what comes
naturally," Tom said, grinning. Dexter saw him give Laura
a look of pure appreciation and wanted to take the other
man by the scruff of his neck and kick him out of his own
garden.

"They are destroying my Michaelmas daisies," Sir

Monty wailed, as another of the flock enthusiastically chewed the violet flowers from a nearby bush. "And my late roses! This is appalling!"

"Just like the Dames' Tax," Laura agreed. "Quite appalling."

"And the grass!" Sir Montague ran a shaking hand over his brow. "My gardeners have tended it carefully to prepare it for the winter!"

"It is so much richer than the grass on the fells," Laura agreed. "The sheep will enjoy it very much." She smiled warmly at Sir Montague. "Now that the nights are starting to draw in they will also benefit from having a proper fold."

"In the stables," Lady Elizabeth added helpfully.

"But I keep my hunters in there!" Sir Montague expostulated. "I can't have sheep in with my horses!"

"I am sure they will get along famously," Laura said. She smiled impartially at the group, her gaze lingering on the brandy glass in Nat's hand. "Do not let us keep you from your entertainments, gentlemen. What is it this afternoon? Dreaming up new taxes with which to cheat the ladies of Fortune's Folly?"

"Touché," Dexter murmured, as Sir Montague spluttered ineffectually. He met Laura's gaze and she gave him a small smile of triumph, her beautiful, generous mouth turning up irresistibly. Dexter felt the impact of it like a kick in the gut. He found himself thinking of what it would be like to kiss her. He had already taken a step toward her before he managed to kill the urge and get himself back under control. But Miles had noticed and cast him a curious glance. Dexter shifted uncomfortably, aware of his body's growing arousal and his

utter inability to prevent it. This passion for Laura had to be conquered before it led him from his rational path for a second time. He did not need to understand why it kept happening. All he needed to do was vanquish it. The difficulty was that he had no idea how.

"I do not think you should be too sure of victory yet, your grace," he said slowly. "The game has only just begun."

He saw Laura's smile fade to be replaced by a look of cool, steely determination. Unfortunately he found her sternness equally arousing. There was something about Laura being strict, as she had been with Miles in the ballroom on the night of the assembly, something that made him think of her bed and twisted satin bonds. Her voice dragged his imagination back from the brink of erotic chaos.

"Well," she said, in clipped tones, "we shall leave you to your brandy and return to our council of war. Good luck, gentlemen."

Dexter watched her slender figure stalk away through the gate with Elizabeth and Alice following along behind.

"There go three women intent on causing havoc," Miles Vickery muttered.

"In more ways than one," Dexter agreed. He was amused to see that Miles could not stop staring at Alice Lister, who had turned to latch the gate and had given Miles an extremely quelling look when she caught him watching her.

"I think you might be wasting your time there, old chap," Dexter said. "Miss Lister seems refreshingly immune to your so-called charm."

"We'll see," Miles said. He smiled. "You know I relish a challenge, Dexter. The greater the difficulty the more pleasure in the game and—" his smile grew "—I do find Miss Lister well-nigh irresistible."

"Thirty guineas says you won't succeed," Tom Fortune said cheerfully.

"In seducing her or marrying her?" Miles questioned.

"Both," Tom said. "Either. Monty, will you sub me thirty guineas?"

"Done," Miles said. "You might as well hand the money over now, Fortune."

"Show some respect," Dexter snapped.

"What, you think the wager should be higher?" Miles questioned. He looked at Tom. "He could be right, you know, Fortune. Thirty guineas seems a bit paltry for a lady's virtue."

Dexter made a sound of disgust. "You're a scoundrel, Miles. Nat—" He appealed to Nat Waterhouse. "You've known Miles the longest. For pity's sake talk some sense into him."

Nat shook his head. "I'm just waiting to see him fall, Dexter, and I have a feeling—"

"Never mind the women," Sir Montague interrupted, grabbing Dexter's arm. "My garden is far more important! What am I to do, Dexter?" He wrung his plump hands as a sheep demolished the last of his late-flowering honeysuckle. "This is a disaster!"

"Send for a shepherd, round them up and take them back to the fells," Dexter said. "It's simple, Monty."

"Not to me," Sir Montague wailed. "Elizabeth will never permit it."

"Come on, Monty," Nat Waterhouse said. "Brace up.

What we need to do is plan our response. More brandy for you first, though. You look as though you need it."

Once he had been revived with another glass and was installed in front of the fire, Monty Fortune seemed to take strength.

"It is all the fault of the Dowager Duchess of Cole," he grumbled. "You all saw that she was the ringleader. Miles," he appealed to Vickery, "her grace is your cousin. Can you not prevail upon her to desist?"

Miles shook his head. There was a rueful smile on his lips. "I don't think so, Monty. As you said, Laura is a dowager duchess. One doesn't tell dowagers what to do."

Nor highwaywomen, Dexter thought, even retired ones. Not if one valued one's life.

"Nonsense! She should do as she is bid," Sir Montague said sharply. "Disobedience is most unbecoming in any female, regardless of rank."

Looking at the others, Dexter could tell that they were all thinking of Lady Elizabeth, whom Sir Montague had so spectacularly failed to keep in check himself. Sir Montague was singularly incapable of practicing what he preached.

"If you would like to tell the dowager duchess of your feelings on the subject, Monty," Dexter said dryly, "I am sure she would give you a fair hearing."

Sir Montague subsided, grumbling. "Perhaps I could exempt her from the Dames' Tax and then she might be prevailed upon to see sense," he suggested.

"Wouldn't make any odds," Miles said. He sighed. "Laura hasn't any money of her own, anyway. She's doing this for the others, Monty, not for herself. She always was one to embrace a cause." He lay back in his chair, hands behind his head. "Even when she was a child I remember her campaigning for days off for the servants and fairer wages for the farm laborers. She was a wild child. She could ride any horse in the stables and she drove my aunt and uncle to distraction. All they wanted was for her to be a proper lady."

There was no doubt, Dexter thought, that on the surface at least the Earl and Countess of Burlington had succeeded in shaping Laura into the perfect, proper lady. It was only beneath that surface that she was very improper indeed, as Dexter knew. But Miles's insight into Laura's character was interesting. It underlined the fact that she was passionate about causes and about helping people. She *cared*. It was the justification she had given him for her work as Glory—the need to right the wrongs that society could not address. Once again he felt admiration for her and repressed it ruthlessly.

A frown of perplexity was wrinkling Sir Monty's forehead, suggesting to Dexter that he did not really understand the concept of people who acted out of altruism.

"And so she should be a proper lady," Sir Monty said piously. "Days off for the servants? Dangerous, seditious ideas! Devilishly inappropriate."

Dexter shifted a little in his chair. He realized that Sir Montague's dismissal of Laura's philanthropy made him feel surprisingly angry and protective. He had seen for himself all that Laura had done for the poorest of tenants and workers at Cole. Her generosity had been well known and she had had no ulterior motive.

Ignoring Sir Monty, he turned directly to Miles.

"You sound as though you admire your cousin," he said.

"I do," Miles admitted. "There aren't many members of our family who have any principles."

"I do not think it very principled to ruin my garden," Sir Montague grumbled. He appealed to the others. "Tell me what I am to do, gentlemen. My flowers! My beautiful lawn! They will all be destroyed!"

"Well," Dexter said, his patience deserting him, "I suspect that there are those who would say that it is fairly unprincipled of you to instigate the Dames' Tax, Monty, and now you are getting what you deserve." He saw Miles, Nat and even Tom hide their grins at the bald truth of this statement. There was no sympathy for Sir Monty, even from his own brother.

"But I am within my rights in enforcing the Dames' Tax!" Sir Montague's double chin quivered indignantly. "It is the law."

"So is foldage, apparently," Nat said, his gaze on the slender figure of Lady Elizabeth as she came back through the gate into the gardens with a bucket of feed for the sheep.

"As I see it," Dexter said, "you have two alternatives, Monty. Either you back down now and repeal the Dames' Tax—"

"Never! I will lose too much money."

"—or you fight fire with fire."

"But how?" Sir Montague wailed piteously. "Those dashed females!"

Nat was laughing. "Invoke some more of your powers as lord of the manor, Monty."

"There's always the *droit de seigneur,*" Sir Montague said eagerly.

Miles spluttered into his brandy. "Steady on, Monty, you can't do that! You'd get arrested if you abducted all the brides on their wedding nights. Sounds like the kind of thing I would do," he added thoughtfully. "Dashed tempting idea."

Dexter thought so, too. The idea of carrying off Laura Cole and having his wicked way with her was temptation incarnate.

"Forget the *droit de seigneur,*" he said testily, trying to concentrate. "Monty, you need to exploit the other tithes at your disposal."

"What I really need is for some of my tenants to die," Sir Montague said thoughtfully. "That way I would be entitled to the Soul's Scot and could take their second-best chattel in lieu of a tithe."

"Would that be their wife or their horse?" Tom murmured.

"That depends on the tenant," Miles said, with a wicked grin. "And the wife."

"And the horse," Tom said, laughing.

Dexter put down his coffee cup with a snap. He had had enough of Sir Montague's self-inflicted problems and the endless debate they were causing. He had no desire to help the man cheat half the population of Fortune's Folly out of their inheritance.

"I will see you all later, gentlemen," he said abruptly. "I have bespoken dinner at the Morris Clown and then I am to attend the harp recital at the assembly rooms."

"No doubt in company with the charming Miss Cole," Tom said. "Such virginal innocence, Dexter, and allied to money, too! How very tempting."

"Thank you, Tom," Dexter said coldly. He deplored the other man's crass assessment but could hardly cut him dead whilst accepting his brother's hospitality.

"And her less than charming mama," Nat added. "I admire you enormously, Dex."

"To knowingly tie yourself for life to Faye Cole as well as her daughter takes extreme courage," Miles agreed.

His friends' mockery did nothing to soothe Dexter's irritation. As he walked back into the village, across the bridge over the River Tune, he reflected that Nat and Miles were full of congratulations for him on making such good progress in capturing his heiress—and equally glad that they were not the ones heading for the altar with Lydia Cole.

Thoughts of Lydia inevitably made him think of Laura. He was obsessed, infuriated. She had done this to him in the space of a week. Within a fortnight he would be in shreds, mind and body. It was no way for a man of sense to conduct himself.

He wondered if he was really cad enough to marry Lydia when all he wanted was to make love to Laura. Many men would not see the problem, would not even hesitate, but he was not one of them. He had the unnerving feeling that he would be in bed with Lydia on their wedding night and be totally unmanned, unable to make love to her because she was the wrong woman in the wrong place at the wrong time. Either that, or he would be fantasizing about Laura when he was with her cousin. Damn it, he had too much conscience to be a true rake. He had realized that years before when his angry passion for Laura had led him into more bedrooms and boudoirs than a man had a right to see in a lifetime. That was not his true nature. For the first time in his life he wished he were more like Miles Vickery, whose sense of honor seemed to be permanently missing when it came to women.

Yet what choice did he have but make Lydia Cole an offer? His entire family depended on him making a good match. He had no realistic alternative. And Lord Liverpool had as good as given him an ultimatum to find a rich wife or find another job. He could not fail in this.

Swearing under his breath, he crossed the street into the market square. It was a cold night with the wind howling in from the north, but the village was still bustling with activity even though dusk was falling now. The flower sellers, who had been doing a roaring trade from the moment so many London gentlemen had arrived in Fortune's Folly a-courting, were starting to pack up their stalls. There was a delicious smell of roasting meat floating toward Dexter from the inn, reminding him that his dinner would soon be ready.

He was crossing the cobbled square to the inn when he saw Laura disappearing along the lane that led toward the priory ruins and The Old Palace. The green of her gown paled to gray in the dusk. She was holding her bonnet firmly to prevent it blowing away. Dexter hesitated, turning away toward the inn, but even as he did he saw that someone had fallen into step behind Laura and started after her down the lane. They looked furtive and they kept in the shadows. The hair on the back of Dexter's neck prickled and stood up on end. His professional instinct took over. Without further thought he slid into the shade and followed the figures into the dark.

CHAPTER EIGHT

LAURA PLACED HER LANTERN carefully on a stone slab and reached up to retrieve a bottle from the shelf. She kept all her wine here in the cellars of the ruined priory, preferring it to The Old Palace where the steps down to the basement were dangerously steep and Carrington had almost fallen on more than one occasion. Here she kept her own recipes that brewed and bubbled gently in the corner and also the remnants of her grandfather's collection of fine wines. Laura seldom had cause to entertain these days and usually ended up drinking on her own, which she thought was no doubt the last resort of a sad old dowager duchess, sipping her sherry in the armchair before the fire, like an old soak. Tonight there was a harp concert in the village but she had had no wish to attend to see Dexter Anstruther and her cousin Miles and their friends fawning over the Fortune's Folly heiresses. Instead she would sit at home with a glass of wine, read a good book—not an improving one but something amusing—and plan further vengeance for Sir Montague Fortune. The sheep plan had worked rather well and now it was time for something new.

Laura selected a bottle of her elderflower champagne and looked at it critically. In the flickering lantern light it glowed as golden as straw in the sun. It was definitely ready to drink. Next to it on the shelf was a space and a dusty smear where it looked as though something had recently been removed. Laura frowned. She also kept her sloe marmalade and her jams in the cellar because the fruit was preserved for longer in the cool room. She was certain that she had not taken any of the pots away recently but she could not imagine who else had been down in the priory ruins looking for marmalade.

A sudden sound in the dark corridor behind her set her spinning around, clutching the bottle like a weapon. It would be a shocking waste of good champagne to break it over an intruder's head, but she would do it if she absolutely had to. She reflected that creeping around the priory ruins at night was probably not a good idea. She was not one of the credulous folk who believed that the spirits of the dead abbots walked through the ruins but even so, her grip on the bottle tightened.

The shadows shifted and Dexter Anstruther stepped into the circle of light thrown by the lantern. Laura was so surprised she almost dropped the bottle on the floor.

"Mr. Anstruther!" Her voice came out with a strangled squeak, revealing more vulnerability than she would have liked. "What on *earth* are you doing here?"

Dexter looked from her face to the bottle in her upraised hand and back again.

"Please could you put the bottle down?" he said. "You are making me nervous."

He did not look remotely nervous, Laura thought. He looked tough and uncompromising even though his tone was very polite. For a moment she caught sight of the other Dexter Anstruther—not the gentleman who had come to Fortune's Folly to court an heiress but the man she had met with at the Half Moon, the man who worked for the government in some shadowy capacity and no doubt had faced far more perilous situations than a jittery dowager brandishing a champagne bottle. Then the dangerous expression faded from his eyes.

She did as she was asked and put the bottle down. There was an odd silence between them as his gaze assessed her from head to foot, not with the overt masculine appraisal that she had seen from men sometimes, but with a more thoughtful calculation. It made her shiver. There was something impersonal about it, as though he were in some way measuring her character, and yet at the same time it felt intensely private.

"Are you alone?" he demanded.

The color flooded Laura's face at the implication of his words. "Of course I am alone!" she said. "Do you think that I entertain gentlemen friends down here in the cellars at night?"

"I don't know," Dexter said. He gave her a look that brought even hotter color searing her face. "Do you?"

"Of course not," Laura snapped. "You are offensive, Mr. Anstruther. And it is no business of yours, anyway." Her tone was sharp, masking her physical awareness of him. The wine cellar was not small but suddenly the walls seemed to press in on her and she felt a little breathless. Being in an enclosed space with Dexter Anstruther had definitely not been part of her plan for the evening.

"Never mind interrogating me when I am on my own land," she said. "You still have not answered my question. What are *you* doing here?"

"I was following you," Dexter said. "It is dangerous to loiter in the priory ruins in the dark, your grace."

"You were following me?" Laura was taken aback. "I didn't see you."

Dexter smiled suddenly. The impact made Laura's knees weaken. "I would not be much good at my job if you *had* seen me," he commented. His smile faded. "I was not the only one following you, your grace. The reason I came to find you was because I saw someone else behind you in the lane. They looked suspicious."

Laura's brows shot up. "How singular of you to appoint yourself my protector, Mr. Anstruther. I am sure you must be mistaken. There is no one else here and I only came down to fetch some elderflower champagne."

Dexter took the bottle, looked at it closely and started to pull out the stopper.

"Don't," Laura said hastily. "You need to turn the stopper rather than pull it—"

It was too late. The cork came free with a popping sound that echoed around the stone walls and the champagne spurted out like a fountain, cascading all over Dexter and soaking his pantaloons against his muscular thighs. Laura tried not to stare. She grabbed one of the cloths that she used to wrap the bottles of brewing wine and handed it to him to mop up. She was definitely not going to attempt the task herself. Patting dry Dexter Anstruther's soaking pantaloons would be asking far too much of her self-control.

"Oh dear," she said. "I did warn you. It is champagne and very volatile."

"So I perceive." Dexter wiped his face with the cloth and flattened down his wet hair. "Next time you need a weapon," he added, "just pull out the stopper rather than plan to hit someone with the bottle."

"I'll bear that in mind," Laura said. She watched as the tiny droplets of champagne that were scattered in his hair caught the lantern light. She wanted to touch them. More specifically, she wanted to lick them up. Heat squirmed low in her stomach. She tried to get a grip on herself.

"Perhaps we should leave now," she said quickly. A horrid doubt grabbed her. "You did not close the door at the end of the corridor, did you, Mr. Anstruther? It was wedged open with a stone."

"Of course I did not," Dexter said.

"Good. The door can only be opened from outside. If it closes—" Laura stopped as a gust of wind roared down the corridor and the lantern flickered and almost went out. "We will be locked in here," she finished.

There was a thud at the end of the passageway as the door slammed shut in the wind. The walls of the priory seemed to tremble for a moment.

"Like that," Dexter said.

"Yes," Laura said, listening to the echo of the crash bounce from the stone. "Like that."

IT TOOK DEXTER all of two minutes to ascertain that they were indeed locked inside the priory wine cellar and that there was no way to open the door. He rested one hand against the unyielding stone and thought back to the moment when he had set off down the stairs. He had checked that his exit was clear before he had gone down. That was an elementary precaution. The door had been held open by a heavy stone, one that could not have moved by accident. Therefore the inescapable conclusion was that someone—perhaps the mysterious person who had been following Laura home—had deliberately locked them in.

Cursing under his breath, he walked slowly back down the corridor to the cellar. Now he was well served for succumbing to the impulse to follow Laura. He knew he should have steered clear of trouble. The thought that if he had left her to walk home alone she might even now be lying alone and injured in the dark only served to make him feel more irritable. Why did Laura attract trouble and why did he feel compelled to protect her against it? First he ruined his best boots leaping into the river to rescue her from drowning and now he was imprisoned with her because of a wayward impulse to make sure she was safe. Whenever he became involved with her the even tenor of his life was disturbed. The smooth running went awry. Logic and reason fled. It was disturbing enough to feel like a callow youth who could not control his physical reaction to her. To want to protect her, as well, felt even more disturbing in a way that he did not want to analyze. After all, any woman who took the role of a highwaywoman was not only able to look after herself but arguably deserved all the trouble that she attracted.

Laura was sitting on the floor, wrapped in her cloak against the chill of the autumn night, the half-full bottle of elderflower champagne at her side. She looked calm and collected, as though she were preparing for a long and unexpected picnic. Dexter wondered if she was really as serene as she appeared.

"It seems that you are correct," he said. "The door cannot be opened."

Laura looked up. The lantern light made her hazel eyes very dark and her expression was inscrutable.

"How tiresome," she said cordially. "How could that have happened?"

"I think," Dexter said, "that someone has locked us in. Whoever was following you earlier may have done it on purpose."

"I am sure that you are imagining things," Laura said, with what Dexter could only feel was a deplorable lack of concern. "Why would anyone want to do such a thing?"

"Perhaps," Dexter snapped, "because you used to be Glory the highwaywoman and in the course of your no doubt reckless and highly colored career in crime you probably made a number of enemies. That seems as good a reason as any."

"I sense your disapproval, Mr. Anstruther," Laura said, "but I cannot agree with you. No one knew I was Glory and thus cannot hold it against me. No one other than you, I mean." She sighed. "And now you find yourself incarcerated for your pains in trying to rescue me! Perhaps you should have thought twice before attempting to help me. Generally I can fend for myself, you know."

Dexter sighed irritably. It was no more than he had been thinking himself a minute before. It was true that it would be difficult to find a more capable or self-contained woman than Laura Cole, and considering that he did not even like her very much it was impossible to understand why he would wish to protect her. He knew that the fault was in him, not in her. He had a hopeless compulsion to help others, even when they did not need it. It was an impulse that had led him to choose the type of work that he did. He strove to try and make the world a better, safer, fairer place and usually he got no thanks for it.

"You feel an overriding urge to bring order out of chaos, Dexter," his sister Annabelle had remarked one day, "and with a family like ours, who can be surprised at it? You have striven all your life to take responsibility for us because Mama and Papa never did and now you seem to have extended that duty to the entire human race."

Dexter was rather afraid that his sister, who was not usually so insightful, had been right in this particular instance. He had to be in control. He had to be able to make life run smoothly and calmly in order to ensure that it never sank back into the terrifying confusion of his childhood again. Someone had to take responsibility and that role had fallen to him.

But with Laura Cole there was something more than a simple urge to protect. With Laura he felt a possessiveness that was nothing short of primitive. It was maddening when she had treated him so badly and he despised her for it.

"Pray do not thank me," he said, his tone all the shorter as a result of his anger at his own weakness. He met Laura's bright gaze. "Sooner or later I will remember not to offer you my assistance when you do not require it. Generally I am not such a slow learner."

"That would probably be better," Laura said. "I am sure this can only be a childish prank. After all, it is Mischief Night in a few weeks and you know that the village lads will use that excuse for all manner of practical jokes. Unless this is Sir Montague's rather juvenile idea of revenge, of course."

"I had thought of that," Dexter admitted, "but it seems

a little harsh of him to make me suffer as well by locking us in together."

Laura smiled. "Perhaps," she said sweetly, "he thought it would be the perfect punishment for me to be trapped in here with you, Mr. Anstruther."

Once again Dexter felt the frustration and the desire fire his blood in equal measure. Punishment was one word for what he felt. Torment was another.

"It is indeed a sore trial for both of us, your grace, when we have agreed that we should avoid one another," he said, "but I am sure that we can both rely on our self-control."

"Oh, of course," Laura said. "Self-control is infallible, is it not? And now that we have established that neither of us wish to be incarcerated with the other, perhaps you could bend your mind to what we are going to do about it."

Dexter sighed, shoving his hands into his pockets. He was not convinced by Laura's argument that this was no more than a practical joke, but he did agree that the best thing they could do would be to get out of there as quickly as possible—for so many reasons. "I take it that there is no other exit from the building?" he said.

Laura shot him another irritated look. "Do you think that I would be sitting here if there were? No, Mr. Anstruther, there are no other doors, or windows, and although there is a privy along the corridor it empties into the moat and I do not relish attempting to escape that way."

"I shall go and take a look," Dexter said. "May I take the lantern?"

"Of course," Laura said. "You shall not be able to see anything without it."

"You are not afraid to be left alone in the dark?"

"No indeed." Laura tilted her head to look up at him, a faint smile on her lips. "Are you, Mr. Anstruther? Many people are. It is nothing to be ashamed of. I do not believe that there is anything worse than spiders and mice down here but I can protect you if you are nervous."

"Of course I am not," Dexter said crossly. "I only wished to make sure that *you* felt quite safe."

"How very kind of you," Laura said brightly. "Of course I feel safe with you, Mr. Anstruther. I am consoled by the fact you are one of the Guardians and are therefore bound to protect me even though you do not like me."

Dexter sighed. He looked from her to the bottle of champagne. "Are you drunk?" he inquired.

"Not yet," Laura said. "Merely a little tipsy." She smiled at him, a luscious smile that made his pulse race. "Have no fear, Mr. Anstruther. I have no intention of ravishing you. I do not even like *you* very much."

Gritting his teeth to hear his own words repeated back to him, and reflecting that the Dowager Duchess of Cole was fortunate that no one had strangled her before now, let alone locked her in a cellar, Dexter bent down and retrieved the lantern from the floor.

"I shall be back shortly," he said.

When he returned it was to find that Laura had broached a second bottle and was looking charmingly bright-eyed.

"How did you get on?" she inquired.

"A small child could probably fit through the gap," Dexter said, "but you are right—neither you nor I could squeeze through."

"I do not agree with sending children up chimneys or

into other small spaces," Laura said solemnly. "It is a barbaric practice."

"Of course it is. Neither do I," Dexter snapped. "I merely meant that you and I are both too large to fit through the opening. I was not advocating child labor."

He sat down beside her. The faint scent of her perfume, a floral fragrance that he did not recognize but found profoundly attractive, wrapped itself about his senses. Dexter knew that it was fanciful to imagine that he could feel her warmth, but now that he knew there was no escape he was starting to feel the cold and damp of the room, and Laura and the lantern seemed the only bright things there. In the pale golden lamplight she looked soft, warm and enticing.

She also looked more than a little tipsy by now with her tousled curls and her flushed skin and her sparkling eyes. It was a tempting combination and Dexter felt a sudden, overwhelming urge to take advantage of her. It was not a course of action he would normally contemplate, of course. The idea of seducing a woman in a wine cellar was dishonorable and immoral, the sort of thing that Miles Vickery would do. Even during the period of his worst excesses, when his disillusion over Laura's betrayal had seared his soul and sent him spiraling into libertinism, Dexter would never have behaved so badly, at least not often. And it was particularly ironic that it should be Laura he was trapped with, Laura who was so damnably appealing that it made him furious with himself that he had such an inexplicable weakness for her. Laura, who was surely so experienced, that for him to have any scruples about seducing her seemed a ridiculous contradiction.

"We can both rely on our self-control..."

He set his jaw firmly. It was going to be a long, long night.

"I think," he said abruptly, "that you have had too much champagne already."

Laura's hazel gaze mocked him. "I suppose that you disapprove of women drinking alone—or perhaps even of them drinking alcohol at all, Mr. Anstruther? I noticed that you did not touch a drop of brandy that night at Half Moon Inn."

"Drinking alone is certainly not advisable for either men or women," Dexter said, a little stiffly. "And drinking alcohol at all only suitable in moderation. The female capacity for drink being so much lesser than the male, it would perhaps be a sound idea for women not to drink at all."

"Of course." Laura inclined her head. "It sounds as though you have studied this phenomenon in depth, Mr. Anstruther."

"Only in my work," Dexter said.

"Of course," Laura said again. "I imagine you are far too self-disciplined ever to become intoxicated, Mr. Anstruther." She waved the bottle of champagne at him. "I do think, though, that you had better have some of this to save me from drinking alone."

Dexter looked at her. "You are taking it directly from the bottle?"

"How else? There are no glasses." Laura laughed. "I suppose you think it unbecoming in a dowager duchess to do so?"

Dexter did not think it unbecoming, quite the reverse. He watched as she tilted the bottle to her lips, closed her eyes and drank deeply. A small trickle of the golden liquid ran from the corner of her mouth and she licked it up with her tongue. It was astonishingly arousing to watch. As she tilted her head back her honey-brown hair brushed the velvet of her cloak with a soft swishing noise that sounded extremely sensuous. Each curl seemed to gleam with gold in the lamplight. Dexter wanted to touch them. He wanted to run his hands into her hair and tilt her head up to his and kiss her on that wide, beautiful mouth until she was sighing against his lips and her body was soft and willing beneath his hands....

Laura held the bottle out to him. "Your turn."

Dexter took the bottle from her and put his lips where hers had been, feeling the lust kick through his body again at the mere thought. Hell, it did not seem to matter what she did. She could probably be mucking out her stables and he would still want to ravish her. Everything she did only served to stir his feelings up even more.

"It is very warming," he said, surprised, as the liquid ran down his throat. "A recipe of your own?"

"Something else I inherited from my grandmother," Laura agreed. "You may wonder why I keep my wines down here rather than in The Old Palace, Mr. Anstruther. Indeed, I am surprised you have not asked already since it would seem a most irrational place to store them."

"I did wonder," Dexter admitted.

"There are several reasons," Laura said. "The first is that the cellars at the house are prone to flooding from the river and the steps are worn and dangerous. But the main reason is that my grandmother moved their cellars down here and I did not trouble to move them back again. She was trying to keep the wine away from my grandfather. By the end of his life he was a terrible toper."

"I am sorry," Dexter said. "You mentioned that he was a libertine. I did not realize that he was a drunkard, as well."

"Oh, he was prodigious on both counts, I fear," Laura said. "But my grandmother realized that if she made it difficult for *him* to get to the wine then he would not drink it. It was quite a cunning plan, I think. He was a very lazy man, you see, and could not be bothered to walk over here every time he wished for a drink."

"Is that why the door is designed as it is? To lock him in if he tried to creep in here unnoticed?"

Laura laughed. "No indeed, that is the original medieval door and I have often thought I should have it changed. Though I do wonder whether the prior who had it designed did so in order to trap any monks who tried to raid the wine."

Dexter took another swig from the bottle. The champagne fizzed against his tongue and sent bubbles effervescing through his blood. He was dimly aware that as an abstainer he should be careful not to take too much as he had no head for drink. Another mouthful would surely not do any harm, however.

"This tastes delightful," he said, handing the half-empty bottle back to Laura.

"Yes, thank you. The recipe is very good." She turned her head and looked at him thoughtfully. "So, Mr. Anstruther, now that we have established that we are definitely trapped in here, is there any likelihood of you being missed and of someone coming to look for you?"

Dexter thought of the paucity of his emotional life.

There really was no one to care whether he returned home or not. He did not even have a valet, as he could not afford to pay one. Previously his lack of ties had seemed a blessing. He had his mother and his brothers and sisters and that was all he required. And when he found his conformable wife she, too, would fit neatly into the pattern and cause no difficulties whatsoever. Except that he did not wish to think of a rich debutante bride when he was sitting here with Laura Cole. It was impossible.

"It is unlikely, I fear," he said. "The guests at the Morris Clown Inn come and go very much as they please. Not that I make a habit of staying out all night, you understand, unless it is in the pursuit of my work."

"Of course," Laura said. "Whatever your past reputation, I would scarcely expect you to be so immoderate these days, Mr. Anstruther. Staying out all night with other women is scarcely the way to win your innocent heiress, is it?"

Looking at Laura as she raised the champagne bottle delicately to her lips again, Dexter felt an almost overwhelming urge to be immoderate with her, there and then, on the wine cellar floor. The heiresses could go hang. He cleared his throat and clamped down ruthlessly on his immoderate lust.

"And what about you, your grace?" he asked. "Are the servants likely to notice your absence?"

"Perhaps," Laura said. "Rachel will certainly be surprised that I have failed to return in time to put Hattie to bed, although I suppose she will merely think that I have been delayed. And Carrington and Mrs. Carrington are probably already abed themselves. They retire very early. It will not be until the morning that anyone will concern themselves over my whereabouts."

"How frustrating," Dexter commented. "Had you thought of employing servants who were a little more active and might notice things sooner? Living on your own as you do, it might be beneficial to have someone you can rely upon."

Scarcely were the words out and he was regretting them, or more specifically the impulse that made him take an interest in Laura Cole's welfare. Perhaps she preferred having servants who seemed deaf and blind to everything that went on. She might be smuggling her lovers up a back stair every night for all he knew, and would not want curious servants with their ears pressed to the keyhole. He did not like to think of it. No, that was too pale a description. He *hated* to think of it.

Laura had flushed pink with indignation at his words. "I do not need anyone else. I know that everyone thinks Mr. and Mrs. Carrington incompetent—"

"Which they are," Dexter interrupted.

"Only because Faye Cole drove them almost to madness with her demands when she became duchess!" Laura protested. "She was appalling to work for. Why, poor Carrington broke down under the strain and Mrs. Carrington's health has never been very strong. It was my fault—I had left the servants at Faye's mercy…" Laura stopped, looked at the champagne bottle and took a deep breath. "I beg your pardon. It is most inappropriate of me to criticize the Duchess of Cole to you."

Dexter knew she meant that it was inappropriate because Faye Cole might become his mother-in-law in the near future, but he was actually more interested in the rest of Laura's champagne-induced outburst. Once again it seemed she was championing the underdog, taking in the Carringtons even though they were unemployable in order to rescue them from illness and poverty. It was kind, generous and utterly impractical, but those were the very qualities that Miles had praised in her. Dexter thought of Carrington failing to hear the bell and staggering down the steps to the kitchen and of Mrs. Carrington so ill she could not even boil a kettle, and he felt a stirring of tenderness for Laura that he could not avoid.

"Anyway," Laura said, and he could hear the defensive tone in her voice, "I rather enjoy doing things for myself. I have never been permitted to do so before."

Dexter looked at her, startled. "How so? Surely the position of duchess gives enormous privileges?"

"You would think so, would you not?" Laura said. She fidgeted with the material of her cloak, avoiding his eyes. "And in some ways you are quite right, Mr. Anstruther. But in others, I would say that being a duchess in the most frustrating business." She paused, sighed. "When I was a child it was an understood thing that I would be a duchess and so my mother trained me from the earliest age. I never went anywhere without at least one servant on each side in case I needed something. It was monstrous inconvenient always to have someone hanging around me."

Dexter was shocked. Even though Miles had said that Lord and Lady Burlington had wanted to banish Laura's wild spirit he had not really imagined what that would entail. "You were *trained* to be a duchess? Schooled for it?"

"Of course. Charles and I were promised from the cradle." A hint of reserve came into Laura's voice. "Then, of course, I *was* a duchess and so I had to behave in a suitable manner."

Dexter realized that he was appalled. His childhood had been a mad helter-skelter affair with parents who could not have cared less what their offspring were doing. He had thought this lack of concern deplorable, but on the other hand Laura's upbringing sounded absolutely dire, with all a child's natural ebullience stifled by protocol and instruction.

"Your mother must have been pleased that everything worked out according to her plans," he said. "Imagine how disappointed she would have been had the arrangement fallen through."

"I believe she was delighted," Laura agreed. There was a slight edge to her voice. "I, on the other hand, was not consulted about what I wanted for my future. So you may understand why I live a slightly less conventional life than that of the average dowager duchess now that I can choose for myself."

"Becoming a highwaywoman is certainly less than conventional behavior for a peeress of the realm," Dexter said.

"I was not referring to that," Laura said. "Will you kindly stop reminding me, Mr. Anstruther? Please do try to move on from this. If Lord Liverpool can pardon me I feel you should be able to, as well."

"Very well," Dexter said, sighing. "What we *should* focus upon is that neither of us will be missed by anyone tonight. What do you suggest that we do?"

"We wait until the morning," Laura said, "and then we shout for help. Someone will pass by once daylight comes and even though the walls here are thick, they may hear us."

"You sound remarkably calm under the circumstances, your grace," Dexter said, stiffening as Laura inadvertently moved a little closer so that the velvet cloak brushed his arm and a curl of her hair tickled his cheek.

"Did you expect me to have the vapors?" she asked. "I cannot see that much would be achieved by that."

"Perhaps not," Dexter conceded.

"But I would be fulfilling your view of how a woman ought to behave, would I not, Mr. Anstruther?" Laura continued. "It is not considered feminine to be so independent. I realize that."

"I know that you think me conservative in my notions," Dexter said, a little stiffly, "but I have to agree that you do not conform to my ideal of female suitability *at all*."

"Oh dear," Laura said, smiling mockingly. "I am quite despondent to hear that, Mr. Anstruther. But I am obliged to ask—suitability for what?"

"For marriage, of course." Dexter struggled a little to achieve clarity in his thoughts. His mind felt blurred at the edges. The truth, he though hazily, was that Laura dazzled him. She held him spellbound but was completely unsuitable in every way. Not that he was contemplating marrying her. Even had she been an heiress there were a dozen reasons, a *score* of reasons, why such a course of action was downright foolish. She called to his wild side, the side that was perilously like his father, the part of him he had tried so hard to repress in the interests of being responsible and sensible and reliable. But she held a strange fascination for him which he could not deny. Dexter looked at the champagne bottle. His mind slipped and slithered as he tried to grasp the nature of

Laura's difference. She was like a bright, wayward star, he thought. She tempted him from the path he thought he ought to follow. That sounded almost poetic. Odd, he thought, for he was not generally a poetic man.

He glanced again at the second bottle of elderflower champagne. It was almost empty. Never mind poetic…

He was drunk.

He blinked at the evidence of the empty bottle. He was not entirely sure how it had happened when he had been aiming at moderation. All he knew was that he felt dazed, slightly unsteady and somewhat cast away. It was a curiously attractive feeling.

Laura shifted again so that her arm was brushing his and they sat side by side against the cold stone wall. The ribbons fastening her cloak had eased and it had fallen back to reveal the slender lines of her throat and the curves of her breasts above the neckline of the green gown. The smoothness and delicious richness of her skin in the lamplight made Dexter ache to touch her. The minute he allowed the thought into his head it crowded out all other thoughts. He was locked in a wine cellar with Laura Cole. He must not touch her. He must not think about kissing her.

He must not think about making love to her.

He was locked in with a woman who made him think about nothing but making love and he must not touch her.

His throat turned as dry as though he had swallowed a mouthful of sand.

"I think that you are foxed, Mr. Anstruther," Laura said.

"I think I am," Dexter agreed.

"I also think that you imagine you want a conformable wife," Laura continued, her voice soft, "and yet if you had one you would probably find it was not what you desired at all." She turned her head to look him in the eyes and suddenly her lips were very close to his. He wondered if in that instant she had any concept of what he really desired and how dangerously close he was to taking it. The restraint he had placed on himself strained close to breaking.

"Believe me," Laura continued, "I was a perfect wife for years, at least on the surface, and neither I nor my husband was happy with it."

"I am not like your husband," Dexter said, feeling an instinctive need to protest against any comparison with the odious Charles Cole. He saw her smile and a tiny dimple appeared at the corner of her mouth and it was almost his undoing.

"No," she said. "That is very true."

Dexter had an unnerving feeling that with every word the conversation was slipping into ever more dangerous territory.

"For a start I would not have ignored you," he said, with what he hoped was appropriate dignity. "I would never have allowed you to gallop around the county righting wrongs and setting fire to things."

Laura's smile lingered. She toyed with the champagne bottle, taking another sip.

"I am glad to hear that you would not have ignored me," she said.

Ignore her? His difficulty would have been keeping his hands off her. Dexter shifted again. His body felt coiled and tight and explosively aroused.

Laura's smile faded. "I was so unhappy with Charles," she said softly. "It drove me close to madness at times. And sometimes I did foolish things or even bad things."

She raised her gaze and met his eyes very directly. He felt his heart clench at the honesty in hers. "The night I spent with you…" she whispered. Her lashes flickered down. "It was wrong in so many ways," she said, "but I wanted it."

Dexter's breath caught in his throat. He raised a hand to ease the constriction in his neck cloth but somehow he ended up touching Laura's cheek instead and she turned it against his fingers in a gentle caress. His stomach contracted with lust and longing. Laura's eyes held the dark, unfocused look of someone who had had far more to drink than was prudent. Her eyelids fluttered shut and her lips parted. Dexter teetered on the edge.

He was drunk.

He was taking advantage.

He was no gentleman, but then, she was surely no lady.…

The need, the hunger and the frustration that tormented him each time he met Laura fused in one irresistible surge of desire. He closed the tiny space between the two of them and brought his mouth down on hers, gently at first then searchingly, wildly, seeking the response he so desperately needed to find in her. In that moment he knew exactly what he wanted. He did not want respectable. He did not want conformable. He did not even want to be in control.

He wanted Laura Cole like a fever in the blood and in that same moment he knew that no matter how he tried the fever could never, ever be cured.

CHAPTER NINE

LAURA KNEW that her mother would say that no lady, still less a dowager duchess, should drink champagne and then find immodest and deeply satisfying pleasure in a man's arms, but by now she was too blissfully adrift to care. It had taken her years to comprehend that there were plenty of things her mother had got wrong, and this was one of them. Once before had she abandoned herself to such heady delights and she had sworn never to do so again but now, with Dexter's body hard against hers, her hands buried in his hair and his lips demanding a response from hers, she had no such doubts. She remembered vaguely that there were reasons why this was a bad idea. She knew there were secrets to be kept. If she let Dexter closer she would run the risk of exposing Hattie's parentage. But she needed him so much. He drove out her loneliness. It felt so right to be in his arms.

She burrowed closer to the heat of his body.

He kissed her again. The impact on her senses was devastating. His mouth was warm and firm against hers, and she could taste the champagne on his tongue and it was absolutely delicious. His hands were equally warm as they slid beneath the velvet cloak to clasp her waist. She could feel the heat in him searing through the silk of her gown. His tongue curled intimately against hers, sweeping her mouth with lazy strokes. There was no hesitation in him and no inexperience. It was Laura who felt like the innocent one, trembling with a mixture of nervousness and desperation as barely remembered feelings and emotions raced through her. She was transfixed by the strength and the command of Dexter's body against hers. As he crushed her against him with relentless demand, she felt her nipples harden and peak against the muscular wall of his chest. There were tremors of delight tingling low in her belly and she stifled a moan against his lips, leaning back against the wall of the cellar for support. Dexter followed her back, trapping her against the stone, deepening the kiss within the softness of her mouth, his tongue caressing hers until her body threatened to melt under the onslaught of such white-hot desire. She thought she had never, ever known such intense pleasure. After four years in the desert it was sweet and life-giving. She thought she would die of it. And then she felt Dexter's hand slide up to free one of her breasts from the confinement of the bodice of her gown. His fingers brushed her bare skin in the lightest but most deliberate of caresses and her body curved like a bow drawn to his touch.

He kissed her again, slow and deep this time, sending her senses spiraling beyond recall, sinking down into pure ecstasy. His palm was warm against the curve of her breast and then suddenly, purposefully, his fingers pulled strongly on her hardened nipple, and then again and again, and Laura arched again as a sweet, molten sensation dissolved through her whole body. The wall was firm behind her, supporting her whilst Dexter dispensed with the cloak and his hands moved to free her other breast. The gown slid to Laura's waist with a soft hiss of silk.

Dexter dipped his head to taken one swollen nipple in his mouth, licking it gently, and Laura writhed against the wall, shocked and fascinated at the instinct within her that made her want to press her breasts against his lips and teeth. She was driven by the need to demand from him the absolute satisfaction that she craved, and yet at the same time she was afraid her body would fracture under the sheer pleasure of the feeling.

"Dexter, please." She struggled for words. "I can't… I need… I can't bear this. You have to stop."

She heard him laugh. "I don't think I will."

It sounded like Dexter and yet it was so *unlike* him, so unlike the careful, conscientious man he was on the surface, that she felt another stab of pure lust pierce her.

"I cannot think…." she pleaded, but he only laughed again, lifting his mouth from her swollen skin a fraction so that she could feel his breath against its dampness.

"Fortunately there is no need for you to think at all," he said, dipping his tongue to stroke her breast again, to tease and curl and flick at the aching peak until her legs trembled uncontrollably and she was afraid she would slump to the ground and only his hold on her waist held her upright.

"This is not like you," she gasped. "Dexter—"

Her words broke off as his teeth nipped wickedly at her breast, making her groan again.

"It is me," he ground out. His voice was harsh. "I don't know myself when I am with you, Laura. I only know that this is what I want."

Laura surrendered. "Then don't stop," she gasped. "Whatever you do, do not stop."

He laughed again and took her nipple between his teeth hard and flicked the end of it with his tongue and Laura almost screamed.

"Ah! *Don't stop*. Please. Harder. Just a little bit harder…"

Was that really her voice begging him in such broken tones to ravish her senses with this blinding pleasure? She felt both his hands clasp her waist tighter as he tilted her back a little against the wall. Her breasts were utterly exposed to his questing mouth. The cold air of the cellar wrapped its chill about her naked skin but the heat in her blood pounded through her and it was that that made her shiver. Dexter was nipping at both her breasts now, pulling her nipples into his mouth, pleasuring them so skillfully with his lips and fingers that the tension gathered and coiled deep within her belly. Her body trembled so violently that she thought she could not stand it.

"Please. I truly cannot bear this—"

He laughed and covered her breasts with tiny little biting kisses that drove a sob from her. She was helpless in his arms, utterly powerless, at the mercy of his strength. She shuddered so much she felt as though she was coming apart. Her body waited in an agony of longing.

The dark, burning pleasure centered deep and low within her, then spun out, turned to ecstasy, and Laura felt her body clench unbearably. She cried out, clutching at Dexter's shoulders, and he kissed her again, his fingers continuing to tug gently on her nipple as a mixture of pleasure and pain racked her. The whole world flooded with light and she was shaken with violent shudders as she climaxed desperately, helplessly, in his arms.

"Dexter!"

It was such exquisite release that she lost herself for a moment, and when her senses finally began to revive she realized that Dexter had wrapped the velvet cloak around her. He held her in the crook of his arm as the little tremors racked her body and died away at last. Her head was against his shoulder and she could smell the scent of his skin, and she felt warm with bliss and turned her cheek against the curve of his protecting arm. She thought fleetingly that perhaps they should talk now but her mind was too fuzzy with drink and sated pleasure. Later, she thought hazily. Later would be soon enough to talk. She felt superbly satisfied and happy. Without further ado she slept.

THE HOUSE RENTED by the Duke of Cole for the duration of his family's stay in Fortune's Folly was, by necessity, one of the grandest in the village. Nothing else would suit his grace's consequence. Fortune Hall and The Old Palace were both already occupied of course, which was unfortunate, but he had still been able to acquire a short lease on Chevrons, a handsome town house built for a rich lawyer whose gout had now driven him south to Bath and a warmer climate.

Miss Lydia Cole, returning from the harp concert at the assembly rooms, tiptoed past the door of her mother's chamber and devoutly prayed that the duchess would not wake. Her mother, who had the constitution of an ox, had unexpectedly succumbed to a chill that afternoon and taken to her bed, consigning Lydia to the chaperonage of one of the other matrons. Lady Bexley was a great deal more lax than the duchess and thus Lydia had been able to escape her after the concert and accept the escort home of a certain gentleman. They had walked back from the assembly rooms quite alone. And then he had *kissed* her when he had bidden her good-night. It had shocked Lydia—she knew it was quite appalling of a gentleman to behave so badly—but she had also been surprised to discover that she had thoroughly enjoyed it. Even now she was still tingling down to her toes.

"Lydia? Come here!" The duchess's stentorian cry gave no indication of a sore throat and with a sigh Lydia eased open the door of her mother's room and went inside. It was stiflingly hot and smelled of the violet creams that her mother enjoyed eating and also of something else—a scent that Lydia did not know well but that she thought smelled rather like alcohol. Yes indeed, it smelled as though the duchess had been *drinking*. But Lydia was sure that was impossible. It must be some concoction her maid had whisked up for the chill that smelled so like wine.

"How was the concert, my love?" the duchess inquired, patting the coverlet to encourage her daughter to sit down. "Was Mr. Anstruther attentive to you?"

"Mr. Anstruther was not there, Mama," Lydia said. Her mind was full of thoughts of another man entirely—of his smile and the glint in his eyes and the wicked touch of his lips against hers. She saw Faye's face darken like a storm cloud and added hastily, "But Lord Vickery was there, and Sir Jasper and Lord Armitage—"

"Which is quite beside the point," Faye snapped. "We shall never get any of *them* to marry you!" She glared at Lydia as though it were her fault Dexter Anstruther had been absent. "How provoking! Go to your room now. I need to think."

Sighing, Lydia went out onto the landing and closed the door with elaborate care behind her. The house was quiet. She knew that her father was not at home. Even in a small place like Fortune's Folly the duke was adept at finding a willing maidservant to service his lust.

Lydia went into her chamber, threw herself down on her bed and lay dreamily gazing into space. It was fortuitous that Faye had dismissed her so abruptly because it meant she did not need to supply her mother with a moment-by-moment description of the evening. On the rare occasions that Faye did not accompany her she always required to know everything, from the jewels the other women were wearing to the precise nature of the compliments the gentlemen had paid her daughter. That part usually took very little time to relate. But tonight... Lydia smiled. Tonight she could relive the memory of that kiss. She could lie here and indulge her memory, with no one to disturb her or nag her or threaten her that if she did not wed she would be cast out of the family.

With a happy little murmur she closed her eyes and gave herself up to her dreams.

WHEN LAURA AWOKE the lantern had burned out and it was dark. Her head ached, her mouth felt dry and she was thirsty. She felt cold and stiff and she needed to go to the privy. She thought there might be more unromantic situations to be in but offhand she could not think of any of them.

She felt wretched.

Her traitorous body was awakened and the quickened

desire stabbed through her as she remembered everything that had happened—the sensation of Dexter's hands and lips on her body, the touch and the taste of him. But in the same instant her mind shrank from remembering the liberties that she had allowed him to take. She had taken too much champagne. She had lost all her self-restraint. Once again she had responded brazenly to Dexter. He knew now just how easily he could command her senses and he would think her response to him proved she was shameless.

Laura felt the chill creep more deeply through her, distancing her from Dexter even as her body still hummed with the intimacy of their physical awareness. The blissful pleasure she had experienced was draining away now, along with her feelings of happiness. She could recall *begging* Dexter to make love to her. She had missed his touch for four long years and it had been heavenly to be in his arms again. It had banished all that cold loneliness that seemed to stalk her. But now she was sober she felt hot with mortification rather than pleasure. Tonight she had reached out to the Dexter Anstruther she thought she had once known, before so much had come between them. She had forgotten all the secrets she was holding and the lies that kept them apart. She had sought the complicated, passionate man who had once cared for her and she had thought that she had found him again. But now she realized that it had been an illusion.

"I don't know myself when I am with you, Laura...."

She remembered now. This Dexter Anstruther was a man determined to be conventional, a fortune hunter wanting a rich bride, in denial of the wild and passionate side of his nature. This was not the man Laura sought, nor the one she needed.

Dexter was asleep. Laura could not see him in the darkness but she could hear the steadiness of his breathing. He was still holding her in his arms but his grip had loosened now and his body no longer warmed her. Only a few hours before he had held her and made love to her with such tenderness and passion as though he truly cared for her. It had felt then that *that* was the real Dexter Anstruther, a man who wanted her for the person she was— not the pattern card duchess her mother had created, nor the dutiful chatelaine of Cole, nor even the wanton whore who had sent him packing after one night of passion. She had thought that when they had made love it had been with honesty and no pretense. But drink had a way of making you think things like that when they simply were not true.

Feeling chilled and disoriented by the champagne, the darkness and her sudden misery, Laura freed herself gently from Dexter's clasp and edged her way along the wall toward the privy.

As soon as she came back into the wine cellar a blast of cold air struck her and set her shivering. The wind was whistling along the outer corridor. Laura was surprised that it had not woken her sooner. Wide-awake now, she groped her way into the corridor that led to the entrance.

The door at the end of the cellar was standing wide open and in the faint light she could see the darker shadows of the priory ruins against the sky and the stars bright and white above them.

For a moment she could not believe it. The cellar door was open. They had not been trapped at all.

"Laura?"

She had not heard Dexter's step behind her but now she swung around to find him standing at her shoulder.

"The door is open! We were not locked in at all!" Try as she might, Laura could not prevent the flat accusation in her voice. He had been the one to check if the door was shut. He must have made a mistake.

"That's impossible." She could not see Dexter's face but there was utter disbelief in his voice. "The door was firmly shut."

"And you can see that it is now wide open!" Laura felt a mixture of anger and indignation. If only she had checked. The events of the last few hours would never have happened. Dexter would not have made love to her in the intimate confines of the cellar. She would not have slept in his arms and felt happy for such a short time before she realized that this happiness was based on nothing but lust and mistrust and could not be hers for so many reasons.

"I am going home," she said.

"Laura, wait!" Suddenly there was an insistent note in Dexter's voice. He put his hand on her arm to detain her, but she shook him off and hurried out the door. Dexter's voice checked her; she heard his urgent step behind her.

"Laura, no—" In the same instant she heard the scrape of stone against stone and the small tumble of pebbles that presaged a rock fall. The moon came out. Laura turned. Something was falling toward her hard and fast and in the last moment she understood and threw herself to one side. Dexter caught her and pulled her to the ground, the weight of his body knocking all the air from hers, and then something caught her shoulder and the pain shot through her like a red-hot knife and she hit her head and everything went dark.

...own, and their home, had come to an end, but she could stop them crying, could hold them and reassure them and comfort and everything would be all right....

CHAPTER TEN

LAURA DID NOT KNOW how long she was unconscious for but it was not long, and when she came round she wished fervently that she had been knocked out cold for good. Her whole body seemed lit from within with a burning pain. It was so bad that for a moment she could not think, could not speak. She could see light behind her closed eyelids and for a second she thought it was day, but then she re-membered what had happened and realized that it was candlelight. Dexter must have carried her home.

Voices echoed through her head and she could feel hands moving over her with infinite gentleness. Each touch brought a fresh wave of agony and made the cold sweat stand out on her forehead. She heard Dexter's voice. "She has broken no bones but the rock fall has put her shoulder out...."

She could see shadow figures moving through the haze of pain. Someone touched her forehead with a cool cloth and Laura made a huge effort and opened her eyes. She was lying against the cushions on the sofa in her drawing room. Dexter's face swam close to her, set in grim lines, his blue eyes so dark and intense she thought hazily that he must be angry with her and she tried to put a hand out to him.

"I'm sorry—" she began.

"Don't try to speak." He sounded frightfully fierce. "Don't try to move."

Laura made another effort. "Carrington... Please don't let him worry.... He takes things so badly these days."

She saw Dexter's face ease into a smile for a moment and there was something in his eyes—some shimmer of tenderness—that for some reason made her want to cry. He touched her cheek with gentle fingers.

"Do not concern yourself. He and Mrs. Carrington were very distressed when I brought you home but I have dispatched them back to bed. Molly has sent Bart to fetch Dr. Barlow. He will be here soon."

"My shoulder—" Laura gasped as she tried to move and a fresh wave of pain broke over her, making her shudder. "What has happened?"

"Try to keep still." Dexter's voice was very calm, at odds with the tension in his eyes. "A piece of masonry fell from the priory tower and hit you. It has put your shoulder out."

"It hurts...like the very devil." She had seen accidents like this before on the hunting field after a fall from a horse, but she had had no idea that putting a shoulder out of joint could be so utterly agonizing. Her thoughts were a jumbled whirl—she knew there were things that she should be thinking about, but even the effort of trying to piece anything together seemed too much. Dexter was there and she felt safe. She closed her eyes and let everything wash over her until the sound of the door opening and Molly's hasty steps dragged her reluctantly out of the darkness again.

"Dr. Barlow's wife says that he is out attending a

confinement and may be an hour or more, sir." Molly's voice had an edge of fear to it. "Oh sir—her grace! What are we to do?"

Laura heard Dexter swear. She opened her eyes. She knew the answer to that particular question.

"You will have to put it back for me, Dexter," she whispered. "I cannot stand this pain and cannot lie here awaiting Dr. Barlow for an hour or more."

Dexter took her hand in his. His gaze was agonized. "Laura, I cannot…." His voice was husky.

"You must have done such a thing before," Laura argued. All she knew was that if she lay there much longer her shoulder would seize up completely and the agony would be intolerable. "Please," she whispered. "I know that it is a great deal to ask of you but I am sure you could do it."

She saw the conflict in Dexter's face. "I could," he said reluctantly. "I have done it before. But…" His eyes lifted to hers and he looked anguished. "I would need to hurt you so much, Laura. I am not sure I can do that."

Laura tried to smile but it came out as a grimace. "Just think how much you dislike me, Dexter. That should make it easier."

His jaws clamped together hard and a muscle tightened in his cheek. "Do not jest about this, Laura," he said harshly. "Not now."

"Very well then," Laura said. "Dexter, I am begging you. Do you think I am not in pain now? Whatever you do could not possibly be worse." She turned her head slightly. "But pray send Molly away—I think she might faint."

"Oh, madam…" Molly said, starting to cry.

Dexter took her arm. "Go and heat some water, Molly, and prepare her grace's bed. I will carry her up in ten minutes."

"Ten minutes!" Laura said. "I doubt I shall last ten seconds." But she felt a relief mingled with the agony. The decision was made. Dexter was not going to fail her.

He brought a glass of brandy across to her and raised it to her lips. "Drink it, Laura." His tone was still harsh, his expression like granite. "You are going to need it."

After that, Laura found that everything became very blurred. Dexter put his hand under her elbow and straightened her arm out. It seemed to take forever. The pain flowered through her whole body and she gripped the arm of the sofa so tightly with her free hand that she ripped the material. Dexter did not look at her; his whole concentration was focused on the job at hand. She thought hazily that perhaps if he saw her face he would be undone, for his body was so taut and tense it felt almost explosive. At one point Laura could not hold back a gasp of pain and she felt Dexter check and look at her. There were deep lines around his eyes and the set of his mouth was hard.

"Go on." Laura forced a whisper. "If you stop now I will never forgive you."

She thought a flicker of a smile touched his lips and then he pulled her elbow across her chest and folded her wrist back toward her right shoulder. There was a horrible crunch but even as Laura steeled herself against it, the pain disappeared and she almost fainted with the relief.

She opened her mouth to thank him but he poured some more brandy down her throat.

"I will carry you up to your bedroom now," he murmured. He gathered her into his arms and she realized that he was shaking. She felt shocked; she knew she had asked a great deal of him but the thought of what it must have cost him disturbed her profoundly. He held her as delicately as though she were made of spun glass and a wave of almost unbearable emotion swept through her then at the thought of what he had been prepared to do for her. She wanted to cry.

"Almost there," he whispered against her hair. "Hold on."

Laura nodded. Her head felt incredibly heavy against Dexter's shoulder. The brandy was fiery in her blood and she was becoming so faint that she could barely stay awake.

"Thank you," she whispered. His face was so close and suddenly she felt so much love for him that it swamped her. It was all-consuming, irresistible. She raised her undamaged hand to touch his cheek.

"I had to make you leave," she said. Suddenly it seemed imperative to make him understand what had really happened when she had sent him away four years before. She could not bear his poor opinion when she loved him so much. The urgency of her feelings wracked her and she struggled a little.

"You have to let me explain—" she started to say.

"Hush." Dexter's lips brushed her hair again. "You don't need to talk now. I understand."

Laura did not think that he did and she strained a little against the waves of darkness that were swamping her mind. "I need to explain," she said again, a little forlornly. She could not form the words to tell him. It felt hopeless. She felt despairing.

But his arms had tightened about her and in that there was comfort. She stopped fighting against the dark and let the warmth and reassurance from Dexter's body wrap about her, and after that she remembered nothing for a very long time.

DEXTER SAT beside Laura's bed trying to read an old copy of *Tristram Shandy* that he had found lying on the window seat. He was not sure why he was trying to read at all, for he had no concentration and precious little light to see by. The candles were burning down very low now and in an hour or so the first traces of dawn would start to lighten the eastern sky. He felt very tired, not so much from being awake for the best part of the night but as a result of the complex, unfamiliar emotions of the past few hours.

He got up slowly and walked over to the ewer on the dresser, splashing some water into the bowl and welcoming the cold shock of its touch on his face. His eyes felt gritty. In the bed, Laura turned over in her sleep and made a soft noise of distress as the movement jarred her shoulder. She did not wake but the sound seemed to skewer Dexter with helpless and protective concern. He rubbed his face fiercely with the towel as though to banish the feeling. If he had felt a stubborn and inexplicable urge to look after her before it was as nothing compared to the violent emotion he felt now.

He was unable to prevent the shudder that went through him as he recalled the moment he had seen the stone from the ruined tower start to tumble toward Laura. When she had fallen and lain so still he had thought for a moment that his heart had stopped. The fear within him had been like a living thing, stifling the breath from him.

Hurting her when he had reset her shoulder had been the most difficult thing he had ever had to do in his life. Her courage and her stoicism in the face of such pain had been extraordinary. And impossibly tangled with his admiration for her were the memories of their lovemaking. The passion that had flared between them had wrenched away his self-control—not that he had ever had a great deal of self-control where Laura was concerned. He turned to look at her pale face candlelit against the pillow and a tender smile touched his lips for a moment before he remembered the reality of their situation and the warmth within him fled. The twin specters of guilt and responsibility smashed through his mind as he remembered his family and his duty to them. He had been intoxicated when he had made love to Laura. That had been an inexcusable lapse in his behavior. He thought of his brothers and sisters relying on him for their future, of his mother spending money like water, of the ghost of his wastrel father mocking him with his affairs and his rakish ways, and he felt almost physically sick. The fear curdled in his stomach. He had come so close to failing them.

Dexter turned back to the bed, resolutely blocking out all the feelings of warmth and gentleness that seeing Laura lying there aroused in him. Watching over her as she slept was intimate and astonishing, even more profound in some ways than making love to her. There was something so vulnerable and giving about Laura it was hard to believe that her passion for him had ever been manufactured. It was almost impossible to believe that she was a whore and a hypocrite, no matter the way that she had treated him in the past.

He shook his head sharply. This was no way to think;

he had his way to make and his family's future to secure. It should not matter whether Laura was innocent or not. His desire for her was a dangerous, uncontrollable force. He had to master it and concentrate on catching his heiress and living a tidy life. That was his future. It had to be. He had no choice.

THIS TIME WHEN she woke, the light hurt Laura's eyes. There were miners hammering in her head and the sour taste of brandy in her mouth.

She opened her eyes gingerly and closed them again immediately as the familiar outlines of her bedroom swam in the light. She was in her bed, and Dexter Anstruther was sitting beside her reading, his head bent, his tawny hair looking tousled in the faint ligh.t…

Her eyes snapped open for a third time and the hammers in her head beat such a chorus that she groaned aloud.

Dexter Anstruther was in her bedroom.

On hearing her groan, Dexter looked up, laid aside the book and leaned over her. Laura's eyes were on a level with his throat, which was smooth and tanned a delicious golden color. Evidently he had removed his stock. Her gaze drifted lower. And he had also taken off his jacket. His shirt was open at the neck and she could smell the clean, masculine scent of him. She remembered it well from their hot, erotic, devastating encounter in the wine cellar.

She also remembered him holding her in his arms the previous night when he had carried her to bed. She remembered the gentleness and the resolve in him when he had reset her arm. She remembered that she had thought in her state of drunkenness that she was in love with him again.

Now that she was sober again she waited for that feeling to disappear.

It did not.

She felt the love for him wash through her in a tide so powerful and deep that she was shaken. She closed her eyes, squeezing them tight shut. Still it was no good. The feeling did not recede. It gripped her heart with a tenacity she knew she could never destroy.

She loved Dexter Anstruther. She always had and she would be a fool to try to pretend otherwise.

She struggled up against the pillows so she could focus on Dexter's face. If it was foolish to deny her love for him it was equally pointless to imagine that anything could come of it and that was the material point she had to remember. But suddenly she felt as tongue-tied, inept and lacking in any kind of experience as a debutante in her first season. Being in her bed did not help. Lying flat, incapacitated, put her at a distinct disadvantage.

"What time is it?" she croaked. She knew she sounded like a drunk after a long night on the town. She probably smelled like one, too. She shrank under the covers in mortification.

She saw Dexter reach for the jug of water on the dresser, splashing some of the liquid into a glass for her. He came over and held it gently to her lips. Laura drank greedily and awkwardly.

"Thank you."

"My pleasure." There was warmth in his voice, though she also sensed some withdrawal in him. "It is late morning," he said.

"Hattie!" The thought of her daughter drove everything else from Laura's mind for a moment. She sat bolt upright, then sank back with a gasp as her shoulder gave a painful twinge.

"Your shoulder will still be sore," Dexter said, "and you have some lacerations to your arm. Molly dressed them for you." He pressed her gently back against the pillows. "Don't worry about your daughter. Rachel came in to tell me that she was taking Hattie into the village and she will be in to visit you when they return."

"Did you see her?" Laura pressed. "Did you see Hattie?" Her headache intensified at the thought that Dexter and his daughter might actually have met. Had he seen Hattie that morning? If he had he might have recognized her at some instinctive level. He might have realized the truth. She felt sick and guilty and afraid to think that Hattie might have been drawn into danger whilst she slept regardless.

But Dexter was shaking his head.

"I did not see her, but she is quite all right," he said. "Rachel has explained to her that you are feeling a little unwell but that you will be much better soon. She assured me that Hattie was not upset and was looking forward to bringing you some flowers from Miss Lister's hothouses."

"Thank goodness." Laura relaxed back against her pillows, limp with relief. She saw the expression on Dexter's face and realized that he had misunderstood her concern. He thought that she had been fearful that Hattie would be upset because she was ill. Suddenly she felt wretchedly guilty that he had hurried to reassure her when she was keeping so huge and unforgivable a secret from him. The grief and remorse filled her, made all the more acute because of her love for him. She was denying Dexter the right to know his own child. It was very wrong of her but her absolute fear for Hattie's future security held her silent. Dexter could never be allowed to reveal Hattie's identity or take her daughter away....

"You look tired," Dexter said softly, his evident concern making Laura feel even worse. "How do you feel?"

"I feel as though I have drunk an entire bottle of brandy," Laura said. She looked at him suspiciously. "You *did* give me an entire bottle, did you not, Mr. Anstruther?"

Dexter's lips twitched. "About half a bottle," he admitted. "You were in a lot of pain."

"And to think that you do not even approve of women drinking," Laura murmured. She turned her head against the pillow so that she could look at him properly. He was looking at her with an expression in his eyes that made her feel very hot and bothered. Suddenly both her respectable dowager nightgown and the thick covers seemed to be smothering her.

"Did you undress me and put me to bed?" she demanded, before she could help herself.

She saw Dexter pause. "No. Molly did that."

Laura relaxed slightly. "Thank goodness."

She saw the wry twist to his lips and knew that he was remembering their encounter in the wine cellar, no doubt in as much vivid detail as she was. He would be thinking that such modesty on her part was somewhat belated. She felt hotter still.

"Do you remember anything about last night?" he asked.

Laura was tempted to take refuge in amnesia. "I

remember nothing after you reset my shoulder," she admitted, "and before that…"

"Yes?" Dexter's gaze was very bright and intense.

"It is very hazy," Laura excused.

"You were talking to me whilst I carried you upstairs," Dexter said. "Perhaps it will come back to you."

Suddenly Laura was not certain that she wanted to remember. She eyed him with misgiving. "What did I say? I am sure it can only have been the brandy talking."

Surely, *surely,* she thought, she had not been stupid enough to swear undying love to him? It would be just the sort of hopeless thing she would do when she was in her cups. She scoured her mind but the memory refused to come. She had no notion what had happened after they had set off up the stair. Color flooded her face, making the blood beat even harder through her veins. Her head throbbed in agony as she thought about the disaster she had made of everything. First she had responded to Dexter with passionate abandon and now it seemed she had crowned her folly with some sort of drunken declaration. She gave a little groan.

Dexter smiled faintly. "There was something that you wanted to explain to me." He straightened up. "When— or if—you remember—"

"I will, of course, let you know at once," Laura said, quickly and completely untruthfully.

Dexter hesitated. "Had you considered," he said, "that what happened last night may not have been an accident?"

Laura stared at him. The headache behind her eyes hammered so intensely that she felt sick. "No, I had not," she said. "Surely it was just a masonry fall? I thought it was simply ill luck—"

Dexter shook his head. "It could have been deliberate. You were lucky."

Laura winced, remembering the agonizing pain of her shoulder. "Surely that depends on how you define lucky."

"Lucky as in fortunate not to be dead." There was an edge to Dexter's voice. "Have you forgotten that we were deliberately locked in?"

"No, but—" Laura's head whirled. "I thought... I assumed it was just a prank—that whoever had locked us in had come back later to release us. And I am sure that the fall of stone was not deliberately manufactured. I saw no one there and it is well known that the priory ruins are dangerous." She shook her head fretfully. "I cannot believe it anything other than an accident!"

For a moment she saw again the hard, calculating look she had witnessed in Dexter's eyes the previous night but then it faded and he sighed. "To my mind it could have been a trap, Laura, cleverly conceived and neatly sprung. They locked you in and then released you, and you were so pleased to be free that you did what nine people out of ten would do and ran directly into a trap."

Laura tried to think about it. She remembered the day on the water the week before when she had been so sure that someone had pushed the boat out into the middle of the river. Was someone trying to hurt her? And if so, why? Might someone try to hurt *Hattie?* It was an intolerable thought. She bit her lip.

"What is it?" Dexter said instantly. He had been watching her face and now Laura realized how close she had come to giving herself away. He was too quick.

"Nothing," she said. She did not want to express her doubts to Dexter, not now, when her head ached intolerably and she could not think straight. She closed her eyes and lay back against the pillows with a sigh.

"Laura," Dexter said, "when you fell in the river last week—"

Laura's eyes shot open. How had he guessed that? She looked at him. He looked implacably back.

"I did wonder," she admitted, capitulating to his unspoken demand for the truth, "whether someone had pushed the boat. I thought I felt something, but the sun was in my eyes and I saw no one. It is little enough." She sighed. "I am sure I am imagining things. As I have said before, you have a suspicious mind, Mr. Anstruther, and now it is firing my imagination, too. There is absolutely no reason why anyone would shut me in my own wine cellar, unless as a practical joke. As for the rock fall, that was definitely an accident—"

She stopped as Dexter gave a derisive snort. "No reason? I thought that we discussed this last night? I begin to wonder if you are utterly in denial over your flamboyant and reckless life of crime!"

"I may be in denial," Laura snapped, "but you make up for it by refusing to let the matter go!" She sighed. "Please—I need to sleep. I do assure you that I am in no danger and you can leave me quite safely."

Their eyes met and held for a long moment and then Dexter sighed sharply. "Devil take it, Laura, but you are a stubborn creature." He ran a hand over his hair. "At least promise me that you will not go anywhere or do anything dangerous."

"I can safely promise that," Laura said, her eyes drifting closed. "I doubt I shall be going anywhere for quite a while."

She turned her head away and screwed her eyes up against a sudden and unexpected sting of tears. It was unlike her to cry. It was only because she was feeling so weak and wretchedly alone. She wanted Dexter to stay with her now, wanted it with a fierce ache of the heart, but at the same time she knew that she had to make him go. Indulging herself when her feelings for him were still so new and acute would not do any good.

"Thank you for all the help you gave me last night, Mr. Anstruther," she said. "I shall always be exceptionally grateful for your medical skills."

"Laura," Dexter said, "speaking of last night—"

"Let us not," Laura said quickly. Her feelings for him were so painful she thought she would choke if she had to talk about it. "Nothing of significance happened," she said. "Let us forget it."

After a moment she heard Dexter sigh again and move away from the bed. "I will talk to you when you are feeling stronger," he said. "We *will* talk, Laura."

Laura did not reply. She heard the door close softly behind him. She felt so bereft then that it was like a physical ache that took her breath away. But she knew that raking over the past, trying to re-create the illusory tenderness she had shared with Dexter for one night, could only lead to danger for Hattie and heartbreak for her. It was better this way. In the clear light of morning and with the aftertaste of the brandy bitter in her mouth, she knew there could be nothing else for herself and Dexter, no love, no future. There was too much to keep them apart. He wanted the calm stability that a wealthy, passionless marriage would bring. She wanted to protect Hattie from the stigma of illegitimacy at any price. And that was an end to it.

CHAPTER ELEVEN

"LAURA! HOW ARE YOU?" Alice Lister laid down a posy of pale pink roses on the hall table and stripped off her gloves before coming over to enfold Laura in an unexpected hug. She stood back and surveyed her friend with her shrewd brown gaze. "Oh dear! You look very drawn. Should you be out of bed today?"

"There is nothing wrong with me," Laura said, laughing as she hugged Alice back. "At least there was nothing wrong until you arrived and told me that I looked like a hag!" She looked her friend up and down. Alice's eyes were very bright and her cheeks very pink though it was not possible to tell if it was as a result of the cold wind or some strong emotion.

"I didn't say you looked like a hag!" Alice protested. She frowned a little. "You look a little pale, that is all, and it is scarce surprising after the accident you had. Rachel told me that you had only just escaped a nasty injury."

Laura wondered just what Rachel *had* told Alice the previous morning—and more to the point what Dexter had told Rachel to say to anyone who asked. It certainly would not be the truth, that he had spent all of the previous night with her. If that rumor circulated in Fortune's Folly her reputation would be in the ditch and his prospects of marrying Lydia with it. She shrugged slightly, trying to shake off a feeling of blue devilment. Her shoulder gave a twinge, reminding her to be careful.

"I was lucky," she said, smiling at Alice. "There was a masonry fall—"

"So I heard," Alice said. "You were knocked unconscious and barely managed to struggle home alone. What a terrible thing!"

"Alone," Laura said slowly. "Yes, yes, I was." So that was the story Dexter had put about. She felt ridiculously disappointed that he had removed all reference to himself from the tale, as though those moments of extraordinary intimacy between them had counted for nothing. But perhaps they did not mean anything to him and anyway, he could hardly take credit for rescuing her without some difficult questions being asked. She swished crossly over to the bell pull and relieved her feelings by almost tugging it from its socket.

"Your cousin told me all about it," Alice said. She bit her lip. "Lord Vickery is a very officious man. I met him in the lane just now and when I expressed my intention to visit you to see how you were, he quizzed me mercilessly about how I had heard of your accident, and who was talking about it and any number of things that are none of his business!"

"I see," Laura said, suddenly understanding the cause of Alice's pink cheeks and militant expression. "I am sorry. Miles can be very protective of my welfare."

"He need not try to protect you against me," Alice grumbled. "I am your friend! I find him very…" She stopped, frowning.

"Very overbearing?" Laura prompted, trying not to smile.

"Well, no," Alice allowed. "Not completely. He is not unpleasant. In fact, he can be extremely charming, although I am in no danger of having my head turned by him, of course."

"Of course not," Laura agreed. She reflected that Dexter must have told Miles of her accident though not, she assumed, the scene in the wine cellar that had preceded it. If he had done, Miles would probably have called him out. She sighed.

"I hear from Rachel that you and Lady Elizabeth held Miles up as he was crossing the bridge this morning and demanded payment of the pontage tax," she added, realizing that Alice was about to ask her what was troubling her and seizing on a change of subject. "That must have tested his fabled charm."

Alice's face broke into a mischievous smile. "Yes, we did. He was very annoyed. And then several of the younger men chose to try the stepping-stones to avoid having to pay to cross the bridge and then they fell in the water! Lady Elizabeth and I thought it vastly amusing."

"We must think of some more medieval laws with which to torment the gentlemen," Laura said. "The Mischief Ball next week may present us with another opportunity." She picked up the roses. "Are these for me? Thank you very much, Alice—they are very pretty."

"I know that Hattie brought some lilies for you yesterday," Alice said, "but one can never have too many fresh-cut flowers about the house. Will Mrs. Carrington put them in water for you, or should I run down to the kitchens?"

"I am sure Mrs. Carrington will do it," Laura said. "Her arrangements are always very elegant. She is feeling a little better today and has baked a simnel cake for us to have with tea. She says it is a medicinal recipe."

"That sounds delicious," Alice said, slipping off her winter pelisse. Carrington had appeared from the kitchens and now tottered away with Alice's coat, gloves and bonnet. He was almost bent double under their meager weight. He had placed the posy of flowers on the top of the pile and it bobbed about rather like a cork in a stormy sea.

"I will bring up the tea tray, your grace," he said. "And may I say how delighted I am to see your grace up and about this morning?" His face shook with horror and shock. "I had no idea, no idea at all, that you were down in the wine cellars the night before last—"

"Please do not worry, Carrington," Laura said, interrupting him as she feared that he was shaking so much he would drop the entire pile. "And there is no hurry for the refreshments."

"Poor Carrington," Alice said, watching the butler with concern as he tottered off. "Can he manage?"

"I expect he will need to carry the cake separately," Laura conceded, ushering Alice into the drawing room, "but he will manage quite well and he does like to do these things for himself. He is very proud."

Molly had lit the drawing room fire and with its bright flames in the grate and the autumn sunshine flowing in, the room was almost cheerful. Alice subsided with a sigh onto the ancient velvet chaise and Laura took her usual armchair at the fireside. She was aware of Alice's scrutiny, as though her earlier reassurances had not satisfied her friend, and now she sighed.

"Stop staring at me!" she said with mock severity. "I am perfectly well."

"If you are sure..." Alice did not sound convinced. "Where is Hattie this morning?"

"She is taking a nap," Laura said. "We played together in the long gallery with the toys that Miles brought for her from London—he gave her the most beautiful spinning top and a new doll whom she has named Emily, and some wooden animals to start a toy farm. Hattie was so excited that she quite wore herself out."

"Lord Vickery does not strike me as the type of man who would have much interest in children," Alice said. "You surprise me."

"Miles is a most doting godfather to Hattie," Laura said, amused at the continued interest in her cousin that Alice was not quite managing to hide.

"And yet he is a rake and a fortune hunter," Alice said crossly. "It is most inconsiderate of him to have any saving virtues for it makes it impossible to dislike him completely!"

"If you remember that he is officious and interfering," Laura said with a twitch of her lips, "I am sure you will not find it difficult at all."

The door opened and Carrington came in with a stately shuffle, bearing the tea tray. He placed it by Laura then retreated to fetch the cake. The whole operation took five minutes.

"Pray let me pour, Carrington," Laura began, as the butler lifted the teapot with a hand that shook so much half the contents splashed onto the carpet.

"Madam," Carrington said with dignity, "I could not possibly permit it."

Laura contented herself with cutting the cake whilst he served Alice tea.

"It is a terrible affliction they both suffer," Alice whispered as Carrington, duty finally completed, withdrew with triumph and the empty teapot. "I am sure the Duchess of Cole must be a monster to have upset them so!"

"It is very sad," Laura agreed. "And pray do not mention to the Carringtons that Faye and Henry are in Fortune's Folly, Alice, or they are like to become completely prostrate."

"Of course not," Alice said, munching on the simnel cake. "I met the Duchess of Cole in the market square when I was on my way here," she added. "Naturally she cut me dead. She had just accosted Mr. Anstruther in the street to invite him to join a house party at Cole Court for a shoot."

Laura felt another twinge to be the recipient of this information, though this time it was her heart rather than her shoulder that pained her. An invitation to Cole would be the next, logical step in Dexter's courtship of Lydia. She wondered why she had not anticipated it. She wished she did not care about it.

"Perhaps Faye thinks that a week of mindless slaughter will put Mr. Anstruther in amorous mood," she said snappishly.

Alice giggled. "Poor Lydia," she said. "Her mama has rather been pushing her in the direction of any gentleman who is remotely eligible, has she not? I am surprised she does not auction her daughter to the highest bidder!"

"For pity's sake do not suggest it to her," Laura said, "for she would no doubt think it a splendid plan. I can see it now—a public sale in the market square!"

"Anyway, Mr. Anstruther refused the invitation," Alice said, with a sideways glance at Laura. "He did not seem very keen at all."

"Strange, when he has been dancing attendance on Miss Cole this se'nnight," Laura said, attacking her simnel cake viciously with her knife. "I think he will make her a declaration soon and he will have no one but himself to blame if he thinks it worth taking on such a mother-in-law."

"He has not known her very long," Alice said, her brown gaze resting thoughtfully on Laura's face.

"They first met years ago," Laura said. "Besides, it takes very little time for a fortune hunter to weigh up the value of an heiress's dowry, Alice, and everyone knows that Mr. Anstruther's prime consideration is to marry a fortune."

Alice smiled. "You seem quite put out by the whole affair, Laura."

"Not at all," Laura said hastily. She had momentarily forgotten just how observant her friend could be.

"Perhaps the duchess will invite him for Christmas instead," Alice said.

"Perhaps," Laura agreed. The thought of Dexter newly betrothed to Lydia and celebrating Christmas at Cole Court caused her a stab of pain, for she could suddenly see that this would be the beginning of her torture, not the end of it. There would be Dexter and Lydia's wedding, and the honeymoon, and the birth of their first child, and the christening—she could only hope that she would not be invited to be godmother—and then the appearance of a whole brood of little Anstruthers. They would be a proper family. They would belong together.

Laura swallowed hard. How would she feel when she watched Lydia walk up the aisle to join Dexter at the altar? It seemed impossible to imagine that she would feel indifferent enough to attend the wedding. Faye and Henry would be sure to invite her, not because they wanted her there but because it would be the appropriate thing to do. She would have to make sure that she and Hattie were taking an extremely long trip when the invitation arrived.

With a huge effort of will she turned her thoughts aside before Alice could sense her unhappiness.

"Are you going to the recital at the pump rooms tonight?" she asked. Her voice did not sound quite right even to her own ears and there was a prickle of tears in her throat.

"I fear so," Alice said gloomily. "Mama has decided it would be a good thing. She enjoys music, whereas I am tone deaf." She looked closely at Laura. "You have turned very pale, Laura. Are you quite well?"

"I am absolutely fine, thank you," Laura said, smiling brightly even as she felt wretched. She had never confided in another person in her life. She realized that she did not even know how to do so. What could she tell Alice, after all? That she had spent the night with her cousin's suitor? That she was in love with him even though he thought her a faithless wanton?

Rachel knocked at the door and Hattie rushed in with shrieks of excitement, upsetting the teacups. She grabbed Alice's hand and dragged her away to see the Emily doll and Laura followed, smiling and chatting, just as she had always done at Cole Court, gracious, guarded, the perfect dowager duchess once more.

CHAPTER TWELVE

DEXTER SAT BACK in his uncomfortable gilt chair in the pump room recital hall, rubbed the back of his neck and tried to relax as he waited for the start of the evening's concert. Conversation had been stilted around Sir Montague's dinner table that night. Every heiress invited had declined the summons to dine, with the inevitable exception of Miss Lydia Cole. In fact there had been only three women present in total: Lydia, her mama and Lady Elizabeth Scarlet, who had claimed that the only reason she was eating at her brother's table was that she would otherwise starve. Sir Montague had been almost incandescent with rage to be snubbed by the ladies of Fortune's Folly and had glowered and growled his way through the entire meal.

Dexter had been seated with Lady Elizabeth on one side and Lydia, inescapably, on the other. Lady Elizabeth had spent the meal baiting Nat Waterhouse, who seemed impervious to her teasing, whilst Miss Cole had been silent for most of the time. She had answered Dexter's pleasantries in monosyllables whilst her mother had craned her neck to watch the progress of the happy courtship from her place farther up the table. It had been stilted and ghastly.

The rest of the day had not been much better. Dexter had met up with Miles and Nat to discuss the most recent developments in the investigation of the murder of Sir William Crosby. There had not, in fact, been a great deal to discuss. Dexter himself had had no success with his inquiries at the Red Lion. Nat had gained little from his discussions with the local constable who had originally investigated the case. Miles had interviewed the gamekeepers and beaters who had been out on the estate with Sir William when he had been shot but none of them had apparently seen or heard anything unusual or remotely helpful. The only thing that had caught Dexter's eye was a note in the transcript of Miles's interview with the widowed Leticia, Lady Crosby, to the effect that an engraved ring had been stolen from her husband's body.

"There was no mention of this in the constable's original report," Dexter had commented.

Miles had looked smug. "Her ladyship said it was too private a matter to tell the constable," he said. "Sir William was a bluff Yorkshire man with a reputation for dispensing tough justice. She did not feel it would enhance his standing for it to be known after his death that he wore a ring with a lock of her hair in it that was engraved with her initials. Sentimental nonsense, he apparently called it, and only did it to please her."

Nat laughed. "How on earth did you get her to divulge that to you, Miles?" He paused. "No, forget I asked that. How stupid of me. I can guess."

"Not my type, old chap," Miles said. "And even I have some standards with regard to the seduction of recently bereaved widows." He stopped. "Though now I come to think of it, do you remember Lady Compton—"

"Spare us," Dexter said. "So the ring was missing when his body was brought back?"

"Correct," Miles said. "Taken by the murderer, presumably."

"Why would he do that," Nat said, "when Sir William's silver hip flask and his snuffbox were not taken?"

"As a trophy, perhaps," Dexter said. "Or to prove to someone else that Sir William was dead."

"To prove it to Sampson," Miles said, "if he were the instigator. Find the ring and we have found the murderer?"

"Possibly," Dexter said. "Although he may have destroyed it, or given it to his mistress, or done any number of things with it."

"Vanity says he would not destroy it," Nat said.

Certainly Warren Sampson was not wearing Sir William Crosby's ring that night. He had greeted Dexter with a firm handshake and his usual bonhomie, and apart from an ostentatiously huge diamond cravat pin he wore no jewelry at all. His gaze had lingered on Lydia Cole for rather longer than politeness dictated and Dexter had seen her blush, but with discomfort rather than pleasure, he thought. The Duke and Duchess of Cole had been very civil to Sampson and had invited him to join their party but Sampson had declined, choosing to sit a few seats away with the Wheeler family instead.

Dexter tried to find a comfortable position on the spindly legged chair. The prospect of the evening ahead was difficult to bear. He had Lydia once again placed next to him and Faye penning him in on the other side. Lydia was habitually silent, her head bent in apparent rapt concentration on her reticule. Faye was staring at him in an attempt to bludgeon him into starting yet another unsatisfactory conversation with her daughter.

"Lydia and I were saying just now how very *ill* the dowager duchess is looking tonight," Faye said. She leaned forward to engage her daughter, obliterating Dexter's view of the room. "Were we not saying that, Lyddy? Did we not comment that Laura looks every one of her *four and thirty years* tonight and then several more?"

"You were saying so, Mama," Lydia said, looking up briefly. "I thought she looked very well and very pretty, as she always does."

"The dowager duchess?" Dexter said. "Is she here tonight?"

Faye leaned back and he was at last afforded an unobstructed view of the recital room. Sure enough, Laura was opposite, taking a seat next to Alice Lister and Lady Elizabeth Scarlet. She was wearing a silk gown in dowager purple, but if that was supposed to be her concession to her status Dexter thought that she had failed spectacularly to look like a respectable widow. To his eyes the gown looked far too rich a hue and far too tightly wrapped about her slender curves to be remotely frumpish. A matching purple silk shawl was draped around her shoulders, dipping down to a diamond clasp between her breasts. She looked like a present that he wanted to unwrap there and then, sumptuous, provocative and gloriously tempting.

Desire and outrage fought a brief battle within Dexter. Surely Laura was still far too weak to be out of her bed let alone attending a public concert. She might look very well indeed—Lydia was quite right—but she had evidently paid no attention *whatsoever* to the warning he had given her to take no risks and stay away from danger, for she had ventured out alone and unprotected except for Alice and Elizabeth, which was just about the most fool-hardy and stupid thing she could possibly have done. The protective fury stirred in Dexter as he thought about it. He had hoped that she had taken heed of his words to her the previous day, yet here she was, defiant, determined and independent, all the qualities that he deplored in the woman he would want as his future bride and yet found strangely attractive in Laura....

Their eyes met. Laura acknowledged him with the barest of nods, as though he was a mere acquaintance, and turned back to her conversation with Alice. Dexter seethed with frustration. She looked so cool, as though their reckless, inflammatory and thoroughly outrageous lovemaking in the wine cellar had never occurred and he had not spent the rest of the night in intimate circumstances with her.

It infuriated him that she was so composed.

He wanted to take her in his arms there and then and smash her self-possession to smithereens. He wanted to shake her and ask her what she thought she was doing to willfully ignore his instructions. He wanted to kiss her until she was breathless.

Faye was still talking. "She never had the looks to carry off the role of duchess, poor ungainly creature. Duchesses should have style and poise...."

Dexter got up and walked across to where Laura was sitting, ignoring Faye's outraged gasp and the ill-concealed curiosity of the other concertgoers.

"A word, if you please, your grace," he said through

his teeth. He took her elbow in his hand, remembering at the last minute not to hurt her injured arm, and pulled her to her feet.

"What on earth do you think you are doing?" Laura uttered, as he drew her a little distance away from the others behind the sparse concealment of a nodding fern.

"I could ask the same of you," Dexter returned. "I hardly expected to see you here tonight. Have you lost your sense to do something so dangerous?"

"Attending a musical recital is scarcely a perilous occupation, Mr. Anstruther," Laura said haughtily.

"Now you are willfully misunderstanding me!" Dexter could feel his temper slipping out of control and his voice rising. "You are barely up from your sickbed and already venturing out without so much as a servant to protect you! Must you indulge your appetite for destruction in such a reckless way? Did I not expressly forbid you to do anything that might put you in harm's way?"

A spot of pink color burned along Laura's cheekbones. Her hazel eyes snapped. "Forbid me?" she said scathingly. "Just who do you think you are, Mr. Anstruther?"

"I am the man you spent the night with not two days ago," Dexter said. "Or had you forgotten? The coolness of your acknowledgment of me might lead me to suspect it."

Laura's luscious mouth tightened to a thin line. "I thought it in both our interests to forget that," she said sweetly. "And as you recall, I am suffering *severe* amnesia over the whole affair."

Dexter's anger tightened to the point where he forgot everything else. "Your apparent amnesia is much exaggerated, I believe," he said, "but I shall be happy to remind you of what happened between us at any time and place you choose—"

"I have come to tell you that the concert is about to start." Miles's smooth voice cut across them. "Also that Fortune's Folly already has a town crier and so does not need you to make any further announcements, Dexter. It is scarce discreet to indulge in an argument behind nothing more substantial than a potted plant."

Laura gave an exasperated sigh, turned her back and walked away and Dexter, suddenly conscious of his surroundings, made his way back to his seat. Lydia avoided looking at him. Faye Cole gave him a look of fury barely masked by a cold smile. The orchestra struck up the first chord and the soloist burst into song.

The concert was almost as poorly attended as Sir Montague's dinner had been. Most of the ladies of Fortune's Folly were absent with the rather odd result that three-quarters of the audience were gentlemen. Half of these left during the interval when they realized that they were baulked of their prey and went to the Morris Clown to drown their sorrows. By the end there was only Dexter, Miles, Lydia Cole and her mother, Laura, Alice, Lady Elizabeth and half a dozen other people left in the room. The German soprano engaged for the evening sang with increasing stridency as her audience diminished and finished by stalking off the stage to a ripple of lame applause.

"A word of advice, old chap," Miles said laconically as he and Dexter prepared to leave. "Try to keep your eye on the main target." Then, as Dexter looked blank, "Miss Cole, Dexter. You have been staring at Laura all evening, rather than at her cousin."

Dexter ran a hand over his forehead. "I need to speak to her grace again," he muttered.

"I really would not advise it, old chap," Miles said, not unsympathetically. "I realize that there is something between yourself and Laura but it can come to nothing. She has no money at all, and I would have thought she was scarcely the type of woman to meet your exacting requirements. She is far too independent."

He nodded toward Lydia, who had managed to escape her mother for a second whilst Faye visited the ladies' withdrawing room and was staring rather fixedly at a group of gentlemen who were chatting by the door. "You could do worse, you know," Miles said. "The mother may be appalling but Miss Cole is a quiet, biddable girl—just what you want—and her fortune is more than respectable."

"I know," Dexter said. Lydia Cole fulfilled every criterion on his list. She was pretty enough, well bred and submissive, and the thought of marrying her turned his blood cold. He could not understand it. A few short weeks ago he would have been glad to marry a woman for whom he felt no more than lukewarm liking. It fitted his notions of how a convenient marriage should operate, with no wild feelings on either side to disturb the surface calm. It was what he had thought he wanted and he could not understand why his feelings had changed so radically. All he knew was that to make an offer for Lydia when he burned for Laura seemed impossible.

"I am not sure whether I can make Miss Cole an offer," he said slowly.

"This is business, Dexter," Miles said, his voice hardening. "Try. You cannot afford to hesitate." He gave

Dexter a consoling clap on the shoulder. "Court your heiress with a bit of passion, old chap. At the moment it's painful to watch. Act the part of the ardent suitor and make it convincing. Sometimes we all have to make sacrifices for the greater good."

A cold breath of wind swept through the room as someone opened the main door and stepped out into the night. The candles flickered and a servant moved swiftly to cut off the draught. And in that moment the coldness of memory trickled down Dexter's spine, setting him shivering. He looked across the room at Laura. She was responding to some comment of Alice Lister's as they walked toward the door together. There was a smile curving her lips. The candlelight shimmered on the hazel of her eyes, making them look warm and deep and mysterious. Dexter suddenly felt very odd, as though a puzzle he had not even been aware that he had been trying to solve had finally slipped into focus.

"What did you say?" he said.

Miles had taken a few steps away but now he turned back, a perplexed look on his face. "I said that we all have to make sacrifices for the greater good." When Dexter did not reply immediately he added with a touch of asperity, "For the sake of your family, old chap—"

"Before that," Dexter said. "You said *act the part and make it convincing.*"

Miles shrugged, clearly puzzled. "Makes the wooing sweeter, even if your heart is not in it. I know it sounds cynical but it's for the best, at least until the knot is tied and it is too late."

After a moment, when Dexter did not respond, he frowned. "Are you quite well, old fellow?"

"Perfectly, thank you," Dexter said, although he felt as though he had been hit over the head with a club. "Don't wait for me. I shall be along directly."

Miles nodded and went out, still looking puzzled. Dexter saw him pause in the hall to speak to Laura and Alice. He saw Laura tilt her head up for Miles's kiss and the light gleamed on the curve of her cheek and shimmered on the golden chestnut of her hair. Then she, too, was gone. The sound of voices died away and Dexter stood in the empty hall whilst the musicians collected their stands and sheet music and the servants started to douse the candles.

"Act the part…make it convincing until it is too late," Miles had said and his words had hit Dexter like a ton of bricks and taken him back to Laura's broken whisper the night before when he had carried her up to bed after resetting her arm.

"I had to make you leave…"

It had not been feverish and drunken nonsense. He remembered that moment in the wine cellar and Laura so soft and sweet in his arms, confiding a little drunkenly that she had wanted him that night at Cole, but that what she had done had been wrong in so many ways.

He felt cold in his bones.

He thought of the Laura Cole who held the respect of all who knew her, who embraced a cause to help others, who was always trying to save people like Carrington. He thought back four years to the Laura who had made such tender, passionate love to him and whispered endearments to him in the heat of the night. That was not the same woman who had turned him away the next day with hard, cold words. He had been so angry that for four long years he had been blind to the truth. But now he knew.

Act the part... Make it convincing... Until it is too late...

They had been swept away by emotion that night, but in the morning Laura had thought that she had done a terrible thing and the only way she could think of to put matters right had been to send him away. She had not wanted him to ruin his life, his career and his family's future. She had pretended that she had not cared, that it had been no more than a game to her. His stomach dropped as though he had stepped off a tall building into thin air.

He knew he was right. He knew it with every instinct he possessed. That was the same Laura Cole who paid incompetent servants in order to save them from poverty, who tried to help the ladies of Fortune's Folly escape the Dames' Tax, whose cousin spoke with admiration of the causes she had embraced and the people she had tried to help.

She had wanted to save him. It was what she did. It was the person she was. Laura tried to help people. She had broken his heart and sent him away because it was the right thing to do and perhaps—just perhaps—she had broken her own heart at the same time.

"I had to make you leave..."

"Excuse me, sir. The assembly rooms are closing now." The servant hovered at his elbow. Dexter realized that the room was almost dark.

"Thank you," he said.

He walked out into the autumn night. The wind was roaring in the trees and the leaves raced across the cobblestones. The lights of the Morris Clown Inn glowed through the dark. He stood in the market square whilst the wind whipped about him and the last of the home-goers cast him curious glances as they hurried through the night.

He tried to tell himself that nothing had changed. The past was gone and he should leave it buried. He did not need to seek Laura out and confront her with the truth because what good would it do? He should merely be grateful that she had seen what he had been too young and too inexperienced to realize at the time—that to run off with her would have been the ruin of them both. He would have thrown away his career and his future and his family's hopes all for love and that was not the ordered way in which he ran his life. He should be thankful that she had saved him from the biggest mistake of his life and leave matters there.

Except that knowing that Laura had ended matters because she cared for him rather than because she was a heartless wanton seemed to change everything.

CHAPTER THIRTEEN

"THERE IS A gentleman caller to see you, your grace," Carrington said, for all the world, Laura thought, as though she were a courtesan entertaining men in her boudoir. "I put him in the library." His voice quavered. "I am very sorry to say, your grace, that it is the Duke of Cole."

For one dreadful moment Laura thought that he was referring to Charles and had lost his faculties completely. Then she saw that the door of the library was open and Henry was standing before the fire, hands behind his back, his chest pushed out importantly, like a fluffed-up pigeon. No wonder Carrington was on edge. He had had no idea that the new duke and duchess were in Fortune's Folly. To see his former employer again would be to bring back all the horror of Faye Cole's incessant demands and his own breakdown.

"Thank you, Carrington," she said.

"I hope, madam," Carrington said formally, "that Mrs. Carrington and I have always served you to the utmost of our ability."

"Of course you have," Laura said, with absolute truth.

"And that there is no possibility *whatsoever* of our returning to Cole Court."

"There certainly is not, Carrington," Laura said firmly.

"Thank you, madam," Carrington said, his face trembling with relief. "We know you cannot really afford us—"

"Carrington," Laura said, interrupting him kindly, "why don't you and Mrs. Carrington enjoy a nice cup of tea and some of that delicious simnel cake in the kitchen. There is nothing for you to worry about."

Shaking her head, she watched him totter off down the servants' stair and walked slowly across the hall to see what on earth the new Duke of Cole could possibly want with her.

"Henry," Laura said, going into the library and closing the door behind her. "What an unexpected pleasure. Do Faye and Lydia not accompany you?"

She sincerely hoped they had not. She had seen neither Faye nor Lydia nor indeed Dexter Anstruther since the night of the concert three days ago. They were all on the list of people she was avoiding, if for different reasons.

Henry looked slightly shifty. "No indeed. They are at the pump room. Faye seems to have developed quite a taste for Fortune's Water."

Or for the company of all those fortune-hunting gentlemen, Laura thought uncharitably. Looking at Henry's slightly uncomfortable demeanor, she realized suddenly that his wife had no idea that he was visiting her. Her curiosity was piqued.

"You have a fine aspect here," Henry said, going to the window and looking out across the gardens to the water meadows and the curve of the river. "I am pleased to see The Old Palace is the sort of environment appropriate for the Dowager Duchess of Cole. It would not fit the family dignity for you to live in a hole-in-the-corner manner."

"It suits me very well," Laura said. She had not forgotten Faye and Henry's snobbery in the past and she wondered now whether Henry had come to The Old Palace purely to make sure that she was not letting the family name down by living in squalor.

"Good, good…" Henry took a turn about the room. "I suppose it is a little shabby here, but nothing that some new fixtures and fittings would not address."

Laura raised her brows. She was certain that Henry had not come to see her solely to discuss home improvements.

"I have been thinking for some time," Henry said abruptly, "that it is a great scandal for Charles to have left you so ill provided for. I am very sorry to say, cousin Laura, that people in the village are *talking,* you know."

"People are talking about me?" Laura asked. Her heart contracted. She felt cold. For one terrifying moment she was afraid that what she had been dreading had come true—someone knew about her encounter with Dexter in the cellars and was spreading gossip about them. Then Henry spoke again and she realized with a pang of relief that she had misunderstood.

"Indeed," Henry said. "They are saying that you are too poor to be considered marriageable under the Dames' Tax, cousin Laura. The fortune hunters consider you negligible."

"Thank goodness," Laura said, with feeling.

Henry's face reddened with disapproval. "But you do not understand, cousin. A *Cole* cannot be considered negligible, not even one who is only a Cole by marriage. It is most inappropriate!"

Laura frowned. "Forgive my slowness, cousin Henry," she said, "but are you saying that you feel it would be more appropriate for me to be a rich widow prey to unscrupulous adventurers?"

"Exactly!" Henry beamed. "With your social distinction you should be the greatest matrimonial prize in Fortune's Folly, not some poor widow scraping to feed her child! I always thought Charles a ramshackle fellow and this confirms it."

"Yes, well…" Laura rubbed her brow. She supposed that with Henry and Faye's particular brand of snobbery there was an odd logic in what Henry was saying. He would feel that it reflected poorly on the family and the dukedom for people to speak disparagingly of her poverty. She herself could not care less as long as she could feed herself, Hattie and the people who depended on her, but it evidently mattered to Henry.

"Please do not let it distress either yourself or Faye," she said. "I can scrape by on the annuity my grandmother left me. My brother, Burlington, has offered me a home with him but you know my sadly independent character, cousin Henry. I prefer to live here."

"Burlington is only an earl," Henry said. "You are a dependent of the Dukedom of Cole, cousin Laura, and as such I have come to the conclusion—reluctantly, mind—that it is my responsibility to make good Charles's lack. You are to have your widow's jointure."

"I am sure it must have been a decision you came to very reluctantly," Laura said dryly. The agreement originally drawn up between her father and Charles Cole had been for her to have an income of ten thousand pounds a year for life. She simply could not believe that Henry, whom some called parsimonious and others plain mean, would reinstate it.

"Dear Henry," she said, "you are all generosity, but I do beg you to reconsider. I know the Cole estates will take years to recover from Charles's profligacy and I would not dream of taking money that could be better used to restore Cole Court."

Henry nodded solemnly. "You are correct, of course. Charles drained the Cole income shamelessly but the estate is recovering now and I am happy to say that my own lands have always been in better shape. I have spoken to your brother and we have agreed—"

"You've spoken to Burlington?" Laura interrupted sharply.

"Of course." Henry looked taken aback. "This is men's business, cousin Laura. I only tell you now what we have decided out of courtesy. I have spoken to Burlington and we have agreed that he will provide five thousand pounds of the jointure and I will provide the other five. Honor will then be satisfied."

Laura could easily picture her pompous brother and equally pompous cousin by marriage sitting down together and planning her whole future. Basil had already vented his displeasure on her that she would not accept his invitation to return home to live at Burlington. He would see a collaboration with Henry as the perfect way to control his wayward sister because once they held the purse strings they would be able to tell her what to do. Neither of them would think it necessary to consult her. And here was Henry presenting her with what he fondly imagined to be the solution to all her difficulties and looking as though he expected her to fall on his neck in abject gratitude.

Laura struggled with her feelings. On the one hand,

to have ten thousand pounds a year would be perfectly marvelous for both herself and Hattie. They could employ a gardener who could help Bart keep the grounds of The Old Palace in check and help her to grow the fruit and vegetables on which the household depended. She could have the drafty windows and the leaking roof mended before winter and she could buy Hattie some new clothes and not be dependent on the charity of the Falconers and Miles and other friends. But on the other side of the coin was the intolerable thought of Henry and Basil forever interfering in her affairs and telling her not only what to spend the money on but also how to live her life…

"I am overwhelmed, cousin," she said truthfully.

"Of course you are! It is only natural that you would be overcome by our munificence," Henry agreed, nodding.

"I assume," Laura continued, "that the terms of the agreement would be the same as before—that is, if I were to remarry, the income would cease?"

Once again, Henry looked remarkably shifty and Laura wondered what, exactly, he was up to. "Burlington and I have agreed," he said, "that were you to remarry the sum of twenty thousand pounds would be settled on you in lieu of the income from the jointure."

Laura almost choked. "But…that is most irregular! There is no provision in the original agreement—"

"Pray do not concern yourself, cousin Laura," Henry said with a patronizing smile. "I know that financial matters are not the province of the female mind so do leave such matters to your brother and myself. We are agreed that it would be too shabby to cut you off without a penny. Therefore we will provide a dowry."

"But the Dames' Tax!" Laura said. "Through your generosity you will make me a target for all the fortune hunters swarming around the village—" She stopped as the full extent of the plan became clear to her at last and literally took her breath away. She had been mistaken in thinking that Henry and Basil wished to tell her how to live her life. What they really wanted was to be shot of her.

"You *want* me to marry!" she said. "You and Basil wish me to make another match!"

Henry put his hands behind his back and rocked back on his heels. He did not seem in the least put out to have had his scheme uncovered.

"A female, unprotected and alone in the world, must always be a burden to her family," he said. "Given that you are unable to accept your brother's hospitality, we felt it would be better for you to be under a husband's guidance and control—"

"Provided that you approve the husband," Laura snapped, her temper rising fast.

"Naturally," Henry said, looking surprised. "I am sure you are aware, dear Laura—and so I do not scruple to mention it—that at your age and with your looks, your prospects of remarriage would normally be severely curtailed."

"But with the money as a bribe and a host of penniless adventurers hanging around," Laura finished, "I might manage to catch someone halfway acceptable!"

"Precisely!" Henry beamed. "Some of the gentlemen in Fortune's Folly are rackety good-for-nothings, it is true, but a few are respectable enough. You might consider Lord Chesterton or Sir Laurence Digby, for example."

"I might consider refusing them," Laura said frostily.

"Sir Laurence has buried four wives already and I have no desire to be the fifth, and there is a reason why Lord Chesterton is unmarried—he has a host of unpleasant habits."

"One must learn to overlook such things in wedlock," Henry said virtuously. "Having been married to Charles, surely you are aware of that?"

"Having been married to Charles," Laura snapped, "I have no wish to put up with another husband's unpleasant habits at all." She looked at him thoughtfully. "Tell me, does cousin Faye know anything of these plans you have for me?"

She had touched a nerve. Henry cleared his throat several times. "This is nothing to do with my wife," he said after a moment. "She concerns herself solely with the disposal of Lydia."

"In marriage, I assume," Laura said, thinking that Faye and Henry seemed frightfully keen to dispose of Lydia in any way they could. She spread her hands appealingly. "Then surely, cousin, you need to keep your fortune intact for Lydia's dowry? You cannot be funding me, as well, generous as you are."

But Henry could not be persuaded. "It seems to me," he said, "that when both you and Lydia are off our hands, cousin Laura, then we shall be able to congratulate ourselves on a job well done."

Laura stood up. "I thank you for your concern for my welfare, cousin Henry," she said, "but I must decline your generous offer. Indeed, I can truly say that you overwhelm me."

"You cannot refuse the money," Henry said, with a certain amount of glee. "We have already written to Churchward to draw up the papers. My dear Laura, I fear you must simply accept your fate." He bowed. "I will see myself out since that fool Carrington is incompetent. I trust that when you receive the money the first thing that you will do is to employ a proper butler." He nodded thoughtfully. "Indeed, I shall put the matter in train myself."

"No, you will not," Laura said wrathfully. "I am perfectly satisfied with the services of Carrington and Mrs. Carrington, Henry, and I do beg you not to interfere in the running of my household. Once again, I insist on declining your money."

Henry merely waved dismissively. " We will see you tonight at the Mischief Ball, cousin Laura, where I am persuaded you will be feted as is appropriate as one of Fortune Folly's finest heiresses!"

He strode from the room and Laura found herself tempted to pick up one of her grandmother's ancient pieces of china and vent her rage by throwing it after him. Instead she reached for the decanter and poured herself a pleasantly large glass of wine. At least there was one thing that Henry did not know. He had not the least chance of recognizing her at the ball that evening, or indeed of recognizing any of the other heiresses, either. Even if word of her sudden wealth spread like wildfire, no gentleman would be able to identify her in the throng.

Not that that solved the problem of the money. She sank down into an armchair and gulped down her wine. She would have to see what Mr. Churchward could do to help her, for she had no intention of accepting Henry and Basil's attempts to bribe someone to take her off their hands. For the moment, though, there was nothing she could do. The Duke of Cole had, against her will, made her one of the richest matrimonial prizes in Fortune's Folly. She wondered how long it would be before the whole village had heard the news.

CHAPTER FOURTEEN

"THERE'S A PROBLEM," Miles Vickery said.

"Another one?" Dexter asked tersely. He had arrived late in Sir Montague Fortune's ballroom that evening, the lukewarm suitor, dragging his feet. He had spent another fruitless day investigating the Crosby case, this time visiting the site of the murder. Sir William, his game-keeper had stated, had expressed the need to make a call of nature whilst out shooting and had disappeared into the woods, which was why there were no witnesses to the crime. Dexter had thoroughly examined the place the body was found but had discovered no further clues. There was nothing but the missing ring to link the murderer with his victim. To add to his frustrations, Laura Cole and Elizabeth Scarlet had stopped him on his way back into the village and demanded payment of the pontage. As he handed over his last few pennies Dexter had wondered what on earth had possessed him to suggest the tax in the first place. Misplaced arrogance, he supposed, just as Laura had claimed.

He had seen Lydia Cole engaged in furtive conversation with a gentleman in the market square as he had entered the Morris Clown Inn. Both Lydia and her beau, if that was who the man was, had melted away when they had seen him. Dexter wondered if Faye Cole had any inkling that her daughter was meeting a man in secret. She was still throwing Lydia in his way at every possible opportunity, apparently oblivious to the fact that neither Dexter nor Lydia wished it. Their courtship had never been more than lukewarm in the first place, Dexter reflected, and now it was stone-cold. Faye, however, was the only person who did not appear to realize this. Even Sir James Wheeler had picked up on the fact that Dexter was no longer squiring Lydia about and had dropped into conversation, with all the subtlety of a sledgehammer, that his daughter Mary was to have thirty thousand pounds on her marriage.

Dexter might want the thirty thousand pounds but he did not want Mary Wheeler, no matter that she was the sort of wife who would not disturb the even tenor of his life. He dreamed about Laura. He ached for her. He had tried telling himself that it was no more than a physical impulse that would burn itself out but he did not really believe it. He did not know how to be free of wanting her. Knowing that she had ended their affair because she cared for him rather than because she cared nothing seemed to have changed all his plans. He wanted to know the whole truth now. He was obsessed.

He looked at the crowds of ladies who thronged the ballroom at Fortune Hall. For this one night it seemed that hostilities over the Dames' Tax had been suspended and every heiress in the town—for the event had been restricted to those ladies only—had accepted Sir Montague's invitation. In their silken dominoes they formed an ever-shifting pattern of glorious color. It should have been an environment rich for exploitation by the unscrupulous fortune hunter. But as Miles had said, there was a problem and Dexter saw it at once.

Sir Montague had decreed that the ball should be a masquerade and so all the guests were masked. There was no way to identify the ladies, let alone to know whether or not they were heiress to fifty thousand pounds.

Dexter groaned. "I might have known that Monty would make a hash of this," he said. "What possessed him to decide it should be a masked ball?"

"He liked the title Mischief Masquerade," Miles said, grinning, "but unfortunately he didn't think of the consequences." He frowned as he scanned the crowds. "There's something else, as well. I didn't think there were this many females in Fortune's Folly, let alone heiresses. It doesn't seem possible."

"It isn't," Dexter said grimly.

Miles stared at him. "Then who are these women? Where have they all come from?"

"I don't know," Dexter said. "Neighbors, friends...all invited by the ladies themselves simply to confuse us, I suspect, and since they are all in disguise it is impossible to sort the real heiresses from the interlopers."

"Well, I'll be damned," Miles said. "How are we to find ourselves a rich wife amongst so many decoys? It's not sporting."

"It is when you want to beat Sir Montague at his own game," Dexter said. He sighed. "It's very clever. I was half expecting no one to attend this evening but instead we get so many ladies in disguise that we cannot tell them apart. I imagine your cousin had something to do with this, Miles. It has all the hallmarks of her planning."

He searched the shifting throng for a glimpse of Laura.

He had no idea whether she was there or not, although Miles had mentioned in passing earlier in the day that Laura might attend. One glance suggested that there were at least a dozen women of the right height and coloring who could be Laura. In theory there was no way that he could tell. Yet something in his blood, a prickle of awareness, an edge of anticipation, told him that she was indeed present and that given time, he could find her even in this anonymous crowd.

I would know her even in the dark….

Rational sense told him that he should not seek her out. He should not even think of it. But his reason was stretched to the breaking point. He wanted to confront Laura and discover the truth of the past. He had to know.

Sir Montague arrived a moment later. His face was a mottled red and behind his mask his eyes were almost popping with annoyance and frustration.

"Dexter, do something!" he besought. "I did not invite all these women to my house! I've been trying to find the real heiresses but every demmed female I approach tells me she is worth fifty thousand pounds!" He looked as though he was about to rend his clothes in his fury. "There isn't enough food for all these guests and I've had to send to the kitchens for more. I won't have it said that I keep a poor table. But they'll eat me out of house and home just like those demmed sheep!"

Dexter started to laugh. "Accept it, Monty. You have been outmaneuvered—again."

Sir Montague's eyes bulged. "I'll demand that they unmask! I'll send them home!"

"You can't do that without appearing even more of a fool…" Dexter stopped and started again. "That would appear very ungracious, Monty. Everyone would be talking about you even more than they are now, and not in a good way."

"Damn them!" Sir Montague was almost crying. "All I wanted was their money!"

"And by now it must be clear they do not wish to give it to you," Dexter said. He smiled. "Excuse me, Monty. There is someone I simply must find."

"That would be my Lydia, I imagine!" The fluting tones of Faye Cole were instantly recognizable even though she was concealed in a voluminous purple domino and frighteningly feathered mask that made her look like a predatory peacock. "She is waiting to dance with you, Mr. Anstruther." She tapped him roguishly on the arm with her fan. "A little clue for your ears alone— Lydia is dressed in a rose-pink domino."

"Thank you, your grace," Dexter said gravely, making a mental note to avoid every wearer of rose-pink dominoes in the room.

He plunged into the crowd. Everywhere he looked, gazetted fortune hunters were trying desperately to ascertain the identity of the masked ladies. The ladies in turn seemed very willing to flirt but equally unprepared to reveal themselves. He saw Nat Waterhouse, languid in a black domino, leaning in a doorway talking to a lady who might or might not have been Lady Elizabeth Scarlet. The lady in question had red hair escaping in curls from beneath her hood, but then so did at least three other ladies nearby. She was peeping demurely at Nat from behind her mask in a manner quite opposite to Lady Elizabeth's forthright style. Nat looked totally dazzled and more than a little confused.

A lady in a green domino approached Dexter and brazenly solicited his hand for the set of dances that was forming. He refused her politely. The ballroom was becoming heated now and the atmosphere was changing from the politely conventional to the feverishly flirtatious. There was something about a masquerade that was uninhibited and abandoned. A number of couples were already drifting away to pursue their dalliance in discreet alcoves. Miles was dancing with Alice Lister and although he was maintaining a perfectly proper distance from her there was something in his eyes as he smiled down at her that was not proper at all. Dexter hoped that Miss Lister was aware of Miles's reputation as a rake and could deal with him as he deserved.

Dexter spotted Lydia Cole, who was indeed in a pink domino and was dancing with a man Dexter did not recognize whilst her mother stood glaring on the sidelines. For once Lydia looked blissfully happy. Her eyes were half-closed, there was a dreamy smile on her lips and she was completely ignoring the duchess's disapproval. Faye made flapping motions to summon Dexter but he bowed and moved on with a slight smile. He saw Sir James Wheeler almost literally push his daughter Mary into the arms of Lord Armitage, who carried her off triumphantly into the dance. His opportunities to marry a fortune were narrowing by the minute, Dexter thought wryly. Lord Liverpool would probably wash his hands of him. His mother's creditors would be baying for blood.

Sir Montague Fortune hurried past pursued by two giggling women who looked suspiciously like Cyprians. Not that Sir Monty was complaining. His temper seemed to have improved enormously. And still Dexter searched the shifting crowds and could not see Laura.

Then the mass of people fell back a little and before him was a woman wrapped in a midnight-blue domino. She was standing with her back to him. His heart leaped. She turned slowly. Beneath the hood he glimpsed a lock of dark hair before she tucked it back and out of sight with one gloved hand. Her eyes, shadowed by a sapphire-blue mask, looked deep and mysterious. Laura. It had to be.

"Madam…" Dexter reached her side in a single step.

"Sir?" The lady turned toward him. Her mouth curved into a smile that was sinfully tempting but at the same time promised nothing to the overeager fortune hunter. Behind the mask her cool hazel gaze appraised him.

"Would you care to dance with me?" Dexter reached to take her hand and lead her onto the floor where the first bars of a polonaise were playing.

She slipped away from him, elusive as ever. "Thank you, but I do not dance tonight." Her tone, cool as ice, sent shivers down his spine. She spoke so low he could not recognize Laura's voice for sure, and she kept the hood close about her face.

"Then if you do not dance, what do you do here?" he asked. "Do you have a passion for the card tables?" He threw her a sideways look. "Would you like to challenge me?"

Once again she smiled that faint and mysterious smile. "Not at cards. I would perhaps challenge you in a game of wits. But I do not gamble, sir, and I suspect that neither do you." She tilted her head to look at him thoughtfully. "You do not look like a gambling man to me, nor indeed a man who would do anything to excess."

"Are you suggesting that I have no vices?" Dexter said.

She laughed. "Certainly not. Which of us can claim that? Not you, sir, from the look of you."

"What can you mean?"

"A handsome fortune hunter on the catch for a rich wife?" Her smile was mocking. "For shame! That is vice enough."

Dexter laughed ruefully. "Are you rich?" he inquired. "I am sure you and I would deal well together since it seems I cannot deceive you."

She cast him another quick glance. "I may be an heiress—who can tell amongst this throng? But if I were I would expect a pretty wooing in return for my money."

"But you would think it no more than a pretense and my compliments insincere," Dexter pointed out, "since you have already divined that I seek a fortune."

"That is true," she agreed. "If you flirted with me I would know that all you really desired was to walk down the aisle with my moneybags."

"That would not be *all* I desired." This time Dexter caught her hand and she permitted him to keep it. The touch lit his blood with sparks of fire in much the same way that crossing wits with her did. It was tempting and seductive.

"I would enjoy courting you," he said. "And I would make sure that you enjoyed it, too."

She opened her eyes wider in amusement. "You are very direct," she said, "and dangerous, too. A less experienced lady than I might be tempted into believing you, whereas I know that, having claimed no interest in flirting with me, that is precisely what you are doing now."

Dexter took two glasses of wine from a passing

servant and steered her to an alcove where there was a cushioned love seat in the deep window embrasure. It was lit by one branch of candles high on the wall. She sat at one end of the seat, maintaining a scrupulous distance from him. When he handed the glass to her she raised her brows.

"Do you then number drinking amongst your vices?" she asked. "I would not have thought it."

"I am getting a taste for it," Dexter said. He looked at her. "Have we met before, madam? I have an astonishing sense of recognition about you, as though we had already crossed swords at least once."

A dimple dented her cheek at the corner of her mouth. Dexter watched, fascinated.

"How can I tell if we have already met?" she murmured. "One fortune hunter can be…" She paused. "Disappointingly like another, I find."

Dexter winced at the setdown. "You are harsh, madam. Do you see nothing here tonight to please you?"

Her gaze lingered on him. Beneath the mask her lips curved into a smile. "Oh, there are some things here that please me." She glanced away at the swirling kaleidoscope of colored dancers in the ballroom. "There are a great many men in black dominoes tonight," she observed. "How interesting. Perhaps they see the lighter colors as being too feminine for them."

"Sir Montague is in bright red," Dexter pointed out.

She laughed. "And I think we all understand what he is trying to convey with a scarlet domino!" She shook her head. "I will allow that it is also most amusing to see the fortune hunters trying to work out which ladies are the heiresses and which are not. To see Sir Montague courting a pair of actresses in the hope that they are rich debutantes…" She laughed. "Well, he will probably end up paying them for their favors rather than them bestowing a fortune on him!"

"Yes," Dexter said. "That was clever. A plan of your own contriving?"

"Perhaps." She inclined her head slightly. "The point, sir, is that every gentleman in Fortune's Folly thinks that every lady is fair game. As long as she has money they care little about anything else. Oh—" Her tone was scornful. "No, I mistake. They care if she is pretty, as well. It is not essential if she is rich, but it is desirable. It is as though they are purchasing a horse. Looks, pedigree, value…" She shrugged. "The ladies of Fortune's Folly do not care to be treated like livestock."

"I think that the ladies of Fortune's Folly have made their disapproval abundantly clear," Dexter said.

"Not clear enough to stop that fool Sir Montague." She sighed as Monty Fortune scampered past again with the two actresses chasing him with hunting cries. "Oh dear, I should have guessed that he would actually *enjoy* this. How very provoking!"

"Not everyone hunts a fortune because they are greedy and covetous," Dexter said. "Perhaps you should not judge all gentlemen by Sir Montague's example."

She looked at him, the smile fading from her eyes. "Perhaps I should not. What are your reasons, sir?"

"I am a fortune hunter because my family is poor," Dexter said slowly. It felt very important to tell her the truth of his situation. "I am the eldest of seven brothers and sisters who require to be educated and launched into the world," he said. "I have a widowed mother who does not understand the meaning of the word *retrench*. I had an unreliable, spendthrift father who was the poorest example a man could have to follow." He sighed. "I feel that I have an obligation to provide for and look after my dependents. My employer also demands my marriage as a sign of my trustworthiness. My family's creditors demand it because we are mortgaged to the hilt and in debt to the tune of several thousand pounds." He shrugged self-deprecatingly. "There you have it."

Her gaze scoured his face as though she was testing his honesty. "Then it is a shame that you are so bad at catching a rich wife," she said. The smile was back in her eyes. "I have observed that about you. Some men see it as a challenge and take pleasure in the chase, but you…" She shook her head. "I do not think that you enjoy it. Your heart is not in it."

"I hate it." Dexter spoke with unaccustomed passion and saw the surprise reflected in her eyes. "It offends my honor," he added, "even when I acknowledge the necessity of it."

Their gazes met and he was snared in the candid warmth of her eyes. She was smiling a little and it felt as though she understood exactly how he felt. It felt as though she knew him through and through: the man who sought to do the right thing for the sake of his family even when it was at the expense of his own principles.… His breath caught. For a full five seconds it felt as though he could not inhale.

"Does it offend your honor to offer marriage without love?" she asked.

Dexter shifted. "I would like to offer marriage with at least a mutual respect."

She took a long, thoughtful sip of her wine. "Mutual

respect is a worthy aim," she said, "and it can grow over time." She looked him directly in the eyes and he felt a jolt of emotion that he could not immediately identify. "But without love, marriage is a long cold business. Believe me, I should know."

"And love is a dangerous illusion," Dexter said. He felt as though he needed to assert his belief in rationality over emotion. He felt as though his careful, logical values were somehow slipping away, undermined by the current of undeniable feeling between them.

She laughed. "How like a man to be so cynical!"

"So you believe in love?" Dexter said.

"Of course." There was a wistful expression in her face that made his heart thump. He reached forward to take her gloved hand and felt the little shiver of awareness that shook her.

"Have you ever been in love?" he said.

She looked at him for what felt like a long time, her gaze shadowed and dark. She ran her fingers thoughtfully over the rim of the glass in her hand and he felt the touch like an echo inside.

"Twice," she said. "I have been in love twice in my life. The first time was with my husband, which, I suppose, is as it should be."

Dexter leaned forward. "And the second?"

Again she raised her gaze to his and his heart turned over at the expression in her eyes. He was back in the parlor of the Half Moon Inn when he had accused her of being a hypocritical whore and in that moment she had looked at him without artifice and he had seen the pain and denial in her eyes. Now he saw again all the grief and hurt that was in her and it made the blood slam through his body.

"The second time I fell in love by accident," she said softly. "I had not intended it. I am not even sure how it happened. But it was the worst thing that I could possibly have done because I was not free."

SHE HAD TOLD HIM too much.

As soon as she had spoken, Laura felt her heart contract with fear. Lured on by the intimacy of their situation, seduced by the look in Dexter's eyes, she had forgotten herself and gone right to the edge of indiscretion. She had been tricked—no, she had tricked *herself* into believing for a moment that she could be honest with Dexter when in fact their closeness was a dangerous illusion.

She had not intended it to be like this. When Dexter had first approached her she had recognized him at once and had been incredulous that he had even thought of trying to flirt with her. Then she had remembered that she was an heiress now and his advances had made a horrible kind of sense. Dexter must have heard the rumors of her newly acquired fortune and with the ruthlessness of the true fortune hunter he had switched his attentions from Lydia to her. His courtship of Lydia had been faltering, anyway, and she was the better bet. She was as rich as Lydia now and she had already shown herself hopelessly susceptible to him. It was distasteful but all too plausible. She had felt shocked, disillusioned and angry.

The more she had thought about it the more Dexter's calculated attempt at seduction had infuriated her and she had been determined to play him at his own game to see just how far he would go, just what sort of a heartless philanderer he really was beneath the facade of the honorable man. He had painted himself as a reluctant fortune hunter out to marry money solely for the benefit of those who relied on him, but Laura thought that was probably all part of the plan to gain her sympathy—and her money.

Yet despite being armed against him, somewhere along the way she had forgotten to be wary of him and to guard her tongue. She had trusted him because he seemed sincere. She could not help herself. She loved him and she wanted to believe in him. And so she had allowed him to lead her too close to intimate disclosure. She had gone right to the edge of admitting that Dexter himself was the other man she had loved. If he knew that—and knew that she and Charles had been completely estranged—it was but a small step to questioning Hattie's parentage. She had put her daughter in danger with her indiscretion. She had compromised Hattie's safety because she had spoken too freely. She thought of the hideous scandal that would ensue if even the slightest hint emerged that Hattie was Dexter's child and not Charles's. Her daughter's future would be tarnished irreparably and it would all be her fault.

"Laura?" Dexter must have seen the sudden anxiety in her for he put out a hand to her. "What is wrong?"

"I have to go now," Laura said. Panic fluttered in her chest like trapped butterflies and she sought to control it. She pulled off her mask and dropped it on the seat. She felt shaken and angry with herself as well as with him. She had been a fool to trust him, even for a moment, and to bring herself and Hattie so close to ruin. And he had been a scoundrel setting out to woo her coldly for the money.

"Excuse me," she said. "That was a pretty flirtation, Mr. Anstruther, but I fear it will not succeed. I am aware

that your courtship of my cousin is not proceeding well."
She looked at him. "No doubt *you* are also aware that I
am now an heiress. But to transfer your attentions to me
with such blatancy even though you have so poor an
opinion of me—"

She stopped. The shock in Dexter's face was so abrupt
and so vivid that it could not be assumed. Her heart
seemed to stumble. He had not heard about Henry's
largesse.

He had not known she was an heiress.

Suddenly Laura had the disconcerting feeling that
she had misread the situation completely. She had
thought Dexter had meant to flirt with her, seduce her if
he could and compromise her for the money. But in that
moment she had the conviction that he had had a completely different aim in view all the way through their
conversation. He *had* been sincere in his distaste for
fortune hunting. He had told her the painful truth about
his family and his obligations. She had misjudged him.

Dexter had also taken off his mask now and the anger
in his blue eyes was so strong that it pinned her to the
spot. "I have no idea what you mean, your grace," he said
evenly, "but I am…disappointed…that you would believe
that of me." He shifted, but the intensity of his gaze did
not waver. Laura could feel her heart beating like a drum
in sharp, vibrant snaps. She felt a moment's chill premo-
nition and then he spoke again.

"I have no interest in whatever fortune it appears you
have suddenly gained," he said. "What I actually wanted
from you was to ask what you really felt on that morning
four years ago when you dismissed me from your bed and
your life." He raised his brows. "I think you lied to me at

the time when you said you did not care for me. I think you were in love with me. I think that I was the man you spoke of just now. Now tell me the truth, Laura."

Laura stared at him in silence. Dexter's words had smashed the last vestiges of pretense between them. She could see now exactly what he had planned. The flirtation between them *had* been a seduction but it had been intended to seduce the truth out of her. He had calculated every question in order to draw her out. He had planned the conversation deliberately to get her off her guard, to tempt her into revealing too much. And she had almost done so.

"Laura?"

Unnoticed by the two of them, Alice Lister had approached and now laid a hand on Laura's arm.

"I do apologize for disturbing you," she said, "but Mama and I are ready to leave and we wondered if you wished to take the carriage home with us? Mama swears that Sir Montague's prawn patties have made her feel nauseous whilst I fear that the attentions of so many fortune hunters have had a similar effect on me. I hope," she added, as neither Laura nor Dexter had taken their eyes from one another, "that I have not interrupted you at a terribly delicate moment?"

"Not at all, Alice," Laura said, shaking herself. "I am quite ready to leave." She turned to Dexter and saw the cynical twist to his mouth as he realized she was going to walk out without answering him.

"Good night, Mr. Anstruther," she said. "I do not believe we have anything further to say to one another."

Dexter got to his feet and bowed to them. His blue gaze was still cold. "Good night, your grace. Good night, Miss Lister."

Alice slipped her hand through Laura's arm as they made their way round the edge of the ballroom. "Gracious," she whispered, "Mr. Anstruther can be extremely cold and cutting when he chooses. Whatever did you say to upset him, Laura?"

Laura let her breath out in a long sigh. She had not even been aware that she was holding it. She felt a little shaky.

"There was something that he wanted to know," she said, "but I did not wish to talk about it with him."

Alice looked at her curiously. "It must have been monstrous important."

Laura shook her head. "It was nothing of importance, Alice. Nothing at all."

IN THE SUMMERHOUSE at the bottom of the gardens at Fortune Hall, Lydia Cole was curled within the circle of her lover's arms. She liked to think of him as her lover although they had not made love with one another. Such a thing was, of course, completely forbidden and utterly out of the question, but she loved him and was almost certain he loved her, too, so they were definitely lovers in that true, pure sense of the word. In fact, Lydia loved him enough to want to be alone with him and therefore risk the scandal of discovery and the even worse danger of Faye finding out what she was up to. The thought of what would happen if her mother knew the truth was sufficient to make Lydia shudder, for there was no possible chance of matrimony with this gentleman. Her parents would never approve. Yet somehow his very unsuitability, and the hopelessness of her passion, made Lydia feel all the more ardent.

It was a cold night with a bright, white full moon, but

Lydia did not notice the sting of frost in the air for she was wrapped in her lover's black domino. It was warm and it smelled of him and the scent made her head spin. She leaned back against his chest and felt him nuzzle her hair gently. She liked that. His kisses were gentle and this soft caress was, too. He never frightened her with violent passion.

His tongue searched out the delicate curve of her ear and the shivers ran down to her toes.

"I love you," she whispered.

"I know, sweetheart, I know...." There was a smile in his voice and it made her feel weak to hear it. He must love her to speak so tenderly to her.

"I have a gift for you," he continued. "Close your eyes and put out your hand."

Lydia did as she was bid. She heard the softest chink of metal and then he placed something in her palm.

"Open your eyes."

The clear, hard moonlight shone on the necklace in her hand, turning the links of the fine golden chain to silver. He must have been wearing it about his neck for it was still warm from his body. Lydia touched it gently, reverently. There was a ring on the chain—a thick gold band—and in the moonlight she could see it had some letters inscribed on it but the light was not bright enough for her to read them.

"They are your initials," he said. "An *L* and a *C*." He sounded very pleased with himself.

Lydia gave a little gasp. "But this is too costly a gift! I cannot accept it. And how could you afford—"

"Hush." He put a gentle finger to her lips. "I want you to wear it about your neck. Do not let anyone see it, for it must be our secret for the time being."

"Of course," Lydia said, overwhelmed. "Of course, but—"

He turned her face to his and stopped her protests with a kiss. Lydia gave a little sigh. He must love her very dearly indeed to give her so precious a gift as this ring. She felt secure and cherished and extremely happy, and relaxed against him with a little sigh. The kiss deepened almost imperceptibly and Lydia surrendered to the sweetest, slowest and most gentle of seductions illuminated by the light of the moon.

CHAPTER FIFTEEN

LAURA EASED OPEN THE wicket gate that led into the paddock and, holding her lantern high, picked her way across the field toward The Old Palace. Alice had been extremely concerned at the thought of her walking home alone in the dark and had wanted to send the carriage out again until Laura had pointed out that the journey took ten minutes by road and only two minutes across the fields on foot and she would not dream of causing Alice further inconvenience. Poor Alice had already been most concerned about her mother, for Mrs. Lister had been *in extremis* with the effects of the prawn patties and had descended from the carriage with more speed than grace in her dash for privacy. Laura had wondered whether Sir Montague's cook had been reduced to serving up the fish that had been intended for the stable cats in an effort to feed all the guests at the masquerade that night.

The moonlight was so bright that the lantern was almost superfluous and Laura could see her way with perfect clarity. She had walked these footpaths since she was a child and it was only the memory of the night in the priory ruins that made her grasp the lantern a little more tightly in one hand and her tiny pearl pistol in the other. At the back of her mind were Dexter's words to take no risks and not to put herself in danger, but nothing moved in the still moonlit landscape. No men in black dominoes stalked the priory ruins, except in her imagination.

She crept up the steps to the front door of The Old Palace, found it unlocked and slipped inside. There was no sign of Carrington. The house seemed asleep.

The hall was silent and shadowed. Laura slipped the cloak from her shoulders, took off her evening slippers and started to tiptoe up the stone stair. She felt relieved to be home. She felt safe.

She had gone no more than three steps when the door to the library opened and Dexter came out. He had her mask in his hands. Laura stopped dead. Dexter's gaze swept over her from her stockinged feet to the pearl pistol in her hand.

He smiled faintly although the smile did not reach his eyes, which remained cold. "History repeats itself," he commented. "Would you mind putting that pistol down? You are making me nervous."

"I was taking your advice not to go out unprotected," Laura said breathlessly, stowing the pistol in her reticule. Anxiety crawled through her to find him here. She had hoped against hope that he would not follow her whilst knowing with an absolute conviction that he was not the sort of man who would let the lies between them go unchallenged. She had thought about it all the way back in the carriage and had known that the reckoning would come. She had just not expected it to come so soon.

"That was not quite what I meant," Dexter said dryly. He took a step toward her. "Tell me, are you always this willfully foolish in your disregard for your personal safety?"

"We have had this conversation before," Laura said. "I was perfectly safe and you know I can shoot straight." She raised her brows. "In fact you are fortunate I did not shoot *you* as an intruder."

"I am sure you were tempted," Dexter said, "but I did not break in. Your butler opened the door to me, as is customary for visitors." He motioned toward the library. "Shall we? I want to talk to you and this is not the sort of conversation to have in the hall."

Laura hesitated and Dexter moved slightly, and she saw the look in his eyes and realized he was still angry. Her carelessness over her own safety had made him angrier still. If she did not walk into the library herself he would in all likelihood carry her in bodily. Her heart skipped a beat. She was very aware of his gaze on her as she passed him in the doorway. She glanced up at him and saw that there was a hard, closed expression on his face.

Dexter shut the door behind them, turned the key in the lock and leaned back against the panels.

"I don't think that we finished our discussion earlier," he said pleasantly. "You know what it is that I want from you, Laura. Now tell me the truth." He shifted a little. "You sent me away from Cole Court pretending that you cared nothing for me. You said that the whole matter had been no more than a game to you. You implied you took lovers to your bed all the time. You lied to me through and through."

Laura felt a spurt of temper. "What if I did? You were penniless. You were at the start of your career and you were eight years my junior. I was married—a duchess. I could not elope with you without ruining both our lives. I had to make you leave." She sighed, the anger going out of her as abruptly as it had jetted up. "It was easier that way, Dexter."

Dexter came away from the door in one fluid movement, trapping her into a corner with her back against the bookcases. Laura pressed herself back against the hard edges of the shelves but she could not escape his physical presence. It almost overwhelmed her.

"It was easier to make me hate you," he said harshly.

"If you wish to view it like that, then yes, it was!" Laura glared at him defiantly. "I knew that if you hated me you would leave and never wish to see me again."

"I see." Dexter spoke very softly. "I see it all now."

"I cannot see why it matters, anyway," Laura said. "What happened between us is all in the past. So far in the past that it is quite irrelevant and I do not intend to resurrect it."

Dexter was shaking his head. "I need to know how you felt, Laura," he said. "You owe it to me to tell the truth."

"Why?" Laura burst out. "It would change nothing—"

"It would give me some peace of mind," Dexter said grimly. "Do you know how it is for me, Laura? I have been courting Lydia Cole this month past but I have found I could neither make her an offer, nor could I transfer my attentions to any other female. The reason? It is because all I see is you. All I think about is you. All I want is you."

Laura put up a hand as though to ward off his words. "Don't," she said helplessly. "Don't say that."

"Why not?" Dexter said. "It is true. I have no difficulty in admitting the truth to you. I wanted to marry Lydia for her money—I told you tonight that I am nothing better than a fortune hunter. Yet I find I cannot offer for any woman because I am still haunted by what happened with you. I think about it all the time and until I can lay the past to rest, I know it will always be the same. I know it will always come between me and the future."

"Forget what happened between us," Laura said. Her pulse was slamming in her throat now. "Forget how I felt! It does not matter. All that matters is that both you and I were saved from making a mistake that would have ruined our lives. Find another heiress, Mr. Anstruther, if you cannot court my cousin. Heaven knows there are plenty of them about! Leave the past behind where it belongs."

"I wish that I could," Dexter said. His face was set and dark. "I have tried. Believe me, I have tried for all the reasons I told you about tonight." He shifted the point of his attack. "You said earlier tonight that you had been in love twice," he said softly. "You said it was a mistake because you were not free. I was the man you loved, was I not, Laura?"

The anxiety caught at Laura's breath, smothering her. Everything was unraveling now. The danger to Hattie was acute. She had known she had told Dexter too much when they had talked earlier. And he was not the sort of man who would forget a single word she had said.

Dexter took her chin in his hand and turned her face up to his. His gaze was intent on her, steady and compelling. Laura trembled beneath his touch.

"Laura, look at me," he said. "Were you in love with me?"

The moment spun out and seemed to stretch forever. Could she look Dexter in the eye and lie to him? Her defenses were at breaking point. But if it were to protect Hattie...

"No," she said. "You were not the man I loved."

She saw some expression flicker in his eyes and then he had released her and turned away. She was so relieved that she took a deep, gasping breath and felt her legs tremble so much that she was afraid she would fall. She wanted to embellish the lie, to lead him away from danger, but the words would not come. Lying just once to Dexter had been almost impossible, one of the most difficult things she had ever done, a horrible echo of the words she had spoken to him four years before when she had sent him away.

"I know that isn't true." Dexter's voice was flat. He did not sound surprised. He did not even sound angry with her. He turned back to her and his speculative expression did more to scare Laura than his anger could ever have done.

"You're lying to me," he said. His eyes narrowed thoughtfully. "I don't know why it is so important to you to deny the truth, but there has to be a reason. What are you afraid of, Laura?"

She *was* afraid and she *was* lying and there *was* a reason and if he took one more step closer to the truth Laura knew that everything she had worked to protect would be finished. He moved back toward her, his gaze intent on her face. It felt as though he could see right through her denials and evasions, and it was terrifying. Laura took a step back and felt the backs of her thighs come up against the edge of one of the bookcases. She grabbed the edge of it for support, her fingers gripping the wood until they ached. He was very close to her now. His physical presence filled her senses. She forced herself to look up at him.

"You are imagining things, Mr. Anstruther," she said, as lightly as she could. "Perhaps your vanity cannot accept that I did not love you?" She gave a little shrug. "I am sorry. But you said that all you wished was to be free of the past. Now you are."

There was a pause. She was held captive by the look in his eyes. She licked her dry lips and saw his gaze drop to them, then his gaze came up to hers and it was hot and glittering with something that made her stomach clench.

"You said that was all that mattered to you," she whispered.

"I lied, too," Dexter said.

He raised one hand from the edge of the bookshelf, slid it around the back of her neck and suddenly his mouth was hungry and hard against hers. The last of Laura's composure splintered under the impact of the kiss. Her gasp of shock was lost beneath the pressure of his lips. He forced his hand into her hair and held her head still, his lips mercilessly plundering hers, the kiss utterly devastating in its emotional force. Laura's head spun and the hot tide washed through her body, leaving her shaking. She placed both her hands against his chest and held him a little way away from her.

"That was what I wanted," he said, his breathing as ragged as hers. "It is what I have always wanted."

"We cannot rekindle the past," Laura said. The raw, ruthless passion was racing through her blood threatening to drive all else away. She struggled for control. "Dexter, we cannot do this. Everything is different now—"

"Maybe it is not."

He kissed her again, more gently this time, his tongue dipping and tangling with hers, teasing out a response from her rather than demanding one. The heat of his body seemed to burn her. The scent of his skin was drugging her senses. It was blissful torment. Laura could feel the whole, hard length of him against her, feel the urgency in his touch, and then he had scooped her up in his arms and carried her over to the green velvet chaise, sitting down with her across his thighs. He brushed her hair back with fingers that shook a little and scanned her face.

"Laura… So beautiful… How can I ever cure this wanting?" Dexter's voice was a broken plea, and the heat and excitement surged within her. To be desired was the most intoxicating feeling of all. It filled her with a heady feminine power. Charles had never wanted her; he had called her cold and had shunned her bed. But Dexter's hands on her body and his lips on hers had worshipped every hollow and every curve. Her scruples were lost in the hot and turbulent emotions he was stirring within her. She needed this comfort just as she had done four years before.

Laura put a hand to his cheek and felt the stubble rough against her palm. Dexter made a sound deep in his throat and then he had rolled her over so that her back was against the soft velvet of the chaise longue and her hair had tumbled from its pins to spread over the green cushions. He was leaning over her now and the smoldering fire in his blue eyes took her breath away.

"You may not want to tell me how you felt," he said, "but I will tell you what it was like for me that night at Cole Court." He raised a hand to her shoulder and slid the material of her gown down, following its path with his lips against her skin. "I wanted to make love to you," he said. His voice dropped to a whisper. She could feel his breath against the vulnerable curve of her collarbone. "It was a dream come true for me. From the moment that I first saw you I wanted you in my bed, Laura. I was young and idealistic and you were a goddess to me. I dreamed about you, with the most vivid and passionate and downright erotic dreams of my entire life."

Laura's heart beat violently against the flimsy cotton of her bodice. She could feel the beats echoing through her body and through the chaise on which she lay. She was transfixed by the glitter of heat she could see in his eyes and by the brush of his lips against her neck and over her bare shoulder. The tiny hairs rose on her skin, which felt so unbearably sensitive as it begged for his touch. Her nipples tightened and she squirmed on the chaise, a movement that only served to inflame her further.

"I knew that you were not free," Dexter continued remorselessly. He bent his head to the neckline of her gown, his tongue flicking across the swell of her breasts as they strained against their confinement, dipping into the hollow between them. "It should have mattered to me but it did not. I was not as honorable as I had believed. Not when it came to wanting you." His lips paused above her breast and then he nipped at the swollen peak that was outlined so clearly against the silk of her gown. Laura smothered a gasp and grabbed his shirt in both hands, arching up toward him.

"I fulfilled my wildest fantasies with the duchess in my bed." Dexter's voice had sunk to no more than a murmur. He drew her bodice down to bare her breasts to his lips and tongue. "It was exquisite. You were exquisite, Laura."

He kissed her again and she slid her arms around his neck and drew him closer, feeling the silkiness of his hair between her fingers and the roughness of his cheek against her softness. Beneath the constriction of her clothes her entire body ached to touch his. She wanted no barriers between them. His words had conjured all the memories of their time together in all their sweet, devastating urgency and Laura wanted that time over again, suddenly, desperately; she wanted to lose herself in the past and in the illusion of loving and being loved.

Her urgent fingers delved beneath his shirt, pulling it from his trousers so that she could run her hands over the muscular planes of his back. Her caresses wrenched a groan from him. She felt a shudder go through his entire body. It roused an answering need within her. She had forgotten where she was, had almost forgotten *who* she was, for her feelings were so caught up in the sensations of the moment that she could think of nothing else. The warmth of the room, the flickering of the fire in the grate, the shadows that danced along the wall all served to create an intimate and private place where the two of them were alone and the world could not touch them.

Dexter shifted slightly and Laura felt cool air touch her thighs as her skirts rode up about her hips. The chill feeling was acute, contrasting with the flare of warmth deep within her. Dexter was kneeling between her thighs now and she felt so desperate that the need for him almost choked her. His face was grave in the shadowed room and when he raised his gaze to hers his expression was intent and urgent.

"Laura…" He sounded dazed.

She knew that he was, somewhat belatedly, making an

extreme effort to regain his self-control and suddenly she did not want him stop. She could not bear to be left wanting again, after so many empty years of missing him and longing for his touch. All her natural desires had been repressed for so long. The loneliness yawned within her. If he left now it would devour her. It would be intolerable. It would break her.

She reached up and brought his lips down to hers and felt the resistance in him before he sighed against her mouth.

"I want you," she whispered. "Don't leave me. Please don't leave me now."

She reached for the fastening to his trousers, not wanting to give him time to think in case he denied her. She fumbled the buttons because her fingers were shaking so much and heard him laugh ruefully.

"Wait." His fingers brushed hers, putting her hands gently aside. Laura sank back against the cushions, closing her eyes, trying to draw him down with her, but he resisted. For a moment she was terrified that he was going to get up and simply walk away, but then she felt him flip her petticoats up to the top of her thighs and she gave a gasp. His hand stroked across the soft skin of her bare abdomen, a gentle caress that sent the tremors rippling deep within her body.

She made a little needful noise deep in her throat. Her skin felt hotter and hotter as he traced a line from her belly to her thigh. He cupped her sex in his hand and she moaned, her whole body shivering uncontrollably as he parted her and teased and explored her. Her breath was coming in shallow little gasps. She ached and shook. But this was not what she wanted. Not this time.

"No!" She grabbed his arm. "This time I want you inside me."

She felt him pause. "Laura…" His voice was so rough she barely recognized it.

"Please." It was the only way she could feel complete. She needed to banish the darkness. "I need you."

She looked at him. His body was so taut with the effort of control that she thought he shuddered with it. His eyes were dark with concentrated desire. She put out a hand to him and saw his self-control splinter.

He was shaking as much as she was as he lowered himself between her thighs and she felt the tip of his erection slide within her. Pleasure drenched her and she reached out to him, kissing him with a desperate hunger, her hands sliding over his back and down to his buttocks to draw him into her. He pushed a little deeper and she was afraid she would come apart with the bliss of it. His hands slid beneath her, tangling in her skirts, raising her up so that he could plunge in deeper, and a sweet agonizing sensation swept through as he drove into her, pushing her close to the brink.

He had seen how close she was. He withdrew a little. His lips brushed her brows before dipping to hers in a kiss that was gentle but hot.

"Wait…"

"I can't!" Laura gave an anguished cry and twisted beneath him.

"Tell me that you loved me when we made love before." His voice was a dark seduction. His lips hovered over the tender skin at the curve of her neck. "I know I was the man you loved. *Admit it.*"

"Ah!" The cry was wrenched from Laura in utter

despair. Ecstasy shimmered tantalizingly close but just out of her reach. She tried to pull his head down so that she could kiss the question away from his lips and banish the thought from his mind, but he held back, bending his head instead to taste the hollow at the base of her throat. The flick of his tongue sent another spike of lust through her. She shuddered on the brink.

"Tell me."

His voice was so quiet, so insistent, so undeniable…

Her feelings for him were too strong now, too exposed, too raw to be denied.

He moved inside her, barely a movement at all, but enough to torment her past bearing.

"No…" She found a flicker of rebellion. "I *won't* tell you—"

But I will always love you…

"Ah…" She heard the anger and the amusement conflicting in his voice. "My Laura, so stubborn…"

My Laura…

His mouth brushed her throat in the gentlest of caresses, then moved to her breast and she felt the echo of that touch deep in her belly. Her body took one shaking step closer to fulfillment. She moaned for more. He held back. She writhed, seeking his body and the completion it could give her.

"Damn you…" She almost hated him for withholding that pleasure from her.

He thrust into her hard, fast, again and again, taking her cries of relief into his mouth in another long, deep kiss. Laura's head spun. The pleasure built irresistibly, shimmered so close.

Dexter stilled again. He held her still with his weight

on her and Laura's body twitched and jumped to feel him still inside her, hot and hard, filling her. She hung on the edge of ecstasy.

"Are you trying to punish me?" she demanded, wriggling desperately to try to achieve surcease, "Because if so, you are succeeding…"

"Perhaps…" She heard the smile in Dexter's voice and her indignant fury mingled with frustrated desire and she groaned aloud.

Dexter moved at last, but only to slide deeper inside her. He raised her up to meet his thrusts. His mouth on hers held her silent. The shock shattered within her. Harder, deeper, relentless… She felt Dexter's mouth curve into a smile against the slick skin of her breast as he licked and tugged at her nipple. Her body shuddered helplessly, screaming for fulfillment, rocking to meet Dexter's thrusts and Laura forgot everything as the world finally spun and smashed about her. Dexter's mouth was on hers again, taking her cries even as he took her body. He did not stop, but plunged into her again and again and Laura's whole body jolted against the rough velvet of the chaise, and she felt his back arch and his muscles lock with tension and he came in violent spasms, his climax pushing her over the edge again to drown in exquisite sensation.

For several long, heavy heartbeats they lay together, and then Dexter shifted a little and tucked her protectively into the curve of his shoulder. Laura had no idea of how much or how little time had passed. She felt sweaty and sticky. She wanted to let go of everything and simply sleep, but she knew that soon she would have to move.

Soon she would have to think.

She had no idea where to begin.

"How can I ever cure this wanting?" Dexter had said, and she understood that for him their lovemaking had been an attempt to exorcise the ghosts of the past and to banish the power she had over him.

But for her it had been an expression of love.

She turned her head and looked at Dexter and he smiled at her. His lips brushed her hair and she felt another huge and helpless wave of love overwhelm her even as she was afraid of what he might say to her. How could she ever deny her feelings for this man?

"Laura—" he began.

"We can't talk now," Laura said. She felt panicky and scrambled up, out of his arms. Her hands shook as she haphazardly rearranged her disordered clothing. She did not want to hear him apologize or diminish all the feelings and emotions that were so jumbled inside her. She was not the sort of woman who could indulge in mindless lovemaking and deal with the aftermath with sophisticated aplomb. Nor could she deal with the practical details, either. She had a sudden horrified vision of Carrington waiting patiently outside the library door for them to emerge before he locked the house up for the night.

"Perhaps it would be better if you left via the window," she said. "The servants—"

"I am not climbing out of the window like a thief and skulking off through the shrubbery," Dexter said. His voice was so angry that Laura jumped. "I arrived by the front door and I will leave the same way."

He stood up. He seemed completely unselfconscious of his nudity. In the firelight his body was bronzed and firm. Laura gulped, forgetting what she had been about to say. He reached negligently to draw on his trousers and slip his shirt over his head. Laura, distracted, groped for words.

"All I thought was that if you leave now we could pretend that nothing had happened...."

"An outstandingly bad idea." Dexter's mouth had set in hard lines. He came up to her and gently fastened the buttons that were slipping through her shaking fingers.

"Laura, you must see that it would not serve," he said, in a softer tone. "You are not thinking straight."

"I cannot think straight around you," Laura said.

"Neither can I with you," Dexter admitted, "which is why we are in this situation in the first place."

"Your neck cloth is ruined," Laura said hopelessly, fidgeting with its folds. "I do not know how to tie it and you look..." She stopped, for he looked dangerously virile and masculine and totally as though he had been making mad passionate love to her, and she knew it was impossible to pretend otherwise.

"Oh dear," she said inadequately.

There was a sharp knock at the library door. Laura jumped violently. The handle turned but fortunately the door remained closed.

"Don't open it!" Laura gasped. "If you are not going to escape out of the window then I think I will."

Dexter ignored her, strolled nonchalantly over to the door and turned the key. For a moment hysterical laughter bubbled in Laura's throat at the thought that she, the gracious, the utterly proper Dowager Duchess of Cole was about to be caught *in flagrante* with her lover and that matters were spiraling with dramatic and spectacular style right out of her control. Then the library door opened and

Carrington stood in the aperture. Not a muscle flickered in his face as he looked them over.

"Lord Vickery and Miss Lister are here, your grace," he said.

"Ask them to wait—" Laura began, but it was too late.

"Lal!" Miles hurried into the room. "I was worried about you. I called at Spring House and Miss Lister said that you had walked home so I thought I should make sure you were quite safe—"

"And I insisted on coming, too," Alice put in, "because it was my fault that you did not have the carriage."

Miles shot her an exasperated look. "Even though," he said, "I assured Miss Lister that it was quite unnecessary and she should stay at home and nurse her mother—"

He stopped. And looked from Laura to Dexter and back again. There was a long, long silence whilst both he and Alice took in the scene before them.

In that moment Laura could see through her cousin's eyes, see her rumpled gown and disheveled hair, see Dexter's state of undress that was more telling than any words could be. And then Miles had crossed the room and before Dexter could defend himself, had struck him a clean and scientific uppercut to the jaw. Alice gave a little squeak of alarm.

"Miles! What on *earth* are you doing?" Laura grabbed her cousin's arm and dragged him away. Dexter had put one hand up to his jaw and was wincing as he touched it, but he made no attempt either to defend himself or to retaliate and Laura understood why. In Miles's eyes he was utterly and completely in the wrong. He would bear the blame for this even though she was the one who had begged him to stay with her and make love to her.

"I am defending your honor since you seem so careless of it, Laura," Miles bit out. He turned on her. "What the *hell* has been going on here? No, on second thoughts, do not answer that. It is patently obvious from the look of you what has happened."

"That is none of your business!" Laura snapped. "I would ask you to leave, Miles, and please take Miss Lister with you." She turned to Alice. "Alice, I am so sorry. This is no place for you."

"Well at least you have some sense of decency left," Miles said. "Miss Lister, I insist that you wait for me in the hall."

"I shall not!" Alice said, raising her chin. "Laura is my friend and it seems to me she may need my help."

Miles shook his head in disbelief. "The only time in my life that I try to protect innocence," he said bitterly, "and I am overruled." He turned back to Laura. "I suppose that you frequently entertain your lovers in the library, cousin?"

"Of course I do not," Laura retorted, firing up. "Do you think I would have made such a mess of things if I made a habit of this? Oh no, if I was *practiced* at this I would have dealt with it all with far more aplomb!"

Out of the corner of her eye she saw Dexter smother a rueful smile. Suddenly she was anxious to finish matters before he could intervene and make them worse.

"Dexter and I—" she began.

"So it is *Dexter* to you now, is it?" Miles said. His tone was murderous. "You do not surprise me."

"Lord Vickery," Alice interposed, "it might be better if you did not keep interrupting—"

Miles shot her another exasperated look. "Thank you, Miss Lister," he said. "You know you will have to marry

Anstruther now that you have been discovered alone in this intimate situation," he added, turning back to Laura. He glanced at Dexter and the anger and dislike flared in his eyes. "I knew that you wanted to marry a fortune, Anstruther," he said coldly, "but I never thought you would sink as low as this! To deliberately compromise Laura on the very day it was announced she was endowed with a fortune—"

Laura felt a pang of shock. In the heated exchange with Dexter earlier she had completely forgotten about the money.

"I am refusing Henry's money, anyway," she said, "so it makes no odds."

Dexter was looking at her, a sudden frown on his brow. "I fear you have lost me," he said. "I had not heard about your fortune earlier when you mentioned it and I do not quite understand—"

"Oh, don't pretend that you did not know," Miles interrupted contemptuously. "It was the *on dit* tonight at Fortune Hall! Everyone was talking about it!" He shook his head. "I never would have thought it of you, Anstruther. I knew that there was something going on between you and my cousin but I thought you had *some* honor. But to set out to compromise a dowager duchess who is practically old enough to be your mother—"

Both Laura and Alice gave a gasp of outraged protest and at the same time Dexter took a step forward so that he was face-to-face with Miles. His mouth was set hard and tight. A muscle flickered in his cheek.

"Do not," he said quietly, "speak of your cousin with such disrespect, Vickery, or I shall be obliged to call you out."

There was something so cold and firm in his tone that after a moment Miles took a step back.

"I beg your pardon," he said to Laura. "That was wrong of me." He turned back to Dexter. "Whether you knew of the money or not, you disappoint me, Anstruther. I did not think you the unprincipled sort of cad who would court a rich debutante and at the same time deliberately seduce a widow for entertainment—"

"He did no such thing," Laura said hotly. She had heard enough. She was terribly afraid that Miles would insist that she was compromised into marriage. She could overrule him, of course—he could not *order* her to marry—but the whole matter was already getting out of hand. She had lost Miles's good opinion and she had very probably ruined the friendship between Miles and Dexter irreparably, as well.

"I shall appreciate it if you do not make a fuss about nothing, Miles," she said quietly, "or put a bullet through Mr. Anstruther, thereby creating a scandal where none exists!"

Miles's skeptically raised eyebrows were all the reply he gave to this. Laura started to speak again, but Dexter put her firmly to one side.

"I appreciate you speaking up for me, your grace," he said carefully, "but I must take full responsibility for this."

"Damn right you must!" Miles said pugnaciously, squaring up to him again.

"No, you must not!" Laura said, inserting herself between the two of them. "I am amply capable of taking responsibility for myself. Besides, nothing of import happened."

Dexter gave her a look that brought the hot color racing

into her cheeks in a scalding tide. "Dear me," he said in an undertone that only she could hear, "that is the second time you have said as much. I must be losing my touch."

Miles looked at her in polite disbelief. "I found you alone in a room, half-undressed, with a man who was once an accredited rake and—forgive my bluntness—you look ravished, Laura. Do you still wish to persist in this fiction that nothing happened?"

"This is madness," Laura retorted. "Mr. Anstruther, I must ask you to go—"

"Certainly not," Dexter said, his blue eyes alight with devilish challenge. "And before you seize on any of your cousin's ludicrous comments as ammunition against me, allow me to tell you that I have *never* considered you old enough to be my mother. The idea is both absurd and mathematically impossible."

"You are not helping, Mr. Anstruther," Laura said through gritted teeth. She could feel the situation slipping well beyond her control now. "I cannot imagine that you could possibly wish to prolong this unfortunate circumstance any further, so I suggest that you simply keep quiet!"

"I beg your pardon," Dexter said. "I was merely pointing out that there is no sense in trying to suggest that you are in your dotage, for you are not."

"Thank you," Laura said starchily. "I am, however, eight years older than you, Mr. Anstruther, and I have every intention of turning down the money my relatives wish to settle on me. Those are both good reasons for ending any association that there might be between us. So I suggest we bring this farce to an end and that you return to courting your youthful heiresses—"

She stopped. There was a smile in Dexter's eyes and Laura felt her stomach drop and her heart turn over to see it.

"Not before we have discussed this properly," he said.

Laura made an exasperated gesture as though to brush away his remarks. "There is nothing more to discuss. We have discussed quite enough tonight. The material point," she added, looking at Miles and Alice, "is that since no one other than the four of us know that you and I have been here together, Mr. Anstruther, there is not the least necessity for this to go any further."

Dexter moved closer to her. "I beg to differ," he said. "I will call on you tomorrow to make you an offer."

Laura's eyes flashed. "And I shall not be at home."

She saw the expression leap to Dexter's eyes and turned quickly to Miles before he had time to speak. "And I thank you for your concern, Miles, but it is unnecessary. I am well able to take care of myself."

"I shall still call on you tomorrow," Dexter said.

"Mr. Anstruther!" Laura said warningly.

"Must you be so stubborn, Laura?" Miles interposed. He gave Dexter a dark look. "Dexter is, I suppose, trying to do the right thing."

"Oh, mind your own business, Miles!" Laura snapped, abandoning her dignity. Suddenly she felt bone tired. Hers was the responsibility for what had happened and the consequence of that dazzling, overwhelming, absolutely blissful moment of passion with Dexter was that he was now obliged to offer her marriage solely because they had been caught. Those were society's rules and not even a dowager duchess was above them. Especially not a dowager duchess inconveniently hampered with a cousin who was determined to defend her honor when she did not want him to.

She looked from Miles's implacable face to Dexter's unreadable one and wondered what would happen if she baldly announced that she was very happy to take Dexter as a lover but that she did not wish to remarry. That would serve Miles right for his interfering. Mind you, poor Alice had probably experienced enough shocks for one night.

Laura was aware that Dexter had not taken his gaze from her for a single moment and now he took her hand and she felt the tiniest tremor of emotion go through her. She knew he had felt it, too, that quiver along her nerves that told him she was nowhere near as composed as she wanted to be. He allowed his thumb to rub gently, almost absentmindedly, over her skin and she tried not to shiver.

"Meet me on Fortune Hill tomorrow at eleven," he said. His concentration was on her alone, cutting Miles and Alice out as though they simply were not there.

"I shall not," Laura said. Her voice was not quite as steady as she wanted it to be.

She saw the expression flare in his eyes. "Yes, you will," he said. He raised her hand to his lips and the touch of them on her skin awoke every sensation she had tried to repress. "You will be there or I will come looking for you. Good night, your grace."

ALICE LISTER, walking back across the paddock toward Spring House, was disconcerted to catch a glimpse of Miles Vickery following her in the moonlight. She had bidden him an abrupt farewell in the hall at The Old Palace and had insisted she did not require his escort home. Indeed she was, at this belated juncture, regretting the impulse that had made her accompany him to see Laura in the first place. She had stumbled into a scandal that had shocked and disturbed her. She felt anxious and stirred up. It would have been so much more sensible to stay at home and tend to her mama, even though Mrs. Lister was now safely tucked up in bed and probably fast asleep.

Alice glanced back over her shoulder once more. Although Miles was not hurrying, his long stride seemed to eat up the distance between them. Seeing this, a strange twist of panic seemed to unravel in Alice's chest and instead of slowing down and waiting for him like any sensible lady would, she chose instead to hasten her pace and positively ran around the corner wall of the orchard and through the gate into the tunnel of trees beyond. There she stopped, panting a little for breath, and chiding herself on the foolish impulse that had taken hold of her. Miles probably wanted nothing more than to make sure that she arrived home safely. There had been no need to make a fool of herself by running away from him. She was a young woman of two and twenty, not a silly miss who could not deal with a handsome gentleman even if he was a rake.

And yet Miles Vickery was so *very* handsome and there was something about that lazy look in his dark hazel eyes that absolutely scorched her with its heat. She knew that he admired her because he had made it plain from the moment they had first met. And she… Well, she liked him, too, much more than she ought to like a philandering fortune hunter. She was feeling hot now just thinking about him, and this was a frosty autumn night with the leaves blowing from the apple trees and scattering about her feet.

She rested one hand on the gate then tried to snatch it away as Miles came abruptly around the corner of the wall and placed his hand over hers to stop her moving away from him.

"Miss Lister," Miles said, holding on as Alice vainly tried to release herself, "may we speak?"

"I... Yes, of course." Alice gave up the unequal struggle to free herself and waited as he let himself through the gate and joined her under the trees.

"I wanted to make sure that you were safe," Miles said slowly.

Alice opened her eyes wide. No one had ever cared as to whether she was safe or not in all her two and twenty years and it was seductive to think that Miles might genuinely mean it. She was so charmed that she almost believed him.

"Did you?" she croaked. "I assure you that it is perfectly safe to walk home alone in Fortune's Folly."

Miles smiled. It deepened the lines about his eyes and Alice felt the warmth curl in her stomach again. She blinked and told herself not to be a henwit. She knew his real intention and that his professions of concern were only a ruse.

"Perhaps," she said, "you were also anxious to ensure that I would not repeat anything I heard tonight concerning your cousin?"

Miles did not deny it. She could feel his gaze on her face like a touch and her skin warmed beneath it.

"I assure you," she said steadfastly, "that I will tell no one. Laura is my friend and I respect her."

"But you must have been shocked to know that she and Mr. Anstruther were lovers," Miles said.

Alice hesitated. It was true that she had been both shocked and strangely intrigued by the frankness of the discussion between Laura and Miles and Dexter. She knew of course that Laura had been married and was no doubt vastly more experienced than she was herself, but Alice had seldom felt so naive, or so disturbed. That was when her imagination had started to somersault and present her with a rather fascinating and wayward set of images involving herself and Miles Vickery, of all people… Which, she thought a little wildly, was no doubt why she had run away in the first place when she had seen Miles following her. She made a concerted effort to exercise some common sense and banish all these wayward thoughts.

"You may have heard that I was once a servant girl, Lord Vickery," she said. "It takes a great deal to shock me. I have seen and heard things that might even shock *you*."

"Which makes it all the more surprising," Miles said, "that you have retained such an air of innocence."

"I do not believe that you would recognize innocence if you tumbled over it," Alice retorted with spirit. "I know for a fact that you are a most accomplished rake."

Miles laughed. "I recognize innocence in you," he said, "and I want it. I want to teach you all manner of things, Miss Lister."

He put a hand up and raised her chin so that she was forced to meet his gaze. His fingers felt cold against her cheek. Alice's eyelashes fluttered. She wondered if he could read in her eyes all the wanton excitement that was making her pulse race. And evidently he could, for he gave a low-voiced exclamation and the expression in his own eyes darkened and he lowered his mouth to hers. Alice gave a stifled squeak. She had never been kissed and suddenly realized that she did not know what to do or how to go about it. Miles's lips were cool and firm against her own, the kiss gentle and yet terrifying for its irresistible undertone of wicked danger. Alice understood instinctively that here was a man who knew exactly what he was doing, a ruthless rake who was treating her gently not because he was kind but because he was calculating the best way to seduce her.

Miles gently parted her lips and she felt his tongue touch the corner of her mouth with the most featherlight and temptingly soft touch. She opened her lips beneath his after only the slightest hesitation, and kissed him back. She thought that she should perhaps push him away but she was honest enough to admit to herself that she did not want to. It was very pleasant to be kissed in the moonlight by a man who was an absolute expert. Or perhaps pleasant did not quite cover the situation. It was utterly delightful.

When Miles finally let her go she felt shaken and weak at the knees. She glanced up at him and thought she saw a look of blank shock in his eyes. It was only there for a fleeting moment and then his expression became completely impassive. She had no idea what he was thinking. Perhaps she had done it all wrong. Perhaps she was hopeless at kissing. She could not tell. What she *did* know was that she should never have got herself into this situation in the first place. One of the lessons she *had* learned as a servant girl was to avoid dangerous rakes.

"Are you all right, Miss Lister?" Miles asked, and once again Alice felt that insidious tug of attraction that undermined all her defenses.

He truly cares…

"I am quite well," she said, although that was not really an accurate reflection of her feelings. "If that is your idea of seeing me safely home," she added, "I think that I should finish the journey alone."

Miles's grim expression lifted slightly and he almost smiled.

"Perhaps you should," he said.

Alice walked away from him, controlling the instinct that made her want to turn to look back. Even though she could not see him she was aware that he stood watching until she reached the garden door and the thought that he was indeed taking care of her almost melted her guarded heart.

You are a fool, Alice Lister, she told herself, for she knew Miles Vickery's very skill lay in persuading her that it was her person and not her money he was interested in. Yet she was afraid that for all her stern common sense, she was falling in love with him.

CHAPTER SIXTEEN

DEXTER STOOD under the pump in the courtyard of the Morris Clown Inn and shivered as the cold water cascaded over his head and down his body, soaking his shirt and chilling him to the bone. It was so cold that it hurt, and the autumn wind that was blowing down from the fells made him shiver all the more. But he had wanted this. He needed the clarity of mind that this coldness brought with it.

The previous night he had told Laura he would make her an offer of marriage. Triumphant in his possession of her, full of raw masculine satisfaction that she had loved him, whether she had denied it or not, and exultant that she was wholly his, he had been determined to claim her publicly as his own. He wanted her and he was going to have her. He was certainly not going to climb out the window like a thief and scuttle off to leave her to face the consequences. Since he seemed unable to control his passion for her he would tame it within marriage. It was a sensible solution.

One sleepless night later, the demons of poverty and fear were on his back again, flaying him alive for his wanton lack of self-control. If he could not persuade Laura to keep the money Henry Cole wished to settle on her then he would be throwing away the chance of making an advantageous marriage. He would be letting down his family. And all because those wayward urges that had ruined his parents' lives were now threatening to play havoc with his own.

He thought back to the previous night and the moment in their lovemaking when Laura had begged him not to stop, not to leave her. From the moment he had first kissed her he had been so shaken by the blaze of their passion that it had taken every last ounce of his strength to restrain his desire for her. Nevertheless, he knew in his heart that he could still have ended it before it was too late, even though it would almost have killed him to cease at that particular point. He remembered clearly that although his mind had been clouded with pleasure and his body had clamored for satisfaction there had a been a moment—two moments, in fact—when he had stopped to think about what he was doing. He had to acknowledge that and to take responsibility. But he had been reckless. He had made the deliberate choice to continue because he had not wanted to stop. Making love to Laura had been as exquisitely pleasurable as he had remembered it. There had been the same sense of completion, of rightness, that he always felt when he was with her. He had thought that he had wanted to break the hold she had over him, but what he had really wanted was to take her and bind her to him forever and claim her as his alone. Each time he made love to her was more intense than the last. He could not make his craving for her cease and to think that he could was futile.

He disliked feeling like this. It was irrational and unhelpful. It reinforced for him how traitorous and untrustworthy physical passion could be. The feelings unleashed in him the previous night had been dangerously close to what he had felt four years before when he had loved Laura with such abandonment. It was easy to see how an impressionable young man might mistake lust for love. Dexter never again wanted to lose his control and his self-respect, lose his *way*, as he had done in his youthful madness. It was too close to the reckless excesses of his parents.

He shuddered under the stream of cold water. In truth it was too late. He had already lost his way. He had failed to exercise sufficient restraint. He had made love to Laura and they had been caught. She might argue that she was no schoolroom miss to lose her reputation, but the truth was that a man of honor—a status that he was hanging on to by the skin of his teeth—was obliged to make her an offer of marriage. If he did not he would be a cad of the first order and, on a more terminal note, her cousin would call him out and try to kill him.

Marrying Laura had clear benefits. He not only wanted her in his bed, but in some way he did not quite understand he knew that he also needed her warmth and openness in his life. He knew that in his determination to be responsible he could also be too serious. Laura teased him out of that, though there was a danger that such frivolity could go too far. In his heart of hearts he was not sure that he wanted to live without the sense of completeness she brought to him. To lose her would feel as though a part of him was missing. It would feel as though he had carelessly thrown away something that made him whole.

But such thoughts were not helpful. He shook his head angrily. To think like this was impractical. He had to admit that to marry Laura ran contrary to all his plans. She was not the heiress he had intended to wed. Although she was now a lot wealthier than he had realized, he knew that she planned to refuse the money the new duke insisted on settling on her and knowing Laura, she would do precisely that. She certainly could not offer him a calm and undemanding life. She was no biddable wife. If he made her an offer of marriage he would be throwing his future into the very turmoil he had sworn always to avoid. It would be reckless and dangerous. Downright irresponsible. He would be letting down those who relied on him to secure a fortune. He did not want to take that risk.

He stepped out from under the pump.

"A word with you, Anstruther."

Dexter rubbed the water from his eyes and opened them to see Miles Vickery holding a towel out to him. It was not exactly a conciliatory gesture; Miles looked as though he would rather punch him. His face was tense, his hazel eyes, so like Laura's own, were hard. Looking at him, Dexter wondered suddenly whether he had permanently forfeited the good opinion of one of his oldest friends through his behavior the previous night. If he had, he could hardly blame Miles for it. If someone had seduced Annabelle or Caro he would kill him.

He took the towel and rubbed hard at his hair. "I know you want to hit me again, or worse," he said, when Miles did not speak for a moment. "I would feel the same in your position. What I did was indefensible."

Miles's tight expression eased a notch. "I can scarcely blame a man for acting the rake when I do so myself," he admitted, "but even so…"

"But even so you would not have acted the rake with my cousin."

This time Miles almost smiled. "No," he said. "I hope I would not, although…" He shrugged. "Well, actually, I probably would have done. But I thought you were the better man."

"And now you know I am not," Dexter said.

Miles squared his shoulders. "Do you really mean to make Laura an offer, Anstruther?"

Dexter stopped. "It would be the honorable thing to do," he said slowly.

"For God's sake do not propose out of chivalry," Miles said. "If this is just a casual affair for you then I would ask you to do the decent thing and end it. I will never speak of what happened nor, I am sure, would Miss Lister. Laura's reputation would be safe."

Then, as Dexter looked at him in astonishment, he said with difficulty, "Laura deserves better than this, Anstruther. She has already been trapped in one unhappy marriage. She deserves someone who truly loves her, utterly, completely and forever. So finish this. Then you can marry Miss Cole for her money as you originally desired, or you can find another heiress, and Laura can find someone who will genuinely love her." A rueful smile touched Miles's mouth. "I doubt Laura would accept you, anyway. You heard what she said last night. She has no more wish to be compromised into marriage than you really have to offer it."

He walked off leaving Dexter wondering if it were possible to feel any more dishonorable than he already did. Miles had put the situation in stark terms. He was suggesting that Dexter abandon Laura now in order to resume his carefully planned strategy of marrying Lydia for her money. Dexter's integrity revolted at what that would make him. Did the phrase *callous, fortune-hunting philanderer* cover the situation or was that too generous? And yet if he was to achieve his original intention of a convenient marriage, that was exactly what he had to do.

Finish this. She deserves someone who truly loves her...

Dexter did not believe in a love like that anymore. He did not want to. Love like that had to be dangerous, leading a man into all kinds of ill-considered actions. To love someone utterly, completely and forever, as Miles had said, would be extraordinary. He had never seen an all-consuming love like that, certainly not on the part of his parents, whose loves had been as undiscriminating as they had been frequent. He was not even sure that such a love could exist. But even if true love did exist, Dexter was not sure it was worth the risk. It was certainly not the way he felt for Laura. He wanted her with a passion, but that was surely a matter of physical possession only.

On that basis he should perhaps do as Miles suggested and step aside so that Laura could find love with another man. As soon as the thought formed in his mind—and it was an entirely rational thought based on a logical sequence of ideas—he realized that he did not like it. In point of fact he had a large problem with it. Specifically he had a problem with any other man marrying Laura, or making love to Laura, or even being within a radius of six feet of Laura. She was his. He wanted her. He needed her. And he certainly was not going to let any other man have her.

The primitive fury of his possessiveness shocked him

even as he recognized that it was part and parcel of all those other turbulent emotions that Laura aroused in him. He thought again of his parents, led astray time and again by the type of uncontrollable lust that he felt for Laura now. It was not a sound basis for marriage. They had proved that with their infidelities and their affairs. He did not want to risk going down the same road. Yet he was already halfway down it. And if Laura had conceived his child in that mad, reckless moment last night then he had repeated all his parents' mistakes. The thought brought him out in a hot sweat even as the last drops of the cold pump water still trickled down between his shoulder blades. No child of his would suffer the slights that he and his siblings had throughout their life. He would not permit a child of his to be in ignorance of their true parentage nor to have any doubt cast on their good name.

He went inside to find a clean set of clothes and prepare to set out to meet Laura, all the time mulling over the terrifying contrast in the paths now before him. He could sacrifice his honor by telling Laura that whatever was between them was at an end and then make his bloodless, passionless marriage to Lydia or another heiress. Then he would run the risk of being twice the scoundrel he already was if Laura gave birth to his child out of wedlock. Alternatively he could sacrifice all his plans for security and fortune and offer for Laura. He would have her and all the wild passion that was between them but he would have no money and no security, he would not have the steady life he craved, and if the desire between them died he would be left with nothing at all. He had to make a choice and he had very little time in which to decide now.

He rode out of the village past the huge bonfire that the children were busy constructing for the celebration of Guy Fawkes Night in the field by the river. The track to Fortune Hill wound upward between walls of gray stone. Pastureland gave way to bracken and heather, turning bronze and gold in the autumn sun, and he rode higher until the whole of the village and the river and valley beyond were spread out before him. The wind was keen in his face.

He saw Laura as his horse breasted the rise at the top of Fortune Hill. He had expected her to be on horseback and maybe even to have brought a groom not so much for propriety's sake but as a defensive gesture. However, she was alone. She had tied up her horse, a beautiful highly bred chestnut with a white flash that he recognized, ruefully, from his one encounter with the Glory Girls, and was seated on a pile of stones from the tumbledown wall. She was staring pensively across the valley to the far fells. She was wearing a riding jacket in deep rust red that matched the fallen autumn leaves.

She looked up as he reined in beside her and dismounted, and their eyes met.

For a long moment they stared at one another. There was something different about her, Dexter thought, an element of vulnerability in her face that he had not seen before. Her eyes looked tired, as though she had not slept. His heart stumbled to see it. Laura so seldom let her defenses down. All the impossible choices he had to make rose up to torment him and without intending to he took her in his arms and drew her close to him. She fitted perfectly against his body and he instantly felt comforted. It felt less like unbridled lust and more like something deeper and much more tender. She instinctively raised her face to his and he kissed her gently, and tumbled straight into the profound depths of his desire for her, made all the hotter by his memories of their night together.

It was several minutes later that he realized she was wearing riding breeches rather than a habit and that beneath them she appeared to be naked. He was so shocked his hand fell away even as his body reacted to the knowledge and he became even more rock-hard than before. This felt more like rampant lust.

"It is easier to ride astride," Laura said, answering his silent question, "and with breeches a lady cannot wear underwear."

Riding breeches. No underwear. Dear God.

He was not sure what showed on his face—the same uncontrollable hunger he felt inside, probably, because she took a step back from him. "I did not expect you to discover it," she said. "I thought we were going to talk." She shook her head slightly. "I suppose I might have realized, given that we do not seem to be able to resist one another. Have I shocked you, Dexter?"

"That hardly describes my feelings," Dexter said.

She met his gaze very directly. "I suppose not. Not after last night. And yet we must talk. We do not appear to have a problem relating to one another physically, do we? It is in other respects that the problems lie."

That went straight to the heart of the matter and he admired her for her honesty even as his body groaned with frustration to be denied. To take her here, now, on the windswept hillside, with the autumn leaves as a bed and the wide sky above them would fulfill his wildest fantasies. But that was exactly where his dilemma lay. To succumb to those feelings again and give himself up to their passionate affair would be irresponsible, reckless and dishonorable. It was marriage—or nothing. It had to be or he would have surrendered the last shreds of his honor.

"I did not come here today to resume our affair where we left off last night," Laura said, echoing his thoughts as she walked a little away from him. "I have been awake all night trying to decide on the best thing to do and I have come to make it clear that what is between us must end, Dexter. I hope you will feel the same and agree with me. You need not for one moment feel obliged to offer for me because of what happened. You are a free man."

Dexter waited for the feelings of relief to swamp him, as surely they must. Laura was refusing to contemplate a proposal from him. She was setting him free.

He waited. Nothing happened. He did not feel relieved. No calm reassurance washed through his veins. He looked at her with the wind in her hair and the pink color staining her cheeks and the jacket and breeches hugging her slender form and the hot, masculine possession gripped him like a vise.

"Is there some other man you would prefer to wed?" he asked. He thought of the fortune hunters lining up to court her now that she had money and the jealousy speared him like a knife. It was another new sensation.

She gave him a scornful look. "Not in the slightest. After everything that has happened do you still think me the kind of woman to take you into my bed—" her lips twisted "—or on my sofa, at least, and then profess a wish to wed another?"

"No," Dexter said. "I do not think you that sort of woman."

She sighed. "It is simply that I do not wish to wed again. How could I, when my previous experience of marriage was so unhappy?" She saw he was about to interrupt her and held up a hand. "I know you are not like Charles. Of course you are not. But I could never wed a man who does not love me and I am not sure you even believe in love anymore, Dexter. I am not sure that you want to. Last night you called it a dangerous illusion and said that mutual respect was all you required in marriage."

Dexter shrugged. "When I was younger I believed in love," he said. "I attributed the feelings and emotions around lust and passion to it. That was my naiveté and now I know that love is just a pretty word for physical desire. It makes it sound more acceptable."

It was only an articulation of what he had been thinking earlier but Laura looked disgusted by this piece of logic. "Congratulations, Dexter," she said. "Somehow you have managed to sound both cynical and stuffy at the same time. I am not at all certain how you achieve it." She snapped a twig of the hawthorn hedge and broke it sharply between her fingers. "I suppose that you see marriage primarily as a business arrangement?" A shade of scorn touched her voice. "It must be, I imagine—your rich, conformable marriage to your biddable heiress bride?"

"Ideally it would be," Dexter said. "I am not a man to indulge in meaningless affairs, so I have always hoped the marriage relationship would also have a physical side. I hoped it would be enjoyable."

"Enjoyable!" Now there was no doubting Laura's scorn. "Is that how you felt about last night, Dexter?" she snapped. "That it was *enjoyable?* You reject the power of emotion and yet you cannot quite eliminate it from your life, can you? So you pretend that love is less important than it really is by calling it by other names and thinking to keep it in a box and under control. You know, I *pity* your poor bride!" She took several angry steps away from him. "You are offering her a fake—a marriage where you want no more than her money and a quiet life—oh, and a *pleasant* time in her bed! What sort of existence is that?"

"A rational one," Dexter said. He looked at Laura's flushed face and bright, angry eyes, and her luscious body stiff with indignation, and wanted to grab her and kiss her even though his attraction to her contradicted every last commonsense principle he held to, and drove him mad into the bargain. "A calm, ordered life is the ideal," he said, trying to keep his voice steady.

"How very tedious!"

"That is rich criticism coming from you, madam," Dexter said, feeling his temper slipping and, as always with Laura, utterly powerless to resist. "Why, from the very first you have hidden behind a facade of propriety when really you are wanton and passionate and shameless and *wild*—" He had unconsciously taken a step closer to her with each word and now he grabbed her upper arms and kissed her with all the pent-up denial and frustration that was in him. His mouth seduced hers relentlessly, plundering its softness, demanding her response.

"I admit it!" Laura wrenched herself from his arms and stood looking at him, her breasts heaving beneath the tight riding coat as she gasped for breath. "I have acted the part of the perfectly proper duchess in public but at least I am honest enough to admit both to myself and to you that I *am* wild and passionate under the surface." She glared at him. "When I marry—if I ever marry again—I would want my husband to understand that and to want me as I am. He would not seek to change me to fit into his conventional view of life. So I cannot marry a man who secretly deplores his attraction to me and wishes he could make sense of it!"

"You mistake," Dexter said. His breathing was ragged. He took her in his arms again. "You will marry me, Laura."

"No, I will not." Laura looked defiant. She wriggled, trying to free herself from his grip. Dexter gritted his teeth at the provocative slide of her body against his.

"You do not really want to marry me," she said. "What you want is to be free of your passion for me so that you can wed a nice quiet girl who fits all your ideas of a perfect wife and a perfect marriage. That was what last night was about, you wanted to break the spell between us!"

"And I failed," Dexter ground out.

She was right. They both knew it. She was not what he had sought in marriage. He did not want his life to be driven by so demanding a passion. But with the insistent pressure of Laura's body against his, Dexter knew only that it was Laura he had to have or run mad, a situation that was even less practical, even less desirable than the one he was in.

"I have no choice, Laura, and neither do you," he said, his mouth only inches from hers. "We have to wed. It is the only way I can have you in honor."

He brought his mouth down on hers again and Laura's gasp of shock turned to a moan as he drank deep from her. He wanted to pull her down onto the soft bed of leaves behind the tumbledown wall and peel away her saucy red riding jacket and the tight breeches. He thought he would burst just to think of it. He knew that he was every bit as driven by the demand of his senses as his foolish, feckless father had been and was equally as powerless to resist. But he could bind Laura to him in marriage. That would make matters right. He could conquer this need in him by keeping her with him forever.

Laura dragged herself away from him. She was breathing hard. She looked frightened. His heart clenched at the expression on her face.

"Laura—" He put out a hand to her. He wanted to reassure her and tell her that everything would be all right. They would marry as soon as possible and then this wild and spontaneous passion between them could be controlled within the bonds of matrimony....

"I cannot marry you," she whispered. "Not when you do not love me and when you do not know—" She stopped. She looked terrified.

"Everything will be all right," Dexter said. "Laura, trust me. We will be wed soon. I will get a special license—"

Laura shook her head. "No, Dexter." She looked at him and made a little hopeless gesture. "There are many very good reasons why I cannot marry you, although being with you almost makes me forget them."

Dexter caught her arm, suddenly anxious not to let her leave on this denial.

"Is it Hattie?" he asked. "I understand it might be confusing for her at first but she is young and children do adapt. And I have six younger brothers and sisters, so I know a little of what to expect. I swear I would be a good father to her and I am sure that in time she would come to accept me—"

He stopped. Laura's eyes were brilliant with tears. It shocked him to see them. There was so much grief and uncertainty in her face that he instinctively tried to draw her into his arms, but she held him back. Her evident distress reminded him of the previous night, when she had struggled so hard to deny her love for him and he had known that there had been something frightening her.

"It is not that," she said. "Oh, Dexter, you are a good man." She gave a little laugh that was almost a sob. "You *are* a good man, despite your misguided views on love." She shook her head a little. "I am sorry. It is my fault, but we cannot wed."

Dexter stood and watched her walk away. He wanted to call her back and insist that she explain to him. His need to understand and to uncover the truth drove him. Yet she looked so sad and so determined that something held him still. He could not rid himself of the feeling that when she had apologized, it had not been for refusing his offer of marriage but for something else entirely, something he did not understand.

CHAPTER SEVENTEEN

BY THE TIME Laura had rubbed the horse down, stabled and fed her, she had started to feel a little better. The stifling guilt that had gripped her when Dexter had spoken so gently about Hattie had ebbed a little.

She wondered if she might have given a different answer to Dexter's proposal if he had said that he loved her. She had loved him for four years and she was in love with him still but she knew that he did not feel the same. He desired her but that was not the same as love. And Dexter was, at heart, deeply conventional. The heat of his lust for her drove out the more conservative elements of his behavior but he was struggling against it all the time. She did not want to be married to a man who fought against his attraction to her rather than celebrated it. One day he might actually succeed in conquering it. Nor did she want to be in another marriage where her husband required nothing more than for her to conform to his ideal of proper behavior. She had already done that and she had not buried Charles in order to do it again.

She thought about telling Dexter that she had borne his illegitimate child out of wedlock. Knowing him as she did now, she could see that he would regard Hattie's parentage as yet another reason why they should wed and regulate yet another irregular situation that had occurred between them. He would be proposing because he wanted to do the right thing but also because it would make matters neat, tidy and appropriate. It would be the responsible thing to do, to provide for her and for his child. It would fit his notions of proper behavior.

She sighed. She had not denied him knowledge of Hattie because she did not want to marry him but because she was fearful that Dexter's absolute conviction of what was right, that very inflexibility within him that had led him to pursue her relentlessly for the truth, would mean that he wanted to acknowledge Hattie openly. She was afraid that he could not compromise nor understand her reasons for wanting to preserve the fiction. She was afraid that he would not understand her reasons for wanting to protect Hattie.

She strode through the front door of The Old Palace to find Alice Lister in the drawing room with Hattie on her knee, the two of them reading *The History of Little Goody Two-Shoes*.

Alice looked up and smiled. "Good morning, Laura. I came to make sure you were quite well this morning."

"That was very kind of you considering what I put you through last night," Laura said, feeling a little inadequate. "I am so sorry, Alice. I am sure that you were most dreadfully shocked."

"Not really," Alice said serenely. "That is, yes, I was somewhat taken aback but I had observed from the first that you had a partiality for Mr. Anstruther. And you must not forget, Laura, that I was not always a debutante heiress. When I was a servant I saw things that would shock *you* to the core."

Laura bent to kiss Hattie's head and her daughter reached up and wrapped her fat little arms about Laura's neck and buried her face in her hair.

"Mama smells like a horse," she announced.

Laura laughed. "Thank you, darling. You are quite right, I do. I need to change my clothes and have a wash and then when I am clean why don't we play with your doll's house?"

"I want a papa for my doll's house," Hattie said. Her hazel eyes were bright as they fixed on her mother's face. "I only have a mama and a Hattie. I'd like a brother and a sister, as well, if you please."

Laura felt a hard lump in her throat. Her eyes met Alice's. Her friend made a sympathetic face.

"Papas and brothers and sisters are not always easy to find, darling," Laura said.

"My fault, I'm afraid," Alice said in an undertone as Rachel took Hattie upstairs to the nursery to set the doll's house up. "Hattie told me that because her papa had died, she was not allowed to have another one. When I explained that sometimes one's mama might remarry she said that that was splendid and that she wanted another papa of her own right away."

For a moment the lump in Laura's throat felt so excruciatingly tight and hard that she could not speak.

"I am sorry," Alice said anxiously. "I thought that if you were to accept Mr. Anstruther's proposal…"

"I understand," Laura said.

"But you refused him," Alice said, watching as Hattie disappeared around the corner of the stair, clutching Rachel's hand and chattering to her about the exploits of Little Goody Two-Shoes.

"Yes," Laura said. "I cannot wed Dexter, Alice. There

are reasons…" She sighed. She wished that her friend Mari Falconer were there to confide in. Mari was the only one who would understand. Mari knew all about Hattie's parentage and Charles's threats to expose her and Laura's absolute fear for Hattie's future.

"Dexter said a great deal about how he had to marry me because it is the only way to have me in honor," Laura continued.

"How vastly romantic!" Alice said.

"But then he also implied that it was against his will and his good sense and there was no rational reason for feeling as he did. Truly, Alice—" Laura threw herself down into a chair "—he is pompous and pigheaded and a stuffed shirt of a man who wants a conformable wife and a well-ordered life—"

"So it is as I suspected all along," Alice said, a twinkle in her eye. "You are in love with him. I thought that you must be. I did not imagine you would take him as your lover if you did not truly care for him."

"He reminded me of my late husband Charles!" Laura said crossly.

"Dear me, the worst possible insult you could pay a man, so I understand!"

"Except," Laura swept on, "that I cannot understand how a man can kiss like Dexter does and make love like he does and yet be so determined to be boring!"

"Hmm. You are definitely in love with him," Alice said. "How amusing that you are so cross with him."

"Well, what difference does it make if I am in love with him?" Laura demanded. She pulled off her hat and cast it aside with a sigh, running a hand through her tumbled hair. "It is over, Alice. I cannot marry Dexter and I cannot have an *affaire* with him because Miles will kill him if I do and anyway, you are right—I am not the sort of woman to have scandalous love affairs. Not really. I have Hattie to think of before I take Dexter as my lover and ruin my own reputation and my daughter's future."

"A pity, when you care for him," Alice said, "but I can quite see that you are not cut out for a life of scandal, Laura. And as for marriage, well…" Her perceptive brown eyes scanned Laura's face and she smiled. "If you tell me that you have good reasons for refusing Mr. Anstruther then I believe you."

"I do," Laura said. "And I should certainly not be speaking of such matters with you, Alice, no matter your worldly experience. I cannot believe we are having this conversation! Your mama would be appalled." She sighed. "I am a terrible influence for a dowager duchess. Oh, I feel blue-deviled."

"And playing at happy families with Hattie will not help," Alice said sadly.

"I suppose not." Laura sighed again. She went upstairs to change. She could hear Hattie talking to Rachel about the people who lived in her doll's house, the mother and father, the two boys and two girls…

I want a papa for my doll's house and a brother and a sister…

Laura sat down a little heavily on the edge of her bed.

Hattie wanted nothing more than to belong to a family and Laura's heart ached to deny her. She thought again about deceiving Dexter over Hattie's parentage and tried fiercely to ignore the customary deep ache of guilt it roused in her. She had acted for the best of reasons. That had to be good enough.

DEXTER HAD BEEN FISHING all afternoon. The quiet run of the river and the cold mist rising from the water had soothed his mood a little but there were matters that still troubled him.

Most infuriating, most galling, was the fact that Laura had refused his offer of marriage. He had thought she might reject him and had been so certain he would feel nothing other than relief to be free to marry another heiress. Instead he had felt a white-hot, possessive fury that knew no bounds. So then he had been determined to persuade her in order to deal with the passion that was between them in a sensible manner. Yet still she could not be persuaded. All of which meant that he was frustrated and dissatisfied and aware that there were matters keeping them apart that he did not understand. He disliked unfinished business. One of the reasons he was generally so good at his job was that he was utterly relentless.

He was walking back to the Morris Clown Inn across the water meadows when he heard the sound of voices. The evening sun was low on the horizon and he put up a hand to shade his eyes. He could see Laura and Alice down by the water's edge, playing with a small girl who was bowling a hoop through the grass. The child was running after the hoop and laughing and Dexter could hear her calling excitedly to her mother.

He realized that he had never seen little Lady Harriet Cole before and he paused for a moment to watch as Laura scooped her daughter up in her arms and spun her around until they were both dizzy and collapsed together in the grass. Dexter smiled ruefully. It felt strange seeing Laura playing with her daughter, to see her utterly unguarded. He felt the same tug of emotion he had felt when she had greeted Miles with such pleasure that first night at the assembly. He felt an outsider looking in. In some way that he did not understand but knew was not remotely rational, he was aware that he wanted that sense of belonging and he wanted it with Laura.

Hattie was giggling with excitement. Dexter could hear her laughter on the evening air as she scrambled to her feet and made a grab for the hoop. Her bonnet had come off and the last rays of the sun were shining on her hair and illuminating her face like a clear-cut silhouette. Her hair was as black as a raven's wing, curly and strong, springing from a miniature widow's peak on her forehead. Even though she was only young there was an intentness in the lines of her face, a determination and sense of concentration as she bowled the hoop along. Dexter had seen that expression before.

His heart turned over. His breath seemed to stop in his throat.

Alice had seen him now. She half raised a hand in greeting but then she must have seen the look on his face because she let her hand fall back to her side. There was apprehension in her eyes and she said something to Laura. A stillness came over Laura and her smile faded. She scrambled up and started to hurry after her daughter, the meadow grass whipping about her skirts.

"Hattie!" Dexter could hear the note of fear in her voice now. "Hattie! Wait!"

Hattie ignored her. She rolled the hoop right up to his feet and Dexter put a hand out automatically to stop it. Hattie tilted her chin up so that she could look at him—another gesture that was so familiar to him that his heart clenched—and he dropped to one knee in the grass beside her so that they were on a level.

"Hello!" Hattie said. Her eyes were wide and fearless, hazel like Laura's own. Dexter felt something twist within him. "Who are you?"

"I'm Dexter," Dexter said.

"My name's Harriet," Hattie said, "but you can call me Hattie." She looked from Dexter to the fishing line lying in the grass beside him. "What have you been doing?"

"Fishing," Dexter said.

Hattie smiled. It felt to Dexter as though a fist had closed around his heart and squeezed so tightly he thought he would die.

"Mama and I go fishing," Hattie said. "I catch things in my net. Then we let them go. Did you catch anything?"

"No," Dexter said. His voice was husky and he cleared his throat. "Not this afternoon."

"Good," Hattie said. "When you do you must let them go." She smiled again and Dexter's heart did another painful flip. "I like you," Hattie announced.

"Hattie…" Laura had reached them now and picked Hattie up, whisking her protectively from under Dexter's nose. She sounded out of breath. She held Hattie tightly, defensively, as though she thought Dexter would snatch her away. Her eyes were scared. Hattie was the only one who had not sensed the tension between them for she was laughing, the same intent look on her face as before, as she twisted in her mother's arms and pulled at the ribbon holding Laura's hair back. It spilled from its confinement, settling in a russet halo about her face in the sunset. Laura brushed a few strands back with fingers that shook.

Dexter got slowly to his feet. A huge tide of anger welled up in him as he looked at Laura. He had never felt anything like it before, not even when she had sent him away from Cole Court like a whipped dog. He felt hot, furious and on the edge of losing control.

He kept his voice as steady as he could for Hattie's sake.

"I think," he said, "that there is something that you forgot to tell me when you were being so honest with me last night."

Laura's hazel eyes were wide and terrified as they met his across Hattie's oblivious, down-bent head.

"How did you know?" she whispered. "She does not look like you and no one would ever have told you—"

There it was. No denials, no prevarication, no apology, no excuse. Other people evidently knew about his daughter whilst he did not. Dexter's mind reeled as he tried to grapple with the implications.

"Who knows that she is mine?" he asked harshly.

Laura looked dazed. "Her godparents, Nick and Mari Falconer. And I think Miles suspects, though he has said nothing…"

The rage exploded in Dexter so violently he was afraid of what he might do. The Falconers were friends of his. Miles had been, too, until Dexter had seduced Laura and forfeited Miles's good opinion. He looked at Laura as she stood there holding his child.

"We cannot talk about this now," he said. "Not in front of the child." He dragged in a breath. "I will call on you in one hour. Be there."

Laura's chin came up. "I cannot. Miles is joining us for dinner—"

"Then get rid of him," Dexter said. "I mean it, Laura."

He was afraid that if he stood there much longer his control would break and he would say something in his distress and anger that he would later regret. He was afraid of what she must see in his face. He had never before known such terrifying lack of control. He turned away without another word but when he reached the gate he looked back. Alice, who had been hanging back out of earshot, an unwilling observer, had taken Hattie's hand and they were walking away toward The Old Palace. Hattie had stopped to pick some of the late marguerites that starred the meadow. Her excited little voice faded away.

Laura was still standing where he had left her, her gaze fixed on his retreating figure. The fury, the pain, the utter *agony* scalded Dexter, turning his insides to a seething mass. He was astonished that anything could hurt so excruciatingly. He thought of Laura keeping from him the truth of his daughter's existence and of Hattie bearing the name of a man he despised. Laura had fed him nothing but secrets and lies. He had thought that everything had been laid bare between them but even then she had held back. He had started to trust her again but she had never had any intention of trusting him with the truth of his daughter.

He felt something snap within him. He had always tried to use sense and reason to protect him against such excesses of emotion. Now that protection was gone. The hurt roared through him again and he knew he had to stem it before it ripped him apart. There was only one thing he could do now and as soon as he thought of it he felt better, calmer, more controlled, rational again.

He had to insist that Laura married him.

She had refused his proposal that morning but now there was a child involved. He closed his eyes and the images of his own childhood danced against the lids: the bewilderment on the faces of his brothers and sisters as they heard the gossip about the Anstruther miscellany, the scars that all the scandal had laid on his heart and the way he had tried to ignore the hurt, the endless doubts about his parentage and whether he was truly his father's son.

He would insist that he and Laura wed. Hattie would be part of his family then. She would be officially his stepdaughter but he would make her true parentage known to her as soon as she was old enough to understand. By marrying Laura he could make everything right and bring some order out of this chaos. He would claim them both as his own.

He would have Laura as his wife and the wild passion that had led to the birth of their illegitimate daughter would at last be under his control. All would be ordered and calm again. For a moment he wondered how he could live with Laura now when she had hurt him so badly, but once again his calm logic came to his rescue, telling him that it need make no difference. What mattered was that he should be in control of the situation. And he would be. Everything would be well.

WHEN LAURA REACHED HOME the house was quiet. Rachel had taken Hattie upstairs to the nursery for supper. Alice had left a note on the hall table that she would call on Laura the following day. Laura's eye fell on a small glass vase of marguerites drooping on the windowsill. She swallowed a lump in her throat. She went into the library, poured herself a glass of brandy and drank it down like medicine. She hated the spirit but it revived her, steadying her shattered nerves and calming the racing beat of her heart. Suddenly she felt exhausted. She sank down into a chair and put her head in her hands.

How had he known?

She was sure that none of the people who knew about Hattie would have told Dexter about his daughter. Even if they disapproved of the secret Laura was keeping, they would never betray her or place Hattie's future in jeopardy. Did someone else know the secret of Hattie's parentage? Icy fear crept along Laura's skin to think of it. Was someone watching and waiting, stirring up trouble, ready to expose the past? She could not bear to think of her daughter in such danger. But if no one had told Dexter, how could he have known?

She had never seen Dexter so angry. She had seen his fury, his disbelief and his pain etched so clearly on his face. It had shaken her to the soul because she knew he was a man who sought to protect others, not to harm them, and yet he had looked at her as though he wanted to hurt her as much as she had hurt him. She had been so afraid when she had seen the rawness of accusation in his eyes. Afraid of what he might do to her, afraid of what might happen to Hattie now that her father knew the truth.

Laura raised her head and stared through the window at the dark closing in outside. How had she expected Dexter to feel? Shock must be the least of his emotions. She tried to imagine what it must be like for him to discover so suddenly and so shockingly that he must have fathered a child. It was impossible to guess the depth of his pain and betrayal. She had hurt him badly, beyond forgiveness. The fact that she had done so for Hattie's sake would not make Dexter's pain any the less. She could only hope that she could explain it to him and make him understand.

The long case clock in the hall chimed the hour of five. Laura straightened her shoulders, stood up and smoothed her gown. She needed to change. She needed to send a note to Miles. And Hattie would be waiting for her to share nursery tea. She hoped she did not smell of brandy. Despite her distress, she had no desire to appear as one of the gin-swigging mothers of a Hogarth drawing.

She had less than an hour until Dexter would call. The clock ticked down the seconds and she felt full of panic. She had so little time and no idea at all what she was going to say.

LYDIA WAS ANXIOUS. She picked at her food and scanned the guests at Sir Montague's dinner table for the twentieth time that evening even though she knew that her lover was not present. She had not seen him that day except for a brief moment when she had caught sight of him deep in conversation with another man at the pump rooms. He had looked through her, cut her dead as though she were of no importance, and Lydia had felt crushed even though she had told herself that it was all part of their secret. She tried to comfort herself with memories of the endearments and assurances he had heaped on her after they had made love the previous night at the masquerade ball, but now that memory distressed her, too. She wondered if she had run mad to allow herself to be seduced in the moonlight. It had seemed so romantic at the time and she loved him so much that she had given herself to him with no thought for the consequences. But now for the first time she felt a chill. He had not said anything about meeting again. Only the warmth of the ring he had given her, as it rested between her breasts on its gold chain, gave her some reassurance.

She toyed with her iced fruit until her mother put out a hand and snatched the spoon from her grip. It fell onto the table with a tinkle that sounded loud in the sudden silence.

"Stop fidgeting!" Faye Cole's whispered hiss seemed to echo from the walls. "Really, Lyddy, what is wrong with you tonight? You are drooping like a wet lettuce!"

"There is nothing wrong, Mama," Lydia said. Faye was particularly cross with her today, having witnessed her dance with her lover at the masquerade the night before. She had badgered and badgered Lydia for his name and when Lydia had pretended not to know what her mother was talking about, Faye had actually thrown a hairbrush at her. Fortunately it had missed but Lydia had known that her mother's temper, always unreliable, was now on a knife's edge.

"Then *smile!*" Faye hissed. "Smile and look as though you mean it or you will never catch a husband!" She accompanied the words with a rictus grin so wide Lydia thought it would not have looked out of place on the Guy on the bonfire.

Lady Elizabeth shot Lydia a sympathetic look across the table. Lady Elizabeth, Lydia thought bitterly, would never tolerate such treatment. She wished fiercely that she had the sort of spirit that had prompted the ladies of Fortune's Folly to defy Sir Montague's Dames' Tax. Her parents had insisted that she come to Sir Montague's house and accept his invitations, all in the interests of marrying her off, when in her own heart she wanted to be as rebellious as Lady Elizabeth. But there was still time…

She stood up and pushed back her chair. "Excuse me," she said to the table in general. "I do not feel quite well."

Faye looked up, astounded. "Lydia! Come back here! Come back, I say!"

Lydia walked to the door with her mother's scolding tones ringing in her ears. A footman opened the door for her and she walked through with a word of thanks and no backward glance. The passageway outside was empty of servants for Sir Montague kept as small a staff as he could in order to save money. The passage was cold because the door to the courtyard was open and Lydia could hear the faint sound of men's voices talking.

As she drew closer, her evening slippers silent on the stone flags of the floor, the conversation ended and a man came through the doorway and into the shadowed passage. Lydia stopped.

"It's you!" she said. "Oh, where have you been? I have been wanting to see you all day—"

He was at her side in a single step, his hand grasping her arm tightly, silencing her. "Hush! I am not supposed to be here."

Lydia realized that he was dressed for the outdoors in a heavy black cloak. He smelled of fresh air and wood smoke. Her head spun at the scent of his skin and the memories it evoked of the previous night. The urgency in him held her quiet and excited her, too.

"But why not?" she whispered. "You live—"

This time he silenced her with a kiss. It was blissful. Her head spun all the more.

"Did you see anyone else?" he asked when he let her go. It seemed like an odd question to Lydia but she was feeling so distracted from the kiss that she barely questioned it.

"I thought I heard you talking to someone," she confessed, "but I was not sure."

He kissed her again. This time she could feel relief in the way that he held her, before it gave way to a different kind of urgency.

"Come on," he whispered. He pulled open a door and bundled her through. It was pitch-black but Lydia thought she could smell beeswax and silver polish.

"Where are we?" she asked, bewildered.

"In one of the storerooms." She could hear a smile in his voice even though she could not see him in the dark. His hands were suddenly busy on the fastenings of her gown. Lydia gasped.

"We can't do it here!"

"Yes, we can."

Lydia thought of her mother finishing her dessert in the dining room and felt a huge, wicked wave of defiance. She could be wild after all, she thought. It was easy to rebel.

"So we can," she whispered.

CHAPTER EIGHTEEN

"MR. ANSTRUTHER, YOUR grace."

It was precisely six o'clock when Carrington showed Dexter into the drawing room at The Old Palace. Laura had been trying to read a six-month-old copy of the *Ladies Magazine* whilst she waited, but she might as well have been holding it upside down for all the sense it made, and in the end she had cast it aside with an exclamation of exasperation and had gone to look out of the window. It was already dark and the moon that had shone the previous night was obscured by cloud. The night felt gloomy and threatening. She had let the curtain fall back into place and turned for comfort to the glow of the fire, trying to warm herself before it.

Laura took a deep breath as she turned to face Dexter. She felt anxiety and dread in almost equal measure. The guilt gnawed at her, making her pulse pound and her head ache with tension. In the long moment whilst they waited for Carrington to close the door and leave them alone, she noted that Dexter was looking particularly elegant, as though he had made a special effort with his appearance that night. His linen was a pristine, perfect white, his pantaloons were without a wrinkle and his boots had a high polish. Something about the effort he had made with his immaculate attire combined with the unyielding expression in his eyes made Laura's heart ache with loss.

"Will you take a glass of something with me, Mr. Anstruther?" she asked. She smiled wryly to think of her mother's advice on the appropriate behavior of a duchess at a time like this.

"When your lover visits to discuss the illegitimate child you kept a secret from him, offer him a glass of wine...."

That one had most definitely not been in the dowager duchess's handbook.

"Thank you," Dexter said.

Laura poured him a glass of wine and he took it, but then set it aside immediately as though it was of no interest to him. His entire attention was focused on Laura, silent, watchful, his stance speaking of tension and antagonism.

"Hattie is my daughter," he said and it was a statement, not a question.

"Yes," Laura said.

She saw something ease in his face at her words, as though, despite everything, he had expected her to deny it. She felt again the pang of guilt at the hurt she had caused him.

"I knew she must be as soon as I saw her," Dexter said. His tone hardened. "Had you been deliberately keeping her from me so that I should not guess?"

"Not really," Laura said. "I had no notion that you would recognize her." She cleared her throat. "How did you know? I did not think that she resembled your family at all." She remembered the moment in the long gallery when Hattie had glanced up at her in a way that had been exactly like Dexter. Resemblance was sometimes a matter of small gestures rather than appearance.

"She has something of my air of determination about her," Dexter said. "And then there was this."

He held out a little locket to her. Laura took it, her fingers slipping a little on the catch. Inside was a picture of a child whose likeness to Hattie was so sharp that it made her catch her breath.

"My half sister, Caro Wakefield, when she was five years old," Dexter said dryly. "You may have heard of her referred to as my father's ward. That is a polite fiction to cover the fact that she is his illegitimate daughter and part of the Anstruther miscellany."

"She has the same blue eyes as you," Laura said. Her throat felt thick with tears. Looking at the likeness, accepting for the first time that Hattie was part of a wider family, was an extraordinary feeling.

"Whereas Hattie's are darker, I think. Hazel, like yours."

Laura looked up. They were talking so easily, so superficially, but beneath the surface she could sense all the pain and heartbreak and anger that lay between them. She felt cold through and through.

Dexter ran a hand through his hair, disordering it still further. "I can see that the timing fits," he said. "In fact I am surprised that I did not think of it before. You had told me at the time—at Cole Court—that you and Charles were estranged. But then a year or so later I heard that you had had a child and I thought…" He shrugged, his tone tipped with ice. "I thought it was just another lie that you had spun me."

"It was not," Laura said.

Just another lie...

She felt so miserable.

"No. I realize that now. Hattie's resemblance to Caro puts her parentage beyond doubt." Dexter looked at her. "Caro's looks come from the Anstruther side of the family. My brother Roly also has that coloring. The fair hair and blue eyes are from my mother's side."

"I should have thought," Laura said. She hesitated. "Hattie did not resemble you. So I assumed..."

"That I would never know?" There was such hostility in his Dexter's tone that Laura felt as though her heart was shriveling up to hear it.

"I suppose so."

"You did not intend ever to tell me?" The latent fury in his voice pinned her down.

"No."

She felt the accusation in his silence.

"Why should I tell you?" Laura knew she sounded defensive. "Charles was still alive when Hattie was born. Everyone assumed she was his child and I was not going to suggest anything to the contrary. Think of the scandal if the truth of her parentage had come out, Dexter! It would have caused nothing but trouble."

"Still so concerned to preserve your reputation?" Dexter sounded scathing. He paced across the room, the pent-up fury latent in every line of his body. "I know it has been your prime concern all along."

"You are mistaken," Laura snapped. "It was Hattie I have sought to protect all along. That was why I kept the secret. Do you think I wanted her branded a bastard, growing up under the shadow of her mother's disgrace? *That* was why I never told you."

Dexter recoiled from her, dislike flaring in his eyes. "You thought that I would broadcast your so-called disgrace to the world and condemn our daughter to ruin?" His tone flayed her. "What sort of man do you think I am?"

"I never thought that you would do it on purpose," Laura said. She spread her hands appealingly. This was all so much worse than she had imagined. The stark disgust on Dexter's face made her feel guilty and miserable for the choices she had made. "I was afraid," she said simply. "Scandal has a way of leaching out and damaging those who least deserve it, no matter how one tries to keep it secret." She made a desperate gesture. "You know that it would take only the slightest whisper that Hattie was illegitimate to cause a huge scandal."

"I can understand why you did not tell me whilst Charles was alive," Dexter said. "But to keep the secret after his death—"

"What else was I to do?" Laura burst out. "Did you imagine I would calmly write to remind you of our night together and inform you that you had a two-year-old daughter? Besides," she said, turning away from him, "I knew your opinion of me. I thought you would doubt that Hattie was your child and then I would have put her in danger all for nothing."

Dexter's expression was hard. "Well, be assured that I do not for one moment doubt Hattie's parentage." His tone was rough. "That at least is one honest thing between us."

Laura winced. Only that morning he had held her in his arms and shown her if not love then tenderness. Now he sounded as though he hated her.

"Since you were estranged, Charles must have known

Hattie was not his child," Dexter said. "What happened when he discovered that you were pregnant?"

Laura looked at him. She did not want to tell him, did not want to rake up all the terrible things that Charles had done, but she knew she could hold nothing back from Dexter now.

"Charles came back to Cole Court from London when I was six months pregnant," she said. "He was drunk and violent." She swallowed convulsively. "He swore at me for carrying another man's bastard child. He pushed me down the stairs. I fell all the way down. I remember being utterly terrified that I would lose the baby." She clenched her fingers together tightly. "In ten years of marriage to Charles I had never thought to conceive a child and I could not bear to lose her—literally *I could not have lived* if I had lost her, Dexter. And Charles—" Her voice broke. "He stood looking down at me as I lay there and said he hoped the child was dead and then he just walked away."

She saw Dexter make an instinctive movement of shock and revulsion.

"Later," she said, "he wrote to say that he would take Hattie away from me." Her words were coming faster now, spilling out after so many years of restraint. "Charles threatened to denounce Hattie before he died," she said. "He was going to take her away from me and banish me. At first he had said nothing out of pride, but as he grew more bitter and angry, so his threats became more intemperate." She stopped and put her hands up to cover her face briefly. "I was so frightened," she said. "Hattie was everything to me, the most precious thing in the world. I could not have borne it if—" She stopped. "And then Charles died," she finished fiercely, "and I was *glad*."

She felt Dexter touch her arm gently. "I am sorry," he said, "that you were left to deal with that alone."

Laura stood still, stiff beneath his touch, her fear and misery locked deep inside her. She wanted him to take her in his arms but she knew there was no easy absolution for her here. Dexter could not forgive her simply because Charles had been cruel and vicious to her. She had hurt him too much in excluding him from Hattie's life and keeping the secret of her parentage for him for him to forgive her easily now.

She moved away from him and he let her go. "Thank you," she said. "I suppose it accounts in some part for the reasons why I have been so absolutely determined to keep Hattie safe these four years past."

"But not for why you never saw fit to tell me I was her father."

Laura's heart plummeted. "I understand that you must be angry—" she began.

"I doubt that you do understand," Dexter said. His tone was dangerously quiet, but Laura could see the tension in him, barely under control. "Anger does not begin to describe how I am feeling now. To discover that I am the father of your child, to know that you never intended to tell me…" He shook his head. "Well, you may have denied me the right to take responsibility for my daughter before, but you will not do so now, Laura. You will marry me. This time you will accept me." His tone defied her to refuse him. "You will marry me for Hattie's sake. You claim that everything that you have done has been with no thought in mind other than to protect our daughter. Well, now that I finally know about her, that is my responsibility."

Laura put her hand up to her brow. "No! I cannot marry you when I know that you are so angry with me and cannot possibly want to offer us your protection."

Dexter came closer to her. His face was granite hard. "I am doing this for Hattie," he said. "I will not allow her to grow up in ignorance of the fact that I am her father, particularly when she will believe that Charles Cole, a cruel, dissolute apology for a man fathered her instead."

"But that will undo all the good I have tried to achieve," Laura argued desperately. "Once Hattie is in your family circle and people see the resemblance between her and some of your brothers and sisters, they are bound to talk! They will speculate that there was an affair between the two of us before Charles died and drag Hattie's name through the mud!" She put up her hands to cover her face before letting them fall again. "Dexter, all I have tried to do from the very first is keep Hattie safe. You say you want to protect her—well, the best way that you can do that is by leaving us alone."

Dexter shook his head. "There will always be talk," he said. "People can prove nothing. The fact is that Charles was alive when Hattie was born and there was never any suggestion that she was illegitimate. And now that he is dead you will be safer with the protection of my name than without it. I will *not* be excluded from Hattie's life any longer, Laura."

"But that need not mean we have to marry," Laura said. "You could still see Hattie—"

"And think how much conjecture that would cause," Dexter said dryly, "when I am supposed to have no connection with her."

Laura was silent. She could see the truth of that. She

flung up her hands. "But I do not understand why you cannot simply accept things as they are! It is the way that things are done—"

"It is not the way that I do things," Dexter said. His anger was palpable now. The air crackled with it. "I am aware that half of society has affairs and illegitimate children and everybody keeps their peace to avoid scandal. Who would know that better than I, with my family history?" His jaw set. "It is *because* I grew up in such a situation that I am absolutely determined my children will never face a similar state of affairs. I am prepared to keep the pretense of Hattie's parentage outside the family. It is, after all, nobody's business but ours. However, within the family Hattie will know exactly who her father is and there will be no misunderstandings and no lies. And to that end you will marry me."

"I cannot," Laura said. "I cannot marry you." She turned to him. "I appreciate what you are trying to do, Dexter. I admire the sense of honor that prompts you to do what you think is best for Hattie even when you dislike me so strongly. But you need have no concern that she is unprotected. Nicholas and Mari Falconer are Hattie's godparents and they will make sure that she will never want for anything, either materially or emotionally. And I have plenty of other relatives such as Miles, who will help—"

Dexter made a violent move toward her and she stopped abruptly. "Hattie will always lack a father," he said, through his teeth, "and that I cannot permit." His voice warmed into fury. "You would rather consider any other option—anyone else's charity—than accept me, would you not? Do you think that I will stand by and watch another man provide for *my child* when that is my duty and I am willing to undertake it?"

"That is not why I am refusing—" Laura began, but he cut her off.

"Perhaps you will reconsider when I tell you that if you do not accept me I will be the one to tell everyone that Hattie is my child and then all your subterfuge will be in vain."

The room spun. All the breath left Laura's body. She grabbed the edge of the table for support. "So now you seek to *blackmail* me into marrying you?" she whispered.

Dexter smiled mirthlessly. "Yes. You have said that you would do anything to protect your daughter. Well, this is the price you pay for her safety. You marry me."

Laura gaped at him. "You would not do it! You are not that sort of man!"

"You mistake me," Dexter said. His eyes flashed, dark blue and very angry. "I am exactly that sort of man. I would do that and more if that were what it took to get you to accept my proposal. I think I have made it clear that I want you and Hattie living with me, and if the only way to achieve it is to make it plain to the world that she is my daughter, then that is what I will do."

"You pretend that you want what is best for Hattie," Laura said, Dexter's determination firing her anger, "and yet you threaten her and use her as a bargaining counter."

"I only seek to protect her," Dexter said. "You have admitted yourself that you are not close to your relatives, Laura. I want Hattie to grow up within a loving family."

"I cannot imagine that she will be very happy when she realizes that her father has forced her mother into marrying him and they cannot bear to be near one another," Laura said sharply. "Besides, you cannot simply appear one day and start to live with us. Hattie barely knows you!"

"I said this morning that children adapt," Dexter said. "Hattie will get to know me quickly. With six younger siblings I have some experience of children. You can trust me."

Laura looked at him. It was true that Hattie would be more open than she was. When she had met Dexter earlier that afternoon she had accepted him without question. She was a happy little girl because, despite everything that had happened, Laura had worked hard to make sure that nothing and no one had ever threatened Hattie's security. She would give Dexter her unconditional love and Dexter, Laura knew instinctively, would never betray his daughter's love and trust. Laura's heart ached to think of the happiness such a relationship would bring them both. Dexter would make a wonderful father. But the price was that he would also be a husband, *her* husband. He would be a husband who would always hate her for her deception. But if the al ternative was for Dexter to reveal the truth about Hattie's parentage to the world, what choice did she have? Bitter pain twisted within her.

"Very well," she said. "I will marry you for Hattie's sake." The knife twisted within her again. "And I will accept the money Henry and my brother are offering as a dowry for your family's sake. But it will be a marriage in name only, Dexter. It must be. You are marrying me because you wish to be Hattie's father, not my husband."

She stopped. An unsettling smile had touched Dexter's mouth. "My dear Laura," he said, "you delude yourself. I wish to be your husband in every way there is. How could we possibly have a marriage in name only?"

"Because we don't like each other," Laura snapped. It was only partly true. She hated the way in which Dexter had forced her hand but she could not deny that her traitorous body responded to him even when her mind knew how impossible it was for them to be together.

There was a dangerous glint in Dexter's eyes as he pushed away from the wall and came toward her. "I thought we agreed only last night in your library just how much we liked each other?"

"I am talking about trust and respect, not lust," Laura said. "Those are the qualities that you yourself said you required in marriage. You feel none of those things for me."

Dexter did not contradict her. That unsettling smile still lingered on his lips. "Those qualities may be desirable but they are not precisely necessary for an intimate relationship," he murmured.

"So cynical." Laura looked at him, feeling a hopeless mixture of awareness and despair. "I cannot make love with you when I know how much you dislike me."

Dexter shook his head. "I am sure that you can. I still want you and that is all that matters."

He slid a hand onto the nape of her neck and drew her forward until he could kiss her. His lips were cool and firm, almost gentle, except that there was now no tenderness in him for her. Nevertheless she felt the flare of heat within her body and was helpless to part her lips in response to the demand of his. When he let her go they were both breathing fast and there was the glitter of desire in his eyes.

"You see," he said, in the same cold tone, "you do not require trust and esteem and respect from me. I will get a special license and we will wed within a fortnight."

CHAPTER NINETEEN

IT WAS LAURA'S WEDDING DAY, the autumn sun was shining and the gossip in Fortune's Folly was positively deafening. The *on dit* was all about how the Dowager Duchess of Cole was marrying Mr. Dexter Anstruther at scandalously short notice and with a special license. Laura knew that half of the village were suggesting that she had been having an *affaire* with Dexter and was pregnant. The other half thought he was just a handsome fortune hunter and Laura a rather embarrassingly foolish older woman who had fallen for his charms. Both pieces of scandal, Laura thought, were close enough to the truth to make her uncomfortable.

Sir Montague had been so cock-a-hoop that the Dames' Tax had apparently driven its key opponent into marriage that he had had the temerity to approach Dexter and suggest that as he was benefiting directly from the tax he should pay Sir Monty a percentage of Laura's dowry. Dexter had declined the tempting invitation but that had barely dented Sir Monty's glee. If Laura had not been feeling so wretchedly uncertain about her future she thought she would probably have devised another plan to take him down a few pegs, just for Alice and Elizabeth's sakes. If the chance ever arose, she thought, she would return to the fray and help them vanquish the greedy baronet.

She stood before the mirror in her wedding dress. She had not had a new gown made for the occasion. She had not had the time. Instead she had chosen a very beautiful but very old dress that she had not worn since the early days of her marriage to Charles. It was of deep rose-pink silk, embroidered with tiny paler pink rosebuds. It swathed her tightly—she was more rounded than when she had first worn it as a girl of twenty—but the close fit of the silk was by no means unflattering. Fashions had altered, of course, but then Laura had never really cared about that. What was important about this dress was that she had worn it when she was happy, before the canker of Charles's neglect and indifference had eaten away at her and changed her life. It was as though putting the gown on today was a pledge of faith, a desperate hope that she would find with Dexter the happiness that she longed for.

Even so, she experienced a moment of utter panic as she stood staring at her reflection. How could she go through with this sham of a wedding? Dexter did not care for her. It was Hattie he wanted. He certainly did not love Laura the way that she loved him.

In the fortnight since Dexter had insisted on their marriage Laura had blanked out all doubt and hesitation from her mind, concentrating only on the need to do what she had to do in order to protect Hattie. Dexter had come to visit her every day, but they had spent very little time alone in conversation and he had not touched her once. His sole intention had been to start getting to know his daughter and so they had gone out onto the hills to fly

Hattie's kite, or taken a picnic down to the river, where Dexter had fashioned toy boats for Hattie out of twigs and sticks and they had sailed them together. Sometimes Alice had accompanied them, and Rachel had come, too, which had eased the situation for Laura and also, at the beginning, for Hattie, too. But Hattie had accepted Dexter into her life with all the openness of her character and Laura's heart had ached to see the unguarded nature of her daughter's love. To Hattie everything was so simple and easy.

On Dexter's side, too, Laura thought that the love was unconditional. It hurt her to see him watching Hattie with so much pride and affection because it could only serve to emphasize all that she had denied him for the past three and a half years. And then Dexter would look up and see her gaze on him and the softness would melt from his own eyes and Laura would know that he had not forgiven her.

Miles never joined their family outings even though he had remained in Fortune's Folly. Laura had been surprised, for she had expected Miles to be pleased when she had announced her betrothal to Dexter—she had hoped that it would heal the rift that had been between them since the night Miles had discovered them together in the library. It had not. Something had been said between the two of them, Laura thought, and the breach was wider than before.

"You look beautiful, Laura," Alice said, putting a gentle hand on her arm and breaking into her thoughts. "Here—I have picked some of the last roses from my hothouse for you to carry. It's time to go."

Laura picked up the small bouquet and inhaled the faint scent. The roses smelled like the last days of summer.

"Thank you," she said. Alice smiled and Laura realized with a pang that her friend thought she was choosing to marry Dexter because she loved him, not because she had no choice. Alice had been so pleased when the engagement was announced—one of the few people who had accepted the news without judgment. Laura did not have the heart to tell her it was all a sham.

She had deliberately chosen the early evening for the wedding, when most of the curious inhabitants of Fortune's Folly would have gone to their homes. She had no desire for her charade of a wedding to become a freak show, as well, with the whole village staring. The only people she wanted there were Alice as bride's attendant and Miles to give her away. She had not even wanted Hattie to be present, although Dexter had insisted. He had wanted their daughter to be there to see her parents wed but Laura knew the significance of the occasion was for her benefit, not really for Hattie. Dexter was staking his claim to both of them publicly, openly, and with no pretense.

Hattie was with Rachel in the hall, a small, sleepy bundle rubbing her eyes and clutching a smaller posy of thornless rosebuds that were a miniature version of Laura's own. Laura's throat closed with tears as she brushed her daughter's soft cheek with her lips. Miles was there, too, an oddly sober Miles, his face set and stern. He smiled when he saw her and Laura managed a wobbly smile back.

"Are you all right, Lal?" he asked her and Laura nodded, feeling the tears at the back of her throat.

Miles swung Hattie up into his arms and they stepped out into the night, making their way along the path from The Old Palace to the church.

The autumn evening was chill. Laura shivered deep within her cloak with a combination of cold and nervousness. The path to the church was uneven and slippery with dew and she was grateful for the support of Alice's arm. She could see the candlelight behind the windows. The vicar of Fortune's Folly was waiting at the door and inside, in the timeless calm peace of the interior, stood Dexter and his groomsman, Nat Waterhouse. As they approached, Miles exchanged a stiff nod with Nat but ignored Dexter completely.

Laura met Dexter's eyes. He was looking at her and for a moment he looked dazzled and something more, then the coldness swept into his eyes again.

"Dearly beloved..." the vicar began.

The service passed in a blur. Laura knew that she must have made the appropriate responses but she could remember nothing of it.

Dexter kissed her briefly at the end, his lips cool and remote against hers. It seemed there was no emotion in him for her at all.

Hattie wrapped her arms around Dexter's neck and kissed him and it was then that he smiled, a sweet, tender smile for his daughter that had Laura's heart thumping in her chest and her face burning red with grief that he had such uncomplicated love for Hattie and none for her. The love that she felt for him was impossible to dismiss. She had been afraid that, as with Charles, her love for Dexter would wither under the onslaught of his anger for her, but it had not. She saw him with their daughter and felt full of tenderness. She ached for him to love her whilst knowing he did not, but she could not quite eliminate the hope from her heart that one day things might change.

Miles kissed Laura but did not even shake Dexter's hand. He stood looking at his former friend with cold dislike, shoulders squared, aggression in every angle of his body. "I warned you not to marry unless you meant it," he said to Dexter. "If I hear one word that Laura is not happy, Anstruther, I'll come looking for you."

He nodded abruptly to Alice and walked away. For a moment there was an angry glint to Dexter's eyes. Then he picked Hattie up and turned to Laura.

"Shall we go home?" he inquired with scrupulous courtesy.

Alice reached up to kiss Laura's cheek. "I hope you will be very happy," she whispered.

Hattie was so tired by the time they got back that she was asleep in Dexter's arms. Laura watched as he carried her up the stair to bed. It felt extraordinary, as though everything was the same—and yet it could not have been more different. Mrs. Carrington had done her best with a dinner of mutton, but Laura was not hungry. She sat alone in the parlor, the mutton stew congealing on her plate, and reflected morosely that this was more like a wake than a wedding.

The parlor door opened and then closed with a very firm click. Laura was aware of Dexter standing behind her chair.

"Are you tired?" he asked. He touched her cheek, his fingers gentle but impersonal. "Perhaps we should go to bed."

Laura said nothing. The last time he had kissed her—the last time he had touched her—had been in the drawing room when he had sworn their marriage would be a full one in every possible way. In the intervening time he had become almost as a stranger to her, but now that moment had come and she was suddenly afraid. She went out of the room and walked up the stairs in front of him. She didn't turn round. The back of her neck prickled with awareness of Dexter's scrutiny. She could feel him watching her and it was like a physical touch on her skin. As each step took her closer to the top of the stairs, her nervousness increased. Her heart was stumbling in her chest. Her fingers were shaking. The hysterical laughter bubbled inside her. It was her wedding night and she felt like a prisoner taking her last walk to the executioner's block.

On the top step she stopped abruptly and turned to him. "Dexter, I cannot do this. You... I...I feel as though I no longer know you at all."

There was a lamp standing on the armada chest on the landing and it threw a soft light. In that light Dexter's expression was remote and it was that very aloofness that made Laura curl up inside. He was worse than a stranger to her now: someone she loved, someone she *wanted* to love her, except that somehow all the pieces of their lives had been shattered by secrets and lies and she could not see how to put the pattern together again.

He took her hand in his, his thumb moving against her palm, and she felt the tingling of physical awareness through her body and felt even more wretched in her mind that her perfidious senses could betray her when she did not want them to. She had always been wild and with Dexter that wildness was translated into a sensuality over which she had no control and no choice.

"You know me." Dexter kissed her and her lips parted beneath the inexorable pressure of his mouth. His tongue swept hers, sweet and tantalizing. Her body recognized him instantly and filled with a trembling longing. Her knees weakened and her toes curled within her pink silk slippers and his mouth ravished and plundered hers until she had to drag herself away simply to draw breath.

Dexter made a sound of satisfaction deep in his throat and picked her up, carrying her through the doorway of his bedroom, where he dropped her full in the middle of the bed. Her petticoats rode up about her thighs and she sat up quickly to cover herself. The kiss had made her body ripe with wanting but her mind felt detached, cold and afraid. She could *not* respond to Dexter like this. She did not want to. Not when everything else was twisted and broken between them, not with her guilt and Dexter's lack of forgiveness.

Dexter was pulling his neck cloth loose now. He dropped it carelessly on the floor. His shirt followed. Laura looked away quickly, but not before she had caught a glimpse of his broad and muscular chest. The breathless feeling in her body intensified. So did the panic in her mind. She tried to communicate something of her disquiet to Dexter, making a last-ditch effort to make him understand.

"Why are we doing this?" she said desperately. "You do not even like me now, Dexter, let alone love me. And I have told you before that I cannot have sex without love, only for the physical pleasure—"

"And I have told you that I am sure that you can." The blue glitter of Dexter's eyes was implacable. He came across to the bed and the mattress gave under his weight as he sat down beside her. "It will be my aim, my dearest Laura, to prove to you that you can."

Laura's stomach squirmed with an anticipation that both horrified and excited her. Their eyes met and Dexter put out a hand to the rose-pink ribbon that tied the neckline of her gown. His knuckles brushed the upper swell of her breasts above the bow. Laura sat tense and upright, all her senses suddenly sharply alert. Dexter ran the ribbon thoughtfully through his fingers, then he gave a tug and the ribbon came loose.

"You are my wife and I want to make love to you," he whispered, his hand moving to the first button on her bodice. "I am going to make love to you and it will be very pleasurable indeed, for both of us."

His other hand came up to tangle in her hair, drawing her head forward so that he could kiss her intimately, deeply, branding her as his. Laura's head spun. Her senses flared into vivid life. He had taken everything that day, she thought, as he eased her back against the bedcovers, following her down into their soft embrace with the weight of his body on hers. She was his wife, she bore his name, he had his child now and all he needed to do to complete his possession was to take her body. Her soul, which once she would have given so freely, was the only thing that he could not touch now. So why fight this intense, delicious warmth that undermined all her resolutions and defenses? She wanted the physical comfort of his touch and for now that would have to be enough. She did not want to struggle against him or against her own instincts any longer. She was tired and lonely and she wanted the illusion of being loved.

Dexter propped himself up on one elbow and unfastened her bodice in slow, measured movements, pausing to press soft kisses on her pale skin as each button came open. Released from the conflict between her thoughts and her desires now, Laura's body relaxed and unfurled, lying still and quiescent beneath his hands, her flesh warming beneath his touch, a blush heating her exposed skin. Her breath was rapid and shallow. She allowed her eyes to flutter closed and let her mind drift, thinking of nothing now other than carnal pleasure and the slowly spiraling need for fulfillment.

Dexter drew her bodice down so that she was bared to the waist and cupped one of her breasts in the palm of his hand, lowering his lips to its taut tip. Laura did not try to hold back the small moan that escaped her and he paused on hearing it before taking her nipple between his tongue and teeth and sucking gently. Memories of their previous encounter in the library flashed through Laura's mind, inciting a further rush of helpless feeling. She squirmed on the bed, feeling the roughness of the covers against her bare back, wantonly pressing her breast against Dexter's lips as he caressed and stroked her with his tongue.

"How do you feel now?" His voice was low and very gentle.

"I feel warm…" Laura's voice sounded distant to her own ears. "And shivery…"

"Good." She felt the curve of his smile against her naked breast. "So it is quite pleasurable for you?"

"Quite." She gasped the word, arching upward like a drawn bow as he bit down gently on her skin.

His hand slid lower over the gentle curve of her stomach, easing her away from her gown, petticoats, stocking and chemise, and pushing them aside in a tangled pile. She lay pale, naked and exposed on the bed, and although her eyes were closed she knew that Dexter was looking at her, his gaze drifting slowly down every quivering, anticipatory inch of her body. A small part of her mind was still telling her that this was not what should be happening between them and she reached for something to cover her nudity, but he caught her hands and pushed them aside.

"Don't cover yourself. I want to look at you." His fingertips trailed fire over her belly. His tongue curled wickedly in her navel. "You are beautiful, Laura."

His hand slid over the silken skin of her thigh and Laura shuddered. That calculated, deliberate touch was stroking intimately close to the heart of her femininity and she tensed for a second, then allowed him to spread her legs wide and slide down gently to lick the swollen flesh he was caressing.

He raised his head a little. "How do you feel now?"

A groan was wrenched from Laura's throat as she felt the skillfull flick of his tongue over her most secret places.

"I want…"

"This?" He slid his tongue into her heated cleft.

A small cry escaped her and she arched upward again in mute appeal. Slowly, knowingly, he prolonged the pleasure, drawing out every caress, every touch whilst Laura's hips jerked helplessly as she sought release. He was ruthless, utterly controlled. Laura was aware of nothing but the shimmering need pulsing within her.

She became faintly conscious of the moment when he left her side to strip off the rest of his clothes and then he was beside her on the bed, his body hot and hard, and it jolted her out of her sensual dream for a moment. Her palms came up against his chest. She could feel the strong thrust of his arousal against her thigh and felt something akin to shock.

"Take me."

They were his words, not hers, an order rather than an appeal. Her eyes opened wide even as she felt him move and settle between her thighs where her body still throbbed with the demand for satisfaction. He shifted her slightly so that she was perfectly positioned to accommodate him and she felt the tip of his erection touch her a second before he thrust hard into her tight, quivering body.

His mouth took hers again in a kiss of primitive possession even as he drove into her body with sure, strong strokes, allowing her no respite, his demand on her absolute.

"Open your eyes."

There was no tenderness in him, only a total need that she be his and his alone and that she recognize the fact. She opened dazed eyes and saw the taut command in his face, the intense, concentrated glitter in his eyes. Her body burned and ached for surcease as he forced her closer and closer to the edge. She knew he was not going to succumb to his own climax until he had ensured that she had surrendered to him. She felt herself slipping into ecstasy, driven deep into pleasure by the insistent thrust of his body in hers. But then, at the very last moment, she felt herself withdrawing from him so that although her body convulsed with absolute rapture her mind was left cold and untouched and she felt strangely empty.

Her eyes locked with Dexter's. He had paused, watching her. He smoothed the damp hair back from her face and his fingers rested for a moment against her cheek in something close to a caress. But there was no affection in his eyes.

"Do not hold back from me, Laura," he said.

Her body still thrummed with the force of her climax. He was still inside her, strong and hard, filling her. She knew that he had not gained his release; what he had done had been all about showing her pleasure and proving that her denials were empty. Her body would respond to him without love and out of no more than a desire for physical pleasure. It had done. He had proved it. But that had not been enough for him. Now he wanted her mind, as well. He wanted her complete submission.

Now he moved again gently, barely at all, but the friction was enough to send further ripples of sensation through Laura's still-sensitive body. When he withdrew from her she could not help a small whimper of disappointment. He turned her over and canted her bottom in the air and the shock skittered through Laura again as she felt him spread her legs and enter her. The dark pleasure filled her. Exposed, vulnerable to his gaze and to his touch, she nevertheless felt impossibly aroused.

The rhythm built again. This time he penetrated her deeply and withdrew slowly, over and over, Laura's breasts moving languorously with each thrust, her nipples rubbed to unbearable stimulation with the friction of the bedclothes. Dexter slid his hands to cup her breasts before bracing her hip with one hand and slipping the other lower to stroke and caress the tender core of her. The intense, deliberate pressure of his invasion of her body sent the blood pounding through her veins once more as the molten pleasure flowed through her, twisting tighter and tighter within her. Slowly, inexorably it built and then suddenly she could not resist it any longer. It smashed through her and she cried out again and again in exquisite bliss, feeling Dexter finally succumb to his own climax. The sensations fused in her mind in a shower of blinding lights as she let go of everything and allowed the pleasure to sweep through her and take her away.

She rolled over and lay back on the pillows, sated and abandoned, dimly aware of Dexter beside her and the slick heat of his skin and the harshness of his breathing.

She turned her head slightly and a big fat teardrop rolled down her cheek to land with a plop on the pillow beside her, surprising her.

"Laura?" Dexter's voice was very quiet. "Why are you crying?"

Until that moment Laura had not realized that she was. Then her feelings caught up with her body, piercing the languid pleasure that had enclosed her in the aftermath of lovemaking. Her body felt full and heavy and satisfied and her mind felt terrifyingly lonely with a raw, screaming darkness that threatened to swallow her whole.

"I'm crying because that felt wonderful, Dexter," she said, "and really it ought not to have done, not when it had nothing of love in it."

Dexter was frowning now. He lay back on the bed, magnificently naked, making no attempt to cover himself. He looked glorious. She wanted to touch him. *No. She wanted to hold him and feel close to him and revel in their intimacy.*

She wanted to curl up in his arms and sleep, and wake to find him there, holding her against his heart. Whereas he had made it quite clear what he wanted, and that did not involve any element of tenderness. The hopelessness of her desires swamped her.

She rolled off the bed and grabbed her clothes from the haphazard pile on the floor. She was not going to stay here and let him see her cry, or worse, lie beside him and feel lost and alienated and alone.

"You have proved your point," she said quietly. "You can make love to me and not care for me at all and you can give me pleasure, too, but it means nothing. Do you understand that, Dexter? It is empty and worthless. That is your marriage."

She went through the connecting door into her own bedchamber and locked the door behind her. The room looked warm in the candlelight, familiar and reassuring. Almost it was as though nothing had changed. But it had. Everything had changed. Laura scrubbed away another wayward tear from her face, slipped on her nightgown—it was cold because Molly had not warmed it before the fire, evidently thinking she would have no use for it that night—got into her bed and curled up tight against the cold. But the cold was inside her. And it did not go away.

DEXTER WAS FISHING. It was a glorious late-autumn afternoon on the River Tune with the wood smoke hanging on the air and the late sun glittering on the water. He should have been enjoying the peace and the quiet flow of the river. He was not. He should have been happy. He was not.

He cast his line with an unnecessarily vicious flourish. He had everything that he wanted now, neat, ordered and under control. He had his daughter, he had the money, or at least he would have when the lawyer, Mr. Churchward, had finished arranging the marriage settlements. He had written to his mother to tell her of his marriage. He would be able to buy Charley a commission now and pay Roland's university fees and meet all the other debts and obligations that had weighed so heavily on him in the past. He had his work in London, which he was going to return to just as soon as he had made a breakthrough in the Crosby case. He had also written to Lord Liverpool to tell him he was wed and that he now hoped to progress the murder inquiry, assuming that Miles was ever prepared to work with him again.

He had Laura as his wife.

Uncomfortable emotions stirred in him. Conscience, guilt... He was not accustomed to feeling guilty about anything. He had always tried to do the right thing in his life and that had brought with it a belief in his own integrity. Even now, when he was feeling remorse for the way in which he was treating Laura, he told himself that he had forced her into marriage for Hattie's sake and that in time they would learn to live more comfortably with one another. She was his wife and so she fitted into the pattern of his ordered life now.

He shifted uneasily as his conscience prickled again. They had been married for a week, but he was spending no time with Laura and deliberately so. He was punishing her. He still felt so bitter and betrayed that she had kept Hattie a secret from him. He could not seem to help himself. They lived as strangers to one another except that each night he went to her bed and each night they made love with heated, passionate fervor. But that was also a part of his ordered life now. He could keep his physical urges under control by exercising them in the marriage bed. Everything was disciplined and rational and under control.

Except that it was not. A piece was missing from his life and for all his logic and intellect he could not work out what it was. Dexter closed his eyes for a second. When he opened them again the sun on the water almost dazzled him. He knew that he was dissatisfied with his marriage in some way. He, who now had everything arranged exactly as he wanted it, still felt irrationally unhappy. It was inexplicable.

He thought of Laura. He had thought that he could be angry with her and yet could make love to her and remain detached from everything but the perfect physical and sensual pleasure that he always found with her. Yet it seemed to be becoming increasingly difficult to find the satisfaction he craved. It was not that she ever refused him. She responded to his every desire with a passion and wildness that fired his blood. He could not deny that their encounters were exhausting, spectacular and physically fulfilling, but at the same time they left him in some complicated way unsatisfied. His grip tightened on the fishing line so hard that he almost snapped it in two. It felt as though as his physical intimacy with Laura increased, so she slipped away from him in some way, as though she were even less than a stranger to him. The woman he wanted to possess body and soul was eluding him and turning into a phantom. He could not control the feeling and it infuriated him.

With a sigh, he gathered up his line and started to walk along the riverbank back to The Old Palace. As he came out into the water meadows he saw Hattie running toward him through the grass, her nursemaid and a woman in a lavender-blue gown walking behind. For a moment he thought it was Laura and despite everything his heart lifted. The he realized it was Alice Lister and felt a ridiculous disappointment. Alice waved to him, said a farewell to Rachel and Hattie, and walked away toward the Spring House.

Dexter put down his rod and line and picked Hattie up into his arms as she wrapped her plump arms about his neck and shrieked with excitement. Her body felt solid and warm against his and Dexter was swept with such a powerful feeling of love and protectiveness that he felt shaken to the core. With Hattie it was always this easy. She gave her love so generously.

"I am collecting pebbles for Mama," Hattie said importantly. "They are a present." She wriggled away from him and ran across to the stream, picking up little rounded stones and holding them out to Rachel, who put them in her apron pocket.

Dexter walked slowly back toward The Old Palace, threw his fishing tackle into a corner of one of the outbuildings and went inside to wash. When he came downstairs, Hattie was in the hall, arranging her pebbles in a pattern on the carpet. She was wearing the intent, concentrated look he recognized as one of his own qualities. She looked up at him with bright hazel eyes, Laura's eyes.

"Papa," she said slowly, as though trying the word out. Then she smiled and Dexter felt the love he had for her swamp him like a tide.

The drawing room door opened and Laura came out. Dexter thought she looked tired. Evidently she had been writing, for there were ink stains on her fingers. She was looking at them with a certain amount of exasperation and trying to wipe them off on her skirts. There were faint, dark smudges beneath her eyes. She looked up and saw him and he saw the expression change in her eyes to something wary and unhappy. He felt a kick of intolerable guilt inside. He had to do something to put matters right between them but he did not know what. Suddenly he felt as uncertain as he had done in his youth when he had loved Laura and lost her the first time. The instinct to retreat to the safety of his ordered world was incredibly strong, but he knew with absolute certainty that he would find no solace there. He had to do something different. He did not know what. The thought terrified him. He who had faced danger and even death in the course of his work was running scared of his own feelings.

"Dexter—" Laura began when she saw him.

He caught her hand in his and she looked at him, a startled expression in her eyes at the gentle gesture.

"Will you spend the day with me tomorrow?" He asked. He felt as though he was fumbling his way toward something he did not quite understand and had only blind instinct to guide him. "Just the two of us together?" he said. "I would like that."

Laura looked puzzled and a little fearful, and he suddenly felt a complete scoundrel for driving her so far from him. "I am not sure," she murmured, avoiding his eyes, her gaze on Hattie.

"Please," Dexter said. He tightened his fingers until she looked up at him. "Please," he repeated softly. "Laura, I must talk to you. There are things to discuss."

"I agree that we need to talk," Laura said, but she still sounded hesitant.

"Then spend the day with me," Dexter urged. "We could go riding, perhaps."

She smiled a little warily. "That might be...nice."

"I will try to make it so," Dexter said. He saw Hattie watching them and for the first time there seemed to be a shadow in her eyes as she looked at them, as though she had felt the tension between them though she was too young to understand it.

Laura's lashes fluttered down, their shadow spiky and dark against her cheek. Dexter felt a sudden rush of longing, so powerful it took his breath.

"I know we have to make the attempt," she said, "for Hattie's sake."

"Not just for that," Dexter started to say, "but—"

"I want a brother," Hattie said, looking up from her seat on the carpet. "Mama, Papa, I want a brother or sister."

Laura blinked. "She called you papa," she whispered.

"Yes," Dexter said. He pulled her a little closer. "I think," he said softly, "that Hattie feels I have earned the title, but I am not sure I deserve to be called your husband."

Laura's hazel eyes were bewildered, as though she could not quite understand what he was trying to say. Dexter released Laura's hand and crouched down beside his daughter.

"I think it might take a little time to make you a brother or sister, poppet," he said. "I need to get to know your mother better first."

The color stung Laura's cheeks. "Really?" she said. "Do you really mean that, Dexter?"

"Really," Dexter said. "We will start this evening."

"I was going to take Hattie to the bonfire display," Laura said. She glanced at the clock. "It begins in a half hour."

"Then we shall all go together," Dexter said. "I am sure it will be a memorable night. And after that we can talk."

The door to the servants' stair opened and Carrington shuffled out. "Might I beg a word, your grace?" he asked, with dignity. "Mrs. Carrington and I would like to request permission to attend the bonfire display tonight."

"Certainly, Carrington," Laura said, smiling. "I am delighted that you would like to go out. Rachel and Molly are happy to stay at home. Apparently they do not care for bonfires."

"No, your grace," Carrington said. "Their cottage burned down when they were children and they have never liked bonfires since."

"It cannot be a happy time of the year for them," Laura commented. She looked at Dexter and there was something in her eyes that made his heart turn over. "Oh, Carrington," she said, "one final thing—would you please address me as Mrs. Anstruther now that I am married?"

"It will be a pleasure, your grace," Carrington said. He shuffled back to the staircase and closed the door behind him. Laura picked Hattie up.

"Laura," Dexter said, shaken to discover how moved he felt at what she had just done, "wait—"

She shook her head. "We need to get ready," she whispered. "We can talk later, Dexter." And this time she smiled at him and he felt the unfamiliar emotion tighten within him and sweep him further away from reason and sense than he had ever been. It felt dangerous and unfamiliar and frightening. It felt a lot like love.

CHAPTER TWENTY

IT APPEARED THAT EVERYONE in Fortune's Folly had turned out for the Guy Fawkes bonfire that night. Laura glimpsed Sir Montague in the throng along with Miles, Nat Waterhouse, Lady Elizabeth Scarlet and Alice Lister. Mr. and Mrs. Carrington were talking to Mrs. Morton, the village dressmaker. Mr. Blount was roasting chestnuts on the bonfire and had already given Hattie some to eat.

The night was crisp with the stars white and bright overhead. The fire leapt and climbed, crackling and hissing, licking up the ragged trousers of the guy. The village children had done an excellent job. The guy wore a rough wig of straw beneath an old felt hat and had a mask that looked uncannily like Sir Montague Fortune. Laura wondered whether Lady Elizabeth had painted it. She was accounted a very fine artist.

Hattie snuggled close in Laura's arms and watched, entranced, a toffee apple clutched in one sticky hand and a piece of parkin in the other. With Dexter so attentive, as well, Laura felt almost as though they were like any proper family, as though the grief and distrust and misery of the last few weeks had at last lifted. Those brief moments in the hall had given her hope, and even if Dexter did not love her and was making this attempt for

Hattie's sake, so that their daughter would know a happier childhood than he and his siblings had experienced, it was not impossible that in time they might build the marriage of mutual respect that he had once said he wanted. It would be a pale imitation of what she had once wanted from him but it was a start.

Faye Cole was standing a little apart from the crowd, shivering deep within her fur wraps. She did not seem particularly pleased to be there and Laura wondered what had prompted her to attend. Of Henry Cole there was no sign. It was not the type of event that Laura thought Faye would normally grace with her presence but perhaps she saw it as yet another opportunity to attract a husband for Lydia. Certainly she had tried to push her daughter toward Lord Armitage when he had strolled past, but Lydia had refused to budge. She stood beside her mother, looked pinched and cold and very unhappy, her fingers working feverishly on the links of the golden chain that was about her neck.

"You had better be quick there, my girl," Laura heard Faye say, "or that little whey-faced Mary Wheeler will snap Armitage up from under your nose! First Mr. Anstruther lost to your cousin, and now Lord Armitage is paying court to that sniveling girl—"

Laura saw the expression on Lydia's face a second before Faye did and knew exactly what was going to happen. She half turned to hand Hattie to Dexter in the hope that she could intervene, but even as she took a step forward it was too late. Lydia had, at last, been pushed too far.

"I don't want to marry Lord Armitage!" Lydia screamed, making several people who were standing close to her, Laura included, jump with the sheer shrillness of her voice. "Do you hear me, Mama? I did not want to marry Mr. Anstruther and I do not want to marry Lord Armitage!"

Faye recoiled a step. "Be silent, you foolish girl," she hissed. "*No one* will want to marry you if you make such a dreadful scene in public!"

"I don't care!" Lydia screamed. "I am sick of you telling me what to do, Mama. You never ask what I want. *You* bully me and *Papa* creeps about the neighborhood fathering bastards on any willing servant girl he can find, and no one cares a rush for me!"

"No one ever will care a rush for you if you behave like this, you little madam!" Faye screeched in a tone to match her daughter's own. Her face was turning almost purple with shock and anger at her daughter's outburst. "Be quiet! Be quiet, I say!"

The rest of the villagers, attracted by the unmistakable sound of the conflict, had drawn closer, their faces avid and inquisitive in the firelight, but neither Lydia nor Faye took any notice. Matters had already gone too far to be saved.

"Someone cares for me," Lydia shrieked. "Mr. Fortune wants to marry me. He gave me a ring!" She pulled out the golden chain and the ring on it gleamed bright in the flames. Beside her, Laura heard Dexter give a sudden, sharp exclamation.

"Miss Cole—" he began.

Faye grabbed Lydia's arm, ignoring Dexter's intervention completely. "Mr. Fortune!" she said scathingly. "*Tom Fortune* who has nothing to offer, not even a good name? You stoop too low there, my girl."

"How dare you!" Sir Montague interposed now. "I'll

have you know that the Fortunes have an older name than the Coles, madam! We can trace our ancestry back to the Conquest!"

"The Fortunes are mere gentlemen and the Coles are dukes!" Faye shrieked, more piercing now than Lydia in her outrage. "If your brother has tried to mislead my daughter, Sir Montague, then it merely goes to show what bad blood there is in the Fortune family!"

"I love Tom." Lydia had started to cry now. "I was going to run away with him." She was turning the ring over and over between her fingers. Faye grabbed it and wrenched it from her. It spun across the ground, sparkling in the firelight. Miles bent to pick it up. Laura saw him glance across at Dexter and give an almost imperceptible nod.

"You stupid girl!" Faye had turned all her venom back on her daughter now. "Mr. Fortune doesn't love you! I'll wager that he only wanted one thing from you! If he loves you where is he now?"

"I don't know," Lydia wept. Her shoulders had slumped and she seemed to be shrinking into herself. "I don't know. He was to meet me at the tithe barn tonight and we were to run away together, but he was not there…" The rest of her words died in a tangle of sobs and it was Elizabeth Scarlet who went over to put a comforting arm about her.

Hattie had picked up on the malevolence in the air now and had started to wail. Laura drew her close. Everyone was standing frozen, bemused by what they were witnessing.

"Laura," Dexter said urgently, beside her, "I have to go after Tom Fortune. Miles and I must try to find him. I'm sorry."

"Of course," Laura said. She felt bewildered at the speed with which everything had unraveled about them. Lydia's heart-wrenching sobs had quietened now but her devastation had been shocking.

"Is Tom the one you were looking for, then?" Laura asked. "Is he Warren Sampson's henchman?"

"I think he must be," Dexter said grimly. "That ring Lydia had came from Crosby's body." He hesitated, his face tense and hard in the firelight. "I think Tom is the one who tried to hurt you, too, Laura, that day on the river and in the priory ruins. He and Sampson must have known you were Glory and were afraid of what you might know." His tone hardened. "He tried to kill you and for that alone I have to settle with Tom myself." The look in his eyes was suddenly so primitive and so fierce that Laura felt a pang of shock. There was nothing calm or restrained in Dexter's demeanor now, just fury and a violent emotion that almost took her breath away.

She caught his sleeve. There was no time now for pretense or pride between them. "Be careful," she said. "Please, Dexter, take care. For Hattie's sake—and for mine."

She saw the expression in Dexter's eyes soften and for a second it felt as though she was looking at a reflection of all the love that was inside her. It was so powerful that she felt faint.

Dexter kissed the top of Hattie's head. "Be good, sweetheart," he said. "I will be back soon."

He looked at Laura. "I don't want to leave you," he said. His voice was rough. "I *will* be back soon, I swear." He kissed her, a brief, hard kiss that left Laura feeling shaken through and through. Then he was gone.

Now that the excitement was over the villagers had started to drift back to their homes, no doubt, Laura thought, to discuss the sensational news of Lydia Cole's ruin. Only a few people remained, talking quietly in the firelight. Lady Elizabeth and Nat Waterhouse were standing close together. Nat was holding Elizabeth's hands in a comforting grip. Laura felt another pang. She had forgotten briefly that Tom was Elizabeth's half brother. She would feel his desertion very keenly.

Hattie had quietened now and had fallen asleep against Laura's shoulder. Alice came over to her. "I was never so shocked in my life," she said. Her face looked very pale. "Poor Lydia—and poor Elizabeth! Can it really be true that Tom Fortune is a hardhearted seducer? Surely there must be some mistake!"

"I don't think so," Laura said. "He is worse than that, Alice. He is a murderer. It seems that he killed Sir William Crosby. We all thought that it was Mr. Sampson who was responsible for Crosby's death but it seems it was Tom all along."

Alice looked suddenly fearful. "And Mr. Anstruther and Lord Vickery have gone after him?"

"It will be all right, Alice," Laura said, catching Alice's hand as she understood the source of her friend's anxiety. "Miles will be quite safe. I am sure of it."

The fire shifted and snapped and suddenly, with a roar and a crack of breaking sticks, the guy toppled from the bonfire and rolled to the ground. The felt hat came off. The straw wig was burning fiercely and so was the mask of Sir Montague's face, and beneath it…

Someone screamed as the body of Warren Sampson turned over and lay still, staring sightlessly at the night sky.

"A SHOCKING NIGHT, madam," Carrington said, as he brought a beaker of hot chocolate into the drawing room for Laura later that evening. Hattie was abed and the house was quiet. "Who would have thought that young Mr. Fortune was a seducer and a murderer? It quite shakes my faith in human nature."

"Indeed, Carrington," Laura said, taking the cup for him before he dropped it. "Thank you very much. I imagine," she added, "that neither you nor Mrs. Carrington enjoyed the evening much. I am very sorry."

"It was not quite as I had anticipated, madam," Carrington agreed.

"I suggest that the two of you partake of some of this fine hot chocolate to steady the nerves," Laura said, smiling. "Please tell Mrs. Carrington from me that it is delicious and just what we all need after such a shock."

Carrington hesitated. "Thank you, madam." He cleared his throat. "Your grace—" He stopped and started again, his voice shaking a little. "Your grace, there is something that I feel I really should confess to you. Something that you do not know."

"A secret, Carrington?" Laura said. She felt a little puzzled. "What could you possibly have to confess to me?"

The butler shuffled unhappily, his face tense. "Oh, madam," he said. "I was the one who locked you in the wine cellar!"

The surprise was so great that Laura almost dropped her cup of chocolate on the carpet. "You, Carrington?" she said, mopping at the drops she had spilt. "How on *earth* is that possible?"

"Oh, madam," Carrington said again, "it was the most terrible mistake. I thought you were the Duchess of Cole!"

Laura's eyebrows shot up into her hair. "You thought that I was Faye Cole?" she repeated faintly. "But why? I was not even aware that you knew she was in Fortune's Folly at that stage. And why would she be down in my wine cellar?"

"It was all a terrible mistake," Carrington repeated. He wrung his hands. "Mrs. Carrington saw her grace in the village and followed her to the priory one afternoon. She was stealing the marmalade from your cellar, madam! We thought that if we could lock her in and then show the world the sort of person she was—"

"Wait!" Laura besought. "Faye Cole was stealing from my wine cellars?"

"She always did have a shocking appetite for marmalade laced with sloe gin, madam," Carrington confirmed. "When we worked for her at Cole, Mrs. Carrington was driven mad by the number of pots she had to produce. All the sloe bushes were robbed bare! She has an unnatural appetite, madam. It is quite disturbing!"

"It is indeed," Laura murmured, her mind boggling at the thought of Faye creeping through the priory to raid her stores. "I am shocked, Carrington. Even more so at the thought that you and Mrs. Carrington had planned to trap the duchess and reveal her extraordinary habits to the world!"

"Yes, madam," Carrington said miserably. "Oh indeed, madam, it was so very bad of us, but her grace had treated us with the utmost contempt and cruelty!"

"I know," Laura said. "I know what you suffered at Cole and I am sorry for it." She thought about that very night and Faye's vicious public condemnation of her own daughter. It was true that Faye had not a single shred of generosity within her. Her voice softened and she smiled at him. "I do understand, Carrington."

"Oh, thank you, madam!" Carrington said, looking as though he was about to cry with relief. "It was only when I got back that night and Mrs. Carrington said that you had not returned that I realized what a dreadful mistake I must have made. So I hurried back to the priory and opened the door again. But in the process I must have loosened some of the stones in the tower and—" He stopped again, looking as though he was about to expire with the upset of it all. "Oh, madam, when I heard you were injured… I was ready to give myself up to the constable!"

"Well, I am glad you did not," Laura said. "At least that accident is one thing we cannot lay at Tom Fortune's door."

"No, madam," Carrington said, "but if I might ask an enormous favor of you, madam…"

"Yes, Carrington?" Laura asked.

"Don't tell Mr. Anstruther!" Carrington begged, his face shaking. "We have all observed how protective he is of you, madam, and I shudder to think what he would do if he discovered that I was responsible for hurting you!"

"You think he is protective of me, do you?" Laura said. A little smile touched her lips. If it had not been for that moment when Dexter had taken his leave of her she might have been inclined to tell the butler how very wrong he was, but now… She gripped her hands tightly together about the cup and felt its warmth. Now she did at least have a little hope.

"We think that he loves you, madam," Carrington said, with dignity, "which is exactly how it should be." He bowed. "If that is all, madam, and you feel that you can forgive me…"

"Of course," Laura said. "Think no more of it, Carrington."

"Thank you, madam," Carrington said, and he went out and closed the door, leaving Laura alone to think of Dexter and pray he would be safe.

CHAPTER TWENTY-ONE

"LIZZIE, I AM SO VERY SORRY," Laura said. She was taking tea with Lady Elizabeth Scarlet and Alice Lister in the pump rooms. Fortune's Folly was positively bristling with gossip that morning, for everyone was talking about the events of the previous night.

"I always knew that Tom was a scoundrel," Lady Elizabeth said sadly, "but I had no idea that he was in so deep." She was a little paler and quieter than usual, her natural vivacity subdued. "Oh, it was easy to pretend there was nothing wrong because Tom could be so charming and he was so likable—the exact opposite of Monty! But from childhood I remember he was always in scrapes of one kind or another and as he grew older so he became wilder..." She shook her head. "He lost money at cards and almost killed a man in a brawl on more than one occasion. We should have realized then that his propensity for violence would get him into bad trouble."

"You could never have realized that he was associating with Mr. Sampson, nor where it would lead," Laura said comfortingly.

"I suppose not." Elizabeth fidgeted with her teacup. "Lord Waterhouse was telling me that they think Tom took money from Sampson and did his dirty work for him because Sampson paid his gambling debts. He killed Sir William Crosby on Sampson's behalf. Sampson was blackmailing Tom, but in the end Tom turned against him."

"It was truly gruesome when Mr. Sampson's body rolled off the bonfire," Alice said, shuddering. "If I were the type of female to indulge in the vapors, that was the moment I would have chosen."

"At least the Duchess of Cole fainted away and gave us all some peace," Elizabeth said. "Poor Lydia! Tom always had the most terrible reputation, but to seduce the Duke of Cole's daughter! I can scarce bear to think of it."

"I hope that Lydia will be all right," Alice said anxiously. "First to be betrayed by Mr. Fortune and then to be whisked off home in the middle of the night by her parents simply because they wish to avoid the scandal!"

"We must see what we can do for her," Laura said. She had already decided that she would go to Cole and try to help Lydia. Her cousin's reputation was in shreds but Lydia's heart was broken, too, and she would need someone kinder than Faye to comfort her.

"I hope," Laura continued, "that Sir Montague is bearing up, Lizzie?"

Lady Elizabeth looked disgusted. "Oh, Monty does not deserve your sympathy, Laura. I can scarce accept his callousness. Do you know, he has already washed his hands of Tom? He even plans to take Tom's pitiful little estate at Withenshaw and include it in the Dames' Tax. His greed knows no limits!"

"Gracious," Alice said involuntarily, "I knew he was very acquisitive but that is too much!"

"You had a fortunate escape there, Alice," Lady Elizabeth said. "Not that you ever intended to accept Monty's marriage proposal, I know." She smiled wickedly. "And who would, when a man like Lord Vickery would be so much more fun?"

"Lord Vickery is a rake," Alice said, coloring up furiously. She glanced at Laura. "I am sorry, Laura, for I know he is your cousin, but it is true!"

"Oh, do not apologize to me," Laura said cheerfully. "I know exactly what Miles is like but I think he does have his good points, too."

"One would have to look very hard for them," Alice said crossly. "If one were interested enough to do so, which I am not!" She chopped up the sugar furiously with a teaspoon. "Have you had any news from Mr. Anstruther, Laura? Have they found Tom yet? Are they returning home yet?"

"I am afraid it is a little too soon for news," Laura said. She tried not to feel too despondent, knowing that the others were watching her and also knowing that Alice in particular needed her to keep their spirits up.

"I'll wager that Mr. Anstruther is anxious to return as soon as possible," Lady Elizabeth said, smiling. "We all saw the way that he kissed you last night, Laura! A pity that Nat did not go with Lord Vickery instead."

"But then you would have no one to torment, Lizzie," Laura said gently and saw Lady Elizabeth blush before she waved Nat Waterhouse aside with one elegant flick of her hand.

"Oh, Nat and I are old friends," she said airily. "That is why we are forever squabbling with one another. It means no more than that."

Mr. Argyle, the master of ceremonies, bustled past the

table. "Sir Montague's latest declaration on the Dames' Tax, ladies," he said importantly. "Each single lady in the village is to pay a window tax of four shillings per window and a dog tax of two shillings per dog."

"But I have half a dozen spaniels," Lady Elizabeth protested, "and Monty knows it. He has already taken all my allowance this quarter, the wretch!"

"And I have at least twenty-four windows!" Alice said, paling at the thought. "This really is too bad!"

As Mr. Argyle made his way around the room a ripple of anger and disquiet followed him as the ladies heard the news. Laura watched his progress thoughtfully.

"I have been thinking," she said to Alice and Elizabeth, "that since my marriage I have neglected to help you in your struggles against the Dames' Tax. It has been very remiss of me. But now I have an idea." She hesitated. "It seems a little unfair to do this to Sir Montague when he has had such a terrible shock with regard to his brother—"

"Oh, do not let that stand in your way," Elizabeth said bitterly. "Think of the window tax—think of my spaniels!"

"Very well, if you are sure," Laura said. "Only this will hurt one of the things Sir Montague cares about the most."

"Are we to sell off his horses?" Alice asked.

"No," Laura said. "It is not as bad as that."

"Then it must be his wine cellar," Elizabeth said. "That is the only thing he seems to care for now."

"Exactly," Laura said. "I have a plan."

"What will Mr. Anstruther think of you helping us?" Alice asked tentatively. "Forgive me, Laura, but he does not seem the most indulgent of gentlemen when it comes to bending the law."

Laura smiled ruefully. "Well, no, he is not. He will probably disapprove heartily. I am afraid that my plans seldom fit Dexter's notions of proper behavior, but since he is absent at the moment he will not know."

She poured more tea and started to explain her strategy, hoping fervently that she was right and that Dexter would not hear about the plan until it was far too late.

DEXTER AND MILES RODE OUT of Newcastle a week later on the road to the south. Tom Fortune had been apprehended trying to take ship for Germany and was in the city jail. A woman who claimed to be betrothed to Tom Fortune had given them plenty of information on his criminal activities once Miles had told her that Tom had apparently affianced himself to another girl in Yorkshire.

"Lord Liverpool will be pleased," Miles said as the evening of the second day brought them down the Tune Valley and close to home. "Warren Sampson is dead and his murderer arrested. We have done a good job."

"Yes," Dexter said. "It might make up in some small part for my failure to capture Glory on my last case in these parts."

Miles laughed. "You were never going to catch Glory, old fellow."

"No," Dexter agreed. "In her I really did meet my match."

He felt Miles's gaze on him. Their friendship had been much restored through working together and because in true manly fashion they had not been required to talk about anything difficult and had simply been able to get on with the job. But now there was something Dexter wanted to ask.

"Miles," he said slowly. "When did you first know that Laura was Glory?"

There was a silence so long he thought that Miles was not going to answer. The question had raised a slight constraint between them because they had studiously been avoiding speaking of Laura in the whole time they had spent together.

"I did not know at the time," Miles said at last, "but after a couple of years Nick Falconer came to me and asked me to help organize Laura's pardon from Lord Liverpool. I think he did it for Hattie's sake so that there was no danger to Laura in the future."

"So Nick knew," Dexter said slowly, "and you knew and Lord Liverpool knew, and none of you chose to tell me. Why was that?"

"Probably because we knew you were the one who would cut up rough," Miles said, a little grimly. "You have a very clearly defined sense of what is right and wrong, Dexter. You never bend."

"No," Dexter said. "I suppose I do not." He thought of Laura telling him that they had both been on the same side, fighting for justice, but that he was too uncompromising to acknowledge it. She had been right, he thought. He had been damnably stubborn through fear of losing his principles just as his father had done.

The horses splashed through the ford on the road that led to Fortune Hall. Dusk was starting to fall.

"You admired Laura for what she had done, didn't you?" Dexter said. He was thinking back to what Miles had said when they had been talking that day at Fortune Hall about Laura's desire to help those in need.

"I was not the only one," Miles said. "Once he had met

her, Lord Liverpool admired her, too." He laughed. "He was always more pragmatic than you, Dexter, more able to bend the rule of the law if it benefited him."

They turned the horses into the long drive that led to Fortune Hall. The deer were grazing beneath the trees, alongside Mrs. Broad's sheep and various other animals belonging to the villagers.

"You were right in what you said to me that day at the inn," Dexter admitted. "Laura does deserve someone who loves and accepts her wholeheartedly for what she is and not someone who wants to change her to fit in with their notions of sense and rationality and proper behavior. I see that now."

"Someone like you, perhaps," Miles said, with a sideways glance at him. "You're a fool, Dexter. It's taken you long enough." He sighed. "At least I don't have to put a bullet through you now. You had better find Laura and tell her. You've wasted enough time."

"I will," Dexter said. "I'll tell her just as soon as we have broken the bad news of his brother's arrest to Sir Montague." He shot Miles a look. "And will you be seeking out Miss Lister, Miles?"

Miles's expression was discouraging. "Not I," he said. "I'm for London. I hear word of a very, very rich nabob's daughter, whose fortune makes Miss Lister's seem almost paltry." He urged his horse a little ahead before Dexter could reply.

They found Fortune Hall shrouded almost entirely in darkness. There were no servants about and they were obliged to leave the horses tied to the mounting post in the stable yard.

"Devil take it," Miles said, as their knocks on the front

door went unheeded and they let themselves in, "I thought Monty might take his brother's downfall badly but I had no idea it would be this bad."

The two of them stumbled down the barely lit passage and into the hall. Sir Montague's figure was barely discernible, sitting in a large oaken chair before the fire. His head was bowed and when they came in he did not even move.

"Monty!" Dexter said, putting a hand on his shoulder. "Monty, old chap!"

Sir Montague looked up, his face tragic in the firelight. "Dexter. Miles. How are you?"

Miles and Dexter exchanged a look. "Bad news, I'm afraid, Monty," Dexter said awkwardly. "We caught up with Tom at Newcastle. He's in the jail there—" He stopped as Sir Monty nodded gently.

"Well, he can expect no help from me," he said. "Damned scoundrel." He looked up, his tone morose. "Besides, I have more serious matters than Tom's misdemeanors to attend to. Those wretched women! You cannot conceive what they have done now."

Dexter frowned, wondering if the shock of discovering his brother's criminality had turned Sir Montague's mind. "What women, Monty?"

"My own sister!" Sir Montague mourned. "What did I do to deserve such thankless siblings? And Miss Lister, a viper in women's clothing!" His expression dissolved into malevolence. "And *your* wife, Dexter! Your *cousin*, Miles! She escapes the tax through marriage and then she has the downright audacity to lead those women in their worst outrage yet!" He mopped his brow on his sleeve.

Dexter's lips twitched. "Upon my word, you are beset,

Monty. What have my wife, Miss Lister and your own sister done now?"

"My wine cellar!" Sir Montague wailed. "They called it vineage and claimed there is an ancient tax that obliges me to share a quarter of my wine with the villagers in honor of Saint Anand, the patron saint of wine merchants. As though those peasants could begin to appreciate my cellar. The waste of it! They took my claret! They took my champagne! Elizabeth showed them where to find it, Miss Lister helped to carry it out to the carriage and Mrs. Anstruther drove off with it not ten minutes back!"

"Good lord," Miles said, aghast. "But your cellar was the only reason I dined here, Monty!"

"I fear the ladies of Fortune's Folly have gone too far this time," Dexter said.

"Quite right, Dexter," Sir Montague said, nodding virtuously. He suddenly seemed a great deal more animated. "If I don't get my wine back I shall call the constable."

"There's nothing for it, then," Dexter said. "I will have to deal with Laura myself. Leave it to me, Monty." He grabbed Miles's arm and hustled him out of the room. "There's only one way to do this," he said, pausing in the doorway to the stables. "May I take your horse, Miles? Mine's tired and not up to the task in hand."

Miles raised his brows. "With pleasure, old chap, but what are you—"

"And your pistol," Dexter said.

"A pistol," Miles repeated. He looked at Dexter, who looked back at him completely blankly. A smile started in Miles's eyes. "Ah… You do know that highway robbery and abduction are capital crimes, Dexter?" he said.

"I do know," Dexter said. He grinned suddenly. "Just

give me the damned pistol, Miles, and I will be on my way. And should anyone ask you, you know nothing of any matter of highway robbery."

"My memory becomes ever more faulty by the day," Miles said ruefully. He slapped Dexter on the shoulder. "Good luck, old fellow. I'll go and administer some port to Monty—assuming he has any left!"

THE CARRIAGE THAT Laura had hired from the Morris Clown Inn ground slowly along the twisty Yorkshire road and she sat back against the seat to the accompanying chink of Sir Montague Fortune's wine bottles. The incursion into Sir Monty's wine cellar had gone rather well, she thought, and she had been scrupulous to take only a quarter of his stocks though she rather suspected from his reaction that she had taken the best quarter. Certainly Sir Monty had been beside himself, wailing and wringing his hands and demanding that his servants stop them—at which point Lady Elizabeth had countermanded his orders and the poor servants had not known what to do.

Laura smiled. She rather thought that the villagers of Fortune's Folly would enjoy Sir Montague's fine wines. And they had been within their rights to take it. Well, they had been almost within their rights. Sir Montague was meant to *give* the wine to the village under the ancient laws, so technically she had robbed him of it since he had not offered it freely.... Laura shifted a little uncomfortably. She had promised Dexter that her days of righting the injustices of the rich against the poor were over but this was straying perilously close to the line. Dexter would hardly approve. Technically she had committed a crime. It was the reason that she had sent Alice and Eliza-

beth on ahead to tell the villagers the wine was coming.
She did not want them to be accused of the robbery itself
and suffer any penalties under the law. That would be her
responsibility alone.

She sighed. No indeed, Dexter would not approve.
Her behavior scarcely fitted his idea of conduct becoming to a sensible wife. It was fortunate he did not know
what she had done or their fledgling reconciliation would
be in big trouble. If he came back and found that the constable had her under arrest in Skipton Jail for theft he
would very likely hang her himself. Laura shivered and
looked out the window to distract herself. She might jest
about it, in her own mind as much as she had to the other
ladies, but she did not think she could bear to lose Dexter
again.

The road straightened out and the carriage picked up
speed, rattling toward the village. The turnpike road took
a much longer route than the path along the river, but it
was the only way that Laura had thought she could trans-
port the wine into Fortune's Folly. They were cutting
through a narrow gorge where the fells pressed close on
either side. The sun had long since dipped behind the hills
and the air was cold and a winter blue, full of shadows.

"Stand!"

Laura jumped violently at the shouted command. She
could barely believe it. The Dales had been largely free
of highway robbery in the last few years and to stage a
holdup so close to the village was absolute madness. The
hired carriage slewed across the road and the horses
plunged in the shafts. The wine bottles clanked together
in their crates and for a moment Laura was afraid they
would break. She soon realized that the coachman and

groom from the Morris Clown Inn were no heroes. They had not been paid well enough even to think of resistance. The coachman slowed the horses to a standstill and the groom kept prudently quiet.

Someone wrenched open the door of the coach. The cold evening air poured in, making Laura shiver. She realized that she had never been held up on the road before. At any other time the thought might have made her laugh to think that she, the infamous Glory, was the victim of highway robbery. Now she shuddered. It was frightening. She fumbled in her reticule for the tiny pearl-handled pistol she always carried.

"I've got a pistol," she began, "and I know how to use it."

There was a man in the doorway, mounted on a black horse, cloaked in black, too, a pistol considerably larger than hers in his hand. His shadow looked huge and threatening against the darkening sky. She looked up at his face and her head spun.

It was Dexter.

Her heart started to beat in long, hard strokes. Her mind refused to accept the evidence of her eyes. Dexter would *never, ever* hold up a coach. Dexter would not dream of breaking the law. Dexter would not—

She saw him smile though his eyes were cold. The gun in his hand moved slightly. "I suggest you put that toy of yours down unless you want it shot from your hand," he said.

Looking into his eyes and seeing the unyielding purpose there, Laura actually started to believe him. She wondered wildly if the discovery of her latest outrage had turned his mind.

"What are you *doing*—" she started to say, but Dexter grabbed her arm and dragged her out of the carriage without another word. One of his arms was brutally hard about her waist as he lifted her up into the saddle in front of him. He gestured with the pistol toward the coachman.

"Drive on to the village. They will be expecting you." He reached in and grabbed half a dozen bottles of champagne out of the coach, stowing them deftly in the saddlebags. "I'll take these and I'll take the lady, too. Get going."

The coachman met Laura's eyes for a second, his expression furtive and guilty before it slid away. He picked up the reins and the carriage started to move. Dexter dug his heels into the horse's side and they turned away, up a track that led out onto the fells. The sky had clouded over and the first few flakes of snow were starting to drift down. Dexter did not speak. Laura tried to turn around to look up into his face but his arms tightened about her, pulling her back against the hardness of his chest.

"Dexter, what are you doing?" Laura asked breathlessly. "This is abduction and highway robbery. When they get back they will call out the constable."

"Sir Montague will have done that already," Dexter said, his voice hard. "He wants his wine back."

Laura caught her breath. So that was why he was angry. She had been right. He had been to Fortune Hall and he knew the whole story of what she had done. He was appalled that she had gone back to what he saw as her old ways. He would think she had betrayed his trust yet again. With her disregard for convention and her insistence on doing what she thought was right, she was the very opposite of everything he had always wanted in a wife.

Yet that did not quite explain what he was doing abducting her from a carriage and stealing Sir Montague's champagne into the bargain.

"Dexter," she said, thoroughly confused now, "I don't understand. You are too rational to do this. It's madness! And it's dangerous. Even if it is not illegal for a man to abduct his own wife—and if I had my way it *would* be— you threatened those men at gunpoint. You stole Sir Monty's champagne! You could be arrested and your career will be in shreds. Let us go home and talk about this sensibly."

"Save your breath, Laura," Dexter said. "I have realized at long last that the very last thing I need is to be *sensible.*" He said the word through his teeth. "And if you object to being abducted by your husband then you should have thought of that before you decided to break the law!"

Laura fell quiet. She could not quite believe what was happening, but her spirits had begun to revive despite the extraordinary nature of the situation. Dexter held her tightly and she could sense the tension still in him, but there was something else there, too; something of promise and even love, and at one point he turned his head slightly and his lips brushed her hair in a caress.

Neither of them spoke further as the horse picked its way along the track and began to descend toward the pinpricks of light in the village below. As they came into the yard of the Half Moon Inn, Dexter dismounted and lifted Laura down from the saddle, swinging her up into his arms rather than setting her on her feet. Laura was taken by surprise and wriggled like mad as he carried her over the threshold into the taproom beyond, which was packed to the rafters. There was absolute silence as they walked in. Laura was mortified.

"Put me down!" she huffed. "Everyone is looking!" She turned her burning face into his shoulder. "Dexter, put me down! You have punished me quite enough. Oh! My cousin Hester used to come here to pick men up. Everyone will think that I am the same!"

"Then they will be accustomed to this sort of thing," Dexter said, holding her all the more tightly, "and since they are well acquainted with your antics as Glory, they will not be shocked, either." He looked across at Josie Simmons, who was standing hands on hips, watching them.

"There's a room free," she said, jerking her head toward the stairs.

"Josie!" Laura almost shrieked. She caught sight of a thin man lurking behind Josie's massive bulk. "Lenny! Are neither of you going to help?"

"Reckon he doesn't need any help," Josie said admiringly. "Good for you, Mr. Anstruther. Never thought you had it in you. Thought you were too much of a stuffed shirt for this sort of business. Just goes to show."

Dexter tossed Lenny a bottle of champagne. "Sir Montague's finest," he said. "There's more in the saddlebags." He looked round the crowded taproom. "Enjoy it."

"Dexter!" Laura protested.

Dexter grinned. "We don't need it, sweetheart," he said, heading for the stair. Someone cheered.

Laura was even more infuriated to note that Dexter did not appear remotely out of breath as he carried her into the chamber above stairs, kicked the door shut and tossed her down into the middle of the big bed.

"Now," he said, "at last we talk."

"Are you angry with me?" Laura said. "I understand

that you must disapprove about my reallocation of Sir Monty's wine—"

"I don't give a damn about Sir Monty's wine," Dexter said, interrupting her brutally, "nor do I care about the Dames' Tax, nor even my imminent arrest for highway robbery. At the moment all I care about is you, Laura." He cast aside the black cloak and sat down beside her on the bed. He took her hands in his. She could feel the tension in him knotted so tight it felt almost unbearable. There was a pulse pounding in his jaw.

"I love you," Dexter said. His expression eased as though he had let go of an intolerable burden. "There. At last I have said it. At last I have had the courage to admit it openly to you. I love you so much, Laura, I find there is not a single rational thought left in my head and for once I do not want there to be."

"Love?" Laura whispered. Her mind was whirling, unable to accept what she was hearing. She tightened her grip on his hands, not quite believing, not wanting ever to let him go.

"It was wrong of me to force you into marriage in the first place," Dexter said roughly. "I am sorry. I was hurt and angry that you had concealed the truth from me, and I wanted you—and Hattie—with me, but I went about it all the wrong way. I wanted to ensure that Hattie never had to endure the slights and the whispers that have haunted my family for years and that she grew up knowing who her father was. I could not *bear* for her to experience what I had endured, or that I should behave as irresponsibly as my father had behaved."

Laura closed her eyes for a second. "I knew it was dreadfully painful for you," she whispered, "and I would never have denied you the truth if I had not thought I was doing what was right for Hattie. I am so sorry, Dexter."

Dexter shifted, drawing her a little closer. "I was always terrified of making the same mistakes my parents did," he said. "They were forever swearing they were in love and behaving with such profligacy. They would come together and pledge undying devotion to one another and then they would quarrel and run off and find another lover and have a tempestuous affair." He bowed his head. "I clung to order and logic because it was the only thing that seemed safe to me. And the only time I let go of it and indulged in the type of stormy love affair my parents had had, my world ended in chaos."

"The time that I seduced you," Laura said, "and then sent you away. My love, I am so very sorry."

"Hush." Dexter laid a gentle finger against her lips. "You did what you thought was right. You did it because you loved me, not because you did not." He smiled. "When we spoke that time on the hill I said that I did not believe in love any more and you accused me of being afraid," he said. "You were right, Laura. I loved you, but I pretended that what I felt was no more than lust because I was afraid of what would happen to me if I let go of all my restraint and allowed myself to love you as I had before. But now I am not afraid any longer." His gaze was brilliant as he lifted his eyes to hers. "You are the breath of life to me, Laura, and I want that life to be full of passion and excitement and love. I want our marriage to be joyful, not the hollow sham or the emotionless desert I used to think I wanted."

Laura drew his head down to hers and kissed him.

"It will be," she promised.

Dexter's teeth closed about her lower lip, biting gently, his tongue teasing the corner of her mouth. Slowly, hesitantly, she parted her lips against his and he kissed her sweetly, almost reverently.

"I cannot be the pattern card wife you wanted," she whispered when he let her go. Her cheeks were wet with tears. "I am as I am, Dexter—wild and reckless and all the things you used to deplore."

"That is what I love about you," Dexter said softly. He kissed her again, smoothing a gentle hand over her hair. "I love you because you are so committed and passionate and because you feel things so strongly. I could no more try to force you to change than I could leave you, Laura. I realize that now."

Laura pulled him to down to lie beside her on the bed. "Are we really going to make love in an alehouse?" she asked, tracing the line of his jaw with loving fingers. She found that she could not stop smiling.

"Why not?" Dexter said. His hands moved to the fastenings of her gown. Laura gave a little voluptuous shiver.

"Perhaps I am more like Hester than I thought I was," she said. "I did not realize how wanton I was—until I met you."

Dexter's hands roamed over her body, stroking, exploring. "And whenever I made love to you," he said, "I threw sense and reason to the four winds and lost myself utterly in you. I should have realized then that I was fighting a losing battle and one I did not, in my heart of hearts, want to win." He kissed her softly. "I was so afraid to let the emotions in," he said. "Forgive me, Laura, please?"

"I forgive you," Laura said, smiling radiantly, pulling his head down again to meet her kiss. "I love you."

"This could be very, very bad, you know," Dexter said after a moment.

"Bad? With you?" Laura gasped as he let his lips drift over the vulnerable skin of her throat. "How so?"

"Because I love you," Dexter said. "And you love me. And at last both of us are openly and freely admitting it with no secrets and no reservations. You complained because it was good before when we did not trust one another totally—"

Laura arched against him. "I was not exactly complaining, Dexter." She raised a hand to his cheek, reveling in the rough stubble against her palm. "But it is good to know that this time it is with love," she whispered.

"It always was, though I was not honest enough with either of us to admit it," Dexter said. "But now I do. I will love you forever."

His mouth covered hers completely. He drew her close and worshipped her every line and every curve with his lips and his hands and his body, and she cried a little at the end, but this time with happiness, and she thought that he almost did, too.

Hours later, Laura was drawn from a deep and untroubled sleep by a pounding at the door. She could hear the roar of people in the taproom below and knew the alehouse was full with a rowdy crowd, the night well advanced and the champagne probably much appreciated, regardless of what Sir Montague had thought of the populace of Fortune's Folly.

"The militia are here, madam," Josie shouted through the door, "They have come to arrest both of you for stealing Sir Montague's champagne and Mr. Anstruther on the additional charge of highway robbery and abduction."

Laura rolled over in Dexter's arms, skin against his skin, registering the warmth, the sense of rightness, the completeness.

"Please tell them there has been a misunderstanding," she said. "Tell them that I will sort matters out with Sir Montague." She shifted a little as Dexter came awake and started to nibble very gently at her bare shoulder. "Tell them," Laura added, "that I'll shoot them myself if they try to arrest Dexter."

"Right you are, madam," Josie said.

"Oh, and please tell everyone," Laura finished, "that I am paying for the drink tonight. Thank you, Josie."

She rolled over in Dexter's arms, a movement that placed her breast where her shoulder had been. Dexter moved to take advantage but Laura laughingly held him off.

"We should go home," she said. "Much as I have enjoyed my stay here I would rather be at home with you."

Dexter reached a little regretfully for his clothes. "Very well," he said, "but only if we may be wild and disorderly and reckless again very soon."

Laura smiled, too, as he wrapped her up in the black cloak and swung her up into his arms. "We could be all those things again very soon indeed," she whispered. "Hester once confided in me that she had made love in the carriage all the way home."

She saw an answering smile curve Dexter's mouth and he bent his head to brush his lips against hers.

"Well, then," he said. "What are we waiting for?"

EPILOGUE

December 1809

"I FIND IT QUITE incomprehensible," Faye Cole said disagreeably, over the breakfast table at Cole Court a couple of weeks later, "that Laura styles herself *Mrs. Anstruther* these days. Why, one would think she was actually proud of having married a nonentity like Dexter Anstruther. She who was once Duchess of Cole!"

"Perhaps it is incomprehensible to you, Mama," Lydia said, pushing her plate of toast away untouched, an expression of revulsion on her pale face. "I can quite imagine that you would not understand such a thing at all."

Her mother looked at her without affection. "Your views on marriage are hardly the most reliable, are they, Lyddy? Had you forgotten that you were prepared to throw yourself away on a man who is a criminal?"

"I am not likely to be allowed to forget it," Lydia said steadfastly. She took a sip of tea but put her cup down quickly and seemed to turn an even more pasty shade of white. Neither of her parents noticed. The duke was engrossed in his newspaper and the duchess was busy scouring the marmalade pot.

"I am not at all sure how we are to get you off our

hands now that your reputation is so tarnished, Lyddy," she said. "I suppose we could pay someone but I suspect that your dowry will certainly not be enough, even though Mr. Anstruther has returned the money that your father tried to settle on Laura." She shot the duke a venomous look. "Which in itself is quite extraordinary, now I come to think of it."

"Fellah said that he loved her for herself alone," Henry Cole grunted. "Damned fool!"

" Anyway, Lyddy, you look so sickly these days," the duchess continued, returning to her main target. "Really, it is small wonder that no other man has taken a fancy to you. Lyddy?" She stared as her daughter pressed a hand to her mouth, pushed her chair back violently from the table and rushed out of the room. "Lyddy!"

The door slammed.

The duchess looked at her husband. "I do not know what is wrong with the girl these days," she said. "Really, Henry, it is a complete mystery."

IT WAS SNOWING in Fortune's Folly, with huge white flakes floating down from a gray sky. Hattie had run outside, squeaking with excitement, to build a snowman with Rachel. Laura was curled up in the window seat watching.

"I will go out and join them presently," she said, "for it looks prodigious fun, but I wanted to know what was in your letters first."

Dexter broke the seal on the first of the letters and sat back to read it.

The most marvelous news! His sister Annabelle had written, her dashing handwriting even more wild than ever because of her excitement.

Mama is to remarry! She has met an old flame, a gentleman who was an admirer of hers before she married Papa (at the least, I think it was before, but it might have been during, as well.) Anyway, he is a military man and has offered to buy Charlie a commission in his old regiment, the Royal Horse Guards. And Roly has gained a scholarship to Oxford, so his fees will not be too prohibitive. Caro has met up with an old school friend and they plan to open a teaching establishment together. I had no notion she wished to work and think it most odd in her, but she assures me that she will feel much happier with something other than marriage to keep her occupied!

Which just leaves me, dearest Dexter, and I am sure that if you give me the most extravagant and exciting come-out ball imaginable then I will be off your hands in no time at all. I do not scruple to admit that some gentlemen have already been very attentive to me when I have been out and about with Mama in Town. It is no surprise to me because, of course, I am very pretty, so I imagine I will have no trouble in catching a husband...

There was a great deal more in the same vein and Dexter put the letter down with a rueful smile on his lips. Caro's letter was briefer and much more to the point.

Dear Dexter, you will have heard from Belle that your mama is to wed. Mr. Sandforth seems a pleasant enough man, I suppose, a little short on intellect and far too doting on your mama, but neither of those are necessarily bad things. She will likely ruin him in a month, though that is his problem. Fortunately he is very rich.

I do not anticipate it being very long before Belle follows Mrs. Anstruther to the altar. She would like a come-out ball, but you will have to be quick as she is so romantically inclined that she will likely elope to Gretna before long. On second thoughts, if you wish to save money I would simply let nature take its course. As for me, I shall be very happy running a school. It suits my managing nature…

The third letter was from Lord Liverpool, the writing spiky and black, blotched with irritable ink stains.

Anstruther, I demand that you return to London at once. Disturbing news has reached my ears of you abducting your own wife. Whilst not illegal, this sort of behavior is most reprehensible and not at all what I expect of you. The other charges of highway robbery and theft I can only assume were an unfortunate misunderstanding.

And whilst we are on the subject of your marriage it seems that you have made the most regrettable hash of things. I warned you against being distracted, Anstruther. You had a simple task to perform yet I hear you have somehow managed to wed a widow with no money, a dowager, no less, with a daughter of her own, which will be one more mouth to feed. This is quite inexplicable and totally incompetent and if it were not for the fact that the lady in question

is one whom I admire very much, I would dismiss
you from my service immediately…

Dexter dropped the letter, put his head in his hands and
started to laugh. Laura put a hand on his shoulder and he
looked up and met her eyes. She was smiling at him.

"What is the matter?" she asked.

"Nothing at all," Dexter said, passing his sisters' letters
to her. He laughed again. "None of the things that I feared
have come to pass and no one needs my money anymore."

"One more mouth to feed," Laura said softly, angling
her head to read Liverpool's letter as it lay on the table.
"Oh dear, I fear Lord Liverpool is going to be apoplectic when he hears that there is going to be yet another Anstruther to feed, and so soon after the wedding."

Dexter looked at her, the light blazing in his eyes.
"You mean…"

Laura's face was vivid with happiness. "Our family is
expanding, Dexter, and so shall I be soon." A shade of
anxiety touched her eyes. "Is that reckless of us when we
have no money now that you have given my dowry back?"

"Very probably," Dexter said, kissing her, "but at least
I still have a job thanks to you. As you see, Lord Liverpool admires you very much."

"Then he may be godfather to our baby," Laura said.
She grabbed his hand. "Let us go and tell Hattie she is to
have a brother or sister. I am sure she will be delighted."

And they went out together into the snow.

* * * * *

*All's fair in love and matrimony in the second
installment of Nicola Cornick's*
THE BRIDES OF FORTUNE.
Out soon
THE SCANDALS OF AN INNOCENT
*Miles is on the hunt for an heiress...and Fortune's
Folly is a marriage mart fit for a rake!*

The Village of Fortune's Folly
Yorkshire, February 1810

ALICE LISTER WAS NOT cut out for a life of crime.

She had not even committed the robbery yet and already her palms were damp with anxiety and her heart was beating light and fast.

"This," Alice thought as she tried to calm her breath, "is a *very big mistake.*"

There was no going back. That was the coward's way. Bravely she raised her lantern to illuminate the interior of the darkened gown shop. She had broken in to the workroom at the back of the premises. There was a long table with piles of fabric heaped on one end. A half-finished gown was draped across a stool, the pale silk glimmering in the light. Paper patterns rustled and fluttered in the draft from the open window. Ribbons uncurled on the floor. Sprays of artificial flowers wilted in a corner. Lace trimmings wafted their ghostly fingers against Alice's cheek, making her jump. The whole place with its unnatural silence and its darkness made her think of a sinister fairy story in which the gowns would come to life and dance in front of her—and she would run screaming from the shop straight into the arms of the night watch. Yes indeed, burgling Madame Claudine's gown shop was not for the fainthearted.

Not that this was theft, precisely. Alice reminded herself that the wedding gown she was hunting had been bought and paid for. It would have been delivered in the normal manner had Madame Claudine not gone out of business so abruptly and shut up her shop in the face of all inquiries from her anxious clientele. The modiste had disappeared one night leaving nothing but a pile of debts and bitter words for those of her aristocratic customers who lived on credit. The contents of Madame Claudine's gown shop had been declared the property of the money-lenders and all the stock impounded. This was particularly unfair to Alice's friend, Mary Wheeler, for Mary's father had paid the bill already with the same promptness he had paid a gentleman to marry Mary. Sir James Wheeler had been one of many to take advantage of the Dames' Tax, the wholly outrageous edict leveled the previous year by the squire of Fortune's Folly, Sir Montague Fortune. Sir Monty had discovered an ancient tax that entitled him to half the dowry of every unmarried woman who lived in the village of Fortune's Folly—unless they wed within a twelvemonth. Sir James Wheeler had been only one of many fathers who had seen this as an opportunity to get his daughter off the shelf and off his hands, parceled away to the first fortune hunter who asked.

Mary Wheeler had been distraught to hear of the gown shop's closure and had taken the whole thing as a bad omen. And to be fair, Alice thought, marrying Lord Armitage was a poor enough proposition without getting off on the wrong foot....

"Alice? Have you found it yet?" The urgent whisper brought Alice back to the present and she raised the lantern again, scanning the piles of clothing hopelessly, for there were so many gowns and they were as tumbled as though an autumn gale had blown through the shop.

"Not yet, Lizzie." Alice tiptoed across to the open window, where her coconspirator, Lady Elizabeth Scarlet, was keeping watch in the passage at the side of the shop. It had been Elizabeth's idea, of course, to simply *take* Mary's wedding gown.

Alice shook her head to have been so easily led. Naturally, once they had reached the shop it became apparent that Lizzie was too tall to squeeze through the window and it was Alice who was the one who had to break in.

"What is keeping you?" Lizzie sounded decidedly testy and Alice felt her temper prick in response.

"I'm doing my best," she whispered crossly. "There is a mountain of gowns in here."

"You are looking for one in white silk with silver lace and silver ribbons," Lizzie reminded her. "Surely it cannot be so hard to find? How many gowns are there, anyway?"

"Only about two hundred. This is a gown shop, Lizzie. The clue is in the name...."

Sighing, Alice grabbed the next pile of dresses and hurriedly sorted through them. Silver with pink trimmings. White with green embroidery... Golden gauze... That was pretty.... White and silver with silver ribbons... Alice snatched up the wedding gown even as Lizzie's agonized whisper floated up to her.

"Alice! Quick! Someone is coming!"

With a muttered and very unladylike curse, Alice ran

for the window, squeezed through the gap at the bottom of the sash and struggled to climb out and down into the street. It was only a drop of about four feet and she was wearing boy's breeches, borrowed from the wardrobe of her brother Lowell, which made movement a great deal freer and easier. But as she tried to ease her leg over the sill the breeches caught on something and stuck fast.

"*Alice!*" Lizzie's hissing held a note of panic now. "Come on! Someone is almost upon us!" She caught Alice's arms and tugged hard. Alice heard the material of the breeches rip. She wriggled free for a few painful inches and then stuck fast again. She was not a slender girl and every one of her curves currently felt as though it was squashed into too small a space. The edge of the windowsill dug painfully into her hip. She dangled there helplessly, one leg out of the window the other on the sill. She could hear footsteps coming ever closer, their measured tread loud on the cobbles of the road.

"He will see us," Lizzie groaned.

"He will certainly *hear* you," Alice said crossly. Lizzie's idea of being quiet seemed to equate to behaving like a bull in a china shop. "If you will cease that pulling and pushing and keep still and quiet for a moment he will pass by the end of the alley. And put the lantern out!" she added fiercely.

It was too late.

She heard the footsteps stop. There was quiet for a moment, quiet in which Alice's breathing seemed loud in her own ears and the window ledge creaked in protest beneath her weight. She lay still like a hunted animal. Instinct told her that the man, too, was watching and waiting....

"Run, Lizzie!" Alice gasped. "I am right behind you!" She gave her friend a shove that sent Lady Elizabeth stumbling off down the passage even as everything seemed to explode into noise and movement around her. A man came running out of the darkness and Alice wrenched herself free of the ledge and tumbled headlong on top of him, wrapping them both in the silky, voluminous folds of the wedding gown as they fell to the ground. As an ambush it could scarcely have been more effective had she tried.

Alice scrambled up, lost her footing on the slippery folds of material and fell to her knees. The man was quicker. His arms went about her, scooping her up and then holding her fast against him, so that all her kicking and pummeling was quite in vain. His grip was too tight to break, as taut as steel bands about her waist and back. Her struggles were embarrassingly puny against such quiet, almost casual strength.

"Hold still, urchin," he said. His voice was mellow and deep, and he sounded carelessly amused, but there was nothing careless in the way that he held her. Alice could tell she was not going to be able to break his grip. She also sensed by instinct that this was no drunken lord returning home after a night's entertainment at the Morris Clown Inn. There was something too powerful and purposeful about him—something too dangerous to dismiss easily.

She was in deep trouble.

HQN™

We *are* romance™

All's fair in love and matrimony in
the second installment of
the Brides of Fortune series by

NICOLA CORNICK

Insufferably attractive Lord Miles Vickery intends to gain
Miss Alice Lister's fortune by seducing her into marriage.
But his charming lies deceived Alice once before and
it will cost this handsome rake three long months of
complete honesty to get a second chance at her heart!

The Scandals of
an Innocent

Coming soon!

www.HQNBooks.com

PH-NC389

HQN™

We *are* romance™

The Corwin family curse continues....

New York Times bestselling author

carly phillips

When Mike Corwin wakes up in Vegas $100,000 richer and
married to gorgeous Amber, he thinks he's hit the jackpot.
Until she takes his money and runs.... But Mike wasn't business
as usual for Amber, and he might have been The One—if
she hadn't been forced to betray him. Now he's hell-bent on
divorce, she's on the run, and they're both in need of a

Lucky Streak

Don't miss the sequel to LUCKY CHARM,
available now wherever books are sold!

www.HQNBooks.com

PHCP375

**Don't miss the sizzling new Lone Star Sisters
series by *New York Times* bestselling author**

SUSAN MALLERY

Sibling rivalry takes on a whole new meaning as the
high-society Titan sisters vie for their tyrant father's
business and respect...and fall unexpectedly in love
with three sexy men along the way!

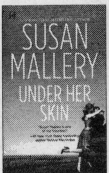

Available wherever books are sold!

**And don't miss the final Lone Star Sisters tale,
HOT ON HER HEELS, coming this winter!**

HQN™

We *are* romance™

www.HQNBooks.com

PHSMT2009

HQN™

We *are* romance™

On this rainy night a mystery beckons....

GEORGETTE HEYER

When Captain John Staple is mired on the moors on a dark and stormy night, he hardly expects to find a young, frightened boy who's been left alone to tend a toll gatehouse. But as John investigates the suspicious disappearance of the lad's father, he begins to unravel a far more complex mystery. And at its center is a woman—the very one to tame John's reckless spirit....

The Toll-Gate

Available now in trade paperback!

www.HQNBooks.com

PHGH412

REQUEST YOUR FREE BOOKS!

2 FREE NOVELS FROM THE ROMANCE/SUSPENSE COLLECTION PLUS 2 FREE GIFTS!

YES! Please send me 2 FREE novels from the Romance/Suspense Collection and my 2 FREE gifts (gifts are worth about $10). After receiving them, if I don't wish to receive any more books, I can return the shipping statement marked "cancel." If I don't cancel, I will receive 4 brand-new novels every month and be billed just $5.74 per book in the U.S. or $6.24 per book in Canada. That's a savings of at least 28% off the cover price. It's quite a bargain! Shipping and handling is just 50¢ per book.* I understand that accepting the 2 free books and gifts places me under no obligation to buy anything. I can always return a shipment and cancel at any time. Even if I never buy another book from the Reader Service, the two free books and gifts are mine to keep forever.

185 MDN EYNQ 385 MDN EYN2

Name	(PLEASE PRINT)	
Address		Apt. #
City	State/Prov.	Zip/Postal Code

Signature (if under 18, a parent or guardian must sign)

Mail to **The Reader Service:**
IN U.S.A.: P.O. Box 1867, Buffalo, NY 14240-1867
IN CANADA: P.O. Box 609, Fort Erie, Ontario L2A 5X3

Not valid to current subscribers of the Romance Collection,
the Suspense Collection or the Romance/Suspense Collection.

Want to try two free books from another line?
Call 1-800-873-8635 or visit www.morefreebooks.com.

* Terms and prices subject to change without notice. Prices do not include applicable taxes. Sales tax applicable in N.Y. Canadian residents will be charged applicable provincial taxes and GST. Offer not valid in Quebec. This offer is limited to one order per household. All orders subject to approval. Credit or debit balances in a customer's account(s) may be offset by any other outstanding balance owed by or to the customer. Please allow 4 to 6 weeks for delivery. Offer available while quantities last.

Your Privacy: Harlequin is committed to protecting your privacy. Our Privacy Policy is available online at www.eHarlequin.com or upon request from the Reader Service. From time to time we make our lists of customers available to reputable third parties who may have a product or service of interest to you. If you would prefer we not share your name and address, please check here. ☐

BOB09

HARLEQUIN® *Blaze*™

Make Me Yours

by *New York Times* bestselling author

BETINA KRAHN

Between a prince and a hot body…

The Prince of Wales chooses Mariah Eller for the "honor"
of becoming his next mistress. However, she needs to be
married in order for the affair to proceed, so he tasks his
friend, Jack St. Lawrence, with finding Mariah a husband.
But little does the prince know that Jack has found a
husband for Mariah—*himself!*

Available in July wherever books are sold.

red-hot reads

www.eHarlequin.com
HB79483

NICOLA CORNICK

77303 UNMASKED	___ $6.99 U.S.	___ $6.99 CAN.
77211 LORD OF SCANDAL	___ $6.99 U.S.	___ $8.50 CAN.

(limited quantities available)

TOTAL AMOUNT	$	_____
POSTAGE & HANDLING	$	_____
($1.00 FOR 1 BOOK, 50¢ for each additional)		
APPLICABLE TAXES*	$	_____
TOTAL PAYABLE	$	_____

(check or money order—please do not send cash)

To order, complete this form and send it, along with a check or money order for the total above, payable to HQN Books, to: **In the U.S.:** 3010 Walden Avenue, P.O. Box 9077, Buffalo, NY 14269-9077; **In Canada:** P.O. Box 636, Fort Erie, Ontario, L2A 5X3.

Name: _____

Address: _____ City: _____

State/Prov.: _____ Zip/Postal Code: _____

Account Number (if applicable): _____

075 CSAS

*New York residents remit applicable sales taxes.
*Canadian residents remit applicable GST and provincial taxes.

HQN™

We *are* romance™

www.HQNBooks.com

PHNC0609BL